SO4ED

How to Seduce an Heiress

SARA ORWIG
LUCY ELLIS
HEIDI BETTS

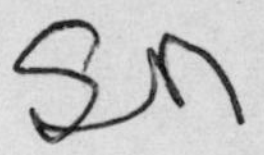

First Published in Great Britain 2016
By Mills & Boon, an imprint of HarperCollins*Publishers*
1 London Bridge Street, London, SE1 9GF

ISBN: 978-0-263-92073-4

05-0716

Our policy is to use papers that are natural, renewable and recyclable products and made from wood grown in sustainable forests.The logging and manufacturing processes conform to the legal environmental regulations of the country of origin.

Printed and bound in Spain
by CPI, Barcelona

THE RELUCTANT HEIRESS

BY

SARA ORWIG

Sara Orwig lives in Oklahoma. She has a patient husband who will take her on research trips anywhere from big cities to old forts. She is an avid collector of Western history books. With a master's degree in English, Sara has written historical romance, mainstream fiction and contemporary romance. Books are beloved treasures that take Sara to magical worlds, and she loves both reading and writing them.

Many thanks to Stacy Boyd and
Maureen Walters.

Prologue

"I don't have a clue why I'm here," Garrett Cantrell, company CFO, said at the family gathering in the Dallas office of Delaney Enterprises.

"Because Sophia Rivers is our father's child. She's as stubborn as Dad ever was," Will Delaney stated, combing his fingers through his black hair.

"We won't give up. There's too much at stake," Ryan Delaney added, resting one booted foot on his knee. "We can be as stubborn as she is. There has to be a way to reach her."

"We need to outsmart her instead of the other way around," Zach Delaney grumbled.

"Right," said Will. "That's why I asked Garrett to join us."

"I'm sure finding out you have a half sister at the reading of your dad's will was a shock," Garrett said, "but you should face the fact that she doesn't want to meet any of you. I'd say give it up."

"If we don't get her on the board of the Delaney Foundation, we can kiss our inheritances goodbye," Zach snapped. "Also, she's family. We have a sister—all these years."

"I agree," Will added. "She's part of our family and we'd all like to know her."

"Even if she doesn't want to know you?" Garrett asked.

"I think that's because of Dad and not anything we've done. We just want to unite this family and we don't stand a chance if she won't speak to us," Will said. "Each of us has tried and failed to make contact with her. I think the next thing is to send someone neutral."

Garrett straightened in his chair, his good humor vanishing. "Go through your dad's lawyer. She communicates with Grady."

"Her attorney communicates with Grady," Will replied drily. "Grady has never met the lady."

"The bottom line is, we want our inheritances," Ryan stated. "She's costing each of us four billion dollars. Too much to blow off."

As Garrett looked at the Delaneys, he reflected on how his life had been tied to theirs from the day he was born. His father's life had been closely linked with the family patriarch, Argus Delaney. Besides ties of work and family, Will Delaney, the Delaney CEO, was Garrett's best friend. Garrett had been raised to feel indebted to the Delaneys, just as his dad had felt obligated. As he thought about what they were about to ask of him, his dread grew exponentially. "I suggest the three of you try again to meet her," Garrett said.

"C'mon, Garrett. You can contact her because your

name isn't Delaney. Spend time with her, get to know her, find out why she's resisting, and we'll take it from there," Will said. "Just open the door for us. Go to Houston. You have a family business and a house there. It's a perfect plan."

"I own the property management business in Houston—I don't work there. Give it up, guys. Don't ask me to do what you can't do."

"We think you *can* do this," Will argued. "You've been our spokesperson many times. We'll make it worthwhile for you. Help us get her on the board and it's another five hundred million for you."

Garrett was already wealthy— He didn't care about the money. But he couldn't turn down the brothers because his obligation to the Delaneys ran deep. He sighed as Will handed him a manila folder.

Garrett looked at a picture of a raven-haired, brown-eyed beauty. *Maybe their request isn't so bad after all,* he thought.

"If she cooperates, she will inherit three billion dollars. It's not like you're trying to cause her trouble," Ryan pointed out.

"How can she turn down that kind of money?" Zach asked, shaking his head.

"She must be angry as hell," Garrett remarked. "That kind of anger isn't going to change easily."

"We have to try," Will stated. "Will you do it?"

Garrett glanced at the picture again. He had just inherited three billion from their father. Will was his closest friend. How could he refuse to help them now?

"Garrett, we're desperate. And we have a time limit," Ryan said.

"All right," Garrett replied reluctantly. "I can't say no to any of you."

There were thanks from all and a high five from Will, who grinned. "Everything's going for you. You're not a Delaney."

"I might as well be one," Garrett grumbled. "I don't think your half sister will be one degree happier with me than she was with any of you." Garrett shook his head. "Meeting Sophia Rivers is doomed from the start."

One

Sophia Rivers sipped champagne and gazed beyond the circle of friends surrounding her. Her small Houston gallery was filled with guests viewing her art and helping her celebrate the second anniversary of her gallery's opening. The crowd was the perfect size, and she was completely satisfied with the turnout.

"Sophia, I have a question."

She turned to see Edgar Hollingworth, a father to her and a mentor, as well as a man whom she and her mother had been friends with before she ever moved into the art world. "Excuse me," she said to the group around her, and stepped away.

"Edgar, what can I do for you?" she said to the tall, thin man.

"You looked as if you needed rescuing," he said quietly. "You also look ravishing. The black and white is striking on you, Sophia."

"Thank you," she replied, shaking her long black hair away from her face.

"Shall we at least act as if I've asked you about a painting?" Edgar motioned toward the opposite side of the room and she smiled as she strolled with him. "You have a sizable crowd tonight. I'm glad you were able to make it. I haven't seen you in a long time."

"I hadn't planned to come until about three hours ago. I've been in New Mexico, painting. Who's the couple ahead to our right?" she asked.

"The Winstons. They're probably on your guest list because they bought a painting recently."

"Now how do you know that?"

"I sold it to them," he said, smiling at her, causing creases to fan from the corners of his blue eyes. "I still think you should move your gallery nearer mine. Our galleries would complement each other."

Sophia smiled at the familiar conversation that always ended with her saying no. "I do appreciate your gallery carrying my art. You were the first and I'll always be indebted to you for that."

"You would have been in a gallery anyway whether it was my place or another's. You have a fine talent."

"Thank you, Edgar," she said.

Sophia glanced around the room again and was slightly surprised when she saw another unfamiliar face. Except this one took her breath away.

Perhaps the tallest man in the room, he stood in profile. His brown hair had an unruly wave to it and his hawk nose and rugged looks made her think instantly that he would be an interesting subject to paint. He held a champagne flute in his hand as he looked at a painting.

"There's someone else I don't know," she said.

"His name is Garrett Cantrell. We talked awhile. He

has a property management business here and he's a financial adviser. He, too, bought one of your paintings last week. Another satisfied customer."

A woman approached Edgar, who excused himself, leaving Sophia to contemplate the tall, brown-haired stranger, strolling slowly around the gallery. She suddenly found herself crossing the room to stand near him.

"I hope you like it," she said.

"I do," he replied, turning to look at her with thickly lashed eyes the color of smoke. Her breath caught. Up close he was even more fascinating—handsome in a craggy way—and his gray eyes were unforgettable.

"That's good," she replied, smiling and extending her hand while still held in his compelling gaze. "Because I'm the artist. I'm Sophia Rivers."

"Garrett Cantrell," he said, shaking her hand. His warm fingers wrapped around hers and an uncustomary tingle ran to her toes. She gazed into his smoke-colored eyes and couldn't get her breath. Her gaze slipped lower to his mouth. She wondered what it would be like to kiss him. The temperature in the room rose. She knew she should look away, yet she didn't want to stop studying him.

"The artist herself. And even more beautiful than your paintings," he said as he released her hand. "You've caught the atmosphere of the West."

"It's New Mexico, around Taos. And thank you," she added. Her pulse jumped at his compliment and she was keenly aware of him as they moved to view another painting.

"You're very good at what you do. I look at these and feel as if I'm there instead of standing in a steamy metropolitan city."

"That's what I hope to achieve. So this is the first time you've been to my gallery."

"Yes, but I own one of your pictures," he said, moving to the next painting. "You must spend a lot of time in New Mexico. I assume you have a gallery there?"

"Actually, I don't. I intend to open one early next year, but I haven't launched into that yet. It will take time away from painting."

"I understand." He sipped champagne and moved to another painting. "Ah, I really like this one," he said and she looked at a familiar work. It was an aged cart in front of a brown adobe house with bright hollyhocks growing around it. A small mesquite tree stood at one corner of the house.

He looked at the next series of paintings. "These are my favorites. The Native American ones," he said, indicating a man with a long black braid standing beside a horse in an open stretch of ground dotted with mesquite. Overhead, white clouds billowed against a blue sky and a large hawk sailed with widespread wings.

"That's a great painting," he said. "The light and shadows are an interesting contrast." Happy with his compliment, she smiled. "I'll take this one. Any chance the artist will help me decide where to hang it? A dinner is in the offering."

Again, she had a flutter in her heartbeat. "We're strangers, Mr. Cantrell."

"It's Garrett. We can fix the 'strangers' part. When you can get away tonight, why don't we go around the corner to the hotel bar and have a drink? Tomorrow evening we'll hang my painting and then I'll take you to dinner."

"You don't waste time. I'd be delighted to have a drink tonight. I should be through here in another hour."

"Excellent," he said, glancing at his watch.

"I'll get one of my staff to wrap your painting and we can deliver it tomorrow if you'd like."

"That will be fine. The delivery person can leave it with my gatekeeper."

She smiled and left to find one of her employees. "Barry, would you help Mr. Cantrell? He wants number 32. Please take care of the sale and get the delivery information."

She had to resist the temptation to glance over her shoulder at Garrett.

Instead, she strolled around, speaking to customers and friends, meeting Edgar again.

"I see Cantrell bought a painting."

"Yes. I'm having a drink with him after this."

"That was quick," he said, glancing across the room. "Seemed nice enough. Wealthy enough, too. Last week he bought your painting from me without hesitation. Now, a week later, he's buying another one. The man knows what he likes."

"I see the Santerros. I have to speak to them."

"Have fun this evening," Edgar said as she left him.

"I intend to," she stated softly. "Garrett Cantrell," she repeated, glancing back to see him at the desk, handing a business card to Barry. Her gaze drifted over his long legs while her heartbeat quickened. Dressed in a navy suit with a snowy dress shirt and gold cuff links, the handsome man was a standout even in the well-dressed crowd.

She spent the next hour all too aware of where Garrett stood.

When she saw him talking to a couple she recognized, she waited until he moved away, then worked her way around to them.

"How are the Trents tonight?" she asked.

"Fine," Jason Trent answered.

"We love your new paintings," Meg Trent said. "Thanks for the invitation."

"Thank you for attending. I saw you talking to Garrett Cantrell. I just met him, but it looked as if you two already know him."

"We do," Jason replied. "I lease a building from his company. He keeps up with whether everything is going smoothly, which it is. Good bunch to work with."

"We're getting one of your watercolors for the family room," Meg said. "It's the one with the little boy and the burro."

"I'm glad you like that one. I hope you enjoy having it in your home."

"You're a prolific painter," Jason remarked.

"I enjoy it."

"More than the financial world," he said, smiling.

"I have no regrets about changing careers."

"That's what I keep trying to talk Meg into doing—She'd love to have a dress shop."

"Accounting seems to hold fewer risks. You're established now, but weren't you nervous when you started?" Meg asked.

"I suppose, but it was absolutely worth it," Sophia said. "It was nice to see you both," she added, moving on, aware of Garrett across the gallery talking to two people. She wondered whether he knew them, too.

She stopped at the desk to look at his card. "Cantrell Properties Inc." It was a plain card with a downtown address, logo and phone number, but little else. She returned it to the drawer.

Garrett appeared at her side. "Can you leave? You still have quite a few people here."

"I can leave. My staff can manage quite well. They weren't expecting me to be here tonight anyway."

"I'm glad you are," he said.

"We can go out the back way and it'll be less noticeable." She led him through a door, down a hallway that opened onto offices, a mailroom and a studio and out the back into a parking lot where five cars were parked. Four tall lampposts illuminated the area as brightly as if it were day. A security guard sat in a cubicle watching a small television. He stepped to the door.

"Good night, Miss Rivers."

"I'll be back after a while to get my car, Teddy."

"Sure thing. Evening, sir," he said, nodding at Garrett who greeted him in return.

"My car is in front," Garrett said, taking her arm.

"It's a nice night. We can walk if you want," she said, pleasantly aware of his height because she was taller than some men she knew and as tall as many.

"I saw you talking to Meg and Jason Trent. Jason said he leased property from you."

"Yes, he's a good tenant," he said. "They like your art."

"I've had a gratifying response from people," she said.

They entered the bright hotel lobby, then the darkened bar where a pianist played a ballad for couples who were dancing.

Garrett got a booth with a small lamp at the end of the table. It spilled a golden glow over his fascinating features, highlighting his prominent cheekbones and leaving the planes of his cheeks in dark shadows. She felt breathless again, a steady hum of excitement that she couldn't explain.

They ordered drinks—a cold beer for him and an

iced soda for her. When they came, he raised his glass in a toast. "Here's to a new friendship. May it grow."

"A toast to friendship," she repeated, touching his cold bottle lightly. She sipped her soda and set the glass down.

He reached across the table to take her hand, his warm fingers enveloping hers. Again, a current streaked through her like lightning. "Shall we dance?"

As she stood, he shed his coat and tie, folding them once on the seat of the booth.

Sophia followed him to the small dance floor and stepped into his embrace. Her hand was in his, her other hand on his shoulder, feeling the warmth of him through the fine cotton shirt. She enjoyed dancing around the floor, aware of how well they moved together. He was agile, light on his feet.

"I've been waiting all evening for this moment," he said, setting her heart fluttering again. She had never had such an instant and intense reaction to a man. "I'm glad I decided to come tonight. I didn't expect to see the artist, but I knew I would enjoy looking at your art. Now, the whole world has changed."

She smiled. "I don't think it's been a world-changing night," she said, though she actually agreed with him. She wasn't sure things would ever be the same after having met Garrett Cantrell.

"The night isn't over yet," he reminded her, obviously flirting.

She slanted him a look. "Perhaps you'll change my mind."

"That's a challenge I'll gladly take."

The ballad ended and a faster number began. Garrett released her and she put a little distance between them. The man had sexy moves that set her pulse at a faster pace. She was unable to tear her gaze from his until she forced herself to turn and the spell was broken.

By the time the music finished, she needed to catch her breath.

Garrett took her hand. "Shall we go back to our drinks?"

They returned to the booth. He loosened the top buttons of his shirt. The temperature climbed a notch and her desire revved with it.

Her cell phone chimed. She looked down, reading a brief text from Edgar.

How is your evening with G.C.? Call me when you get home. I promised Mom.

She had to laugh. "I have a text from my friend Edgar. You bought a painting of mine from him."

"Yes. I remember."

"He once promised my mom that he would look out for me and he's been like the proverbial mother hen ever since. He's checking on when I'll get home."

Garrett flashed a breathtakingly handsome smile. "Is he jealous?"

Shaking her head, she laughed. "Definitely not. Edgar always loved my mother. They dated some, but for Mom it was a good friend sort of thing. Then as my interest in art developed, Mom told Edgar. He became a friend and mentor, helping me in so many ways."

She sent a text back.

Go to bed, Edgar. I'm fine and he's fun.

"I let him know that I'm okay and we're having a pleasant time."

"A pleasant time. I'll have to try harder if I want to move that into the 'world-changing' arena."

She smiled as she put away her cell phone. "So tell me about yourself," she said.

"I grew up with the proverbial silver spoon. Well, my dad began to make big bucks when I was about seven years old. Life was easy in some ways."

"What wasn't easy?"

"My mom died when I was fifteen. My dad and I were close. I lost him this past summer."

"Sorry. It hurts. My mom died a couple of years ago."

"Your dad?"

"I never knew him," she said, her eyes becoming frosty as she answered him.

"I'm glad you and your mom were close. So how did you get into art?"

"It's my first love. I went to college, got a degree in accounting, got a good job, moved up. I began to invest my own money and did so well, I finally took over managing my mother's finances, which was far more than I had. Finance became my field, but art was—and is—my love. We have something else in common—our financial backgrounds."

"So we do."

"The difference is, you love it and pursue it. I wanted something else."

"Sometimes I think about something else, but I'm locked into where I am."

"What else do you think about doing?" she asked.

"Nothing serious. I'm where I should be, doing what I've been trained to do and have a knack for doing."

"There's something else you like," she persisted, tilting her head to study him. "I don't think it's art. I'll bet it's far removed from the world of property management."

"Yes, it is. It's not that big a deal for you to even try to guess. Someday when I retire, I'll make furniture. I like working with my hands."

"It's getting a little scary how alike we are," she said, noticing how his thick lashes heightened the striking effect of his gray eyes.

"Perhaps it's an omen indicating we will get along well."

"Usually, it's the other way around. Opposites attract."

"Well, I'll see where we're opposite—one thing, you're living your dream. I won't leave the business world."

"Why not?"

He shrugged a broad shoulder. "I was raised to do this. When Dad was alive, I wouldn't have changed for anything because it would have hurt him terribly. He hasn't been gone long and I just can't think about changing when I know how badly he wanted me to do what I'm doing. There are other reasons, too, but that's the biggest."

She nodded. "We're different there, all right. My mom was okay with the change I made. I'm sorry she didn't live to see the success I've been lucky enough to have, especially since she's the one who told me to chase my dream."

"Be thankful. I've been told the opposite all my life."

"I am thankful," she said, wondering about his life as the topic of conversation shifted. As she looked at him, desire smoldered, a steady flame. She knew he would kiss her tonight and she wanted him to.

"So there are no other men in your life?" he asked, tilting his head.

"No, no other men and you're not exactly in it either since I've known you all of a few hours."

"I'm in it now," he said in a tone of voice that stirred sparks. "So Mr. Right has not come along. And there's no one vying for that title."

"I'm definitely not looking for Mr. Right. The past few years I've been incredibly busy and my social life has suffered."

"I can understand about incredibly busy. And I'll see what I can do to remedy that a little for both of us."

"And what about the women in your life? You can't convince me there are none."

"There isn't anyone special, or even anyone really 'in' my life at this point. I'm free as a bird, as they say."

"Workaholic?"

"I'm not arguing that one."

When her phone chimed again with a text that the gallery was cleaned and closed, she noticed the late hour. "I didn't know the time. I should go home."

As they walked back to the gallery, Garrett stopped her. "Why don't I take you home? I'll pick you up for breakfast and bring you back to the gallery to get your car."

"That seems a lot of trouble for you."

"No trouble at all," he said, unlocking the door of a black sports car.

After a moment, she climbed in, gave Garrett her address and watched him drive, studying his hands with neatly trimmed nails. A gold cuff link glinted in the reflection of the dash lights.

They drove through a gated area and up the front drive of her sprawling house. He parked and came around to open the door for her. They crossed the porch and she unlocked the door before turning to face him.

"You have a nice home."

"Thanks. As you said, it's comfortable. It's too late to invite you in but I had a great time tonight."

"It's too early to exchange goodbyes," he said, slipping his arm around her waist to draw her close.

Sophia's heart raced as she looked up at him. His lower lip was full, sensual. She leaned slightly closer, pressing against him and closing her eyes as his mouth covered hers lightly, then firmly, his tongue thrusting into her mouth. A wave of longing rippled, tearing at her while she felt as if she were in free fall. Her breathing altered, heat pooled low in her. His kiss was demanding, enticing and she returned it. She moaned softly, the sound taken by his mouth on hers.

Her heart pounded so violently she was certain he could feel it. When she pressed against his lean, hard length, his arm tightened around her. Leaning over her, holding her tightly, he didn't let up. She was lost, consumed in kisses that were magical, that set her on fire.

One hand slipped down her back, a light caress, and the other was warm on the nape of her neck. His kisses were earth-shattering, rocking her world. She had never been kissed this way. She wanted to stay in his arms for hours.

Finally she leaned away to look at him. "Garrett, slow down," she whispered, caution and wisdom fighting to gain control over desire. All she wanted was to kiss him endlessly.

As he gazed at her intently, she realized that his ragged breathing matched her own.

"Sophia," he said, her name a hoarse whisper. "I

want you." The words—stark, honest and direct—set her pulse galloping.

"We have to say good-night," she declared. She had just met him and barely knew him. She should not fall into his arms instantly and lose all control.

Locks of his dark, unruly hair had tumbled on his forehead, escaping the neatly combed style he'd worn when she first saw him. She ached to run her hands through them.

Instead, she took a deep breath and stepped back. "We have to say good-night," she repeated. "I had a wonderful time."

"It was world-changing for me," he whispered, his voice still only a rasp. He framed her face with his hands. "I mean it. Tonight was a special night that I never, ever expected. I'd hoped to meet you but I never once thought I'd have an evening like this." As he spoke, his fingers combed lightly through her hair. His words carried a sincerity that made her heartbeat quicken again, his smoky, intense gaze consuming her.

"I didn't expect anything like this either," she whispered, wanting him with an urgency that shook her.

"When I walked into your gallery, I wanted to meet you for one reason. After meeting you, I want to be with you for an entirely different reason," he said.

He leaned down to kiss her again, passionately. When he released her, he stepped away, but his hand stayed on her shoulder as if he didn't want to break the physical contact with her.

"I'll see you in the morning. How's seven?"

She nodded, and he turned and strode away. She stared at him—broad shoulders, narrow waist, long legs, thick brown hair, handsome. The man took her breath and set her heart pounding.

"Good night, Garrett," she said softly. She closed the door and switched on lights while her lips tingled. Desire was a scorching flame. Garrett Cantrell. She would be with him again in just hours and yet she couldn't wait.

Her cell phone's tune signaled a call. She looked at the number with curiosity as she answered. Her heart missed a beat when she heard Garrett's deep voice.

She laughed. "You do know that we just parted?"

"We did. It now seems like a serious mistake. Tell me more about growing up, your dreams, your day tomorrow."

Smiling, she sat in a rocker in her bedroom, gazing at her shelves of familiar books and pictures. "I grew up in Houston. I've always dreamed of painting and having my own gallery. Tomorrow—"

"Wait a minute. Back up. You grew up in Houston. House? Apartment? Best friends through your school years or did you move a lot? Tell me about your life, Sophia."

When he said her name in his deep drawl, her pulse beat faster. "It can't possibly be that fascinating. I grew up in one house, went to neighborhood elementary schools and then private schools later. I had the same close friends through elementary and then new friends in the private school. See? All very routine and ordinary."

"There is absolutely nothing ordinary about you," he said, stirring another thrilling physical reaction in her that threw her completely off base. She wasn't used to feeling like this because of a man.

"What about you? You said you had it easy growing up?" she asked.

"I always went to private schools. I've had the same

best friend all my life since I was too young to remember. Our fathers were best friends. I've had the same family home my whole life. I'm an only child."

"We're so much alike, I'm surprised we can stand each other, Garrett." When he laughed, she felt her stomach drop, like she was in free fall. He was turning her inside out with just the sound of his voice.

"You're already living your dream. Do you feel fulfilled, complete?" he asked.

"I think people always want more and keep striving. I am very happy with my life, though, and what I do."

"Surely there's something else you want."

"Another successful gallery in Taos. I'd like to live in Santa Fe. But I already have a home and studio, and I have a cabin in the mountains near Questa, where I go for solitude to paint."

"The Questa cabin sounds isolated."

"No cell phone reception whatsoever, which is a plus. I have a caretaker. He and his family have a cabin close to mine, so there are people nearby. He has four dogs. Two take up with me when I'm there, so that's a bit of company. It's a good place to work with no interference—a good place to improve my skills as a painter."

"I'd say you can settle for how well you paint right now."

"No, I can definitely improve. So tell me about you, Garrett. Do you really dream of building furniture someday?"

"It's pushed to a burner so far back, it will take years to get to it."

As they talked, she moved to the window, switching off a lamp and gazing outside at the full moon. By the time she glanced at the clock, she was shocked to see it was half past three.

"Garrett, we have to get off the phone. It's after three a.m., and you're picking me up at seven."

"All right. Sophia, you're a remarkable woman," he said in a solemn tone. She suddenly had a funny feeling that he had expected something different from her.

"And you are a remarkable man," she replied softly. "Good night, Garrett. I will see you soon—very soon."

"Night, Sophia," he said, and was gone.

She turned off her phone and crawled into bed, Garrett dominating her thoughts completely. "Garrett," she whispered, enjoying saying his name while she thought about his magical kisses. She had never expected to meet someone like him tonight. This wasn't a time in her career to be distracted, yet he made her feel things she had never felt before. Morning couldn't come quickly enough. She was already anxious to be with him again.

Two

Setting aside his phone to strip to his briefs, Garrett replayed the night, thinking of the first moment he had seen Sophia at the gallery. In high heels, she had to be six feet tall. Her midnight hair was straight and fell freely over her shoulders in a black cascade.

A dramatic black-and-white dress left one tan shoulder bare. The slit in the straight skirt revealed long, shapely legs with each step. Her mother's Native American blood had given her smooth, olive skin, beautiful raven hair and her prominent cheekbones, yet she bore a striking resemblance to Will and reminded Garrett of Zach in her forthright, practical manner.

From the first moment she had captivated him. Dancing with her had fanned his desire until he ached to kiss her.

He shook his head to clear his thoughts.

While he hadn't lied to her, he had still deceived

her by not mentioning his ties to the Delaneys and his mission in Houston. At the moment she could be at her computer, looking him up and discovering he was an executive with Delaney Enterprises. A chill slithered through Garrett, turning him to ice. By breakfast time, she might already know the truth.

He didn't want her to find out that way. He wanted to tell her about his relationship with the Delaneys himself. But if he did, he wouldn't see her again, and neither the Delaneys nor she would get their inheritances.

His thoughts drifted to her soft, lush curves, her silky, midnight hair and her large, dark brown eyes…

After twenty more minutes of tossing and turning, he went to his indoor pool and swam laps, trying to stop thinking about Sophia yet wanting morning to come so he could see her again.

What if he did tell her about the Delaneys at breakfast? Maybe they already had enough of a connection that she'd agree to meet them.

Who was he kidding? Anyone who felt strongly enough to turn down billions wouldn't change her mind because of a few kisses and one exciting night.

Glumly, he executed a flip-turn and mulled it over as he swam another lap. Three billion dollars—no one could turn down money like that, yet she had. Why? Was her anger at Argus Delaney that deep?

From what the P.I. had unearthed, Argus had continued seeing her mother until she died. At the end of her life, he had done everything to keep her comfortable, taking care of her medical bills and seeing that she had the best care possible. Why was Sophia so bitter? She didn't seem a bitter, grudge-holding type. Sophisticated, intelligent, an inner core of steel, obviously hardworking, optimistic—all were qualities that he would use to describe her. It seemed difficult to imagine that she would have enough anger and hate to give up a three-billion-dollar inheritance.

He had to confess or risk Sophia discovering on her own the deception that grew larger with every passing hour.

Yet if he told her now, it was the end of what they'd only just started. And the termination of hope for the Delaneys.

Trying to shut off his nagging thoughts, he swore and swam harder.

It was another half hour before he was dry, sitting in his bedroom and staring out the window. Sleep eluded him. Worse, he was no closer to a decision about what he would do in a few hours when he saw her. Either way—tell her or wait—their relationship was doomed.

In spite of his disturbed sleep, the next morning he was eager to see Sophia again. His uncustomary inability to reach a decision about her added to his restlessness. Before he left to pick her up, Garrett phoned Will and gave him an update.

"Fantastic. So she can be civil and you like her," Will said. "That's promising."

"Will, for her to cut all of you off and lose her inheritance, her anger must run really deep. I can't imagine being able to persuade her to change her mind."

"We're counting on you to work a miracle. You're already getting close to her."

"Not that close," Garrett snapped and then curbed his impatience. "I wanted you to know that I'll be with her tonight so don't call."

"I'll wait until you call me. You're doing great—I knew you would."

"Will, stop being the ultimate optimist. She doesn't have a clue yet about my connections. Everything will change when she learns the truth."

"Maybe. Maybe not. Thank heavens women can't resist you."

Garrett had to laugh. "Oh, hell. Goodbye, Will. I'll call when I can."

Garrett ended the call and tried to get Will out of his thoughts and stop worrying about him. As he headed to his car, he focused on Sophia, his thoughts heating him to a torrid level.

When Sophia opened the door, her heart missed beats. Dressed in a charcoal suit and matching tie, Garrett looked as handsome as he had the night before.

His warm gaze roamed over her and he smiled. "You look gorgeous," he said.

"Thank you," she replied, thinking about all the different outfits she had tried on before settling on a plain red linen suit. Her hair was tied behind her head with a matching red scarf and he gave it a faint tug.

"Very pretty, but if we were going out for the evening, I would untie that scarf and let your hair free, which is the way I like it."

"But I won't," she replied lightly, locking up and walking to his car with him. "I have to go to the gallery and it needs to be tied and out of my way."

As he held the car door, she noticed he watched her legs when she climbed in. He closed the door and went around to slide behind the wheel. "So how did you sleep?" he asked.

"Great."

"I must be slipping if my kisses didn't keep you awake a little."

"You think I would tell you if I had stayed awake all night?"

As they both smiled, she felt the sparks between them, that electrifying current that had sizzled the whole time they were together last night. She hoped he never realized what a strong impact he had on her. She had a busy life and a time-consuming career. Garrett had come into her life at a time when she was trying to make a name in the art world. She didn't want him to realize how he affected her. She didn't want to lose control of her emotions.

At the restaurant, they were seated on an outdoor patio—the breezes were cool, the sun bright. As soon as they had ordered and were alone, Garrett smiled. "So when will my painting be delivered?"

"This afternoon."

"Excellent. Let me pick you up, we'll go to my house to hang the painting and then I'll take you out."

Her heartbeat quickened yet again. "You really don't waste time, do you," she replied.

"I'll pick you up around seven. So how much time do you spend in New Mexico?" he asked.

"Most of the summer. It's cool at night and I enjoy being there part of the year. Do you have a home anywhere else?"

"My home is in Dallas and I have a condo in Colorado because I like to ski. I also have a place in Switzerland."

"Nice."

"Painting is a reclusive occupation. Do you get out much in Santa Fe?"

"Sure, when I want to. But I enjoy the quiet and solitude. Chalk that up to being an only child." As Sophia talked, she couldn't help but study Garrett. His brown hair had been neatly combed, but the breeze soon shifted the locks and they tumbled over his forehead. His rough handsomeness—his hawk nose and firm jaw—and his spellbinding gray eyes fascinated her. When he began to speak, her gaze lowered to his mouth and she recalled his kisses, not hearing what he was saying as heat suffused her and the temperature of the cool morning changed.

He touched her chin with his fingers. "I don't believe you're hearing a word I'm saying. What could you possibly be thinking about?" he asked in a husky voice as if he guessed exactly why she hadn't heard a word he had said.

"My mind drifted, sorry," she said, embarrassed, looking into his knowing gaze. She felt the heat flush her cheeks and couldn't do anything to stop it.

"So, Sophia, where did it drift? What were you thinking?"

She gave up because he knew full well what she had been thinking about.

"I don't think you need me to tell you that, do you, Garrett?" He gave her a slight smile as she changed the subject. "Do you travel much with your job?"

To her relief he moved on with the conversation and the moment passed. But she suspected it had not been forgotten.

After breakfast Garrett took her to the gallery and parked beside her car. As he walked her to the door, he said, "We're early. May I come inside with you in case your building is empty?"

"Actually, people should start arriving in about ten minutes, and there is a guard outside."

"I'd rather stay until someone does arrive."

"Garrett, it's safe, and I'll lock the door once I'm inside." She turned to unlock the door and reached inside to switch off the alarm. When it became clear that he had no intention of leaving, she headed down the hall and said over her shoulder, "I'll show you my office."

She stepped into her office and he followed, taking in the beige room with bright splashes of color from her paintings. He studied the paintings for a moment, and then turned to her, making her pulse skip. "I expect people any minute now."

"I'll wait and be certain. Why don't you give me the key and I'll unlock the front and switch on lights."

She handed him the key and he caught her wrist, drawing her to him. Her "no" died on her lips before she ever uttered a sound. His arm banded her waist and he looked down at her. "I didn't sleep well and I suspect you didn't either. This is what I've wanted since I woke up this morning." His mouth covered hers, his lips warm and firm as he kissed her.

Her heart thudded while heat made the room a furnace. Wrapping her arm around his neck, she combed her fingers through his thick hair while their kiss turned to fire. Forgetting her surroundings, she held him tightly.

She never heard the car but Garrett raised his head and stepped away. "I hear one of your employees."

Garrett's erratic breathing matched hers. She felt disoriented, trying to ignore her desire and get her focus off Garrett and back to the real world.

He left to unlock the front for her just as she heard a car door slam. One of her male employees came in the back door, and Sophia introduced him to Garrett when he returned to the office.

"I'll pick you up at home tonight. How's six? Too early?" he asked.

"It's fine," she said, still slightly dazed, thinking six o'clock sounded eons away. "Thanks again for breakfast." He gave her an incredible smile, said goodbye and closed the door behind him. Sophia felt like she was in a daze until her phone rang.

"You were out late last night," Edgar said.

"Hello to you, too, Edgar," she said, amused. "I can't recall having a curfew. I don't think this is what Mom had in mind when she asked you to look out for me."

"I think it's exactly what she had in mind. You didn't answer the text I sent you this morning."

"Sorry, Edgar. I went out for breakfast."

"Uh-huh. With the Cantrell fellow?"

She laughed. "Yes, with the Cantrell fellow—Garrett, to be exact."

"Oh, dear," Edgar said, sighing audibly. "I suppose I will have to remember his name. So you're seeing him again?"

"Correct. Am I going to have to check in, Mom 2?"

He chuckled. "No. I'll keep tabs. Just answer your text messages."

"Yes, Edgar."

"Last night seemed a huge success."

"I'll hear shortly when everyone arrives at work."

"I'm certain I'm right. Have lunch with me and we'll celebrate your success."

"Thanks. That'll be nice." She made arrangements with him and a minute later, her assistant appeared to show her the receipts from the gallery.

Last night had indeed been a success—in more ways than one.

Sophia pulled on a blue wool-and-crepe sweater with a deep V-neck, a straight, short skirt and matching pumps. She put her hair up in a French twist. She was nervous, anxious, excited.

Get a grip, she silently lectured herself.

It wasn't easy. Garrett captivated her more than any other man she had known. He was exciting, handsome, interested in her life. If she let herself think of kissing him, she could get lost in memories of the previous night. But she didn't want that to happen. She needed to stay in control.

When she was ready, she studied herself thoroughly to make certain she was at her best for the evening.

When she opened the door to face him, her heart raced, despite all her commands to the contrary. In a navy suit, he looked breathtakingly handsome and commanding. His smile warmed her as his gaze drifted slowly over her.

"You're gorgeous," he said in a husky voice that was like a caress. She smiled, glad for the effort she had taken to get ready. "You have a nice home," he said.

"Sometime you'll get a tour, but right now, we're headed for your house."

"I'll hold you to that. Shall we go?"

Nodding, she closed the door behind her, hearing the lock click in place. Garrett took her arm to escort her to a waiting limo where the driver held the door while she climbed inside. She was surprised Garrett wasn't driving. Did he always travel in limos? Was she seeing another facet of his life? Garrett sat facing her.

"How were the gallery showings?"

"Very good. I'm gratified. I'll paint whether people buy my work or not, but when my paintings sell, I feel good about it. I keep the ones I don't want to sell. Some are just for me and they're not going to a gallery." As she talked, she was intensely aware of Garrett's smoky gaze on her. His fascinating gray eyes and knowledge of what his kisses could do kept her tingling with anticipation.

"If it suits you, we'll go out to my house to hang the painting. When we're through, we'll have dinner."

"Sounds like a great evening."

In a short time they drove through an exclusive residential area with acres of tall pines and estates set back out of sight. Black wrought-iron gates swung open to allow them entrance.

She was curious about his home, interested in finding out more about him. When the trees cleared, she saw the sprawling, three-story stone mansion.

"Garrett, your home is beautiful." A long narrow pool was centered in the formal gardens in the front yard. Various fountains held splashing water and sunlight spilled an orange glow over the house. Tall, symmetrical Italian pines stood at opposite ends of the wide porch that led to massive double doors.

The limo halted and the driver held the door as they exited. The door opened before they reached it and Garrett introduced her. "Sophia, meet Terrence, who is my right-hand man. He's butler and house manager and keeps things running smoothly here. Terrence, this is Ms. Rivers."

"Welcome, Ms. Rivers," Terrence said, stepping back and holding the door wide.

Garrett took her arm as they entered.

"Somehow this surprises me. I imagined you in a different type of home," she said, realizing Garrett had far more wealth than she had thought.

"Maybe I better not ask what kind."

"Something less formal, maybe more Western. Although this mansion has enough rooms to have all types of decor."

"I'll show you my shop and then we'll find the perfect spot for your painting."

He led her down the wide, elegant hall with potted palms and oils in ornate frames hanging on the walls. They entered another wing of the mansion and finally turned into a large paneled room that smelled of sawdust. The terrazzo floor was rust-colored with dark brown stones. Beautiful pieces of furniture in various stages were scattered throughout the room. The framework for an ornate credenza stood on a worktable, above which tools hung. One wall held handcrafted cabinets containing more tools.

She walked around the room, inhaling the sawdust smell, taking in the furniture in progress, lumber, power saws, a stack of sawhorses. "This is what you love, isn't it?"

He stood watching her and nodded. "You're the first woman who has ever been down here."

"I'm honored," she said.

"Sophia," he said and stopped. He stared at her intently.

"Yes?"

"I just wondered what you think about all this. Although I suppose I need to show you a finished product before I ask you that," he replied.

She had the feeling that he had been about to say something else, and she wondered what it was. The slight frown on his face made her curiosity deepen but she was certain if she asked, she would not get the answer.

She walked to a table to run her finger along the smooth finish. "This is beautiful, Garrett."

"That still needs a lot of work. It's intended to be a

reproduction of a French walnut refectory table. I also enjoy history."

"So do you do this when you can't sleep?" she asked.

"Do you paint when you can't sleep?" he said, by way of answering.

She smiled at him.

"C'mon. I'll show you some finished pieces."

As they made their way out into the hall, she still felt as if he towered over her—a unique sensation and one she enjoyed.

They paused by an elegant reproduction of a 19th-century French sofa with embroidered rosebuds in beige damask upholstery. "Here's a finished piece," he said.

She had expected his work to be nice, but this was beyond nice. "Garrett, this looks like a well-preserved antique. It looks like the real thing." She ran her fingers over the smooth wood. "This is truly beautiful," she said, impressed. "You could make another fortune from your craft."

He smiled. "That's the best compliment I've ever received," he said. He placed his hands on her shoulders. "You do look stunning, Sophia. Do you mind?" he said while he reached up and pulled a pin out of her hair. Locks spilled on her shoulders as she gazed up at him.

He stood close, removing pins, causing a gentle tingling sensation on her scalp. She looked at his mouth and her heart drummed. She wanted him to kiss her right now and was tempted to pull him to her.

Instead, she kept quiet while Garrett finished and her hair cascaded across her shoulders. She moved her head slightly, shaking out her hair and letting it swirl across her shoulders. She still watched him while he gazed into her eyes. His attention shifted to her mouth.

"Garrett, show me more of your work," she said, her

voice breathless. She wanted his kisses, yet she felt she should resist and have some control. Garrett had come into her life like a whirlwind and she needed to show some resistance before he totally uprooted her career and schedules. Deep down, she had an instinctive feeling that Garrett was more than just an appealing man who excited her.

"Better yet, come with me and I'll show you where I want to hang your painting. There are two possible rooms—one is the billiard room, the other is a large living area. I entertain there and it's not as formal as some of the other rooms."

She followed him down the wide hall. "You really need a map for this mansion."

He smiled. "Your place wasn't small either."

"I'm so accustomed to it, I don't give a thought to the size."

"Nor do I." He motioned toward open double doors. She entered a large room that had two glass walls. One end of the room bowed out in a sweeping glass curve, giving the room light and a sensation of being outdoors. The other end featured a massive brick fireplace. Leather furniture and dark fruitwood lent a masculine touch.

"This is a livable room. Very comfortable," he said. "I'm in here a lot." He led her across the room and she saw a familiar painting she had done a year earlier.

"I like it there," she said, looking at her painting on his wall with others in a grouping. "A prominent spot in a room you like and live in. Now you can think of me when you see it," she added lightly, teasing him.

"I'll always think of you when I see it," he said, his solemn tone giving a deeper meaning to his words.

"Sure you will," she said, laughing. "Is this the room where you'd like to hang the other painting?"

"Yes, possibly. Where do you think it should go?"

Aware of his attention on her, she strolled around the room, selecting and then rejecting spots until she stopped. "I think this is a good place."

"It is. One other possibility you should consider is over the hearth. It's a sizable painting. I think it fits this room."

"That would be the most prominent spot in the room," she said, surprised and pleased.

"I think it would look good there." He shed his coat. "Let me hold it up and see what you think."

She watched as he picked up the painting and held it in place.

She smiled at him. "It looks great there. Are you sure?"

He grinned. "I'll get tools and hang it."

"What can I do?" she asked.

"Let's have a drink and you can supervise the hanging."

"I can get the drinks," she said, moving to the bar in the corner of the room. "What would you like?"

"I think I'll have beer."

"And I'll have red wine," she stated. While she got a wineglass and opened a bottle, he disappeared. By the time he returned, she was on a leather couch in front of the fireplace with the drinks on a table. He placed an armload of tools on a chair and pulled off his tie. He twisted free the top buttons of his shirt—something so ordinary and simple yet it filled her with heat and she longed to get up and unbutton the rest for him. He picked up his beer, raising the bottle high.

"Here's to improving the looks of my house by adding a Sophia Rivers painting."

"I'll drink to that," she said, standing and picking up her drink to touch his cold bottle. Again, when she looked into his eyes, her heart skipped a beat. Each time they almost kissed, her longing intensified. How soon would they be in each other's arms?

Sipping her red wine, she stepped back. His gaze remained locked on hers. Watching her, he sipped his beer and then turned away, breaking the spell.

He picked up the painting. "I'll hold this and you tell me when I have it in exactly the right spot." He held the painting high, and then set it down. "Just a minute. I can put myself back together later," he said as he took off his gold cuff links and folded back his immaculate cuffs. "Now, let's try this again."

Slightly disheveled, he looked sexy, appealing. She tried to focus on the painting, but was having a difficult time keeping her attention off the man.

"To the right and slightly higher," she said. After several adjustments, she nodded. "That's perfect."

He leaned back to look while he held the picture. Setting it down, he picked up chalk to mark a place on the bricks before pulling the tape measure out.

She sipped her wine while he worked. In an amazingly short time he had her painting hanging in place and he stepped away.

"Let's look at it."

He took her arm and they walked across the large room to study the result of his work. She was aware of the warmth of him beside her. He looked at his watch. "Shall we go eat now, or should I just throw some steaks on the grill?"

"If we eat here, it's fine with me."

He leaned down to look directly into her eyes. “Are you certain you don’t mind my cooking?”

“Now I’m curious,” she said. “I’ll view it as an adventure.”

“Steaks at home it is.” He draped his arm across her shoulders. “It’s a nice evening. We’ll eat on the terrace.”

They carried their drinks outside, and Sophia was again surprised by the house.

“This isn’t a terrace, Garrett—it’s another kitchen, plus a terrace, plus a living area, plus a pool.”

“With Houston’s weather, it works well through the fall and winter,” he replied, crossing to a stainless-steel gas grill built into a stone wall. In minutes he had the grill fired up and he sat with her on comfortable chairs in the outdoor living room.

“So where are you going, Sophia? What do you want out of life?”

“To pursue painting. To do charity work. I’d like to help with literacy. Also, try to do something to aid in getting more opportunities in school for children to take art and learn art appreciation. I want to open a gallery in New Mexico.”

“Marriage and family?”

She shrugged. “I don’t think about that. I’m accustomed to being on my own. I don’t ever want to be in the situation my mother was in—in love with my dad who never returned that love fully.”

“Your dad—you knew him?”

“What I told you last night wasn’t completely accurate. He was around off and on all my life,” she said, feeling a stab of pain and anger that had never left her. “My dad wouldn’t marry my mother. He practically ignored me except for financial support.”

“You said he was married?” Garrett said.

"Not by the time I was a teenager, but he didn't want to get tied down again. Whenever he came to visit, it tore her up each time he left. She would cry for several days. He was the only man she ever loved," Sophia stated bitterly. "He had a family—boys. He would go home to them. I couldn't do anything to help her or stop her tears. When I was little, we both cried. I cried for her and she cried over him."

"That's tough," Garrett said. "He ignored you?"

"In his way he provided for me. But looking back, I don't think he knew how to deal with a little girl. He brought me all kinds of presents. I can remember reaching an age where I smashed some of them to bits. Mom just started giving them to charities. I didn't want anything from him."

"How old were you then?"

"Probably about eight or nine. He was polite to me and Mom saw to it that I was polite to him, but we weren't together a whole lot. He never talked to me other than hello and goodbye. I rarely heard him say my name. When I was little I wondered whether he knew it. Often, I would be sent to my grandmother's, which I loved, or out with my nanny when he was coming. Worked fine for me. I didn't want to see him."

"Yet your mother always loved him."

"She did. And I don't ever want to fall into that trap. The best way to avoid it is to keep relationships from becoming too deep."

"Maybe you shouldn't base everything on the actions of your father."

"That's the legacy he left me—a deep fear of any relationship that isn't totally committed."

"Sorry, Sophia," Garrett said with a somber note.

"How'd we get on this?" she asked, wanting to avoid

thinking and talking about her blood father. She wanted him out of her life and thoughts as much as humanly possible.

"I'm interested in your life and finding out about you. Did he ever try to make it up to you?"

She thought of the inheritance Argus Delaney had left her. "He always showered Mom with money. Money was his solution for everything. He paid her medical bills, but by the time the end of her life came, we had enough money to manage on our own. No matter what happened, she always loved him. And I've always hated him," she said.

"At least he was good to her," Garrett said gently. "And generous."

"I suppose I should be grateful, but I can't be. He left money when he died—money I don't want one penny of," she said.

"He's gone. He'll never know whether you take his money or refuse it. Why not take it and enjoy it? It should be yours."

She shook her head, feeling the familiar current of fury that she had lived with as long as she could remember.

"I don't want anything to do with him."

"You could do a lot with your inheritance."

"I'll never touch it," she said, trying to shift her focus off the past and onto Garrett, thinking he would be fascinating to paint. His rugged features gave him a distinctive individualism and his unique gray eyes were unforgettable. Desire stirred and once again, she struggled to pay attention to their conversation.

He was studying her intently. "Sophia—" He paused, his eyes holding secrets. She couldn't tell what he was thinking.

"What? What were you going to say?"

He looked away. "I'll check on the steaks." She watched him stride to the cooker and she wondered for the second time this evening what it was he'd been about to say to her. Probably more advice about taking her inheritance, which she'd already heard enough of from Edgar.

"The steaks are ready."

She stood, going with him to help get tossed salads, potatoes and water on the table. Soon they sat on the terrace to eat thick, juicy steaks.

"It's a wonder you ever travel for pleasure. It's gorgeous here and you have every convenience."

"I like it here, but I like my other places, too."

"I guess I can understand since I enjoy Santa Fe and Taos and even the cabin in the mountains as much as living in Houston." She took a bite of her steak. "You're a very good cook. The steak is delicious," she said, surprised because he'd seemed to pay little attention to his cooking.

"I'm glad you think so."

"I should have watched you more closely. I invariably burn them."

"You can watch me as closely as you want," he replied with a twinkle.

"I opened the door for that one," she said, smiling at him. "So how did you get into property management?" she asked, picking up her water glass to take a sip. A faint breeze caught his hair, blowing it gently. His hair was thick, and she thought about how it felt to run her fingers through it.

"My dad had the business," he was saying. "He was into property management and finance. I was raised to follow in his footsteps and groomed to take over his businesses."

"Businesses? There are others?"

"Yes, but I'm not directly involved in most of them. Hardly involved at all. They're investments."

"And that leaves you free to play around," she said. "So what do you actually do?" she asked, flirting with him while trying to satisfy her curiosity about him and his life.

He smiled at her. "More than play around, although I hope to do that tonight. Dinner—get to know you—kiss you. That's what I want to do in the next few hours," he said, his voice deepening and making her tingle.

"I don't really know you. Do you work, Garrett, or does the playboy lifestyle fit you?"

"I work, but not tonight, so we can get away from that subject. You aren't eating, and I've lost my appetite for this steak. Let's sit where it's more comfortable to talk. We can take our drinks with us."

She was leaving a half-eaten steak, yet she couldn't resist his suggestion. Her interest in food had disappeared with Garrett's flirting. He took her hand and she stood, going with him, her insides tingling the moment he touched her.

Garrett sat close on the couch. Her perfume was an exotic fragrance and he liked the faint scent. Her long hair was silky in his fingers as he twisted and toyed with the strands. She was stunning and he couldn't get enough of her. And yet, he was racked with guilt.

When she had talked about Argus Delaney, Garrett felt awful that he wasn't telling her the truth about who he was. Twice he had been on the verge, almost confessing and then pausing, waiting because it seemed the wisest course to follow. If he confessed the truth now, he was certain he would be finished. It was too soon, but knowing that didn't ease his conscience.

"What about you and marriage?" she asked.

"I'm a workaholic, I suppose," he said, stretching out his long legs. "I haven't ever been deeply in love," he admitted. "I don't feel ready for marriage or getting tied down. Right now, my life is devoted to my work."

"Pretty ordinary attitude when someone is tied up in work," she stated.

As he gazed into her eyes, he wondered what it would be like to come home to her every night—to make love to her night and day. His thoughts surprised him. Sophia stirred him in a way no woman before her ever had. He had never had long-term thoughts or speculation about a woman before. Not even when he had been in a relationship. "I owe you an elegant dinner and dancing instead of sitting at my house and eating my cooking and helping me hang your painting," he said, trying to get focused again on the present and stop imagining a future with her. That kind of thinking disturbed him. Because it was totally uncustomary.

"I'm enjoying the evening. You don't owe me an elegant dinner," she said. "This has been nice and you're an interesting man, Garrett Cantrell."

Garrett smiled at her. "You barely know me. And I lead an ordinary life."

"Why do I doubt that statement? You've bought two of my paintings. That alone makes you interesting."

"Next time we go to your house and I get to see where you paint," he said.

"It's a typical studio with brushes and paint smears. I don't think it's quite as interesting as your workshop."

"If it's yours, it's interesting. Have you painted all your life?"

"Actually, yes. I loved drawing and painting. Of course, what little girl doesn't?"

As she talked about painting when she was a child, his mind returned to the problem. He hated not telling her about the Delaneys, yet he had heard the bitterness, felt her anger smoldering. He wanted to be up front with her—his guilt was deepening by the minute.

He realized she was staring at him with a quizzical smile. "What?" he asked.

"You haven't heard one word I've been saying, Garrett. Is there something you want to tell me? What are you thinking about?"

He focused on her lips before looking into her eyes again while desire consumed him. He didn't want to admit the truth yet and the burden of guilt was becoming unbearable, but one way to avoid both was to stop her questions with kisses.

Three

Sophia gazed at Garrett, waiting for an answer to her question, wondering what he had on his mind. Was it his business that had him so lost in his own thoughts?

Was it her?

"Garrett, what is it?" she asked, looking into his eyes.

Lust was blatant, causing her pulse to race. Perhaps it *was* her.

He leaned close, slipping his arm around her waist to pull her to him, ending her questions as his mouth covered hers. Her heart slammed against her ribs.

She inhaled, winding her arms around his neck while she kissed him in return. When he pulled her onto his lap, she was barely aware of moving.

He wound his fingers in her hair and she clung to him. Her body tingled, an aching need beginning. She moaned softly as he ran his hand down her back, over the curve of her hip to her thighs. He pushed the hem of her skirt higher to touch her bare skin. Hot, urgent longing consumed her. Her fingers worked free the remaining buttons of his shirt and she pushed it away to touch his sculpted chest. She ran her fingers lower over his muscled stomach. The touch caused the fires within her to blaze. She gasped over caressing him, realizing she had to stop or she would be lost in lovemaking, complicating her life in a manner she had always intended to avoid. She had never slept with a man and she didn't intend to take that step now.

She caught his wrist and raised her head. "This is crazy, Garrett. I barely know you. We're going too fast."

"We're getting to know each other, and I'd say the chemistry is pretty hot." As he talked, he ran both hands through her hair on either side of her face. "You're beautiful. You take my breath away. Sophia, I want to make love to you," he whispered hoarsely.

Her heart thudded but she forced herself to slide off his lap. "Let's take a breather and slow things down," she said, standing to face him.

He stood, his desire obvious. His shirt was unbuttoned to the waist and pushed open to reveal his broad, muscled, masculine chest. Her mouth was dry and she had to fight the urge to fling her arms around his neck and kiss him again.

"I haven't felt this way about anyone before," he said, sounding surprised, frowning slightly as if he weren't happy about it.

"Please sit, Sophia. We'll just talk," he said.

She sat, turning so she could face him. The moment he was seated, he wrapped his fingers in her hair. "We can sit and talk, but I can't keep from touching you."

"Garrett, I meant it when I said I'm not into affairs.

I watched my mother shed a million tears over my father. I won't put myself in that position."

"I can understand that completely. But we're not having an affair. We're kissing."

"I know. But things are escalating quickly," she said.

"Well, now I'm duly warned about your feelings," he said with a smile.

"I figure it's better to be forthright and upfront with you. Why are you smiling?"

"I didn't mean to. You just remind me of a friend who is forthright," he replied, combing his fingers slowly through her hair, caressing her nape and then picking up long strands to wind them in his fingers again. "Sophia, I already feel as if I've known you a long time."

"I like that," she said, trying to focus on their conversation, yet more aware of his hand lightly toying with her hair.

"So. Let's talk. Do you have other relatives?" he asked. "Did your mother have any brothers or sisters?"

"I have two aunts, one uncle and eight cousins, all scattered around this part of Texas. I see them at family events, but otherwise, we haven't been that close since she's been gone. I never knew my father's family, nor did I want to," she said coldly.

"You might be making a mistake there," Garrett said.

Sophia felt her blood turn to ice, and she glared at Garrett. "No, I'm not. His family was the reason he wouldn't marry my mother. I don't want to know them or have anything to do with any part of him."

"Sophia, *you're* part of him. And they couldn't help being part of him any more than you could."

She hadn't ever thought about how innocent they were of what their father did, and the thought startled her, but she pushed it away. His sons were still his blood.

"Even so, they grew up with him. They have his name and he's honored them." Why did Garrett keep taking Argus's side? She disliked talking about her father or even thinking about him. "Garrett, let's find something else to discuss. Do you have any other hobbies besides the furniture?"

"Sure. I work out. I ski. I play tennis, play polo and I swim. You?"

"More things we have in common. I love rodeos, country dances. I also like to ski, swim and I play the piano," she answered.

"With the storms that have gone through recently, they've already had enough freezing weather in the upper levels of Colorado mountains to ski. Fly up there with me for the weekend. We can leave early in the morning and come back Sunday evening."

"You're serious," she said, surprised by his invitation.

"Why not? We'll have fun, ski, nothing big. Just a fun getaway. My condo is large. You can take your pick of bedrooms."

"You are serious." A weekend with Garrett. Excitement bubbled and she wanted to accept, yet common sense reminded her again to slow down with him. He had come into her life like a whirlwind.

He leaned closer and held her chin. "Come with me. No strings. I'll bring you home anytime you want. We'll ski, relax, talk. Do whatever we want."

Her heartbeat quickened. She was surprised at herself because his offer held some appeal. On the other hand, years of being wary of getting too close to someone were ingrained in her.

"I don't think flying to Colorado with you is a good idea."

"Sophia, you're not going to risk getting hurt by spending the weekend skiing with me. We're not getting into anything remotely serious."

"But this is exactly how you get into something serious. Moment after moment together and then it's too late."

"Take a risk and live a little. This is simply two days. We're not going to fall in love over the weekend."

She blushed. She hadn't been worried about falling in love.

Had she?

"If you're worried, we can ask Edgar to join us."

She couldn't keep from laughing. "You're willing to invite Edgar, too?"

"If that's what it takes to spend the weekend with you, yes, I'll invite Edgar, too."

"Now you're making me feel foolish."

"That's not my intention. Listen, I understand why you don't want to follow in your mother's footsteps, but I don't think you run any risk of that happening with me."

Her eyes widened. "I guess I've lumped all males into the same group as my father."

"I can't blame you for being hurt, Sophia," he said solemnly and her heart warmed. He gazed intently at her while she debated, waiting quietly.

"I'll go with you," she said, smiling at him.

"Excellent. It'll be fun. No big deal."

It was a big deal because she didn't even spend weekends with men she knew. All she had to go on with Garrett was the information she had received about him from others and her own feelings.

"I'll tell Edgar I'm going, but we're not inviting him along. He hates cold weather and he can't imagine fastening his feet to 'long boards,' as he calls them. Thank you, though, for the offer to invite him," she said.

"Good. I'll check the weather right now. I don't fly into storms if I can possibly avoid it."

She watched as he pulled out his phone. He smiled broadly, sexy creases bracketing his mouth. "Good weather—cold nights, sunny days. I'll call my pilot. How early can we go?"

"Name your time."

"I'll pick you up at seven."

"Fine with me," she said. She'd surprised herself, she thought as eagerness bubbled in a steady current. The weekend with Garrett. Foolhardy, risky for her heart.

Exciting.

Walking away, Garrett talked with the pilot and made arrangements. When he was done, he sat beside her again. "We're set to fly at eight."

"So one of your traits is impulsiveness," she said. "I'm learning more about you."

"I don't think I'd describe myself as impulsive. Usually I'm predictable and methodical."

"If we get to know each other, I'll weigh in on that."

"We'll get to know each other, Sophia," he said softly in a husky tone that sent a tingle spiraling in her. "I definitely intend that we do."

Desire was constant with Garrett, keeping her intensely aware of him in a physical manner. Despite her concerns, she couldn't deny that she loved being with him, hearing about him, learning about him. In some ways, she, too, felt as if she had known him a long time. They talked until one and she promised herself by half past she would end the evening. Finally, when it was almost two, she stood.

"Garrett, I must get home."

"You don't have to go if you don't want." He waved his hand toward his house. "Needless to say, there is plenty of room here. Take any bedroom you want. Close to mine, far from mine or in mine with me," he teased. "I'll even promise to not wake you in the morning. Particularly if you make the last choice."

Shaking her head, she laughed. "It does seem silly for you to drive me home, but that's what I want. If I'm going to Colorado to ski, I want to go home and get some things."

"All right. Home it is. I told my chauffeur we'd take you home tonight."

"See, I should have driven."

"I would insist on taking you home even if you had driven. It's way too late for you to be out driving around by yourself."

"That's an old-fashioned notion."

"It's not the first time someone has accused me of having old-fashioned notions."

"I think old-fashioned is rather nice if it isn't overdone. Edgar gets a little carried away— I'll probably have a text waiting from him when I get in. He's probably running background checks on you as we speak."

She expected a laugh but Garrett merely gave her a smile and stood. "Shall we go?"

When they arrived at her house, the limo waited while Garrett walked with her to her door. He stepped inside, waiting while she switched off the alarm and then pulling her into his embrace to kiss her.

With her heart racing, she wrapped her arms around him and kissed him in return, pouring her feelings into her kiss, wanting to spend the rest of the night with him, wanting to touch and caress and make love, yet knowing she should do little more than what they were doing unless she wanted to risk losing her heart.

How much time passed, she didn't know or care. They were breathless, wanting more. Need became a raging fire. When Garrett's hands began to roam over her, she stopped him and stepped back.

"We'll say good-night," she stated. Her voice was breathless as she gulped for air. "Garrett, tonight has been so much fun," she said softly. His gray eyes had darkened to slate, desire burning in their depths. "Thanks for a grand evening."

"I'll see you in the morning, Sophia," he said, giving her a smile that nearly stopped her heart. He turned and left, the lock clicking in place behind him.

For a moment, she could barely move, resting against the door, trying desperately to catch her breath, wondering if she was about to make the biggest mistake of her life.

Garrett swore under his breath. He liked Sophia more than any woman he had known. He wanted to call Will immediately and tell him that he hated deceiving her and it had to end. But he knew that as soon as he told Sophia thc Dclaneys had sent him, she would break it off.

He was torn between admitting the truth to her and running the risk of losing her, or continuing the deception until he felt she liked him enough that they could weather the storm that would break when he told her the truth.

More than once he had mulled over resigning from Delaney Enterprises and devoting himself to building furniture. Sometimes he thought of working with his hands, living in a place near the ocean, creating instead of acquiring. He often wondered if the notion of changing careers was merely a pipe dream, yet Sophia had successfully done just that.

Only her situation had been different. He had been raised to do this kind of work and he felt he owed the Delaney family his services. Argus Delaney had taken his father out of poverty, given him a job and paid for his education because he said he saw potential in his dad. His father had worked hard and risen fast and Argus had helped him all along the way, opening doors and paying him well. In turn, his father had absolute loyalty to the Delaneys and had raised Garrett to feel the same. If he left Delaney Enterprises, Garrett felt he would be turning his back on all his father had wanted for him, and on Will's friendship. And he was inheriting a fortune from Will's dad.

Even so, the thought was tempting. Especially after being with Sophia.

For the first time he considered actually going through with telling Will he was resigning. If he resigned, he might have hope of some kind of future with Sophia.

How tempting. He could tell Sophia everything with a clear conscience.

Could he do it?

At his estate he glanced at his watch and picked up his phone to call Will. "Sorry for the early hour."

"I hope it's because you have good news."

"I don't, and I don't know whether I ever will. She told me more about your dad. She's incredibly bitter."

"Are you making any progress?"

"We're flying to Colorado to ski for the weekend."

"I call that progress. Just hang in there—sounds as

if you two get along fine," Will said, his voice rising with enthusiasm.

"We do," Garrett said in clipped tones. "I don't know what will happen when I tell her the truth. Will, I hate not being up front with her on this."

"You're doing her a favor, too—don't forget that."

"Dammit, Will, she's been hurt. She isn't going to change easily and I can't keep up this deception," Garrett said, startled by how deeply concerned he had become over Sophia's feelings. He cared more for her than he would have dreamed possible when he first took this assignment.

"You don't need to feel guilty. You're doing your job. Do your best is all we all ask—your best is mighty damn fine. We're counting on you."

"I know. I'll see how it goes today."

"Don't rush. Get her so close she'll do what you want."

Garrett hated the sound of that. "I'll talk to you tomorrow or Monday," he said.

"Have a real good time."

He hung up, wondering why he'd even bothered to call Will. He stared at the phone with Will's words echoing in his thoughts. *We're counting on you.* All his adult life they had counted on him. He couldn't toss that aside.

Doubting if he would sleep at all, he skipped bed and headed to the shower, thinking of being with her again, of her dark eyes and midnight hair, her laughter, her kiss. A whole weekend. By the time they flew back to Texas, he hoped to be closer to her.

The big question was: What would happen if he told her the truth? Would he lose her forever?

* * *

Sophia rummaged in her closet for ski clothes and other things she would need. Still marveling at the thought that she had accepted Garrett's offer, she decided to wait to text Edgar until the morning.

Anticipation kept a running current of excitement humming through her body. She kept glancing at the clock, anxious to see Garrett again. Was she falling into the same trap her mother had fallen into? Was she doing what she had tried all her adult life to avoid—falling in love?

A text message broke into her thoughts.

Are you home? I've been worried about you. All OK?

She fired back an answer.

I'm home, Edgar. Flying to Colorado tomorrow to ski with Garrett. Back Sunday. Don't worry about me. Go to bed.

Minutes after she sent the text, her phone rang. "Edgar, do you know what time it is?"

"I know you're still awake," he answered. "I hope you keep in touch. Sophia, this isn't like you. How important is Garrett Cantrell to you?"

"I like the guy and we're becoming friends. I can do that," she said, hoping she could hold true to her words. "We'll be back home early Sunday evening."

"I just want to keep my promise to your mother."

"Stop worrying. Mom had no idea you would take her request to this extent. I'm grown, Edgar. I can take care of myself."

"All right, I'll buzz off. Let me know when you're back in town. You can tell me all about your weekend."

Smiling, she put away her phone and climbed into bed.

Just a few short hours later, Garrett was at her door. As he stepped inside, his gaze roamed over her.

She smiled while her heart jumped. Each time they were together, she thought he was more handsome than the time before. Dressed in a cable-knit navy sweater and jeans, he took her breath away.

"You look gorgeous," he said, wrapping one arm around her waist and leaning down to kiss her. She wound her arms around his neck to kiss him in return.

With an effort she moved away. "This is not a weekend for seduction," she said with a smile.

"That's simply a good morning kiss," he said. "And I know what I promised you. We'll keep things light. Unless you change your mind," he added with a grin. "The weather report is good so we're on our way." He picked up her skis, shouldering her bag as she gathered her purse and jacket.

"Sorry, the tour of my house will have to wait," she said.

"Something to look forward to in the coming week. Perhaps Monday night."

She laughed at his attempt to make plans with her for Monday even though they hadn't even gone away for the weekend yet.

At the airport, they boarded a waiting jet that was far larger than she had expected. Its luxurious interior made her forget she was on board a plane for a few moments.

As they flew, Garrett sat facing her, their knees almost touching. It was difficult to keep her mind on the conversation because she was lost in looking at him. She still marveled at her reaction to him, alternating between enjoying it and being concerned by it. *Remember, it's just a fun weekend,* she told herself.

Far sooner than she expected they were driving through the small Colorado resort town to Garrett's condo.

His condo was built of stone with panoramic mountain views. Polished plank floors gleamed beneath high, open-beamed ceilings. Garrett built a roaring fire in the massive stone fireplace.

"What a change this is. It's a picture book," she said, looking out the window that covered almost the entire front wall.

Garrett stood behind her with his arms lightly around her. "We can hit the slopes or wait, if you prefer."

"We came to ski. I vote to ski."

"All right. I'll meet you back here in twenty minutes."

She went to the bedroom she had selected on the opposite end of the hall from Garrett's, which had made him smile. She changed into her gear, finally gathering her parka, sunglasses and gloves. They spent the rest of the day on the slopes, discovering they were well-matched skiers. They returned as the sun was setting.

"When we're changed, I'll take you to my favorite restaurant," Garrett said, stomping snow off his feet inside the entryway.

"Sounds good to me—I'm starving."

"Meet you here in, what?"

"Give me thirty minutes," she replied.

Certain he would be ready in far less time, she hurried. Thirty minutes later she made one last check. Her red wool pants and sweater were warm, as were her fur-lined boots. She let her hair go unpinned. With a toss of her head to get her long hair away from her face, she went to meet him.

As she entered the room, only one small lamp burned

and she could see the view of the sparkling lights through the picture window. The view was spectacular with twinkling lights below spreading out toward the snow-covered mountains that glistened beneath a rising full moon. But when Garrett entered the room, she only had eyes for him. He wore a bulky sweater that emphasized his broad shoulders, tight jeans and Western boots. He stepped closer and his direct gaze held her. Desire shone in the smoky depths of his eyes.

"Now this is best of all," he said. "You look beautiful. I love your hair down." He wrapped his fingers in her hair and his arm circled her waist as he pulled her close. "This is perfect," he whispered before he covered her mouth with his.

Ending their kiss, she tried to catch her breath, noticing that his breathing was as ragged as hers. Taking his cue from her, he stepped back.

"Shall we go?" he said in a husky voice while he caressed her nape.

He held her parka and she pulled on her gloves as they went downstairs to the car. During the ride she looked at the charming snow-covered town, but her thoughts tumbled over the excitement of being here with Garrett and the worry of how important he was becoming in her life.

At the restaurant they sat close to a blazing fire while piano music played softly. They ordered cups of steaming cider and hors d'oeuvres. Garrett had been famished when he finished dressing, but now his appetite had dwindled. He longed to hold Sophia, to kiss her. He ached to just touch her, to physically keep contact. Her hair fell loosely over her shoulders and around her face. Her luminous brown eyes were thickly lashed and captivating. And she looked happy.

Which made what he had to do even harder.

This withholding of information had gone on long enough. The closer they got, the more important it was to be honest with her. He had never been devious in his dealings before and he didn't want to start now.

It was a miracle she hadn't already discovered his connection with the Delaneys. But he was certain he would know when she had.

How he wished he didn't have this big secret. If only he were free to pursue her honestly the way he wanted, in a manner he had never dreamed of before.

Candlelight on the table reflected in her dark eyes. Each day he had been amazed by how much he wanted to be with her. She was becoming more important to him by the minute. Which meant he needed to tell her.

"You're an excellent skier," she said.

"I was going to tell you the same."

She smiled. "I think you held back to stay with me. It was invigorating, a real change from my regular life. You've turned my world topsy-turvy."

And there it was—the perfect opening to tell her about the Delaneys.

But he couldn't. He realized he didn't want to tell her in public. He wanted to be alone with her. And he also realized that no matter how guilty he was feeling, he should wait until they returned to Houston. It would give him the weekend to get closer to her and hopefully create a stronger bond between them that would be harder for her to break.

A voice inside him told him that that was a cruel thing to do, but he ignored it.

He didn't want to lose her. From the first moment he

had seen her, he'd been drawn to her and the thought of losing her made his insides churn. He had never expected to find her fascinating, to want a relationship with her.

"Maybe you've turned mine topsy-turvy, too."

"I seriously doubt that," she said. "All of this is scrumptious," she added, taking a bite of a mini-beef Wellington. I can see why this is your favorite restaurant."

"Good—I'm so glad you like it. So tell me, do you go to your gallery every day?"

"Not at all. I have a competent manager and excellent staff. They run the business so I can stay at the studio and paint."

"I don't blame you. If I ever build furniture full-time, I'll do the same."

"Why do you stay in property management? With your talent for woodwork, you could build a following very quickly."

"Blame my father for that one. I was raised to be in a productive, lucrative business. It was instilled in me as far back as I can remember."

"But your father is gone now, and you've already proved yourself in that area. Your furniture would be productive and lucrative."

"I'm wound up in obligations. Imagined or real, they are as much a part of me as my breathing. To Dad, who hasn't been gone that long, my fascination with building was entertainment and silly."

"Too bad," she said, shaking her head. "What did your dad want for you in your personal life?"

"The usual. Marriage and kids. But I've watched too many people have miserable marriages, and I'm not ready to get tied down."

"Tied down," she repeated, smiling. "So no long relationships in your past?"

"None. And evidently, none in yours."

"Absolutely not."

When he had first met her, her answer would have pleased him—a woman who did not want any deep commitment. Why now did he feel jolted slightly by her answer? Was Sophia weaving a web around his heart—something no woman had ever done?

It was nine before they left the restaurant. When they stepped outside a light snow fell, big flakes drifting, glistening in the light.

"Look, Garrett, this is enchanting," she said, spinning around with her arms spread wide. Her long hair flew out behind her, swirling around her face. He couldn't resist wrapping his arms around her to kiss her, tasting a wet snowflake on her lips.

When he released her, she stepped away. "We're in public."

"I couldn't resist," he admitted, thinking he would always remember her spinning around in the snow, a beautiful woman whose exuberance and zest for life were contagious. He looked up at the falling flakes and took out his phone. "We weren't supposed to have this kind of weather."

"It's gorgeous. I can't keep from being glad we have it."

"Even if you're snowbound with me?" he asked.

"Even if. I'll manage."

"Chance of a trace of snow," he read off his phone. "Clear Sunday." On impulse he glanced up. "Do it again. Let me get your picture."

Laughing but humoring him, she did and he took a picture that he expected to be a blur, a disappointment.

Instead, the picture was clear with her dark hair swinging out behind her head. He had caught her big smile and the essence of the moment. It would have been a perfect moment if it weren't for this big secret between them. He put away his phone, shaking off the thought. "A trace of snow tonight won't make any difference except to please you."

"It definitely does," she said. "Hey, wait. You're not the only one who wants a picture of this." She yanked out her phone. "Smile, Garrett."

He grinned while she took his picture and then flashed it briefly so he had a glimpse of himself. Linking his arm in hers, he waited for the valet to bring his car.

They stomped snow off their boots at his condo and he built another fire, which gave a low light. When he turned away from the hearth, he faced her.

Sophia stood at the window with the flickering orange flames playing over her. As his gaze drifted down over her lush curves and long legs, his heartbeat quickened. His longing was intense. He crossed the short distance to take her in his arms.

Four

Sophia's heart thudded as she wrapped her arms around Garrett. The day had been magical and she had grown closer to him, learning more about him and enjoying herself. All through dinner she had wanted to be alone with him so they could be together like this again.

Snowflakes had been the perfect touch, landing in his dark hair, sprinkling across his broad shoulders. His kiss had tantalized her. She wanted more of him, so much more.

She didn't believe in love at first sight, or second or third for that matter. She thought if she ever fell in love it would be with someone she had been friends with for years, yet Garrett shook her theories because he was already more important to her than anyone else she had ever dated. He was pure temptation.

He made her want to risk her heart.

She stood on tiptoe, her heart pounding while he

held her tightly against his long frame. His hand slid down her back and up beneath her sweater. She moaned softly, the sound muffled by his mouth on hers. His fingers trailed up her back in a feathery touch that was electrifying.

He picked her up and carried her closer to the fire, setting her on her feet while he still kissed her as flames crackled. Garrett stepped back and pulled her sweater over her head, tossing it aside. He unfastened her lacy bra and removed it, dropping it to the floor.

With a deep sigh he stepped back, cupping her breasts in his hands. "So beautiful," he said, his gaze as sensual as his caresses. His thumb traced circles on her nipples that sent currents streaming from his touch.

She tugged his sweater over his head to toss it aside. She moaned in pleasure again while her hands roamed over his broad, muscled chest, her fingers tangling in a thick mat of chest hair that tapered to a narrow line disappearing beneath his belt.

Firelight spilled over him, highlighting bulging muscles, leaving dark shadows on flat planes. His handsome features captivated her, and in some ways she felt as if she had known him for years instead of days, just as he had said to her.

Desire wracked her. She wanted to make love. She ran her hands over his flat stomach until he leaned down to kiss each breast, his tongue tracing circles. She gasped again with pleasure, closing her eyes and clinging to him while fire raged within her.

She wanted him with an urgency she had never felt before. Garrett was special, unique in her life and she didn't think Garrett would ever hurt her. It was a night, not a relationship. Was she succumbing in the same foolish way to temptation, just as her mother had done in allowing a man to become irresistible?

All her logic fled, driven away by passion when his arm banded her waist again, pulling her tightly against him. He picked her up again to carry her to a sofa, settling her on his lap. Her bare breasts were pressed against his warm chest, the thick mat of chest hair sensual against her naked skin. As they kissed his hands roamed over her, light caresses that scalded.

Kisses became hotter, deeper and more passionate and she didn't notice his hands at the buttons on her pants. He pushed them down, standing and setting her on her feet to let them fall around her ankles.

He paused, stepping back to lift one of her feet to remove her boot and sock and then he moved to the other foot, standing to hold her hips while his gaze drifted slowly over her. "You're lovely, so beautiful," he whispered. He yanked off his boots and socks, tossing them aside. When he stood, she unfastened his belt and pulled it free, dropping it and unbuttoning his jeans to push them off. As he kicked them away, he pulled her into his arms.

This was the time to stop if she was going to, but she had already made a decision that went against everything she had practiced. Take a chance with Garrett tonight. Tomorrow she could say no. She had never had a weekend like this one and might not ever again. She gazed into his gray eyes that were heavy-lidded, filled with sensual promises. She wanted him to an extent she had never wanted any man. She wanted to be loved by Garrett. She could take what she wanted, and then go back to her resolutions and her safe life.

Garrett drove all thoughts away with his kisses and caresses.

Her insides knotted, fires building low in her. He sat and pulled her onto his lap against his thick rod, caressing her while one hand dallied lightly along her legs, moving to the inside of her thighs, heightening desire.

Continuing to kiss her, he leaned over her while his fingers went beneath the flimsy bikini panties. She spread her legs slightly, giving him more access, moaning with pleasure and need.

He touched her intimately, kissing her, his other hand caressing her breast while his fingers were between her legs. Pleasurable torment built as he stood again to peel away her panties.

Freeing him, she removed his briefs, caressing his hard manhood, stroking and then kissing him. He closed his eyes, his hands winding in her hair while he groaned. In seconds, he raised her up, looking into her eyes.

He picked her up once again, carrying her to the bedroom, placing her on the bed and then shifting to her ankle to kiss her, trailing kisses along her leg to the back of her knee. Gradually, his tongue moved up the inside of her thigh. Writhing, she closed her eyes while he moved between her legs, driving her wild with his tongue and fingers.

She sat up swiftly, wrapping her arms around him and pulling him down. He held her tightly, kissing her fervently.

"Garrett, I don't have any protection," she whispered.

"I do," he answered. He left, and in seconds returned with a small packet, which he opened. He spread her legs and knelt between them to put on the condom and then he lowered himself.

He started to enter her and she wrapped her legs around him. As he lowered himself and thrust slowly, he stopped. "Sophia," he said, frowning and sounding shocked.

She held him tightly. "I know what I want," she whispered.

"You're a virgin," he said, starting to pull away.

"Garrett," she whispered, holding on to keep him from leaving. "Love me," she whispered. "I want you to," she said before kissing him passionately. He hesitated a moment and then slowly pushed into her, sending a sharp pain that was gone when he filled her and slowly moved in her.

In seconds she rocked with him, lost in desire. The tension increased. Garrett was covered in sweat, moving with her, trying to pleasure her while urgency grew. And then all control was gone. He pumped fast and she met him, clinging to him as relief burst and rapture poured over her.

"Garrett," she cried out, holding him tightly, spinning away in ecstasy, oblivious of all else.

He shuddered with his release and then showered kisses on her, slowing as his ragged breathing calmed.

They were finally still, wrapped together, her heartbeat returning to normal. She held him tightly while her fingers played over one muscled shoulder.

"You should have told me," he said.

"It didn't matter."

"Yes, it did. I tried to avoid hurting you."

She framed his face with her hands and kissed him lightly. "You couldn't hurt me," she said and saw something flicker in the depths of his eyes that was like a warning bell to her, yet had it been her imagination? The warmth in his eyes now enveloped her and she pushed away her worry.

He rolled over, keeping her with him, their legs entangled. He combed long strands of hair away from her face and smiled at her. "You're beautiful," he whispered, kissing her lightly.

"Garrett, when I flew up here, I was certain this would never happen," she said, running her fingers over his bare shoulder.

He showered light kisses on her temple down to her ear. "I actually hadn't planned on it either. I didn't think you'd want to make love." He propped himself up on an elbow to look down at her, gazing intently. "I'll never hurt you, Sophia. I'll never be like your father."

"Shh, Garrett. Let me enjoy the moment now," she said lightly, touched by his statement. She noticed his voice had deepened, his words sounding heartfelt. She combed his brown hair back from his forehead. "This was a one-time thing. I'll go right back to my former resolutions because that's the safe way to live and protect my heart," she said.

He kissed the corner of her mouth lightly. "We'll see what the future brings," he whispered, placing more kisses on her throat.

She ran her fingers along his jaw. "This was perfect. I'll always remember it."

"I agree with that. Monday night I want to see your house, particularly your studio."

"That's a deal. But I think you'll be disappointed. My studio is just an art studio with all the mess that goes with painting."

"It'll be fascinating."

"If it is, you do lead a boring life." She smiled at him and shook her head in wonder. "I'm amazed there isn't one particular woman in your life right now."

"There is definitely one particular woman in my

life right now." He kissed her again on her throat and shoulders.

Through the night they made love and at dawn she fell asleep in his arms. Sometime later, she stirred and looked down at Garrett. The sheet was across his waist, leaving his chest bare. Even in sleep, his looks fascinated her.

She had no regrets. Garrett excited her more than any man she had ever known. He was intelligent, interesting, fun to be with, exceedingly sexy. She thought she could still keep her heart intact as long as she ended the intimacy when they returned to their regular lives in Texas.

But could she do that? She was realistic enough to know that she was not wildly in love. She was certain she could say no to intimacy.

She leaned down to kiss his shoulder so lightly her lips barely brushed him. His arm circled her waist, pulling her down against him as he slowly opened his eyes. He rolled over while she opened her mouth to tell him good morning. Before she could say a word he kissed her and all conversation was lost.

It was almost two hours later when he held her in his arms while sunshine spilled into the room.

"I have a suggestion for the day," he said. "I'll cook breakfast and then we can ski. Or I'll cook breakfast and then we'll stay right here in the cabin."

She laughed. "I say we cook breakfast and ski because that's what we came here to do. And we've been loving it up for hours."

"And I'm ready to love it up some more," he said, rolling over on top of her to end their discussion.

He finally cooked breakfast at one. They ate beside a

window with a view of the mountains that surrounded the small town.

"Do we have time to ski for an hour?"

"Of course," he replied, looking amused. "It's my plane. We can ski for three hours if you want, or longer."

"One hour will be sufficient and then I'll be ready to go back to Texas."

"One hour it is. But there's no need to rush back to Texas."

"Garrett, it's over."

He paused, gazing into her eyes. He cocked his head to one side. "Don't make up your mind hastily. You might change how you feel."

She shook her head. "No. Last night was special and I wanted it to be with you, but we won't pursue it because that could to lead to heartbreak. I'm not taking that chance."

"You're scared to live, Sophia." His gray eyes darkened slightly. He looked away and a muscle worked in his jaw, a more intense reaction than she would have expected. For an instant, anger flashed like a streak of lightning and then was gone.

"Maybe I'm just exercising caution and waiting for a deep, true love. This weekend was a brief idyll in my steady life."

"You're an artist and I doubt if there is any way you can describe your life as 'steady.'"

"Let's clean up and go ski."

"I have someone who will come in and clean after we're gone. We'll spend our time on the slopes."

She hurried to dress, thinking about their conversation and wondering if she could stick by her declarations. She had never expected to have this night of love and yet she had made the decision clearly and rationally and she had no regrets.

But she began to wonder: Was one of the consequences of her actions last night falling in love with Garrett?

She mulled over the question, unable to answer it. She didn't feel the same toward him as she had before they'd made love for hours. And to her surprise, the night simply made her want to be with him more, not less. Could she stand by her resolutions, do what she knew she should do?

Could she avoid a heartbreak with Garrett? Or was she blindly ignoring the truth that she might be falling in love with him already?

Or, more likely, that she had fallen in love with him that first night she met him?

They skied and returned to his condo by five after eating burgers on the way back. Garrett made a call to his pilot. "He'll be ready. I told him we can be there by six."

"I can be ready in just a few minutes. After all, I didn't bring much."

"I'll call him back and make it thirty minutes from now. Or maybe I won't," he said, his voice dropping. He tossed his phone on a table and crossed to take her into his arms, holding her tightly as he kissed her.

Their passionate kiss lengthened until clothes flew and they made love again with a desperate haste.

By seven, they were airborne. She looked below as twinkling lights disappeared and the night swallowed the plane.

"Garrett, it was a wonderful weekend," she said.

He leaned close to kiss her briefly. When he straightened up, he met her gaze. "It *was* a wonderful weekend," he repeated. "An unforgettable one, Sophia. I hope we have more unforgettable moments together. A lot more," he said.

"I don't think that will happen," she said. "We've both avoided any lasting relationship so I don't expect one to happen now."

"The heart is unpredictable."

"You sound like a romantic," she said, amused.

"That's the first time in my life I've ever been accused of being a romantic."

"Maybe I see a different side to you."

He smiled at her.

"When will you let me paint your portrait?"

"I'd love to have anything you paint, except a painting with myself as the subject. I can't exactly see hanging it in my house."

"Everyone should have a portrait painted. It's for posterity. You'll change your mind, and when you do, remember that I'd like to paint it. You have an interesting face."

"Another first. I've never heard that before either. I think you're seeing different things in me from what everyone else sees."

"I see good things."

"Sophia, listen. I want to be in your life for a long time."

"I'm all for continuing to get to know each other, Garrett," she said carefully.

He leaned close, plăcing his hands on both arms of her chair. "I hope you never change your mind," he said, startling her with his sincerity, a look of deep sorrow on his face.

"What is it, Garrett?"

He sat back and smiled at her, looking himself again. "I just hope we can keep spending time together."

While they talked, she thought about the past twenty-four hours and was still amazed at how her life had taken an unexpected turn since meeting Garrett.

It was after ten by the time they reached her house. "If you have a moment, come in and I'll show you the studio."

"Sure. Why put off until tomorrow what you can do today?" he teased.

They walked through a wide entry hall that had a twelve-foot-high ceiling. A circular staircase curved to the second floor. Double doors opened to a dining area on one side of the front hall while columns separated the hall from a formal living area.

He paused to look at Louis XVI furniture on the polished oak floor and an elegant marble fireplace. "I'm surprised. I expected you to have something rustic to match your paintings." One of her landscapes hung above the mantel. "That's a superb painting. No wonder you kept it."

"Thank you. I enjoy it. Mountains and a stream—I've been there and I like to look at the painting and remember."

She took his arm. "Come on. I'll show you the kitchen and my studio."

They entered a blue-and-white kitchen with ash woodwork and a casual dining area. "Now I can picture you in your house when I talk to you on the phone," he said.

Switching on lights, she led him into another spacious room. "Here's where I spend most of my time."

He stood looking at her studio with easels, drawing boards, a wide paint-spattered table. Paintings hung on the walls and stood on the floor. Empty frames of various sizes leaned against a wall. Garrett prowled the room and then paused at the large windows overlooking her patio and pool area. Crystal-blue water filled a free-form-shaped pool that had two splashing fountains.

He turned to her. "I like to see where you work. Now do I get to see the bedrooms upstairs?"

She smiled at him. "No, you don't. It's getting late and we've had a long weekend."

"So I'm not allowed to see your bedroom."

"You don't need to," she said, smiling at him as she linked her arm in his.

"I'm having the grand tour tonight but I still want to take you to dinner tomorrow."

"I look forward to it," she said as they walked to her front door.

Before they reached it, he stopped to face her, placing his hands on her waist. "This weekend was incredibly special," he said in a husky voice.

"It was for me," she said, looking up into his gray eyes that mesmerized her as always. Desire filled them and her heart drummed loudly.

"You're special, Sophia. I mean what I say. I never expected to feel the way I do toward you. From the first moment, knowing you hasn't been at all what I expected. So quickly, you've become important to me," he added with a solemn expression.

"So you had expectations about meeting me? That's interesting." In some ways, she wanted to cover her ears and stop hearing his words because she was falling in love with him and it scared her. But Garrett's words wrapped around her heart. He, too, looked as if he were wrestling with something, so their attraction was taking an emotional toll on him, too. "You've become important to me, too, Garrett," she whispered. She stepped close, going on tiptoe to kiss him.

Instantly his arms banded her waist and he leaned over her, kissing her hard.

As if unable to control her own actions, she twisted free his buttons swiftly, her fingers shaking, while she still kissed him.

He tossed off clothes and peeled away hers and in seconds, he lifted her while he kissed her.

"Protection, Garrett?"

"I have it," he said. When he picked her up again, she locked her long legs around him as he lowered her on his thick rod to make love to her.

Crying out, she climaxed, going over an edge while colors exploded behind her closed eyelids.

He shuddered with his release. "Sophia, love," he said in a gruff, husky voice. The endearment made her heart miss a beat.

She moved with him until they both began to catch their breath. He gave her light kisses and finally set her on her feet.

"Now I do need to be directed to a bathroom somewhere in this house."

"There's one in the guest bedroom at the back of the hall, across from my studio. Clean towels will be out."

He leaned down to kiss her again, then gathered his clothes. She picked up hers, pausing to watch him walk away. He was muscled and fit. He looked strong, masculine, sexy. Her gaze ran down his smooth back, over hard buttocks and then down his muscled legs. He was hard, solid and breathtaking.

She gathered her things and headed to her own bathroom off her studio.

In a short time she returned to the front hall to find

him waiting by the door. When she reached him, he pulled her close to kiss her tenderly.

"I don't suppose I'm going to be invited to stay the rest of the night."

"As adorable as you are, no invitation is forthcoming."

"Let me take you to breakfast again. I'll want to see you in the morning."

She laughed. "Garrett, that's crazy. And I can't go. I have appointments."

"I want to be with you."

"Again, Garrett, this has been a special weekend I'll never forget."

He kissed her again. When they moved apart, he opened the door and stepped outside. "Thanks for going with me."

After he left, she locked up and went upstairs to her bedroom.

Had she just done the most foolish thing of her life by making love with him? She hoped not. There was no denying he was becoming more significant to her all the time. In her room she spun around just as she had outside the restaurant in the falling snow in Colorado. Exuberance, excitement, memories dazzled her. Shoving aside worries, she thought about their loving, remembering Garrett in moments of passion, his magnificent body, his tenderness, his heat and sexiness. His kisses held promises and temptation. It had been one of the most wonderful weekends in her life.

She sang as she hurried to shower, moving as if by rote while she replayed the weekend in her mind.

Was this love? Was she already wildly in love with him?

Five

A car was parked at the gate of Garrett's estate. As his lights shone on it, the door opened and Edgar stepped out, patiently waiting.

Garrett's heart dropped. He knew why Edgar was waiting for him.

He put the car in Park and stepped out to walk to Edgar. His mind raced. Had Edgar already told Sophia? Was he here at Sophia's request or because of his own anger over Garrett's duplicity?

The gatekeeper stood in the doorway of the gatehouse. "I tried to reach you on your cell," he said.

"It's all right," Garrett said. "I know Mr. Hollingsworth." He turned to shake hands with Edgar, relieved slightly to see Edgar offer his hand.

"Sorry, Garrett," Edgar said. "I know this is a late hour, but I want to talk to you in person. This isn't something to deal with over the phone."

"That's fine. Come up to the house and we'll talk. You can follow me in."

"Thanks."

Garrett returned to his car to drive through the gates. Edgar turned in behind him. At least he had been civil, which was a hopeful sign. More than he expected from Sophia when she discovered the truth about his connections.

At the house, he led Edgar into the library where a decanter of brandy and small crystal glasses sat on a mahogany table.

"Would you care for brandy?"

"Yes, thank you."

Shedding his jacket, Garrett poured two brandies although he had no interest in drinking. He handed a glass to Edgar.

"You're more than CEO of a Houston property management firm," Edgar said. "You're CFO of Delaney Enterprises in Dallas. I assume the property management business here is a sideline of yours."

"It actually was started by my dad," Garrett said. He looked at Edgar, waiting for the rest. When Edgar didn't continue, Garrett asked, "Have you told Sophia yet?"

"No."

"I'll tell you what I'm doing here and why I haven't told her about my connection," Garrett said, proceeding to run through his history with the Delaneys and his purpose in meeting Sophia.

"I intended to get to know her so she would at least let someone talk to her about meeting with Will Delaney. So far, she won't even talk to their lawyer, much less to any of them. Edgar, I don't know what details she's told you, but she stands to lose an enormous inheritance and cost the Delaney brothers theirs. They are as innocent in this as she is."

"I know," Edgar said, swirling his brandy in the snifter and then looking up to meet Garrett's gaze. "She's told me. That's why I'm here. First, I don't want her hurt."

"I don't want to hurt her either. I hate keeping this secret from her. I've come to care very much about Sophia. To be honest, I've thought about resigning, but I have deep obligations to the Delaney family."

"Don't resign. I want you to succeed. I want Sophia to get her inheritance. It's absurd for her to toss aside that kind of money. I came to see you to learn what you intend and to make certain you're not going to hurt her. I feel like a father to her."

"I will try in every way I can to avoid hurting her."

"Sophia is very cautious with men. Therefore, she's rather naive. As far as the Delaneys go—I hope to heaven you succeed in making her listen."

"They want to know her and want her in their family. But they didn't even know she existed until the reading of Argus's will."

"Why am I not surprised. That man was arrogant."

"There's one grandchild, Caroline Delaney, who is five years old. This will hurt her, too," he said, pulling out his phone and touching it. He crossed the room to show a photo to Edgar.

"Great heavens!" Edgar exclaimed, taking the phone to stare at the picture. "Except for the curly hair, she looks like Sophia. Actually, Sophia and this half brother bear a strong resemblance."

"Yes, they do."

"Does Sophia know about the child?"

"She has to because Caroline is in the will. There's a

trust for her. Caroline's mother walked out when Caroline was a baby and the oldest brother, Adam, was her father. When he was killed in a plane crash, Will became Caroline's guardian. Caroline has lost enough in this life." Garrett put away the phone, retrieved his brandy and sat again.

Edgar sipped his brandy. "I'll do what I can, but I can't keep her from looking you up. I'm amazed she hasn't already. She must like you and take you at your word."

"I think she's been reassured because Jason Trent knows me. She knows I have a business here and you had already met me. I've had her to my house and now we've spent a weekend together."

"Believe me, that's unlike her. She's very cautious and I'm sure she's already told you why."

"Argus again and his treatment of her mother. I'm not Argus or even close, and not one drop of his blood runs in my veins."

"True. I hope you can talk some sense into her for her own sake. It's absurd for her to toss aside that fabulous inheritance. She doesn't have the kind of money to be so blasé about it."

"Thanks for letting me try to work this out. I just want her to talk to Will and to think about what she's doing to them and herself."

"If I can help in any manner, let me know." Edgar took another long sip of brandy and set down his glass. "I'll go now. I'm relieved to hear your purpose and I hope you succeed. I'll stay out of this until I'm asked to do otherwise."

He offered his hand and they shook again. "Thanks, Edgar. I appreciate it. I intend to tell her soon and I hope that doesn't end her speaking to me."

"I can't help you much if it does. Sophia has a mind of her own and is quite independent. She grew up that way."

At the front door, Garrett walked out on the porch. "Take care, Edgar. The gates will be open."

"Good luck. I will try to get her to listen to reason. Sooner or later she will tell me when she learns the truth about you."

As Garrett watched him drive away, his cell phone rang. It was Will Delaney.

"How did the weekend go?" he asked.

"It was fine. But suppose you had called in the middle of a moment when I would not have wanted to talk to you?"

"You wouldn't have answered your phone," Will said with a laugh.

"I'm actually glad you called. I've been thinking about it, Will. I don't want to accept any pay for this."

"What the hell? Is there something in the water in Houston that makes people not want money? She won't take her inheritance. Now you don't want your pay."

"Just accept that I am off the payroll on this. I'm doing the Delaneys a favor. It's free, gratis," he said, feeling a faint degree better that he wasn't taking money for keeping his purpose from Sophia. But he still hated being secretive.

"I'm not going to argue with you. You're a big boy now and if you don't want money, okay. We can renegotiate your salary."

"Don't push me, Will," Garrett said. He knew Will was teasing and being flip, but he didn't feel like horsing around.

"Sorry, Garrett, if this has turned sour for you. Okay,

no pay. We're all grateful as hell, as usual. So it went well?"

"Yes, it went well. I'll call you when I have something solid to report. Night, Will."

He clicked off. His thoughts shifted to Edgar and then to Sophia. Tomorrow night he had to tell her the truth. Would the intimacy they had shared this weekend be a strong enough bond to keep her from despising him? He couldn't answer his own question.

Sleep eluded him again. He mulled over the fact that she had been a virgin. He was the first man in her life, which shook him. She had strong feelings about intimacy and had avoided it all these years. He hadn't expected that and now, not telling her his connection to the Delaneys seemed even worse.

Why had she changed her mind this weekend? How deep did feelings run between them? Were they deep enough to withstand the shock she was going to receive?

Could she forgive him? If she did agree to meet the Delaneys and give them a chance, would it mean that she was willing to give her relationship with him a chance? Garrett clenched his fists. He was anxious to tell her while at the same time, he dreaded the moment. The fact that she had let him make love to her made him feel a bond with her that he hadn't experienced before. Thinking about making love last night, his thoughts shifted and memories flooded him until he had to get out of bed and do something physical because he couldn't sleep. The prospect of flying home and resigning still tempted him, yet he couldn't do that either. Obligations to the Delaneys, to Will, to memories of his father's wishes were all too strong. Now the Delaney legacy made him sink even deeper into his obligations to them.

He had to stay and confess his ties to the Delaneys to Sophia.

Not one thing about meeting Sophia had turned out the way he had expected. The most certain thing he knew, though, was that he wanted her with him. He missed her and wanted her in his arms and in his bed right now. He conjured up the memory of her spinning around in the snow, big flakes on her silky black hair and lashes and coat, her smile, her bubbling enthusiasm and zest for life. He ached to hold her again and he would remember the weekend all his life.

Would the truth destroy his budding relationship with Sophia? Or could he make her see how much he wanted to be with her even though he had kept this secret from her?

He had basically lied to her about who he was. How could he make it up to her? Would she even let him try?

Sophia tossed restlessly in bed. She missed Garrett, but she was annoyed with herself for reacting in such a manner. The weekend still dazzled her, memories bubbling up constantly that enveloped her and carried her away. Garrett had changed her feelings about intimacy. Had her feelings for Garrett become so strong, she was changing her basic views of life?

They would be together again in less than twenty-four hours. He would have stayed tonight if she had let him. Those two things made her wonder: Was she rushing headlong into a life like her mother's? Had Garrett so easily demolished all the barriers she kept around her heart?

Realizing that she needed a distraction from thinking about Garrett, she switched on a light and got up to paint, losing herself in her task and driving all thought of him away until morning came.

Monday night she dressed eagerly, trying various outfits and finally selecting a red crepe blouse with a low-cut rounded neckline and straight skirt that had a slit on one side. She pinned the sides of her hair up, letting it fall in the back.

Her pulse raced with anticipation and she was impatient to see him.

When she greeted him, he stepped inside and swept her into his arms. Words were lost as he kissed her. She locked her arms around him and kissed him in return.

Finally she stepped back. "Another minute and I won't look presentable to go out to dinner."

"That's impossible." He held her waist and stepped back to look at her. "You're beautiful, just perfect."

"I think you're the perfect one," she said, thinking his charcoal suit made his gray eyes appear darker. "I'm ready."

"So am I," he said in a husky voice, referring to more than just dinner.

"We're going to dinner. You promised," she reminded him.

"Yes, I did. We'll go eat and then we're coming back here and I'm going to kiss you the way I want to."

His words made her tingle and she smiled at him.

He took her arm to escort her to a sleek black sports car. She was surprised it wasn't his chauffeur and his limousine, wondering why he preferred driving. Was it because he expected to stay at her house a long time tonight when he took her home?

She wasn't exactly sure how she felt about that, despite the desire for him that had been burning through her since they'd last made love.

They drove through posts and a wrought-iron fence, winding up a drive past splashing fountains and tall pines with lights high in the branches. As they stopped in front of a canopied walk and he gave the keys to a valet, he took her arm. Lights twinkled in all the bushes and over the restaurant, creating a festive atmosphere.

Inside, a large bouquet of four dozen red and yellow roses in a sparkling crystal vase on a marble table stood in the center of the entryway. A maître d' met them, talked briefly to Garrett and led them to a table in a secluded corner that overlooked the dance floor on one side and a terrace on the other. Beyond the terrace were sloping grounds to a well-lit pond with more lights in the trees. Soft piano music played and a few couples were already on the small dance floor.

"I've never eaten here before, Garrett. I've heard of this place, but just haven't been here. It's lovely."

"The food is great. I think you'll like it." A candle flickered in the center of the linen-covered table. Garrett reached across to take her hand. Candlelight was reflected in his gray eyes and her gaze dropped to his mouth. "The weekend was special," he said in a husky voice.

"It was for me, you know that," she replied breathlessly, studying him as he watched her. He had one of the most interesting faces and she wished he would let her paint his portrait. The only problem was that she would want to keep it, and that was the last thing she needed in her house right now, especially if she was trying to slow things down.

"I brought you something to remind you of the weekend and to let you know that it was special for me," he said, handing her a small package.

Surprised, she looked up and smiled. "How sweet you are. You know you didn't need to do this."

She untied a silver ribbon and then unwrapped blue paper on a small box. When she opened it, another velvet box was inside. She removed it and took out a thin gold filigree bracelet.

"Garrett, it's beautiful," she said, touched and surprised. She looked up at him and then took it out to slip it on, turning her wrist as the candlelight highlighted the gold. "Thank you. It's lovely and I'll treasure it."

"Enjoy it, Sophia, and remember the fun we had."

"Of course I will," she said, picking up his hand and leaning forward to brush a light kiss across his knuckles. He inhaled, his chest expanding while desire burned in the depths of his eyes.

All through dinner and later as they danced, desire kept her tingly. Dancing with him was as much fun as everything else. She enjoyed the fast dances; the slow dancing was sexy, tantalizing, making her want to love again. When they stopped and she looked up to meet his gaze, he appeared to be thinking about the same thing she'd been thinking about.

Garrett had a thick steak while she had lobster tail with white wine. Her appetite fled as she watched him in the flickering candlelight. Garrett had ensnared her heart. There was no way she could keep things light with him or hold to her resolution to avoid a relationship. He was important to her and he turned her insides out just looking at him.

By ten, when Garrett asked her if she was ready to leave, she nodded.

At her house, she invited Garrett inside.

"You've had the tour, so would you like a drink—a cup of hot chocolate, soda?"

"If you have iced tea, I'll take that."

"Two iced teas it is," she said, heading for the kitchen. She crossed the room to get out glasses.

"Have a seat and I'll get our drinks. We can go where it's more comfortable."

Garrett moved closer and turned her to face him. "Sophia," he said in a husky voice, and her heart skipped. He leaned down to kiss her while his arm held her waist tightly.

The moment he touched her, her insides clenched and her pulse jumped. She hugged him tightly in return while her intentions to say no to making love vanished.

Nothing seemed as important as kissing and loving him.

"Now you'll have to show me a bedroom," he said, kissing her throat.

"There's one down the hall on this floor," she said, taking his hand to lead him to the bedroom where he stood her on her feet as he continued kissing her. His hands moved deftly over zippers and buttons, and her skirt floated to her ankles where she stepped out of it.

"This time we're taking it nice and slow," he said, taking time to shower kisses on her. He loved her with deliberation, trying to pleasure her and heighten desire every way he could until she was writhing beneath his touch, aching for him.

"Garrett, come here," she whispered, reaching for him.

He slipped on a condom and lowered himself, slowly filling her, withdrawing and entering again while she arched beneath him.

His loving was slow, a sweet torment that fanned the fires he had already ignited.

He was beaded with sweat, trying to maintain control until finally he let go and loved furiously.

She cried out as she climaxed and in seconds he shuddered with his release.

Gradually her heartbeat returned to normal and her breathing grew quiet. They helped each other up and went to shower together, drying each other off only to return to bed. He pulled her into his embrace, holding her while he combed her hair with his fingers.

"Garrett, I didn't know it could be this way," she confessed. "I couldn't say no to you."

"I hope you never can," he whispered, kissing her temple while he held her against his heart with his arms wrapped around her. "This is perfect, Sophia."

"You might as well stay tonight. There's no reason not to."

"I'm glad to hear you say that. I'm surprised you asked me."

"I surprised myself, but it seems logical. And my bracelet is beautiful. Thank you again."

"Just remember our weekend together."

"I will always. There's no way I can forget it."

He gazed into her eyes. "I hope you don't. It was special to me." He kissed her lightly. Though he'd told her many times before, his words thrilled her. She ran her hands over his shoulders, relishing being with him.

At two in the morning, he partially sat up. "I'm ready now for that cup of hot chocolate you offered. Is it still in the offering?"

"Of course. You have to wait a minute because I'm putting on a robe."

"That takes away the fun."

"Otherwise, we'll never get to the hot chocolate."

"True enough."

She stood, wrapping herself in a comforter and going to get a robe. "I'll meet you in the kitchen."

He grinned and waved, his gaze roaming over her as if mentally peeling away the comforter.

"You look gorgeous."

"It's my beautiful gold bracelet," she replied, holding out her arm and letting the bracelet catch glints of light. Smiling, she left to go upstairs and get her best robe, a black velvet robe with a silk lining. She brushed her hair and went down.

When she entered the kitchen, Garrett already had mugs with steaming cocoa on the table. Dressed in his white shirt and slacks again, he gazed at her, then walked to meet her and place his hands on her waist. His white shirt was unbuttoned halfway and she wanted to run her fingers through the hair on his chest. He had turned the fancy French cuffs back and he looked sexy.

"You look far too gorgeous for that to be called a bathrobe. And far too sexy for that to not be for the benefit of some man."

"You know absolutely there hasn't been a man—until now. It's my best warm and comfy bathrobe."

"I'm glad you said 'until now' and I hope it stays that way."

"Garrett, I've warned you about that from the beginning."

He leaned down to kiss her long and hard. Her heart raced as if it were the first time. She couldn't get enough of him. Fighting an inner battle between what she wanted and what she thought she should do, she shifted away.

"We're going to drink hot chocolate, remember?" she said breathlessly, placing her hand against his chest.

He still held her. "Sophia, you're important to me.

I know we haven't known each other long, but that really doesn't matter. You're essential and I want you in my life."

While her heart drummed, his words held her enthralled. "Saturday night wouldn't have happened if you hadn't been very important to me."

"I'm glad. Don't forget what I've said."

"Garrett, you've said that to me before. What am I missing?"

"Before we sit to drink our hot chocolate, I want to talk to you and I hope you'll listen to everything I have to say."

She looked at him and realized that whatever it was he was about to tell her, it wasn't good. "What is it, Garrett? Go ahead and tell me what's troubling you," she said, puzzled, wondering what he wanted to talk about.

"We've become friends, haven't we?"

"Yes, of course. But more than friends, Garrett. Lovers."

"Good. I want to keep it that way."

"What are you getting at?" she asked, growing chilled. What had he been keeping from her that might change her feelings for him? "What do you want to talk about?"

"I want you to promise me you'll listen and keep an open mind."

"I'll listen and I'll try to keep an open mind unless you're going to tell me you're married with a family," she said stiffly. Suddenly, all her fears about rushing into intimacy with him came back to her. All her life she had been cautious, but she threw caution to the wind when Garrett came into her life. And she had a feeling she was about to find out that she'd made a terrible mistake.

He shook his head. “Nothing like that.”

Relief was slight because whatever he intended to tell her, it was serious. “I’ll try to keep an open mind,” she said, though she could already feel the walls closing down around her heart. “But I can’t make any promises.”

Six

Garrett framed her face with his hands and she watched as he took a deep breath. "I was asked to meet you and get to know you. I was hired to do so, actually, but I've told them I won't take the money. I swear I never expected it to turn out this way at all. I didn't dream I would get any closer to you than I had to in order to talk to you."

"You were hired? To meet me? I don't understand," she said, confusion flooding her. Garrett was struggling with his words, and he wasn't giving her information fast enough. "Answer me, Garrett! Who hired—" She stopped speaking and stared at him, her confusion changing to burning fury. There was only one group of people in the world who would have to hire someone to try to get her to meet with them. "No! It's the Delaneys, isn't it?"

"Yes, it's the Delaneys. Please, Sophia, you have to believe me. I never thought I, we would—"

"Damn you, Garrett," she said, astounded at his pretense and the advantage he had taken of her. She was furious with herself for letting down her guard. "I promised to listen and keep an open mind, but I'm not going to now. Everything you've done has been a sham. You've been conniving and false from the start," she accused. "All that asking about my family, listening while I told you about my father—you're as bad as he was," she said, shaking with rage. "You knew! You knew all the time who Argus was and what he had done! You knew how I grew up. You knew everything when you met me and passed yourself off as a Houston businessman."

"I am a Houston businessman. I own that business."

"How are you connected with the Delaneys?" she blurted, startled to hear he actually had the Houston business.

"I'm the CFO of Delaney Enterprises."

She felt as if he had delivered a blow to her. "So the best friend you talked about, the family obligations—that's all the Delaneys, isn't it?" She clenched her fists. "I'm not going to listen to you. Everything you've done has been underhanded and low. How could you?" she cried.

"Sophia, by denying your heritage and your inheritance, you're hurting innocent people and you're hurting yourself."

"You can't possibly justify your actions." She thought of what had happened between them in Colorado, devastation washing over her like a crushing wave. "How you must have laughed after this weekend. You seduced me for the Delaneys," she said, grinding out the words, tears of anger and hurt threatening, adding to her fury.

"No, I did not. I meant what I've said to you, Sophia. I swear. I meant what I said about how special this weekend was for me—about how special you are to me."

"Oh, please," she snapped, hating him for what he'd done and angry with herself for tossing aside all caution where Garrett had been concerned. She was shaking and hurting all over, and she wanted nothing more than to get rid of him and make sure she never had to lay eyes on him again. "You can get out, Garrett. Out of my house and out of my life."

"I'm not going until you listen to me and hear my side of the story."

"Get out of here," she cried. "I don't want to see you or talk to you. I want you out of my life." She tried to slip the bracelet off her wrist, her hands shaking as she fumbled. She finally succeeded, throwing it at him. He caught it and slowly put it into his pocket, never taking his eyes off her.

"I just want you to listen for a moment," he said, speaking quietly. "You're harming yourself as much as you're hurting them and they haven't done any more than you have. All they did was end up with Argus Delaney as their father. You can't select your parents, and neither could they. So why are you doing this to them, Sophia?"

"I already told you. I don't want anything from Argus Delaney. He never gave me love or attention or even acknowledgment that I was his daughter. Never," she declared bitterly, tears over Garrett's betrayal blinding her eyes as they spilled faster than she could wipe them away. "My father gave us money as a man gives cash to a prostitute. I'm not turning down the money to hurt my half brothers. I'm refusing it because it's the only way I can reject Argus Delaney. He gave it out of guilt at the end of his life, and I will do nothing to exonerate the way he treated me or my mother."

Garrett reached out to touch her and she jerked away from him as if he had scalded her with his touch.

"This isn't about them," she said. "It's about him. All those years from the time I was born until I was in my twenties, he treated me as if I was nothing. I'm not trying to hurt them."

"But you are hurting them. Can't you see? And not just your half brothers. Sophia, there's a grandchild. An adorable little girl, Caroline, who someday will inherit Delaney money. You're hurting that child."

Momentarily startled, she stared at Garrett. "There's a grandchild mentioned in the will. A trust was left for her, which has nothing to do with these inheritances. So how could this affect her?"

"Eventually, she'll inherit money left by her uncles. It's not as big a thing with Caroline, but she's in the family and will inherit family money," he said, pulling out his phone and holding it out for Sophia to see. "Here's Caroline with Will, who is her guardian since her father was killed. Look at it, Sophia. Here are two of the people you're hurting."

She snapped her mouth closed and looked at a picture of a beautiful child with long, black, curly hair and huge brown eyes. Shocked, Sophia stared. The little girl looked like her at a young age. She could see the family resemblance between herself and both the child and the smiling, handsome man in the picture.

"I hadn't thought about the future for her." She continued to stare at the picture, suddenly struck by the fact that she had a family, a family that she had never met, a family that looked very much like her. There was no doubt they were all related. Shaken, she couldn't stop staring at the picture—until she looked at the man who was holding it. Her hurt deepened and she walked away from Garrett to put space between them.

"They have money. The Delaneys are worth billions. This isn't going to hurt any of them." She spun around to glare at him, her anger returning. "If they don't get this inheritance, they'll still be enormously wealthy. They are young and into enough enterprises. They will make more money than they even know what to do with. I want no part of my father or anything that belonged to him. Not a dollar—not a fortune. I will have no part of him."

"He'll never know," Garrett answered, putting away his phone. "Your father is dead now, Sophia. You're not hurting him. The people whose lives you are affecting are Will, Zach, Ryan and Caroline," Garrett said quietly. "Sophia, they didn't even know about your existence— Don't punish them when they haven't snubbed you. When they found out they had a sister, they wanted to meet you. They feel you're part of the family and all of you should be united. Aside from the money, they would have tried to meet you and bring you into the family. They are great guys in spite of their father. They don't want to hurt you. They want you to have your money as much as they would like to have theirs. And they want to meet their sister."

"So they sent you to trick me into meeting them."

"There was no tricking you. They tried to meet you openly. Will called. Zach flew here. You've rejected every contact, including their attorney."

Sophia was losing her patience with Garrett, and

she couldn't stand here and have this conversation with him any longer. "I don't see why you are still standing here when you know you're unwanted," she said coldly, her eyes still blurry from tears that streamed down her cheeks. "Once again, I don't care about the Delaney brothers' inheritances or about meeting them. I don't want to see you again, and I never want to see the Delaneys. I want you to go. You deceived me, Garrett."

"You're not going to listen or give me any kind of chance, are you?"

"How could you do this?" she lashed out, her voice a hiss. She wanted him to get out of her house and her life. Why couldn't he understand?

"I did it because those guys are important to me. And all they want is for you to give them a chance. But I don't want to lose you," he said. Her burning anger had turned to a chill. She shook and couldn't stop tears from falling.

"Get out, Garrett. Just go. You can't change my mind, and you and I are through."

"Sophia, don't do this. You're being stubborn and foolish. If you don't want the money for yourself, give it to charity and do some good with it. You don't have to keep it or live on it."

"There is nothing you can say that will make me change my mind. I don't ever want to meet my half brothers. The only thing we have in common is Argus Delaney and nothing else. Garrett, get it through your head—I don't want to have anything to do with any part of my father, and those half brothers are all part of him."

"You're part of him, Sophia."

"Don't remind me. If I could do anything to erase that, I would." She walked toward the door, opening it to make it very clear that she needed him to leave. "You have to go now."

"Why the hell are you being so selfish about this?" he said. Momentarily, she was taken aback by his harsh accusation and then her anger surged again.

"Selfish? Haven't you been listening when I've talked about my father? His world revolved around him. He thought only of himself. His ego was enormous. Don't accuse me of being selfish. He took the prize."

"But what would it hurt to meet them? There's no way you can be harmed by a meeting. You're being stubborn and unreasonable about this—spiteful and hurtful for no reason. Argus will never know, Sophia. You are not getting back at your father," Garrett said, his voice rising.

"How dare you. How dare you call me spiteful and hurtful after what you've just done to me. In case I haven't made it abundantly clear, Garrett, I don't want to see you again ever."

"Sophia, I don't want to lose you. You're important to me and I thought I was to you. I thought we had something special between us. Other than my connections with the Delaneys, I've been open and truthful with you."

"Other than your connections with the Delaneys? How can you discount that? That is actually the first thing you should have told me about yourself. Because the problem now, Garrett, is that I don't believe you or trust you, and I never will. Get out of my life."

"I'm sorry, Sophia. I'm sorry about everything. About the way this worked out, about how long I kept the truth from you. Just please promise me that you'll think about this and stop having such a closed mind."

Sophia wasn't even going to grace his request with a

response. Instead, she walked out of the room. He followed and caught up with her at the door.

"Just think about what I've said to you. Give some thought to your half brothers who have done nothing to you." When she refused to look at him, he paused for a moment. "Maybe, Sophia, you're more like Argus than you care to admit."

"How dare you, Garrett!" she cried. His words cut like a knife. How could she possibly have given this man her body? Her heart? What on earth was she thinking? "Get out of my life!"

"That isn't what I want to do. I don't want things to end this way between us."

"There is no 'us,' Garrett."

"There was, and there can be, if you'll just give me a chance to explain. I put off telling you about the Delaneys because I was scared of losing you. What I feel for you is real."

"I can't believe you care."

He clenched his fists. "What I want is you in my arms, and in my life. What I feel for you, I've never felt for any woman. I can't tell you how many times I thought about calling Will and resigning. But I didn't, because I believed I was doing the right thing—both for you, and for them."

"Goodbye, Garrett," she said, unwilling to listen to another second of his plea.

"I wish you viewed this differently. You're stirring up a storm when you could have so much joy and give so much joy. And you're doing it for the wrong reasons. Actually, reason doesn't even enter into it. You're blindly striking out and trying to hurt whoever you can. Listen, if I had thought I could be up front with you from the first moment, I would have been. But I can see now that I was right. You wouldn't have talked to me, and so I did the only thing I could to get near you. You have a closed mind. You want me out of your life? I'm out," he stated coldly. He turned and left in long strides.

Sophia slammed her heavy door and sagged against it, sobbing and shaking. She hurt badly in every way.

Garrett had betrayed her—she couldn't perceive anything else. Their lovemaking had simply been a means to an end, nothing more. When they had made love, he hadn't been emotionally involved—he had been working. But as swiftly as that thought came, she replayed the pain in his voice as he confessed to her, and she believed his emotions were real.

Yet how could she trust him now?

She heard his car and then it was gone. And with that, Garrett vanished out of her life.

She sat on the nearest chair and cried. Hurt was overwhelming. Heartbroken, she hated herself for being duped just as much as she hated Garrett for deceiving her. How blind she had been to Garrett's purpose.

His accusations echoed in her thoughts—*you're selfish*; *you're blindly striking out and trying to hurt whoever you can.*

Was he right? Was she being selfish?

He had not succeeded or even come close to getting her to consider meeting the Delaneys. So would Garrett continue trying, or was he giving up?

Would she ever see him again? And could she admit to herself that after everything he had done to her, after everything that had happened, the possibility of never seeing him was the worst part of all of this?

Garrett slid behind the wheel and took deep breaths. Desperate at the thought of losing Sophia, he had been tempted to just grasp her shoulders and force her to talk to him. But where the Delaneys were concerned, Sophia had shut off reason.

Her actions shocked him even though he had known about her feeling rejected beforehand, and had heard her bitterness when she talked about the Delaneys, particularly her father.

Anger churned his insides. Along with fury was an uncustomary hurt. He had enjoyed being with her more than any other woman he had known. He wasn't ready for the hurt of losing her. He wasn't ready for the fallout from telling the truth, yet he had been compelled to do so. How could she be so stubborn?

Clenching his teeth until his jaw hurt, he drove home, charging into the empty house and tossing down his keys. Yanking off his jacket as he headed to his room, he tried to compose his thoughts and get a grip on his stormy emotions.

He'd always thought Will was the most stubborn Delaney—until now. Sophia was more stubborn than Will because Will would at least listen to reason and if you got through to him, he would cooperate. Sophia, on the other hand, turned deaf ears to his arguments.

He thought about the night and her passion. It was as if he had been with a different woman when they had made love. A warm, loving, passionate woman. He hurt and hurt for her.

He swore quietly, pacing his room, glaring at the phone. He needed to break the news to Will, but he wasn't ready yet.

Would she ever give him another chance to talk to her about the Delaneys—or to make it up to her? He doubted it and he didn't care to hang around with unreasonable expectations.

He went to the kitchen to get a cold beer. Reeling with anger and frustration, Garrett popped the top and took a drink, feeling the cold liquid wash down his throat.

Procrastinating, Garrett stared at the window. He did not want to call Will or any other Delaney. Yet he had to. What would he do if he were in Will's place? What could he suggest Will and his brothers do now? In future years, after the inheritances were dispersed to other places and no longer an issue, then would she meet with the Delaneys? The brothers truly wanted to know their sister, and Garrett knew they wouldn't stop trying. Surely then she would think more rationally about them and give them a chance.

But would she ever give *him* another chance?

Garrett paced the floor and sipped his beer while he thought. All the time he had argued with her, he had wanted to just wrap his arms around her and ask her to forgive him, believe him and go back to the way things had been. He knew that was unrealistic, but he wanted her badly and he hurt now in a manner he had never hurt before in his life.

Reluctantly, he picked up the phone. Will answered on the second ring.

"Will, it's Garrett."

"You're running true to schedule, waking me in the wee hours of the morning. What's the deal?"

"Here's the latest," he said, pausing. This was the second-hardest thing he had ever had to tell someone. "I did what I could for you with Sophia."

"Whoa, Garrett. You told her who you are?"

"Yes, I did. I had to. I think waiting longer would have made it worse and it's bad enough anyway."

"Go ahead," Will said, his voice becoming gruff, the

disappointment showing. “I’m not sure I want to hear, but I know I have to. This doesn’t sound good.”

“It’s not,” Garrett declared. “She’s adamant about her decision. She still won’t meet with any of you,” he said, pain rippling through him as he remembered her cold remarks to him.

“Dammit, I thought you were getting close to her—I thought this would work.”

“I did get damn close to her, but the instant she learned the truth… You can’t imagine her fury. She doesn’t want anything to do with me or any Delaney. Will, I did my damnedest with her.”

“I’m sure you did. I’m disappointed, but not with you. You always give a job your best.”

“We were getting along great and I thought I could safely tell her. I was wrong, but I don’t think she would have been any different if I had waited a year. She won’t listen to reason. She’s stubborn, determined and filled with hate for Argus. Because of that, Sophia will pass up the inheritance and hurt herself along with all of you. I’ve been shocked by the depth of her anger toward your dad. It’s monumental.”

“Garrett, I gotta ask,” he said. “I’ve been thinking about you giving up your pay for this. Do you care about her?”

Silence stretched between them. Garrett didn’t want to answer Will, but he knew his silence was telling.

“Dammit,” Will said. “We didn’t want you getting hurt in the cross fire.”

“Forget it, Will. None of us—not any of you, Sophia or even I—expected us to get involved. That’s beside the point here.”

“Sorry. That’s bad news. When the time is up on the

inheritances, and we still want to meet her, do you think she'll at least meet us and let us try to be a family?"

"I can't answer that."

"We all want to know her. You liked her, so in the right circumstances, I suppose we would, too."

"Yes, you would. She's like you in some ways, like Zach in others. She's stubborn as hell—definitely a Delaney."

Another heavy silence ensued. "What do you suggest as a next step?" Will finally asked.

"I've been thinking about it and the only thing I can come up with is to go back to your lawyer. Or get a different lawyer and see if he can reason with her."

"Like I said, she won't even talk to our attorney. She has her attorney talk to our attorney."

"All right, but get him to tell her attorney everything you want her to know. Try to get him to convince her attorney this is in her best interests, which it is. Also, try to get across that you want to know her and include her in the family."

"We'll do that."

"How can her attorney not want to argue in your favor when the size of the inheritance is so huge?" Garrett asked.

"I don't know. Maybe a female attorney might get farther."

"I don't think it'll matter. Man or woman, just get someone who is very clever and competent."

"We'll try. Don't come home yet. Stay a few days longer and see if Sophia relents and has a change of heart."

"Will, I'm coming home. Sophia doesn't want to talk to me or see me again."

"How could she be this bitter when he provided for them and her mother was in love with him?"

"She hated seeing her mother hurt by him, especially when he wouldn't marry her. As a child she felt shut out and ignored by him."

"That wasn't so different from how he dealt with us. We had nannies, boarding schools. It wasn't until we were adults that he began to show real interest in us."

"She doesn't know that and won't care. Since she's never met any of you, you're not real to her and she is lashing out at him. She's financially independent and she's content with what she has."

"The one person on earth who doesn't want more money and she has to turn out to be our sister."

"Sorry, Will. I failed all of you, but I tried," Garrett said. "Will, other than this facet to her personality, she's great. She truly is. You would like her."

"Too bad she's not one of those people who wants to be reunited with her long-lost relatives."

"Work with your lawyer. Beyond that, I can't think of any way to reach her."

"Thanks, Garrett. I know you tried. I still say you might hang around in case she has a change of heart. Miracles happen and you had a chance to say some good things about us."

"Will, I couldn't say anything about you, much less sing your praises."

"You surely did a little tonight."

"I didn't have much of an opportunity. I'll wait a few days but it's hopeless as far as I can tell."

"Okay, I'll let the others know," he said, and paused. "Damn, thanks seems inadequate if the two of you had something going and then this killed the relationship."

"Don't worry about me."

"Hang in there, Garrett. And keep in touch."

"Sure. Sorry, Will. I'm damned sorry," Garrett repeated.

He told Will goodbye, then raking his fingers through his hair, he swore. As bitter as Sophia had been and as stubborn, he couldn't imagine her changing.

He looked at his phone and pulled up the picture he had taken of her. His anger transformed to pain as he stood mesmerized by the picture of the moment that remained magical in his memory. She looked breathtaking, happy, sexy. He remembered reaching out to pull her into his arms and kiss her, and he longed to feel her against him now. Even though he was angry with her stubborn refusal to open her mind a little, he was torn with guilt about making love to her when he had been deceiving her. There were reasons he deserved her anger. He wanted to hold her right now.

He hurt for the loss. While he hadn't known her long, it had seemed as if she had become a permanent part of his life.

He shook his head and swore again. The familiarity and closeness had been pure delusion. For her to become so furious with him, he must have meant nothing to her.

He couldn't stop glancing at the picture even though he knew the futility of longing to see her. Wasn't going to happen. He ran his thumb over her smiling image. Tonight would she think over what he had said? Or was she almost as angry with him as she was with Argus? Garrett missed her far more than he would have dreamed possible.

There was no going back, no setting aside the Delaneys and having something with Sophia. He might as well start trying to move on with his life.

* * *

Sophia painted until six, knowing she was merely going through the motions until she had to get dressed for some appointments. Her anger was overshadowed by pain over the break with Garrett and the deceit he had practiced. She couldn't believe it— Argus Delaney was still causing her pain even after his death. Garrett's arguments nagged at her, but she didn't want to think about them or consider them in the least. He had completely betrayed her trust—in more ways than one.

She didn't believe for a second that the Delaneys wanted to meet her and would still want to after the deadline had passed. They had to be just like their father and after more money. She was certain greed ruled their lives.

When she went to her closet, she barely glanced at her red suit that she had worn with Garrett. Pulling out a black suit that matched her mood, she stepped out of her robe and began to dress. She tried to put last night out of her mind as she got ready to go to the gallery.

She called Edgar and they agreed to meet for lunch. Friday was the anniversary of the opening of his first gallery and he was celebrating with an open house. He had planned to send invitations to clients with a listing of the artists who would be present, including her. Now she wished she could cancel so she could go to Santa Fe and try to forget Garrett, the Delaneys and everything that had happened since Garrett had come into her life. She wouldn't do that to Edgar, but it was a tempting thought.

At her gallery, she tried to get things done as quickly as possible so she'd be ready to leave Houston as soon as she could. Also, she found that the gallery held memories of being with Garrett.

She had to rush to meet Edgar on time. Standing beside their table, he smiled as she approached.

"Oh, my," he said as soon as she was close. He held her chair for her. "Something is wrong. I take it this is not just a fun lunch."

"You're too astute, Edgar," she said lightly. She sat and picked up a menu although she ate there often with Edgar and knew what she liked. She just needed a moment behind her menu before she told Edgar the whole story. It wasn't going to be easy. Their waiter came and they both ordered. As soon as they were alone, she met Edgar's curious gaze.

"I'll give you a clue. When you're upset, you always fasten your hair up in a tight knot," he said.

Startled, she glanced at him. "I don't," she replied and he shrugged. She could tell he didn't want to argue, but he was probably right. "I didn't even realize."

"We don't notice ourselves sometimes. So tell me—what's the problem?"

"I would really like to go back to Santa Fe. Will it be too big an inconvenience for me to cancel my appearance at your anniversary party? Have you already sent invitations with the names of the artists who will be present?"

"Actually, I have. But if you need to miss, you may be excused."

"I can wait until after the party and then go."

"Is there an emergency?" Edgar asked, looking at her closely.

"No, not at all. I just wanted to get away."

"Taking Garrett Cantrell with you?" Edgar asked and she sucked in her breath.

"No, I'm not," she snapped and then wished she had

not answered so abruptly. "It's over with him, Edgar. He's from Dallas and he was sent by the Delaneys."

"So how did you learn this bit of information?"

"He told me. He was sent to get me to talk to them. I told him how I felt about the Delaneys, particularly my father. I don't want the inheritance. I don't want to meet my half brothers. Garrett tricked me and I never want to see him again," she said.

"Seems as if he didn't trick you if he told you that they sent him."

Just as she opened her mouth to answer, their waiter appeared with lunches. She had no appetite for her tossed salad. She sipped water as she watched the waiter place chicken salad in front of Edgar.

"Edgar," she said as soon as they were alone, her curiosity growing. "You don't sound offended and you don't sound surprised."

Edgar sighed. "Garrett told me, Sophia. I knew why he was here."

"Why on earth didn't you warn me?" she asked, aghast at another betrayal from a man she had trusted all her life.

"You know why, Sophia," Edgar stated, putting down his fork and gazing at her intently. "You and I have been over this and I dropped it because it is your decision, but since it has come up again, I'll make another plea. I hate to see you hurt yourself. And you will be hurting yourself in a huge, lifelong manner that I think you will come to regret. You may be hurting yourself terribly in losing Garrett. He seemed like a good man, Sophia."

"Edgar, I'm shocked. You're my friend. Why did you side with the Delaneys on this? When did you turn against me?"

"Far from 'turning against you,' I want what's in

your best interests and I was thankful when Garrett told me why he was here. Sophia, stop being a wounded child about this."

Edgar's words stung. He had always been a mentor, her champion, always supportive and helpful until this argument about the Delaneys and even then, until now, he had backed off and kept quiet.

"Edgar, you know how Argus Delaney hurt Mom and me."

"That has nothing to do with your brothers."

"They're grown men and probably just like their father. They're half brothers, and they're strangers to me."

"You know there is a grandchild. A little girl who looks very much like you."

"Edgar, these people are worth billions. They're all going to be just fine."

"You don't really enjoy money the way some people do. But you do know how to help others with it. You could put it to so much good use. And what did you do—send Garrett packing?"

"Yes, I did. And he deserved it."

"Sophia, I got the impression that he cares for you deeply. Don't throw everything away because of his mistake. Someday, you might look back with enormous regrets that you may not be able to live with. You can take this inheritance and help so many others who have never been as fortunate as you."

"Edgar, I'm shocked that you and Garrett talked and you didn't tell me. I'm finished here. I don't want to argue this with you. I've had enough arguing with Garrett." She stood, tossed her napkin into her chair, grabbed up her purse and left. She couldn't believe Edgar had known why Garrett was here. Another betrayal that cut deeply.

Tears stung her eyes, adding to her anger. She rushed outside the restaurant.

"Sophia—"

She turned as Edgar appeared. Startled he had caught up with her, she stopped. "Leave me alone, Edgar," she snapped, wiping her eyes.

His blue eyes narrowed. "I daresay those tears are not over me. We've known each other too long. You're crying over Garrett."

"I am not," she blurted, knowing as she said the words that Edgar was right.

Edgar bent down slightly to look into her eyes. "I think you're in love with him."

"Edgar, you're not making me feel any better."

"That's what I'm trying to tell you. You're making a mistake and you'll be miserable. Sophia, don't mess up your life this way. Life can be harsh, cold and lonely. You're tossing away opportunities and family with both hands. And maybe tossing away love."

"I have to go and I don't want to hear this."

"You may not want to hear it, but you know I'm right," he said gently. "I told Garrett that I hoped he succeeded not just because you need to accept your legacy, but because it's time you let someone love you."

"Goodbye," she said, turning away.

"Sophia." Edgar's commanding tone was so unusual she stopped instantly and turned to face him.

"I'll be here if you want me. I suspect Garrett would be, too, if you let him."

She rushed to her car, climbing in and locking the door while tears poured down her cheeks. She couldn't stop her crying. It took several minutes, but finally when her emotions were more under control, she started the car and drove carefully.

When she got home, she changed and went to her studio, losing herself in paints, brushstrokes, colors. As she worked, she thought of the things both Garrett and Edgar had said to her about the Delaneys. *You're harming yourself as much as you're hurting them.... You can't select your parents and you didn't pick Argus.... Why are you doing this to the brothers?*

Garrett's gray eyes had been dark as he'd spoken. His words had cut, yet she couldn't deny that there was truth in them. Was she making mistakes she would regret the rest of her life? Should she take the inheritance and then distribute it to worthwhile causes?

Should she let these brothers—these Delaney men—into her life?

She stopped painting to clean her brushes and then continued cleaning tables and doing housekeeping tasks she had put off. It was all she was suited for at the moment. Her concentration on her painting was poor with her thoughts continually returning to her conversation with Garrett. His words rang in her ears. *I don't want to lose you....*

But he had lost her. She didn't think there was any way she could forgive him for not telling her his purpose from the start. He had been as intimate as a man could be without revealing the truth about himself. That was what hurt most of all. It was the first time she had trusted totally, let go of her caution and doubts, and then found that the whole time she hadn't known the truth about him or why he had wanted to meet her.

Take the money and give it to charity. Do some good with it. You don't have to keep it or live on it.

Edgar had said the same in his own way. But she couldn't see that she was hurting herself— She had no real need of the money.

You're being stubborn and unreasonable about this—spiteful and hurtful for no reason.

Stubborn and unreasonable, spiteful and hurtful. Both Garrett and Edgar had accused her of being selfish.

She washed her hands and put away her brushes, going to her room to look at the letter from the Delaneys' attorney.

You are not getting back at your father.

Was she wrong and both men were right? Would she have huge regrets?

She rubbed her forehead, feeling the beginnings of a headache coming on. Everything had seemed so clear to her when it had first come up, but now she was beginning to wonder.

"Garrett," she whispered, angry with him and missing him all at the same time. Garrett had caused her to rethink her feelings about relationships. Was she about to rethink the whole Delaney situation because of him? She rubbed her hands together in anguish.

Had Garrett gone back to Dallas now, to his life there?

Had there been a woman in his life already? Had his declaration that there wasn't a woman been the truth—or another deceitful statement?

She spent a miserable, restless evening with little sleep that night. The next day, she got out the information from the Delaneys and their attorneys, and the copy of her father's will, which told of the bequest and the conditions.

She sat at her desk and read, studying the legal documents in her quiet house, weighing possibilities that she thought she never would have considered.

Edgar always had her best interests at heart. He had

backed Garrett, hoping Garrett could persuade her to take her legacy.

What she longed to do was see Garrett and talk to him. Facing the truth, she was shocked by her wish. When had Garrett become so important in her life? Could she forgive him? At the moment, she felt no inclination to do so. And even if she did, was he still angry with her? Garrett might not be forgiving. Her spirits sank lower. The pain of her argument with him was not only monumental, it kept growing.

She had never felt so lost in her entire life.

Friday night, for Edgar's anniversary celebration at his gallery, Sophia dressed in a plain, long-sleeved black dress. The neckline dipped to her waist in the back and the skirt ended above her knees. Her hair was looped and piled on her head, held in place with combs. She remembered what Edgar had said about when she wore her hair knotted on her head, but she didn't care. Tonight she felt better with her hair secured and fastened high.

Feeling numb, barely aware of what she was saying or the people present, she greeted old friends, talked briefly with people about different paintings and was pleased for Edgar that he had a good turnout.

Edgar appeared at her elbow in a gray suit with a pale blue tie that brought out the blue in his eyes. He looked his usual friendly self, as if their last conversation had never occurred.

"To anyone who doesn't know you, you look as if you're having a good time," he said. "To me, you look as if you're hurting. Sophia, you've made an appearance. You don't have to stay."

"I'm fine, Edgar. Thanks, though, for telling me I can go."

"Have you thought over what I said to you?"

"Of course."

"I won't ask your conclusions. Have you seen Garrett?"

"Not at all. I haven't talked to him or seen him this past week, which is what I told him I wanted. Whatever I do, Edgar, I do not intend to pursue a relationship with Garrett," she said, thinking her words sounded hollow and false to her own ears.

"That decision is solely yours and I have no comments to make. I don't usually interfere in your life."

"No, you don't, and I appreciate that as much as I appreciate the comments you make concerning my paintings and the art world."

"Good. We're getting another good turnout tonight."

"You are. The flowers are beautiful," she said, glancing around the room at baskets of flowers that held anniversary cards.

"Lots of people accepted my invitations and responded. We've sold two of your paintings and the evening is quite early."

"That's gratifying."

"Are you still going to Santa Fe?"

"Probably, but I haven't made arrangements yet."

"Good. I think you should stay here this time of year." He glanced around. "The crowd is growing. I'll go greet the new arrivals." He moved away and she walked along, greeting people she knew.

As she made her way through the gallery, she glanced toward the front door and her heart skipped. She looked into Garrett's gray eyes and it was as if they were alone in the gallery. All noise, surroundings, people—everything faded from her awareness except him.

Seven

Without breaking eye contact, Garrett walked through the crowd toward her. In a dark suit and tie, he looked as handsome as ever and every inch the part of the wealthy, commanding executive. The closer he came, the more her heart pounded. With an effort she looked away, turning to gaze at a painting and keeping her back to him.

Her emotions seesawed from joy at the very sight of him to the familiar anger she had borne for nearly a week.

"Sophia."

His deep voice sent electricity racing over her nerves. She turned to face him.

"Why are you here?" she asked. In spite of her simmering anger, her voice held a softer tone she couldn't hide.

"I knew you'd be here. I received an invitation a while back from Edgar."

"We have nothing to say," she said stiffly and turned her back. Garrett stayed beside her.

"I have something to say. Have you thought about our conversation?"

"Of course I have. I've thought constantly about all of it, about what you said and what you did."

"You can't blame the Delaneys for trying to meet you. All they ask is a chance to talk with you. Frankly, they're curious, too, about their half sister."

"I have no curiosity whatsoever about meeting them. Particularly if any of them would remind me of my father," she said, yet her words sounded hollow and empty. She clung to her old argument out of habit, but it was beginning to lose strength. Garrett had stepped in and changed her life.

"They'll all remind you of him, just as you'll remind them of him."

She shot him a look as anger welled up. "That wasn't what I wanted to hear."

"Sophia, let go of your grudges and just give them a chance. You can give yours away and after a year on the Delaney board, if you still feel the way you do now and don't like them, you can go on your way and never see them again. But if you give them a chance, I think you'll find a family that you will grow to love." He stepped closer and she turned away slightly.

"I sent you some brochures and annual reports. You'll see all the good the Delaney Foundation is doing. That all started when Will stepped in. Argus built that fortune, but Will and his brothers are the ones who have put Delaney money to many good uses. If you cooperate, more wealth can be poured into charitable causes, good causes that Argus never gave a dime to. That is sweet revenge right there, Sophia."

She looked up to meet his gaze.

"Spend Argus's money in a manner he never did," he urged.

Without commenting, she moved on to look at another grouping of pictures and was aware that Garrett followed, moving close beside her. She detected his aftershave, a scent that triggered unwanted, painful memories of being with him. Memories that tormented her.

"I'm glad you've thought about our conversation. If you change your mind, let me set up a meeting. I'll fly you to Dallas and back whenever you want. Or if you prefer, any or all of them will come to Houston and meet whenever and wherever you want."

"Garrett," she said, her voice so low it was almost a whisper. "If I decide to see them, I will not go through you. As I already said, I don't want to see you or talk to you again," she said. Even as the words left her mouth, she remembered Edgar's warning that she was letting go of a good man.

"Have you once thought about if our situations had been reversed? What would you have done?"

Startled again, she glanced up and looked away, clamping her jaw closed and refusing to answer.

"I didn't think so," he stated. "I didn't have to tell you who I work for or anything else when I did. I voluntarily told you when you knew nothing about it."

"That doesn't win you any points. I still feel deceived. I trusted you in the ultimate way, which I wish I could undo or at least forget."

A muscle worked in his jaw and his gray eyes seemed to consume her. Her pulse raced and even as she was lashing out at him because she hurt, she remembered his kisses too well.

"I'm sorry you feel that way. I don't. I can't forget

and I'd never want to undo the moments we spent together."

She should stop him or walk away—anything to reject him—but she couldn't move, trapped in his compelling gaze. His focus shifted to her mouth and she couldn't get her breath. In spite of her anger with him, there was no way to forget his kisses. She grew hotter with fury because she could not stop reacting to him physically.

Taking a deep breath, she turned away, breaking the mesmerizing spell. She moved on, no longer seeing him in her peripheral vision. Finally, she couldn't keep from looking. When she glanced around he was gone.

Her first reaction of disappointment stirred a surge of anger. She should be glad he had left. She tried to forget him, but it was impossible. Feeling unhappy and forlorn, she gathered her things and left without interrupting Edgar, who was talking to people.

At home, she sank in a chair. Her unhappiness grew, settling on her like a dense fog that shut out everything else. Garrett had looked so handsome tonight. She thought of being in his arms, the shared laughter and the passionate moments. She reminded herself that she was not in love with him, but she still felt betrayed. Impatiently, she changed clothes and went to her studio, pouring herself into her work, trying to shut out memories and longing. But once again, she had to stop because she was doing a poor job, ruining what had started as a satisfactory painting.

She spent the weekend in misery, with Garrett's arguments constantly nagging her. Everything he had said, Edgar had echoed. She had always tied the Delaney sons to their father, but they'd simply ended up with him, too, through no fault of their own, just as Garrett had pointed out.

Monday morning the brochures and reports Garrett had sent arrived in the mail. Clipped to the annual report was an envelope. She opened it to shake out the contents.

Snapshots fell on the table. She couldn't keep from looking at them as they tumbled out of the envelope and she saw the Delaney brothers. And there were pictures of the little girl, Caroline.

Sophia's insides clutched and she drew a deep breath. She picked up each picture, starting with one of Caroline. In a pink sundress, she had a huge smile and held a furry white dog in her arms. Sophia set aside the picture and picked up one of four men smiling at the camera. She recognized Will from the picture Garrett had showed her.

She stared at all of them. She bore the most resemblance to the two older brothers, Will and his deceased brother, Adam. For a while she pored over them before setting them aside and pulling out an annual report to start reading. A lot of money was going to help Dallas schools and parks, autistic children, medical research, various university scholarships. There was a long list.

Next, Sophia pulled out the will and read, seeing what would occur if they did not claim their legacies. It was a clear paragraph in which Argus stated that each inheritance would go to the church Argus attended and to the city for art projects—both worthy charities, but that money could do so much more if she cooperated with the Delaneys.

Rubbing her forehead, Sophia continued to think. When she considered meeting with them, should it be one or all of them? Would she feel overwhelmed by them? She could request they meet in Houston where she was at home. When the possibility began to overwhelm her, she went to her studio to inventory her paints and repair a broken chair, trying to think about something else, but she kept seeing the picture of Will and Caroline—the two people who looked the most like her.

Would it hurt to fly to Dallas and meet them? In spite of her anger with Garrett and what she had said to him, she imagined telling Garrett she would go with him. Even though she didn't want to go back to the relationship she'd had with Garrett, she knew she would feel better if he was with her.

She shook her head. She couldn't do it and she wanted to spend more time thinking about it.

In the late afternoon Edgar called to ask her to dinner.

"Thank you," she replied, smiling faintly. "But I don't want another lecture on why I should see the Delaneys. I think I'll pass, Edgar."

"Sophia, you and I go way back. I feel like a father to you. Whatever you decide, I do not want it to come between us."

"It won't as far as I'm concerned. But you may be unhappy with my decision."

"I'll live with whatever you decide. I really have your best interests at heart, though."

"I know you do," she replied with a sigh. "I've been giving it consideration today."

"Excellent news. Somehow I thought you would eventually let reason take charge. Usually you're quite levelheaded and sensible, and I expected the moment to come when you could stand back and see what you're doing here."

"Edgar, I'm getting the lecture again."

"All right, I apologize. If you don't want dinner, I'll try again another time. But don't go flying off to Santa Fe. Running isn't going to help on this one."

"All right, I'll bear your suggestion in mind."

"'Bye, Sophia."

She put away her phone and gazed into space. She didn't feel like eating. The sun slanted in the western sky and in another hour twilight fell. With it her spirits sank and nothing could get her mind off the Delaneys—and Garrett. She thought about the time she had spent with him, going back over their moments together, their lovemaking. Had he really cared about her? Or had it been a tactic he used while he tried to get close to her for his own purposes?

Even though his deception hurt badly, she missed him and his dynamic personality. Her life had been different with him, more exciting even through the most ordinary moments.

Have you once thought about if our situations had been reversed? What would you have done? His words had echoed continually in her memory. If she had been the one to try to get to know him with secret intentions, would she have had the same kind of reaction?

Had Edgar been right—was she making a mistake she would regret forever? Worse, had her anger with Garrett been misplaced? Had he been working toward a solution that would help them all, including her?

Garrett flew home Monday morning and went to see Will in the afternoon. Entering Will's office, Garrett carried a wrapped package under his arm. He crossed the room to place it on Will's desk.

"What's that?"

"It's for you, from me."

Will gave Garrett a puzzled, searching look and picked up the package to open it while Garrett settled in a leather chair across from the desk.

He tossed aside wrappings and paper and lifted out a painting in a simple wooden frame. "Garrett, this is excellent."

"It's one of hers. Now I don't have to tell you that she is truly talented—you can see for yourself."

"Damn, I'll say. This is a great picture. Looks like Santa Fe."

"It probably is."

"I'll put it here in the office. Give me a sales slip and you don't need to bear the expense."

"Forget it. It's a gift. Of course, she knows nothing about it."

"Yeah, too bad," Will said. His smile faded as he set the picture on a nearby table and then picked up the wrapping to dispose of it in the trash. He sat and faced Garrett.

"I did my best, Will. Sorry I didn't come back with Sophia."

"We all know you did what you could. What do you think? Any chance she'll appear?"

"I don't think there is, but she *was* taken aback when I showed her your picture with Caroline and told her this was Caroline's future inheritance, too."

"She must have really hated the old man. He didn't abuse any of us, he just ignored us until we were young adults. Even then, it was never a deep relationship. But once I started in this business that all changed."

"From what I could glean her anger toward him came mostly from him ignoring her. And she's angry over how much he hurt her mother. He merely liked her mother, but her mother always loved him."

"I don't know where we go from here."

"I'll think about it. In the meantime, keep hope alive because I sent her annual reports and brochures about the companies. I sent a few family pictures. I've said a lot to her that she can't keep from thinking about."

"Good. Maybe your efforts will pay off."

"It may be Caroline who does it."

"I don't care how it comes about, but we'd all like to know her. We'd like to have her in the family, which is where she belongs. Give her time and then you can try again."

"Next time, Will, get someone else. She's made it clear she doesn't want to deal with me."

"Garrett, sorry if this job assignment interfered—" Will started.

Garrett shook his head. "I'm ready to start catching up here. If you want me, I'll be in my office."

As Garrett stood, Will came to his feet. "Garrett, we all appreciate what you did for us. Time will tell. It may be too soon to judge."

"Even though she hasn't yielded on this, she's a great person. She's a very talented artist. I bought five paintings, including yours. I liked her."

"Evidently you had something going with her and this killed it. I'm sorry for that."

Garrett shrugged. "She was happy to tell me goodbye."

He walked out, feeling as if his story with Sophia was now officially over. He went back to his office in long strides and closed the door, crossing to his desk to start on the backlog of email. He only got through two before he stopped to pull out his phone and retrieve the picture of Sophia in the snow. His insides clenched as he looked at her picture. Memories engulfed him of that night and that moment when he could not resist kissing her.

He ached for her. Realizing where his thoughts were going, he put away his phone and concentrated on trying to catch up on work that had piled up while he had been away. But all through the day, memories of Sophia were distractions. His thoughts would drift to her and then when he realized he was lost in reminiscence and forgetting his work, he would try to focus.

Wednesday night, when he returned home from work, Garrett swam laps and worked out before going to his room to shower. As he dressed, he pulled on sweatpants and a sweatshirt. Glancing at a bedside table, he picked up the delicate gold bracelet he had given Sophia. He turned it in his hand, remembering it on her wrist. He recalled the moment she had thrown it at him. With a sigh, he laid it back on the table.

He wasn't hungry so he skipped dinner and went to his workshop to start building a rocking chair, sawing and losing himself in the labor, finding a respite from memories for a short time only to stop working to think about her.

He shook his head and returned to building the chair, a task that at any other time in his life would have given him real pleasure. But not now, not tonight.

Thursday came and he hadn't talked to Will about Sophia since Monday. She apparently had held to her original decisions and his disappointment was heavy. As he sat in his office, his cell phone beeped. He glanced at the number and frowned, growing nervous and curious. He touched it to say hello and heard Sophia's voice.

"Good morning," he said cautiously, hope flaring.

He struggled to keep from speculating on the reason for her call.

"You win, Garrett," she said, and he closed his eyes. Just her voice made his heart thud. He wanted to see her and be with her to such an extent it took a second for her message to register. His eyes flew open.

"How's that?" he asked, holding his breath.

"I've decided that I will meet with the Delaneys."

Relief swamped him, and along with it, his yearning to be with her intensified. "Sophia, you won't regret it," he said. "I'll arrange the meeting wherever you want."

There was silence and his heart drummed as she hesitated. "I'd like you to come with me. This is not something I expected to be doing and I don't want to meet them alone."

"Of course I'll go with you if that's what you want. How about Saturday evening for dinner, if that gives Zach time to get back from wherever he is?"

"Whatever you work out," she said in a quiet, forlorn voice that didn't sound like her. "I haven't decided what I'll do, but I will talk to them. I would prefer to avoid having attorneys present for this meeting. This is just to meet and get acquainted."

"That's all I asked. Then it will be between you and the Delaneys. I don't think you'll be sorry. You're doing the right thing—the unselfish thing."

"We'll see."

"You can stay at my house. We can keep out of each other's way. If that doesn't suit you, I know you can stay at Will's."

"I'll stay at your house," she replied, surprising him.

"Excellent. How about flying Saturday early afternoon?"

"That's fine."

"I'll pick you up at one. It'll take little more than an hour to get here."

"I know."

"Sophia, thanks," he said, meaning it, his heart racing with joy, relief and longing. He would see her in two days. "I'll be glad to see you."

"I'll see you Saturday," she said. Noncommittal words spoken in a noncommittal tone. Was she still angry? Or did staying with him mean she might give him another chance? He had no idea what to make of her tone or her plans. "My house at one."

"That's great. The Delaneys will be overjoyed that you've agreed to meet them. And, Sophia, I'll be glad to see you. I've missed you."

"We'll see each other Saturday," she said in the same noncommittal tone.

"I can't wait," he said. "See you soon."

"'Bye, Garrett."

She was gone. His pulse raced. He tried to curb his excitement because it was a baby step in the right direction, but not a commitment.

Saturday. Eagerness lifted his spirits.

He called Will on his cell. Before Will could even say hello, Garrett spoke. "I just had a call from Sophia, Will. I'm picking her up Saturday afternoon at one, and you all can meet with her Saturday night. I figured it would be easiest to do this over a dinner because it will be more relaxed than meeting in an office."

"You did it, Garrett!" Will exclaimed. "I knew you could. You got her to agree to meet with us. We couldn't get along without you. Thank you beyond words. I'll call Zach and Ryan and get them here. Saturday night we'll have dinner at my place. Fantastic, Garrett. Way to go. Talk to you later."

Will was gone and Garrett had to laugh and shake his head. He thought about Sophia and his laughter faded. He wanted more than just to see her, fly with her, go to Will's with her. Saturday night she would stay at his house. He couldn't wait to see her and wished he had asked if she wanted to come tonight. Saturday seemed far too distant in the future.

Eight

On the sunny Saturday afternoon, Sophia heard a car motor and looked out to see Garrett park in front and hurry to the front door. With a final touch of her hair that was tied back by a white scarf, she glanced briefly at her image. Her gaze ran over her white crepe dress and high-heeled white pumps,

When she opened the door, Garrett smiled. "Hi."

When Sophia told Garrett hello, her heart missed beats. She still had mixed feelings about what Garrett had done, about seeing the Delaneys, about accepting her legacy. But she had the same intense, instant reaction to him, stronger now than ever. She ached to be in his arms.

An uncustomary nervousness disturbed her over meeting the Delaney sons. She was glad to have Garrett at her side even though she continued to deal with her smoldering anger at his betrayal. However, she had to finally agree he was right. The Delaneys could not help who fathered them any more than she could. And she had never knowingly hurt anyone in her life the way she had been about to hurt all the Delaney principal heirs.

"I'm glad you agreed to come with me," she said quietly. "I don't expect to be in Dallas beyond this weekend, so I only have this bag."

"I'll carry it," he said, taking it from her to put it on his shoulder. His fingers brushed hers and a tingle sizzled through her. She continued to have the same volatile physical reactions to him, maybe more so because of being away from him.

He drove to the airport where they boarded a waiting private jet. Even though she was intensely aware of him beside her, she sat quietly looking out the window below at a long bayou lined on one side by tall pines. When they were at cruising altitude, she turned to find him watching her.

"You're doing the right thing."

"I suppose, Garrett. I'm nervous about it," she admitted, looking into his fascinating gray eyes. In spite of all that had happened, she still thought he would be incredibly interesting as a subject for a portrait. She had to struggle to keep her mind from imaging what it would be like to paint him, how intimate it would be…

"Why?" he asked, his eyes widening. "There's no earthly reason for you to be nervous."

"I suppose it's another carryover from childhood. My father also intimidated me. If and when he paid any attention to me, he would fire questions at me about how I was doing in school. I never seemed to give him the right answer."

A faint smile played on Garrett's face. "Argus Delaney could be intimidating. I know what you're talking about—I was grilled in the same manner. 'What are your grades this semester, Garrett? Why did you just make a 98 on a test instead of a perfect score? Your dad tells me you don't want to take a third year of Latin. Why not?'" Garrett said, imitating her father in what seemed an accurate portrayal. She had to smile.

"You sound the way I remember him. Didn't your dad work for him?"

"Oh, yes. So why did Argus quiz me about grades? He took an interest in my dad, therefore he took an interest in my life. My dad was happy to have Argus on my case as well as himself, so I was caught between the two of them, which I viewed as totally unfair. My dad never quizzed Will or gave him a hard time and I resented Argus for working me over when I wasn't his son."

"That sounds like him," she said, finding it difficult to imagine the commanding, decisive man seated by her as a boy who was intimidated by the same man she had been. "Was he hard on his sons?"

"Yes. If he was around. Frankly, a good deal of the years they were young, he probably ignored them as much as he did you. They went to boarding schools and Argus traveled."

"Yes, to see us," she said bitterly.

"Usually, Argus wasn't a lovable man—an exception was your mother. Maybe with women he was lovable, but in his other relationships, I doubt it. Intimidating, domineering, he got people to do what he wanted them to do."

"Are any of his sons like him in that manner? If so, it would have been better to bring my attorney to this meeting."

"I don't see it, but I've grown up knowing all of them. Will is my age, Zach and Ryan are younger. Will is as kind as can be with Caroline. She had a lot of problems after her father died. She shut herself off in her own world. She wouldn't talk to anyone. Will tried everything he could think of—doctors, counselors, tutors. Finally, he found a teacher who got through to Caroline and she opened up and became the child she was when her father was alive. Then Will married the teacher."

"Caroline looked like a happy little girl in the picture you showed me."

"She is now."

"I suppose I expected all three sons to be like Argus and my reaction to them to be the same. And I wasn't looking forward to encountering three carbon copies of my father."

"You won't, I can promise. The Delaney brothers are charming and delighted to meet you. They'll be as nice as they can be to you."

"My mother always said my father could be charming. I never saw that side to him."

"You'll see it in Will and that's what his dad was when he wanted to be. Frankly, I never found Argus to be charming. I was raised to call him Uncle Argus. I was quite delighted to learn that he was not my true uncle and that that was merely a title of respect. I didn't want to be related to him, probably any more than you."

"You surprise me. I wouldn't have guessed. If I had known that from the first—"

She broke off, remembering she had had no clue that Garrett had known her father, and that Garrett had had no intention of telling her.

"Do you understand yet why I did what I did?" he asked quietly.

"I suppose I do, because I wouldn't have seen you if you had told me you were sent by my half brothers," she said, looking into his gray eyes and trying to ignore the current of desire that simmered steadily. In spite of the division between them, she found him as appealing and sexy as ever. She had missed him and didn't want to look too intently at how strong her feelings ran for him. She was forgiving him easily, the same way her mother had always excused Argus and forgiven him. She was falling into the same trap her mother had, doing everything her mother had done—having an affair, forgiving the man, losing her heart to him no matter how he treated her. A chill ran down her spine. She was doing all the same things. Would she end up in the same situation as her mother—or worse?

He leaned close and she felt as if she were drowning in depths of misty gray. His fingers brushed her cheek. Tingles spun outward from the contact while she felt consumed in his direct study. She wondered whether he could hear her drumming pulse.

"Do you forgive me, Sophia?"

Her heart lurched. How easy it would be to say yes and go back to where they were before, but she couldn't do it. "Maybe. It isn't quite the same yet. That hurt, Garrett." The words came out sounding more sharp than she intended. Yearning showed in the depths of his eyes, stirring too many vivid memories.

Watching her, he slowly leaned closer. She couldn't get her breath. Her lips parted and her heart thudded. Garrett's gaze drifted down to her mouth, heightening her longing. He had to hear her heart pounding. He placed one hand on her knee and his other hand went behind her head to hold her as he continued to lean closer.

She could back off, tell him no, move away, refuse him. Instead, she leaned forward and closed her eyes.

His mouth covered hers, opening hers wider to give him access. He pulled her closer while her heart slammed against her ribs. Blazing with a need for so much more of him, she couldn't help but kiss him in return.

"When we get off this plane—" he whispered.

She shook her head. "I didn't intend for that to happen," she said. "Slow down. You're still going too fast."

"I missed you," he said. "Stay over longer to go out with me, even if it's only one evening."

She inhaled deeply, knowing she shouldn't while at the same time wanting to more than anything else.

"Sophia, I did what I had to. And it will give you an inheritance worth several billion dollars. That's not the same as deceiving you to hurt you. If you go through with this, you'll give the Delaney brothers what they want and set up money for Caroline so she will never have a worry. You saw the charities and how much they've given. So this is different—vastly different from deceiving you to do something underhanded or hurtful. I know you can see the difference whether you admit it or not."

"All right, Garrett, I can. It doesn't stop me from feeling deceived, or feeling my trust in you has been betrayed."

Her gaze lowered again to his mouth and she thought of his kisses. Her heart started pounding once more. She wanted to kiss him while at the same time she didn't want to see him again—it was confusing, overwhelming. With a deep breath, she leaned back.

"Garrett, we better stop this and get on a less personal note for now."

"I know what I want, Sophia. I want you in my arms and I want to make love to you again," he stated in a husky voice that made her shiver with anticipation. His gray eyes conveyed his desire, holding her mesmerized as he could so easily do. "We *will* make love again."

"You're so confident," she said.

He unbuckled his seat belt to lean forward and kiss her again, a hard, possessive kiss that made her heart pound until she longed to be alone with him. She ran her hands across his broad shoulders while she moaned softly.

He stopped abruptly and she opened her eyes to find him watching her with desire and satisfaction both clearly in his expression.

"I'm going to love you, Sophia. We'll finish what we've started."

She looked away, thinking about all that had happened between them. He was buckled back into his seat when she turned back. "Garrett, nothing has changed about my feelings concerning an affair and you have clearly convinced me you will not consider marriage for years. I don't want a casual affair. We had a night of passion. That's all. I will not get into a relationship like my mother had. You may have forgotten what I told you."

"I haven't forgotten," he said.

She looked outside again, her emotions stormy. She wanted him, wanted his loving, wanted to make love with him in every way, yet she still harbored anger over what he had done. She wondered if he thought her turnaround about the Delaneys meant she had changed her attitude about an affair with him, but she had not.

"How is the painting going?" he asked as if they had been separated months instead of days.

"I'm as busy as ever," she said. "How's the furniture?"

He smiled. "I've started a chair. Building something relieves tension. I'm enjoying the paintings I bought. They remind me of you."

"I'm glad. When I return home, I'm going to Santa Fe." He nodded. After a moment of silence, she said, "I told Edgar about this meeting and he was pleased. He agrees with you about this whole thing and he has my best interests at heart."

"I know he does."

"He's sort of a tie with my mom even though she's gone. Edgar is the father I wished I'd had in some ways."

"Remember, Sophia, this meeting isn't about Argus. It's about you and your brothers and the future."

"I've studied the Delaneys' pictures so I'll know which one is which."

"You won't have any difficulty with that. You'll know Will at once."

"Tell me about them again, please."

"With Adam gone, Will is the oldest surviving brother. He's always acted the oldest anyway. He's a decisive, take-charge person. Zach is forthright, practical, but at the same time, he's a renegade, the wanderer who never settles. Ryan is the youngest, outgoing, enthusiastic, an optimist, a cowboy at heart."

"They don't sound formidable when you talk about them. I'm so nervous about this, Garrett."

"Don't be. They're nice guys and they're going to like you. They're still in shock to discover a half sister."

"How could he have kept my mother and me from them all these years? Especially after they were grown."

"I don't think any of them were keenly interested in where he spent all his time as long as he stayed out of their lives and wasn't meddling. He's one of the reasons all of them have been so leery of marriage. The divorce was ugly. They fought and it upset his sons. Later, Adam married and she walked out early on. She was a party person. She wasn't interested in Caroline. It helped build a strong case against marriage."

"You said all that has had an influence on you."

"I guess it has. People change, though. Will fell in love and married, and he seems happier than I've ever seen him. Ava is great and so good with Caroline."

The pilot announced the descent into Love Field in Dallas. Sophia couldn't keep her nerves calm. Three half brothers she had never met. Argus's family. Garrett had been reassuring, but they were still Delaneys. Too clearly she could remember cold snubs or cutting remarks from her father.

Chilled, dreading the meeting in spite of Garrett's reassurances, she looked at Dallas spread out below. The sprawling city had long gray ribbons of freeways cutting through town. The aqua backyard pools were bright jewels set in green. Garrett's home was down there. All the Delaneys were there, waiting to meet her.

She was quiet on the ride to Garrett's home even though he kept up a cheerful running conversation. She suspected he was trying to put her at ease and he was succeeding to a certain extent.

As in Houston, they passed through a gated area and a gatekeeper waved. They wound up a long drive surrounded by oaks. When the mansion came into view, she was startled by his colossal home. "You're in a palace here," she said. "This is far more palatial than your Houston home."

"I spend a lot more time here," he said. "I'm in Houston only occasionally. This is where I call home."

"It's magnificent," she said, her gaze roaming over tile roofs above a mansion that had wings spreading on both sides and angling around out of her sight. A formal pond with three tiered fountains was flanked by tall oaks. "This is beautiful, Garrett. Far too fancy for my paintings here."

"Oh, no. I already have one of your paintings hanging here."

"When did you do that?"

"Earlier this week when I came back from Houston."

"You've been back here? Where were you when I called you to tell you that I would talk to the Delaneys?" she asked, realizing for the first time that he might have flown from Dallas to get her.

"I was in Dallas," he replied with a faint smile.

"Why didn't you tell me? I could have flown to Dallas by myself."

"This was infinitely more fun. I wanted to see you again and be with you." He picked up her hand to run his thumb over her knuckles. "I wanted to kiss you and hold you again. I was more than happy to fly to Houston and ride back with you."

"Thank you," she said, smiling and shaking her head. "When I called your cell phone, I never thought about you being in Dallas."

"I know you didn't and that's fine," he said as he parked at the front door. "Leave your bag. I'll get someone to bring it in," he said as he climbed out and came around.

At the top of wide steps they crossed a porch with a huge crystal-and-brass light hanging overhead. One of the massive twelve-foot double doors opened before they reached it and a man stepped out, smiling as he greeted them.

"Sophia, this is Roger, who has worked for my family for over thirty years now. Roger, this is Miss Delaney. She has a bag in the car."

"Yes, sir. Welcome to the house, Miss Delaney," he said.

"Thank you," Sophia replied as she entered a wide hallway with a staircase winding to the second floor and a twenty-foot ceiling.

"Garrett, Roger is older," she said. "I can get my bag or you can—"

"Forget it, Sophia. Roger works out every day. I've played tennis with him since I was a kid and I still can't beat him. If you saw him lift weights, you wouldn't be concerned. He worked for my folks and now he works for me. Actually, he's more like a relative to me than an employee. I grew up knowing him, which makes the relationship different from just employer and employee."

"That's nice, Garrett," she said, seeing another facet to Garrett in his relationships with the people in his life.

"I'll show you your room so you can change for dinner," he said while they climbed the stairs to the second floor and walked down a wide hall. They entered another wing. He continued, finally motioning toward an open door. She entered a beautiful suite with ornate fruitwood furniture.

"I hope I can find my way back where we came from."

"You will, and my room is down the hall. I won't let you get lost."

"Do you really live here alone?"

"On this floor. Roger has a large suite of rooms on the third floor. So does my chef, Larrier. There are two more suites where Andrea and Dena live. They're in charge of the cleaning crew. They have another entrance to that wing and we can all avoid getting in each other's way. There's an elevator farther along the main hall. I have a finished attic above the third level where luggage and various items are stored. I can give you a tour tomorrow."

She laughed. "Show me your studio and your furniture, but skip the tour. This place is far too big."

"Is there anything you need?"

"No, thank you."

He crossed the room to her to untie the ribbon holding her hair. She shook her head and her hair swung over her shoulders. Her pulse drummed now that she stood so close to him. She looked up at him, reminded again of how tall he was.

"Garrett, I can't keep from being nervous about this. The whole thing seems weird. I was six when my father divorced their mother. If he had married my mother then, as she wanted him to, I would have suddenly had four brothers. I would have grown up with them. Now I'm finally going to meet them. Suppose they don't like me?"

"They're going to love you. Are you kidding? Sophia, you're the key to them each inheriting four billion dollars. That will make them love anything you do."

"When you put it that way, it sounds ridiculous for me to worry. Also, it sounds as if money is the most important thing in their lives."

"It's not, I promise you. But what is this? You are so cool and poised in the art world and you're falling apart here?"

"This is entirely different. I've never had a close family except Mom. To suddenly know I'll be face-to-face with half brothers gives me the jitters."

"You can relax. Forget your father. His sons are very

nice guys. Ava is wonderful and Caroline is a little doll. The Delaneys are blood relatives, Sophia. You'll find they're like you."

She inhaled deeply as she gazed into Garrett's eyes. His words reassured her, but now that Garrett stood close and rested one hand casually on her shoulder, her attention shifted to him and she forgot her concerns about the Delaneys. Her nervousness vanished, replaced by awareness of Garrett and growing desire.

"Thanks for coming to get me and for sticking with me tonight."

"I missed you," he said solemnly and she could only nod. He slipped his hand in his pocket and picked up her wrist, turning her palm up. He placed the gold bracelet in her hand. "I want you to have this. Will you take it back?"

She looked down at the fine filigree gold in her hand before closing her fingers over it and looking back up at him. Her answer would mean forgiveness. She hesitated another second, knowing the path she was taking.

"Yes, I want it. Thank you, Garrett," she said. She was letting him back in her life and that would cause a whole different set of problems.

He slid his arm around her waist and pulled her to him as he leaned down to kiss her.

The instant his mouth touched hers, passion burst into flames. It was as if they had never been apart or had any angry words between them. Wrapping her arms around him, she clung tightly, kissing him with a fierce hunger.

While her heart pounded, she lost awareness of anything except Garrett, wanting him with all her being, holding him as if she feared losing him again. She let go of her anger and let her pent-up longing surface.

His hand drifted over her, sliding down her back and over her bottom, drifting up to her nape to caress her until she stopped him.

"Garrett, I need to get ready for tonight," she said, gasping for breath.

He looked at her a long moment and then he turned to go. "I'll come get you here when I'm ready." She nodded, watching as he walked out and closed the door behind him.

She turned to look at the elegant sitting room that looked like a formal living room. The floors were polished oak with furniture that looked antique, each piece a gem. She strolled to the bedroom, which was a beautiful room with a king-size canopied bed.

Turning her bracelet, she thought about Garrett. She could no longer deny it— She had fallen in love with him. She had never before felt this way about someone. No other man had ever been as important to her.

I'm not ready to get tied down. She could remember his words clearly yet it was impossible to resist Garrett. The struggle was growing. The more she wanted him, the more important commitment became.

She pulled off her sweater and gathered her things to head for the shower, hoping to clear her head before tonight.

When Garrett rapped lightly on her door, she was dressed and ready. Trying to be conservative, she wore a plain black dress with a high neck and long sleeves. The dress ended above her knees and she wore high-heeled black pumps. Her hands were cold and some of her nervousness had returned. She crossed the room to open the door, catching her breath at the sight of him in an open-necked shirt, a charcoal sports jacket and gray trousers.

When Garrett smiled, her nervousness dropped slightly. As his gaze took a slow inventory, his expression revealed his approval. “You’re beautiful,” he said.

“Thank you,” she replied, feeling slightly better again.

“Shall we go?”

“If we have to,” she answered.

“Stop worrying. You’ll see.”

“I hope you’re right.”

During the drive on the chilly fall night, Garrett kept up the cheerful chatter again. They didn’t have far to go and soon she found herself at another palatial estate with lights ablaze and a party atmosphere already in the air.

Inside they were shown to a reception room that she barely noticed. Across the room stood a brown-eyed man with thick, wavy black hair. Handsome, he was slightly shorter than Garrett. Even she could see a family resemblance, realizing if she had seen him in a crowd on the street, she would have looked twice because he had the same bone structure she had, the same eyes.

As he smiled and crossed the room to her, she extended her hand. He accepted it, his hand closing around hers in a firm clasp. “Welcome to the Delaney family,” he said and hugged her lightly. He released her and continued to smile. “We’re strangers in a way, but one look at you and I know you’re my sister. And we’re not going to be strangers ever again. We’re family.”

“Thank you, William,” she said, her nervousness and concern evaporating because he was as welcoming as Garrett said he would be.

“Please, call me Will. Everyone is coming, but I

wanted to meet you first. Sophia, thank you for meeting with us and giving us a chance here. I have to admit, we're all curious about our newly discovered sister. Unfortunately, we knew absolutely nothing about your existence. My dad kept things to himself."

"I didn't know that none of you knew about me, because I've always known about you. I never saw any pictures, though."

"That's enough about him. I want you to meet the family. They're waiting for us. One more thing—don't blame Garrett for what happened in Houston because we really pressured him. He's like a brother to all of us and we took advantage of that."

"I'll remember," she said, glancing at Garrett, wondering if she had been far too harsh with him.

"Everyone is in the family room," Will said, taking her arm lightly. "I'll show you."

They walked past various large rooms and then Will entered an open area with Corinthian columns and a glass wall giving a view of the veranda and pool area. Two handsome men stood talking to a tall, slender, sandy-haired blonde. To one side a little girl with black curly hair sat playing with a small brown bear. She glanced at Sophia and looked down quickly at her bear. She was even prettier than her picture had been.

Will introduced Sophia first to his wife, Ava, and they shook hands briefly. Ava had a welcoming smile as she greeted her. "We're all so happy to meet you."

"This is something I never expected to be doing," Sophia admitted.

"They've been eager to meet you," Ava said, smiling at Will. Sophia felt the current that passed between Ava and Will, realizing they were deeply in love. She ignored the twinge of longing she felt as she observed them.

Will turned to Sophia. “Ava, excuse us and I’ll continue introducing Sophia.”

“Of course,” she said, giving Sophia’s hand a squeeze. “We’ll talk later. I’ve never met a famous artist before.”

Sophia smiled, instantly relaxing a degree as she shook her head. “I don’t know about fame,” she said. “But thanks, Ava,” she added, more for being nice than what she had said.

Will steered Sophia to the child. Caroline’s brown eyes were filled with curiosity as she gazed at Sophia, who smiled.

“Sophia, this is Caroline,” Will said. “I know you’ve heard about her. Caroline, meet your aunt Sophia Rivers.”

“How do you do, Caroline,” Sophia said, smiling at her. “You look very pretty, Caroline. How old are you?”

“I’m five.”

“Is that your favorite bear?”

Caroline nodded. “Yes, ma’am,” she answered, hugging the bear.

“I guess you sleep with your bear.”

“Yes, ma’am,” Caroline said, smiling at her.

“And you have a dog, don’t you?”

“I have Muffy.”

“I’ve seen your picture with Muffy who is a very cute dog. Sometime I’ll meet Muffy, too.”

Caroline nodded.

“Caroline looks like you,” Will said. “Excuse us, Caroline, while I introduce your aunt Sophia to your other uncles.”

They crossed the room. “Garrett showed me pictures

of all of you. Let me guess," she said, standing in front of the two remaining Delaney brothers. "You must be Zach," she said, extending her hand to a curly-haired man with startling crystal-blue eyes that were so unlike the rest of the brown-eyed family.

"The brother who does not look like a brother," she said. "I'm glad to meet you."

"It's about time. Welcome to the Delaney family."

"Thank you," she said, turning to the youngest brother, another handsome man with brown hair. "You have to be Ryan."

"Indeed, I am. Thanks for coming to meet us. We've looked forward to this since the moment the attorney read Dad's will. Let me get you something to drink. We have everything from beer to champagne to cocktails—whatever suits you."

"I'd love a piña colada," she said.

Garrett appeared at her elbow. "Zach, bring me a martini, would you?"

In a short time, Sophia felt drawn to all of them. They shared stories of childhood, which she guessed were being told for her benefit. They were at their best, she was certain. All of them were entertaining, polite, friendly. Garrett was relaxed and happy here with his lifelong friends.

It was almost eleven when she saw an opportunity to change the subject of the conversation. "I really should go soon, but before I leave I want to say something while I'm with all of you." She glanced at Garrett who gave her a faint smile.

"I'm thrilled to meet my half brothers and relieved that you've welcomed me into the family. I'm happy to discover that I like all of you," she said with a nervous laugh. "Even though he was very good to my mother,

I did not have a satisfactory relationship with your father. In financial matters, he was generous, I will give him that. But that's the past and really has little to do with the current situation. I know your legacies hinge on me accepting my inheritance. Well, after meeting all of you, I'm happy to cooperate with all of you."

She was drowned out by thanks and cheers.

"We really appreciate this, Sophia," Will said.

"I blamed all of you for things that none of you did or had any control over, and it was wrong. I'm sorry, but this should make up for it."

"Don't give all that another thought," Zach said, smiling at her. "We're glad to know you. We all had our problems with our dad, so we understand a bit about how you feel. We just say a giant thank-you for doing this."

"I stand to benefit, too, in a very big way," she said, smiling. "The most important thing is that I'm not alone any longer. I feel I have a family now. Thanks to each of you for being so nice and welcoming me. I'm really overwhelmed and owe you an apology for being so uncooperative." She was quickly drowned out by them telling her to forget the past.

She felt a knot in her throat. They were being incredibly nice to her and she hated to think how cold she had been to them, and how angry she'd been with Garrett when he had tried to get her to see their side.

"I think it's time I go home before I get really emotional over all this. The evening has been delightful."

The goodbyes were long and it was almost midnight before she was in the car with Garrett. He reached over to squeeze her hand. "You were fantastic tonight and you did the right thing, Sophia."

"You were right, Garrett. They were all charming.

Ava made me feel as if I've known her a long time and Caroline is an adorable little girl. It's hard to imagine her going through all she has."

"Ava has been the biggest blessing for Caroline and probably for Will, too."

"I had a wonderful time. I know they were at their best, trying every way possible to please me. Well, they succeeded. That was the most delightful dinner party I've ever attended."

"You know you can keep part of your money and do so many things you want to do—the house and gallery in Santa Fe, the gallery in Taos."

"I have my own money. The Delaney money will go to charities."

"You'll make a lot of people incredibly happy."

At his house, he walked in with his arm across her shoulders. "Sophia," he said in a husky voice that made her pulse jump before they'd barely closed the door.

Nine

As she wrapped her arms around him, her heart pounded. Longing swamped her, making her tremble while his kiss melted her. She clung to him tightly, yielding to mindless loving, swept away by desire.

He wound his fingers in her hair and tipped her head back. “I missed you and have dreamed about you, thought about you, wanted you constantly. Forgive me.”

“Garrett, I do. I shouldn’t have been so harsh—thank heavens you made me see that.”

“Sophia, will you trust me again?” he asked. She gave him a searching look and slowly nodded.

“I missed you,” he repeated.

“We haven’t been apart that long, Garrett,” she whispered, his words making her heart beat even faster. His gray eyes were dark, stormy with passion. He had faint stubble now on his jaw and his hair was in disarray on his forehead. Her gaze lowered to his mouth and she wanted to kiss him. She pulled his head down and his lips covered hers, hard and demanding. Her pulse thundered, shutting out other sounds.

She had missed him dreadfully, more than she had wanted to admit to herself. Now she was desperate to love and be loved, to kiss and caress him once again.

He drew the zipper down the back of her dress. As cool air rushed over her shoulders, she felt his hands moving on her. He peeled away the dress and it fell in a whisper around her ankles. She kicked off her shoes and he held her back to look at her.

"You're so beautiful," he whispered while she tugged free his buttons and pushed his shirt off.

His hands drifted over her. When her lace bra fell, he cupped her breasts, his hands warm, his fingers a torment.

Wanting to get rid of any barriers between them, she unfastened his belt and then his trousers, shoving them off. In seconds she was in his arms, naked, warm, feeling his solid, hard body. While he kissed her, he picked her up to carry her to a bedroom. She was not conscious of where he took her—just that he placed her on a bed, kneeling to shower kisses on her while he drank in the sight of her and caressed her.

She moaned and pleasure heightened until it was torment for her. She rolled over to kiss him, knowing that she did love him.

He rolled her gently on her stomach and knelt to continue trailing kisses on her legs as she writhed and whispered endearments. When he reached her back, she rolled over, reaching for him. He stepped away to get protection and then returned, ready.

Kneeling between her legs, he lowered himself to enter her. Crying out his name, she wrapped her legs around him. She held him tightly, turning her head to kiss him and he filled her and withdrew, moving slowly, a tantalizing loving that heightened her need.

Writhing with passion, she clung to him as she cried out. "Love me, Garrett," she gasped. "Love me now."

"You are fabulous, perfect," he whispered in her ear as he slowly filled her again. Trying to pleasure her, his control stretched. Sweat beaded his shoulders and chest. Finally his control went and he pumped furiously as she moved with him.

He shuddered with release when his climax came and she thrashed wildly, soaring over a brink, caught up in rapture. "Garrett," she cried, clinging to him, unaware of anything beyond his body and hers together.

She held him tightly as they slowed, finally growing quiet. Keeping her close, he rolled on his side.

"I want you in my arms every night."

"That's impossible."

"It's not." He kissed her with light, feathery kisses on her temple, her cheek, down to her throat, lower until she stopped him.

"Just hold me, Garrett. I want you close."

"I want to hold you constantly, to kiss you, to love you," he said, kissing her between words. "What I'd like right now is for you to agree to go back to Colorado with me again next weekend."

"Garrett, I don't want to think about schedules or weekends or anything else right now except you."

"Good enough. We'll put the Colorado discussion off until later. Want to go for a midnight swim? The pool is heated."

"I don't have the energy and I'm surprised you do," she said, laughing.

"How about a hot bath instead? Just sit and soak and hold each other."

"That sounds far more interesting." He led her to a bathroom with a large marble tub.

"Where are we? Are we in your room?"

"No. This is a downstairs guest bedroom. I didn't carry you up a long flight of stairs, if you remember."

"I don't remember. You could have been carrying me outside to the car and I wouldn't have noticed, which means your loving takes all my attention."

"That's good news." He ran water, taking her hand to walk down three steps into the bath. Hot water swirled around her, but she was barely aware of it. All of her attention was on Garrett and his marvelous body with muscles from shoulders to feet.

As the tub filled, she sat between Garrett's legs, pressed against his wet, warm body while he wrapped his arms around her and held her. Another weekend in Colorado with him tempted her—it was something she would love to do—but it went against her good judgment.

Everything was different now. Because she was in love.

Hours later Garrett stirred. Dawn's pale light filtered into the room. He turned his head to look at Sophia who was in his arms, her legs entangled with his. Soft and warm, she took his breath away.

His gaze roamed slowly over her, memorizing her features. She excited him more than any other woman he had known. He wanted her with him—the extent of how badly surprised him. His feelings for her had grown over the weekend. He had missed her when they had been separated, but now he didn't want her to go back to Houston. He wanted her to stay with him.

He had never asked a woman to move in with him, but he wanted Sophia to do so. He ran his fingers through her hair, remembering her stating vehemently that she never wanted an affair. He brushed aside her declaration because they were past that now. She had seemed as eager as he to make love.

He mulled over asking her to move in—a commitment of sorts that he'd never given anyone before Sophia. But the thought of her flying back to Houston and then to Santa Fe and being unavailable for long periods was unacceptable.

It had been far worse than he had expected when she had been out of his life. Which raised a very important question: Was he falling in love with her?

He couldn't answer that. His usual caution and weighing of pros and cons kicked in from a lifelong habit of thinking things through before he acted.

He kissed her so lightly, dropping feathery kisses over her face, finally kissing her on her mouth. Then he lay back beside her, staring into space while he thought about asking her to stay.

When Sophia awoke, sunlight streamed through the windows. She turned to find Garrett smiling at her as he drew her to him.

"I'll cook your breakfast. Are you hungry?"

"Yes. I'll guess it's afternoon?"

"Good guess. I can see my watch," he said, turning to look at his watch on a bedside table. "It's almost one. Explains why I thought of food. Let's go shower and then I'll cook."

"If we shower together, which I think is what you're suggesting, then you won't be cooking for a while," she said, smiling at him. He smiled in return, turning back to kiss her.

"You might be right. Let's try and see," he said, stepping out of bed, picking her up to carry her to the shower. "I don't want to let go of you."

"That's fine with me," she replied. She wished he meant exactly what he said to her. She had fallen in love with him and she wanted his love—his commitment—in return. She felt shut away in their own tiny corner of paradise, yet too soon the world would intrude on them.

He set her on her feet in the shower and turned on the water. He slipped his arm around her waist and pulled her to him. His body was hard, muscled, warm and wet against hers. He bent his head to kiss her and all conversation ended.

Over an hour later they were back in bed in each other's arms. "I told you so, about showering together."

"So you're one of those people who has to say, 'I told you so.'"

"I am in this case."

"You must be hungry."

"Sort of," she replied. "Maybe I should shower on my own."

"Nope. No fun at all. Let's just try again. At some point our hunger might overcome our lust."

She laughed as she stepped out of bed. They showered and he gave her a navy robe to wear. He pulled on jeans and they went to a large kitchen with an adjoining dining area on one side and a living area on another. The house was as elegant inside as outside.

"Your house is beautiful."

"Thanks. I enjoy it. I had it built five years ago."

"Five years—you were young to have a house like this."

He shrugged. "I was fortunate and then I stepped into a job with the Delaneys."

She watched him work, thinking about his past and how neither the Delaneys nor Garrett had even known she existed. "What can I do to help?" she asked.

"You can sit there on a barstool and talk to me. Want coffee? Orange juice? What would you like?"

Barely aware of the answer she gave, she watched him as he moved around, getting eggs and toast. He was shirtless, his chest covered with dark curls. His muscles rippled as he moved and desire ignited again in her.

Instead of yielding to it, she tried restraint, chatting with him while erotic images flashed in her mind.

After breakfast he took her hand. "Let me show you my shop."

They walked to another wing where he entered a workshop much larger than the one he had in his Houston home. There was a wide, overhead door and pieces of wood scattered around with tools on the wall and in cabinets.

"I assume the overhead door leads to a drive, so you can get furniture in and out?"

"Mostly out. You're right."

She walked over to look at pieces on the table. "Looks as if you're starting something."

"I am. It's a rocker for you. I hope you like to rock."

Surprised, she glanced at him. "You're building that for me? You must have expected to see me again—expected us to get back together. A rocker is a big project," she said, suddenly wondering how much he wanted her in his life. To build a piece of furniture took time and effort. Was Garrett falling in love with her?

"Building something for you made me feel closer to you and gave me hope that we'd be together again."

She walked to him to put her arms around him. "I'll love it. I don't know what to say. It's wonderful, Garrett."

"Wait until it's finished. You might not even like it."

"Now you have to let me paint your picture."

He laughed and shook his head. "That one—I can't imagine why you'd want to. Would I hang for sale in a gallery somewhere?"

"Never. Let me take your picture and I can paint from that. Oh, wait—I have one of you already from Colorado."

"If painting my picture gives you pleasure, then by all means, go ahead. You're easy to please."

"Thank you," she said, smiling at him.

"I just wanted you to see my studio. Now's a good time for a swim."

"I don't have a suit."

"You don't need a suit," he said, his gray eyes holding obvious lust.

"You don't live alone," she said, pointing upstairs. "You told me about all the staff who live here."

He shook his head. "Forget it. They are in another wing and we're locked away unless I let them know I'm here and need them. When I do need them, I give them as much advance notice as possible."

"That works, but if we swim without suits, I don't think we'll ever get in the pool," she said.

"I think you might be right," he said, picking her up and kissing her. She wound her arms around his neck and returned his kisses as he carried her back to bed.

* * *

Late Sunday afternoon she was in his arms in his king bed in the upstairs bedroom. He showered kisses on her. “This is paradise, Sophia.”

“I agree,” she murmured, combing her fingers through locks of his unruly hair. “Your hair has a mind of its own.”

“I learned that at a very early age.”

“I love it this way. It keeps you from looking so much the executive and in charge and more like someone approachable and fun.”

He chuckled and wrapped his fingers in her hair. “And I love your hair loose. It’s sexy and gorgeous and makes you look enticing.” As she said thank you, he raised on an elbow to look at her.

“I don’t want you to go back to Houston today.”

“I have to. I planned on it and I have an appointment tomorrow. I’m painting a portrait.”

“I can’t talk you into breaking that appointment?”

“Sorry, I need to keep it.”

He toyed with her hair and studied her. “Sophia, stay with me. Move in with me. I’ll build you a studio and you can fly to Houston or Santa Fe or anywhere else anytime you want. You can open a gallery here in Dallas. A gallery should do as well in Dallas as in Houston.”

Her eyes widened and her heart drummed. A part of her wanted to say yes. If she moved in, would he eventually love her enough to want to marry her?

He was quiet, patiently waiting while his gaze was intently focused on her. His gray eyes were unfathomable and she had no idea what he really was thinking.

She sat up, pulling the sheet to her chin and turning to face him. “Garrett, I’ve talked about this with you from the very beginning. I've told you I do not want to have an affair."

"What do you think we're doing now?" he asked. "But what I'm suggesting would be a whole lot better."

"I'm flying home shortly and I'll go to Santa Fe. We can see each other and go out, but we're not living together. Maybe we'll have occasional weekends together, but nothing intense. Not weeks at a time. I'm keeping my independence and hopefully, my heart intact. I'll not spend my life sitting around getting bits and pieces of a man. We each make our choices," she said, hurting as she said the words. "I want to be with you and you know I do. I haven't been able to resist you. But I need to be on my own."

"You're damn scared to live," he said. "You compare everything with the past. I'm not Argus Delaney and I'd never treat you the way he did your mother. I want a relationship with you. I don't want this to end, and you sure as hell act like you're enjoying it."

"I am, but I want more of a commitment than moving in together." As soon as the words left her mouth, she almost couldn't believe she'd said them.

His eyes narrowed. Sitting up, he stared intently at her. "You want me to marry you."

"I know you don't want that kind of commitment. And I don't want anything less. If I marry, I'll want a family."

"Marriage might happen if we have a good relationship, but I'm not ready for that now. I want to know someone long and well before I make a lifetime commitment."

"I agree that's the best way," she said, her gaze roaming over his bare shoulders and chest. "I think we're at an impasse and I also think it's time to get ready to return to Houston."

"I've never asked anyone to move in with me, Sophia."

Her heart raced and she hurt at the same time. Contradictory emotions clashed. "I'm flattered and part of me wants to say yes and throw aside logic, but I'm not going to. I'm very pleased you told me this is a first invitation from you."

"This is a commitment of sorts."

"It sounds to me like you want a mistress instead of a wife."

"I've never thought of you in terms of a mistress. This is different."

"I can't really see how."

"Think about my offer, Sophia. Don't give me a flat no."

She gazed back, wanting to say yes but fighting her own desire. She had to get away before she gave in. She wanted more from him— She wanted his total commitment, his love.

He reached out to pull her into his arms. His possessive kiss and his hands moving over her, taking away the sheet easily, made her forget their conversation and everything else. She was in his arms and he was kissing her senseless and nothing else existed.

Moaning softly with pleasure, she ran her hands over his smooth, muscled back and was lost to loving him. He was in her arms now and she could pour out her love and try to capture his heart completely so he couldn't let her go.

It was early evening before they were airborne. They were quiet on the flight and she could feel the underlying tension between them. When they were finally at her door, she turned to him. "Want to come in?"

"Yes," he said, watching her unlock and open her door. They walked inside and Garrett closed her door, turning to face her.

"Would you like a drink?"

"What I'd like most of all is to hold you," he answered in a husky voice, pulling her into his embrace.

Just as earlier in the day, she forgot everything else. But this time there was a running hurt that nagged. Because of her rejection, she suspected she was losing him and that he would soon go out of her life for good. She threw herself into loving him, feeling that their times together were numbered.

He stayed the night and she lay in his arms as he slept. She wanted more nights with him, more times for each of them to fall deeply in love. She already was wildly in love with him. Was she making a huge mistake by letting him go? She had almost made a huge mistake in refusing to talk to the Delaneys. Was she doing the same kind of thing here—only more disastrous?

She could imagine living with Garrett, hoping for a proposal, feeling the insecurity of an affair. She would not bring a child into that tenuous situation. With a sigh she tried to set aside her worries.

She turned on her side to run her fingers lightly through his chest hair and stroke him. He was sexy, delightful, exciting—and she was losing him. No matter what she decided to do, she would lose him. If she left for New Mexico, she would lose him now. If she moved in with him, she would lose him later.

What if she moved in with him? She could always move out again if it wasn't working, or they weren't drawing closer. The idea tempted her. Her gaze roamed over him, making her pulse race.

She fell asleep thinking about moving to Dallas and what it would entail. She thought ahead to living there, being with Garrett daily. No one, to her way of thinking, could possibly be as exciting as Garrett was. But then she thought about the years her mother had loved her father, hopelessly. Sophia couldn't move in now with Garrett. She was already doing so many things with him she had said she would never do. Moving in would be the last step, the most disastrous.

It was almost six when she awoke to Garrett showering kisses on her. He soon stepped out of bed and began to gather his clothing. "I have to shower and get back. You have appointments today and so do I."

He left for the shower without asking her to go with him and she felt a separation beginning.

When he was dressed to go, she stood just inside the front door with him while he held her in his arms.

"You've been wonderful all weekend. I think you're going to like knowing the Delaneys. Now you're part of a family."

"It's awesome and mind-boggling. Something I'll have to get accustomed to. I liked all of them. Thank you, Garrett, for getting me to that point."

"You might have gotten there on your own," he said lightly, pulling her closer. "The offer is still open. I want you to move in with me. Don't answer now. Think about it. And I want you to go to Colorado with me next weekend."

She nodded, standing on tiptoe and pulling his head down to kiss him.

Instantly his arms banded her tightly, holding her as close as possible. His kiss ignited passion, branded her as his, became embedded in memory. Shaking, she returned his kiss, trying to convey her feelings in their kisses as much as he had.

"If I had time, we'd be back in bed," he said gruffly. "I'll call you. Go with me next weekend."

"We'll talk," she said solemnly, feeling tears threaten. His gaze searched hers as if he could see her every thought. He turned and left in long, purposeful strides. In seconds he was gone.

"Goodbye, Garrett," she whispered, feeling that she was telling him a final goodbye. In her heart, she felt the budding relationship growing between them was over. Was she ending it? Or would there be this same ending a month or a year from now if she moved in? If that happened, logic indicated a break later, after a long relationship, would be far more devastating than having it happen now. But her heart said a later split with Garrett couldn't cut any deeper than it did now. She wasn't going to move in with him and she needed to make that clear to him.

She closed the door, certain she had ended their relationship. How fragile had it been? How deep did her feelings for him run? Time would tell. It was the first time in her life she had fallen in love. At the moment, she felt like it would be a forever love and that her regret might run incredibly deep.

In a surprising turn of events, she was beginning to have more empathy for her mother, to understand why she had been true to her father all through the years.

As one of his employees approached to park the car, Garrett's cell phone rang. His pulse raced as he answered and hoped it was Sophia with a change of heart.

Garrett tried to hide his disappointment when he heard Edgar's voice.

"Garrett, I haven't talked with Sophia, but I assume all went well in Dallas and her good judgment surfaced?"

"That's right. She's willing to cooperate fully. They all liked each other and got along well."

"She can thank you for getting all this to come about. Thank you for sticking with it when she gave you a difficult time."

"I wanted to for the Delaneys and after I got to know her, for Sophia, as well. She will benefit enormously and now she has a family that really likes her."

"Excellent. I'm glad you're in her life, Garrett. Sophia is a rare gem and deserves someone special. Take care and thanks. I'm greatly relieved."

"Thanks for calling, Edgar," he said.

As he headed for the plane with his thoughts totally on Sophia, he realized he already missed her. He wanted her to live with him. He wanted her where he could be with her daily. How could he entice her to accept his offer?

He flew to Dallas, missing her more with each mile of separation. He had never had a dilemma like this one before. Was he blowing it all out of proportion simply because he wanted her and she had turned him down? It was a first in his life with women.

He entered his Dallas home and for the first time it felt empty. Another first. Sophia had thrown his life into upheaval in too many ways. He swore and called until he found a friend who was free to catch the last half of the Cowboys game.

Twenty minutes into the game from his suite overlooking the field, Garrett realized Sophia had wrapped around his life and he could not shake her out of his thoughts by watching a ball game. He missed her and wanted to be with her. As soon as he got home, he planned to call her.

And say what? What could he say that might change everything for them?

Ten

She was in bed when she heard her cell phone. When she saw Garrett's number, she felt a familiar thrill. "Hi, Garrett," she said, trying to hide her excitement.

"I've been thinking about you constantly since I left you," he said gruffly and her pulse quickened.

"I'm glad you called."

"What have you been doing?"

"Actually, I concluded my appointment about the portrait, and then I haven't done much of anything except get ready for tomorrow." And think about you, she added silently. "What about you?"

"Went to a Cowboys game. They won."

"So you're a Dallas fan?"

"Yes. I barely saw the game. All I could think about was you and wanting to get home where I could call you in private."

Her heart skipped a beat with his answer. "I can't be unhappy with your answer. It's nice to hear your voice."

"This is frustrating. Talking to you causes me to want to be with you more than ever."

"Talking about it makes it even worse."

"I agree. I'll cancel my appointments and fly to Houston early tomorrow if you can cancel your day."

"I can't," she answered regretfully. "I'm leaving for New Mexico."

"Colorado next weekend?" he asked.

She took a deep breath. "Garrett, I'm not going. I'll be in New Mexico for an indefinite time," she said, wondering again if she was making the mistake of her life.

There was silence. "I miss you, Sophia. Really miss you," he repeated in a deeper voice.

"We'll talk when I get back," she said, suspecting that this could be goodbye.

When the call ended, she pulled his picture up on her phone and in minutes was in her studio sketching out a likeness of Garrett.

"I'll have this much of you anyway," she whispered.

She would miss Garrett. The nagging conviction that if she lived with him he might propose disturbed her. Each time she felt that way and succumbed to that belief, she remembered how her mother had felt that way for years, thinking if she did what Argus Delaney wanted, he would marry her. It never happened.

But was Sophia willing to risk losing the only man she had ever loved in order to protect her heart?

Tuesday she flew to New Mexico. She hurt badly over Garrett and missed him more than she had dreamed possible. He hadn't called and she assumed he was breaking things off with her now since she would not live with him.

Wednesday morning she drove to her isolated cabin outside Questa. The caretaker's two dogs came and stayed with her. The afternoons were warm, and the mountain air crisp. She set up her easel to paint outside with the two hounds coming to lie in the sun by her.

She tried to paint, but it was impossible to concentrate. She kept thinking of Garrett, knowing she still could change her mind about moving in with him.

He would soon go to Colorado. She missed him terribly and the nagging knowledge that she could have been with him for another wonderful weekend plagued her. Should she just take chances on life? She could compromise to a degree without moving in, instead of basically cutting him out of her life. Garrett wasn't Argus Delaney or anything like him. She should stop basing her life now on what happened when she was growing up.

She sat in the chair she had placed outside near a tall spruce. She loved Garrett with all her heart, so why not take a chance with him? Life was full of risks—maybe this one was worth taking.

It was worth it. Garrett was worth risking her heart.

Her cabin was out of cell phone range and she usually loved the peace and quiet, but this time, she was restless, steeped in memories of Garrett and missing him every minute until she packed up late Friday and hurried back to Santa Fe, anxious to hear from him.

She discovered she had no messages from him.

Taking off work Garrett flew to Colorado on Wednesday and spent Thursday on the slopes. That night he met friends at a pub, but his heart was not in the evening and he couldn't keep focused on conversations around him. There were women in the group he knew, but he had no interest in even talking to them.

Repeatedly, he reached for his telephone, only to drop it back into his pocket. He missed Sophia far more than he had expected to miss her. What was it about her that made her different from any other woman he had known?

She was beautiful, intelligent, sexy, fun to be with, talented—her own person. Garrett finally said farewell to his friends, grabbed his coat and went back to his place. He built a roaring fire, got a cold beer and sat looking at the flames as he sipped the beer. Was marriage totally out of the question with her?

He had planned to stay single until he was older, putting off a family until later. But why? He was already enormously wealthy as she had pointed out. He loved making furniture. What would happen if he changed his life? He had been a workaholic all his adult life. Will and the Delaneys would manage without him— There were other people capable of doing the job he did.

Sophia had made him look at his life in a different way, to consider the possibilities. The thought of change was exciting, but he could only think about it in terms of her. He wanted her with him if he changed.

Actually, he wanted her with him whatever he did. Marry Sophia whether he stayed at Delaney Enterprises or not. Marry Sophia and have her in his bed every night. Spend his time with her. Was it so impossible? Why not change his timetable? He loved her. He had known he did and tried to ignore how strongly he felt for her. For the first time in his life he was deeply in love.

This week had been pure hell and the thought of her going on her way, finding someone else who would ask her to marry—it was an intolerable notion that made his insides churn.

He grabbed his phone to call her and got nothing. He couldn't leave a message, couldn't even get a ring tone. He tossed his phone across the room and stood up to move closer to the fire while he took a drink of beer. If he had asked her to marry him, she would be with him here now. He drew a deep breath.

He retrieved his phone and called his pilot to see what the weather looked like to fly back to Dallas Friday morning. He couldn't enjoy Colorado and didn't care to stay another night.

After he made arrangements he tried Sophia again and had the same results. He hated being separated from her.

He sat in front of the fire again, thinking about his future and making plans to see her. How long would she be in New Mexico? He had no idea how to find her, but then he realized Edgar might know where the cabin near Questa was located.

Garrett couldn't wait for morning to come. He watched the flames, but saw only images of Sophia, memories spilling through his thoughts of their lovemaking, of being out with her, of dancing with her. He ached to hold her and be with her again and didn't want to spend another weekend like this one.

What was she doing? He couldn't stand to try to guess, hoping she wasn't out with friends the way he had been, meeting guys, seeing some she already knew.

He groaned and tried to think about something else.

He opened his phone and looked at her picture that he loved. That moment had been special, unforgettable. Her hair swirled around her head and she had a huge smile while she looked up with snowflakes on her lashes and cheeks. He wished he had never let her go to New Mexico. How long would she be where he couldn't contact her?

Friday morning he flew back to Dallas, getting in that afternoon. He spent one more night in deep thought about his future. One more night missing Sophia more than ever. During his time away from her, the hurt and loss were growing stronger instead of diminishing.

He had had time for a lot of thought. He wanted Sophia back in his life. Now if he could just convince her and do what he needed to do.

He left his home to drive to downtown Dallas. He had a list of things to do today and one of the first was to call Edgar and find the woman who would be his wife.

Sophia flew home Saturday, arriving in the afternoon. She had had time to think things over away from Garrett. She missed him dreadfully. She showered and changed and then called Garrett on his cell phone.

When he answered, she drew a deep breath. She closed her eyes and thought about him, seeing his gray eyes and locks of brown hair on his forehead.

"Garrett."

"I've tried to call you," he said.

"Sorry, but you can't get through where my cabin is. I'm home now in Houston."

"I'm glad," he said, sounding as if he really meant it.

"I've missed you," she said.

There was a long silence that made her heart lurch and wonder if she had waited too late to call him. "Garrett, I want to talk to you," she said. "And not on the phone. I want to talk in person. What plans do you have?"

"Nothing that can't wait."

"Can we meet somewhere?" she asked. "I can fly to Dallas tonight."

"I think we can find somewhere easier than that."

"I don't mind. I want to talk to you as soon as I can."

"You sound anxious, Sophia," he said.

"I want to see you," she repeated. "Where can we meet?"

"It's not too private, but how about your front door?" he asked, startling her. She leaped up and looked out the front window.

"Garrett!" she cried, dropping the phone and racing downstairs to the front door, throwing it open.

Patiently waiting, looking slightly amused, Garrett lounged against the door frame.

"Garrett," she cried again and grabbed his arm to pull him inside, throwing the door closed as she wrapped her arms around him to kiss him. His leather jacket was cold, but underneath he was warm.

For a fleeting moment he stood still. Frightened that she had waited too late to get back with him, she stilled. Then his arms wrapped tightly around her and he picked her up off her feet.

"Sophia, I've wanted you. I missed you incredibly."

She kissed him, holding him tightly, overjoyed he was in her arms. She leaned away slightly. "Garrett, I was wrong. I should take a chance on us. If you still want me, I'll move in with you and we'll try. I don't want to be alone like I was this week ever again."

"Ahh, Sophia. It's way too late for this moving in business," he said. "I've made my own plans."

"What?" she asked, wondering what he had done during their week apart to make him say such a thing.

Releasing her, he stepped back, reaching into his pocket. Her breath caught. Was he telling her goodbye?

How could he say goodbye and kiss her the way he had? Why was he here if he intended to tell her goodbye?

"Garrett, what—"

He grasped her hand. "Sophia, I love you. Will you marry me?" he asked and held out a dazzling ring.

Eleven

Her heart raced and excitement electrified her. She threw her arms around his neck, hugging him. "Yes, I will. I love you and yes, I will," she said, watching him slip the ring on her finger.

She turned to kiss him and he pulled back slightly. "You're crying."

"Tears of joy," she said, kissing him and ending their talk for a moment.

"Are you home alone?"

"I don't have a staff like you do," she laughed, pulling his head down to continue kissing him. Clothes were tossed aside and in minutes, Garrett picked her up. She locked her long legs around him as she kissed him and they made love passionately.

When she finally stood again, he picked her up and carried her upstairs to her bedroom. As he climbed, she looked at her ring. "I'm impressed with you for carrying me up the stairs. But I'm more impressed with my beautiful, gorgeous, perfect ring. It's wonderful and so are you." She tightened her arms around his neck and smiled at him. "This is paradise. I missed you beyond anything you can imagine."

"I missed you, too," he replied. "I want to marry as soon as possible and then I want to take you on a long honeymoon where I'll have you all to myself. You can't imagine how I missed you, Sophia. I don't want to let you out of my arms."

"Well, you'll have to do that eventually, but hopefully not for too long."

"When would you like to get married?" he asked with a smile.

"Soon. I don't have family to worry about, except the Delaneys, and they won't care what we do."

"They'll help. Let's pick a date. I want to rush this."

"I agree." She looked up at him. "Garrett, how did you know I was home?"

"I was going to fly to New Mexico and go to your cabin to propose. I called Edgar to get directions and he told me you were here."

"I was getting ready to fly to Dallas to see you."

"Then I'm glad we got together before you ended up in Dallas while I was here."

He placed her on her bed and lay beside her, pulling her into his embrace to kiss her again.

Minutes later she slipped off the bed, crossing the room to her closet to get a robe. Finding a calendar, she returned to sit on the bed. He pulled the sheet over his lap and propped himself up beside her.

"Now let's look at dates," she said.

"And then we'll call the Delaneys. I'll ask Will to be my best man."

"I just realized—you don't even know my close friends."

"I look forward to getting to know them. The big question is, how soon can we do this?"

She studied the calendar. "By spending a little more, I imagine I can have a hurry-up wedding. How's two weeks from yesterday? The second of November?"

"I don't want to wait that long, but I will because I want you to have the wedding you want."

"So now I'll live in that castle you call home. I'll need a map."

He laughed. "Tomorrow we can start making plans to build you a studio."

"We'll build me a studio while you think about retiring from Delaney Enterprises and building furniture so we can work at home together."

"We might not get much work done."

"Sure we will. Think about it."

"Actually, I have, a little. I might move it up on my timetable to a few years from now. In the meantime, it's a good hobby."

"If that's what you want. All I want is what makes you happy."

"You make me happy." She looked at him as he talked. His brown hair tumbled in a tangle. He looked fit, strong and handsome. He would soon be her husband—a forever marriage as long as they both would live. Love for him filled her and she placed her hand on his cheek. He stopped talking to focus on her.

"What?"

"I love you, Garrett Cantrell."

"I love you, Mrs. Garrett Cantrell-to-be."

"What happened to your plans to stay single?" she asked, studying him.

He smiled and caressed her cheek. "I met an incredibly beautiful, sexy woman and I had to have her in my life always, so—voilà—marriage."

She laughed and kissed him. When she sat back, she held out her hand to look at her ring, which reflected the light, sparkling brightly. "Garrett, this is the biggest diamond I've ever seen."

"I wanted something to impress you and to please you and to indicate how much you mean to me," he said.

She tossed the calendar on the floor and turned to straddle Garrett as she hugged and kissed him. He playfully shoved her on the bed and rolled over on top of her.

Their wedding plans were temporarily forgotten.

Epilogue

On the second day of November, Sophia stood in the lobby of a huge church filled with guests. The wedding was being held in Dallas since Garrett knew far more people in Dallas than she knew in Houston. The weeks since his proposal had been so busy, she had barely had a moment alone with him. There was a dreamlike quality to the morning. It was strange to think that this was her wedding day.

She carried a bouquet of white orchids and white roses that complemented her plain white satin wedding dress. Edgar had his arm linked with hers and would give the bride away. Before she started down the aisle, he leaned close to speak softly.

"You're ravishing, Sophia, so lovely. I know your mother would be delighted and happy for you."

"Thank you, Edgar," she said, smiling at him.

Trumpets blared and Mendelssohn's "Wedding

March" began. Her gaze went to her tall, handsome husband in his black tux. He took her breath away and she felt as if she were floating down the aisle.

Will was best man while Zach and Ryan, plus two close friends of Garrett's, were groomsmen. Her bridesmaids were all friends, and she had asked Ava to be matron of honor.

The bridesmaids and Ava wore simple pale yellow dresses with spaghetti straps and straight skirts. They carried bouquets of mixed fall flowers.

At the altar, Edgar placed her hand in Garrett's. His warm fingers closed around hers and his gray eyes held love.

They repeated their vows. He kissed her briefly and then they were introduced as man and wife, hurrying back up the aisle together. Her heart pounded with eagerness and joy. She was Garrett's wife, to have and to hold from this day forward. Happiness made her feel radiant.

They patiently posed for pictures and finally left for the country club and the reception. In the limo, Garrett pulled her into his arms to kiss her.

She kissed him, holding him tightly. "I love you, my handsome husband."

"I love you, Sophia. This is wonderful," he said, giving her a squeeze.

They kissed again and then she set about to straightening her dress, despite his best efforts to keep it askew. In minutes they climbed out and joined the reception.

Garrett had the first dance with Sophia. She still felt as if she were floating on air. "I can't stop smiling, Garrett. This is the happiest day of my life." He held her lightly, and she longed to touch his hair, brush it back in place, but she kept her hands to herself.

"I'm glad. I can say the same. You're stunning, Sophia. I have the most beautiful bride ever."

She laughed. "I know you're biased or blind, but I'm glad you feel that way."

"I wish my parents had known you, and known about our marriage. That would have pleased both of them. Dad would have been impressed by your business sense. Mom would have loved you."

"I'm sorry I didn't know them, too. And my mother would have been so happy because I'm happy."

"And very married. No danger of you being treated the way Argus treated her."

She smiled at her handsome husband and thought how wonderful to be married to the man she loved.

The music ended and she danced the next dance with Edgar.

"I'm happy for you, Sophia. This is truly wonderful and I like Garrett. I heartily approve."

"I'm glad, Edgar. I love him very much. How do you like my new family?"

"They're nice men and I think they are delighted to find you and have you marry their friend."

"I hope so."

She glanced across the room to see Garrett talking to the Delaneys. They were all handsome men. Zach had rugged looks, but his riveting blue eyes were as distinctive as Garrett's gray ones. Ryan was laughing at something one of them said. She was thankful that she had changed her mind— She had some wonderful half brothers now. The more she got to know them, the more she liked them, and Ava was quickly becoming a good friend.

Later, Will asked her to dance. As they began to move across the floor, he smiled at her. "We are all happy for you and for Garrett. We had to push and argue to get him to meet you for us, so this justifies our actions."

Smiling, she knew Will was teasing. "Now I'm glad you did. It's been wonderful to get to know all of you."

"Good. You're getting a great guy for a husband."

She glanced across the dance floor to see Garrett talking to Ava. "I know I am. I love him more than I thought possible."

"I wish you all the happiness in the world," Will said.

"Thank you," she replied, smiling at him.

"I see your new husband headed this way."

She danced with Garrett and then Ryan appeared at her elbow to ask her to dance. Unable to dance because of injuring his foot, Zach had given her a toast earlier. Now he sat on the sidelines while he talked to friends.

It was late in the afternoon when Garrett finally took her arm. "I've told the guys goodbye. If you're okay with Edgar, I'd say let's go."

"That's what I've been waiting to hear," she said, smiling at him, her heart racing at the thought of being alone with him.

"Come with me. I know the best escape route and we have a limo waiting." He took her arm and they left through the kitchen. Garrett spoke to each person they passed in the kitchen, calling them by name.

They rushed to the limo and soon were on their way to the airport. They flew in Garrett's private jet to New York City to spend the night. On board she changed to a tan suit and matching pumps. As soon as they were in their suite in New York, Garrett turned to take her into his arms.

"I love you, Mrs. Cantrell."

"I love you beyond measure, Garrett."

He nuzzled her neck. He raised his head to look at her, smiling with love filling his expression. She wrapped her arms around his neck and held him tightly while her joy was overwhelming. She loved her handsome husband with all her being and was ready to begin a life with Garrett that she expected to be filled with happiness.

* * * * *

PRIDE AFTER HER FALL

BY
LUCY ELLIS

Lucy Ellis has four loves in life: books, expensive lingerie, vintage films and big, gorgeous men who have to duck going through doorways. Weaving aspects of them into her fiction is the best part of being a romance writer. Lucy lives in a small cottage in the foothills outside Melbourne.

For Bridie

CHAPTER ONE

NASH as a rule didn't court publicity, so meeting with a publicist went against the grain. But this was for a charity event and he couldn't very well say no.

'I'll meet her at the American Bar in the Hotel de Paris.'

He checked his watch as he approached his low slung Bugatti Veyron.

'I'll be with Demarche until one. I can give her a couple of minutes in the bar. I'll try to make it, but she may have to cool her heels.'

It was one of the few perks of fame. People would wait. He hooked the door of the Veyron and idled for a moment, looking out over the calm Mediterranean water.

Cullinan was talking about seating.

'No, mate, don't book a table. This is a five-minute job. Nobody will be sitting down.'

Blue's management team was headed up by John Cullinan, a savvy Irishman Nash had used in his early racing career when he was thrust onto the world stage. John had protected him from the worst of the media for over a decade and he trusted him to deal fairly with the public and handle the professionals.

He'd need him in the coming weeks. There was already intense speculation about his future. He hadn't said a word during the running of the Grand Prix here in Monaco in

May, but somehow just his presence trackside with current Eagle heavyweight Antonio Abruzzi had sent the media into a frenzy. Not that it took much. Meat in the water and the piranhas swarmed. That was why this meeting with the construction firm Eagle was taking place in the privacy of a hotel room and security barracudas on both sides had elaborate lock-down procedures in place.

He ended the call and jumped into the Veyron, keen to get out of town.

The flip of a wrist and he had the engine purring. His deep-set blue-grey eyes, which one female sports commentator had called *'lethal blue'* as if they not only needed colour coding but branding, assessed the traffic and he pulled away from outside the corporate offices of the business that had been his heart and soul for five years.

He had just tied up a deal with Swiss-based car manufacturer Avedon to produce Blue 22, and whilst every vehicle design was a rush this was the car he'd first conceptualised back in his racing days, when nobody would have taken him seriously if he'd spilled his guts on his future plans.

Fortunately he'd never been overly chatty. Being raised by a mean drunk who'd seen a kid's prattle as an excuse to deal out backhanders had bred in him the habit of silence. To the public he was notoriously impenetrable. 'Self-contained,' one journalist reported. 'A cold sonafabitch,' countered a disenchanted former lover.

But, however else he was perceived, the world took him seriously nowadays even when they weren't intrusively curious. At thirty-four, he'd survived as a professional in one of the most dangerous sports in the world for almost a decade before retiring in a blaze of glory—and unlike so many sports pros he'd parlayed his expertise and a passionate love of design into a second career.

An extremely successful second career.

One that overshadowed whatever fame he'd had as a

driver—which had been his intention. He could command any price for his work and right now he was in demand—at the top of an elite field of specialists.

Yet he was restless, there was no denying that, and several times in the last year he'd caught himself asking the fateful question: What next?

But he knew the answer to that question. It was why the Eagle head honchos had flown in last night.

Yeah, he wanted back in the game, but this time on his own terms. His twenties had gone past in a rush of track groupies and speed as he'd raced against the world's best and outraced his own demons. He'd known when it was time to stop. He also knew this time it would be different. He wasn't a boy any more. His feelings about racing had undergone a change. He had nothing to prove.

The road cleared. He changed gear and took off up the hill.

He had a date this morning up on the Point, with a genuine glamour-girl car who had it all over this newer model he was driving, and even the stumbling block of dealing with meetings all afternoon couldn't dull the edge of what promised to be a very nice find. She was reported to be a sweet little number, with curves aplenty, an all-original and he was finally going to see what the fuss was about.

She'd only recently come on the market, and Nash knew he'd have to move quickly, but he didn't buy without handling the merchandise.

He'd flown in to Monaco that morning after twenty-four hours in the air to hear the news that the owner had loaned her out but she'd be available to look at this afternoon. With the morning to kill he'd decided to take the opportunity to run up the hill and possibly rescue the poor thing from whatever indignities had been visited upon her overnight.

The place overlooked the bay—nice and exclusive. But what address *wasn't* exclusive in this town? The house had a little fame for being a silent-film actress's hideaway in the twenties and he was a little curious to see it. He'd driven past many times, but this was the first occasion he'd had to turn in, idling at the gates—which, to his surprise, were wide open. Security was usually pretty tight in this neck of the woods.

As he eased the sports car down the linden lined gravel drive he slowed to a creep, taking in the state of disrepair. Masses of flowering bougainvillaea couldn't hide the fact that the old place needed a face-job.

And then he saw her.

Nash barely had his car at a standstill before he was out, slamming the door, advancing on the object of his desire.

Sticking out of a flowerbed.

A 1931 Bugatti T51, currently upended in a parterre of small flowered bushes. As if to add to the indignity one of its doors was hanging open.

Every muscle in his body stiffened. He wasn't angry. He was beyond anger.

He was *appalled.*

But he was a man who had made self-control a byword. He reined in the fury—knew it needed to be directed where it could do some good.

Coming towards him was a rotund man in garden greens, shaking his arms towards the sky as if inviting divine intercession.

'Monsieur! Un accident avec la voiture!'

Yeah, that was one way of putting it.

And that was when the shouting started.

CHAPTER TWO

LORELEI St James came awake with a languorous stretch, sliding her bare arms over silken sheets, revelling sensuously in the luxurious comfort. She made a *'mmph'* sound, rolled over and buried her face in the pillow, prepared to sleep away the day, if that were possible—only to hear a deep male voice raised in anger somewhere outside her bedroom terrace.

Ignore it, she decided, snuggling in.

The voice lifted.

She snuggled a bit more.

More shouts.

She wrinkled her nose.

A crash.

What now?

Sighing, Lorelei pushed her satin sleep mask haphazardly up her forehead and winced as she copped an eyeful of bright Mediterranean sunshine. The room did a rinse-cycle spin around her—no doubt the product of too much champagne, inadequate sleep and enough financial trouble to sink this house around her ears.

She shoved thoughts about the latter to the back of her mind even as her heart began to beat the band, and she felt about for a glass of water to ease the Sahara Desert that was her throat this morning. She was greeted by a clatter as she clumsily knocked her watch, her cell phone and a tangle of assorted jewellery to the stone floor.

Easing herself into a sitting position, pushing the fall of chin-length blond curls out of her eyes, Lorelei wrinkled her nose and held on to the mattress as the room did another gentle spin.

I will never drink again, she vowed. *Although if I do,* she revised, *only champagne cocktails...and at a pinch G&T's.*

As if sensing she was at her most vulnerable, the phone on the floor gave a judder and began to vibrate. Her heart did that annoying leap and race thing again. She made a pained face. When the phone rang nowadays there was usually somebody angry on the other end…

To dissuade her from getting out of bed it stopped, but the muted sound of male voices coming up from below her terrace lifted to a crescendo. This was what had woken her. Men shouting. Some sort of altercation going on.

Surely she didn't have to deal with this, too? Not today…

But without the catering staff from last night there was only Giorgio and his wife, Terese, and it was unfair to expect them to deal with interlopers. They'd had a lot of them in the past few weeks—all of them creditors, hunting her down now that her father Raymond was banged up in a low-security prison.

As if she had a cent to her name after two years of legal fees.

It wasn't that she was exactly ignoring her problems—she preferred to think of it as delegating responsibility. She'd deal with the phone calls later, and the emails and the lawyers who wanted her signature on a mountain of documents. Not today. Maybe tomorrow. It was just such a nice day. The sun was shining. She shouldn't ruin it. One more day in paradise and then she'd pay the piper.

Just one more day…

And then she remembered. Not only did she have a client

booked in at noon, she had an appointment this afternoon at the Hotel de Paris. It was about her grandmother's charity: the Aviary Foundation. Every year they hosted an event to raise money for cancer research.

This year the feature was a one-day vintage car rally, and a famous racing driver would be giving kids struggling with cancer the pleasure of a spin around the track in a high-powered vehicle. Their usual publicist was ill, and the foundation's president had personally asked her to do the meet-and-greet with their guest celebrity.

She squeezed her temples. She hadn't even done any research. What if he expected her to know his stats? She could barely balance her own chequebook…

Last year they had lined up a Hollywood actor who famously had a home here in Monaco. Now, *that* one would have been easy—watch a few films, gush… Everyone knew actors had egos like mountains. Frowning, she contemplated racing-car drivers. Weren't they kind of like cowboys? She pictured swagger and ego in equal dimensions. *Blah.*

Reaching for the *eau de nil* silk evening gown crumpled at the foot of her bed, Lorelei tugged it over her head. Really, she was happy to do the meet-and-greet—she'd do anything the Aviary Foundation asked of her—just not today…

She gave a shriek as something small and furry tunnelled its way onto her lap, claws digging into her flesh.

'Fifi,' she admonished, pulling the silk to her waist, 'behave, *ma chere*.'

Lifting her beloved baby, she buried her face in a ball of white fluff.

'Now, be good and stay here. *Maman* has things to attend to.'

Fifi sat up expectantly in the pool of white silk sheets, curious eyes on her mistress as she opened the French doors and went to step outside. Lorelei doubled back as she remembered she wasn't wearing any underwear. She wasn't prudish about her body, but she knew Giorgio was conservative and she didn't want to embarrass him unnecessarily.

Belting her robe at the waist, Lorelei wandered out onto the terrace. It was going to be another one of those perfect early September days, and she inhaled the briny breeze filled with lavender and rosemary scents from the garden. She most definitely didn't want to go and sort this out. As she weaved her way down the stone steps, pulling her sunglasses into place, she told herself that whoever it was couldn't do anything worse than yell at her.

But it wasn't easy being shouted at, and she wondered if she was ever going to become inured to other people's anger. In her defence, she'd been facing more than her fair share lately—and it wasn't getting any easier. Maybe she was suffering from overload, because this morning it felt harder than ever. But Giorgio didn't deserve this either, and the buck had to stop somewhere.

It would just be nice if for once it didn't stop with *her*.

Lorelei saw the Bugatti first and her heart sank. How on earth had it ended up in the garden? On second thoughts, she had a pretty good idea…

And then she saw the man who had disturbed her slumber.

He was… She was…

Lorelei was vaguely aware that her mouth had formed a little 'oh' of wonder. In the next instant she remembered that she hadn't run a brush through her hair, she wasn't wearing any make-up and her panties were upstairs.

Too late now. He'd spotted her.

She couldn't do anything about her wrinkled evening gown, but she smoothed her sleep-mussed hair, glad of the shades—which this morning were hiding a thousand sins. She tried to remember that even if she wasn't looking her best she wasn't without her own certain charm.

Besides, men were so easy.

He headed over, all six foot forever of him, with shoulders that would have served a linebacker, a deep chest, a lean waist, tight hips and long, powerful legs—and one of those classically handsome faces that made her think of old-time movie stars.

Lorelei knew better than to be a sitting target. She took the initiative and approached the Bugatti, giving her scowling uninvited guest her back view, which she knew—thanks to riding and an hour a day on her Stairmaster—wasn't bad, and came up with her best line.

'Goodness me,' she drawled, 'there's a car in my rose bushes.'

On the other hand, maybe humour hadn't been the best direction to take this in. As she listened to the crunch of gravel—big, heavy male footsteps coming up behind her—Lorelei experienced that sinking feeling: the one that told her she'd read the situation all wrong.

Giorgio's expression told her to duck and cover, but after a brief, desperate glance at the older man she decided to stay where she was. It wasn't her style to cut and run, and she'd come this far—she just needed to brazen it out. And the guy had stopped shouting, which was encouraging.

'Are you responsible for this?'

Lorelei took in three things. He was Australian, he had a voice that made Russell Crowe sound like a choirboy, and—as she turned around and looked up into a set masculine face—he clearly wasn't in any mood to be amused or charmed. She couldn't blame him. The car did look pretty bad.

'*Are* you?' he repeated, snapping off his aviators and revealing a pair of spectacular eyes—navy blue rimmed with grey, surrounded by dense, thick, dark lashes.

Those eyes. They were sort of…*amazing.* Lorelei couldn't help gazing helplessly back.

Except they pinned her like a blade to a dissection board. She could almost *feel* him deciding which part of her to excise first. She came back to earth with a thump and tried to ignore the pinch in her chest. It was a look she was becoming depressingly familiar with of late, and it didn't mean anything, she told herself. She would have thought she'd be used to it by now.

He shoved the aviators into the back pocket of his jeans and settled his arms by his sides—stance widened, pure masculine intimidation.

'Anything to say for yourself?'

He was pumping out lots of frustrated testosterone, which was making her a little nervous, but she couldn't really blame him. He wanted another man to punch on the nose and he'd got her.

He clearly didn't know what to do about that.

She lifted a trembling hand and smoothed down her hair.

'Are you *high,* lady?'

Lorelei was so busy staying her ground that his questions hadn't quite penetrated, but now that he was turning away the last one landed on her with a thump.

'Pardon?'

But the guy was already focussing his entire attention back on the car, his hands on those lean, muscled hips of his as he eyed the Bugatti nose-deep in the rose bushes.

Giorgio was muttering in Italian, and the guy said something to him in his own language. Before her eyes the men appeared to be bonding over their shared outrage about the car. Freed from that penetrating stare, Lorelei frowned.

Well, really.

This wasn't how the man-meets-Lorelei scenario was supposed to play out. Her Italian was minimal, at best, and she didn't like the feeling of being forcibly held at bay by her inability to understand what was being said.

She was also a little piqued at being ignored.

And she most definitely didn't like being intimidated.

She cocked a hip, one slender hand resting just below her waist.

'So, do you think you can extract it before it does any more damage to my flowers?'

Giorgio muttered something like, *'Madonna!'*

Good—now she'd get a little action.

The man's broad shoulders grew taut, and as he turned around she felt her bravado flicker uneasily. His movements were alarmingly deliberate—as if this was *his* estate, Giorgio *his* employee and she was trespassing on *his* land. A stone-cold stare slammed into her. He suddenly seemed awfully big, and Lorelei knew in that instant he wasn't amused, he wasn't charmed and he wasn't going to be easy.

'As far as I'm concerned, lady,' he said, his expression giving no ground, 'you're screwed.'

Her reaction was fierce and immediate. She *hated* this feeling. She'd been dealing with it for too long. It felt as if all she'd done lately was shoulder the blame. So this time it was *her* fault, but for some reason his anger felt disproportionate and just plain unfair. It was too much, coming on top of everything else.

Who cared about a silly car when her life was coming apart at the seams?

So she did what she always did when a man challenged her, called her to account or tried to make himself king of her mountain. She brought out the big guns. The ones she'd learned from her beloved, irresponsible father.

Wit and sex appeal.

Lorelei dipped her glasses and gave him full wattage.

'I can hardly wait,' she purred.

CHAPTER THREE

FROM her rumpled appearance she had clearly just rolled out of bed, and for one out-of-bounds moment Nash had a strong urge to roll her back into it.

Hardly surprising. She was a striking-looking woman who exuded a sultry, knowing sensuality that could have been a combination of her looks and the way she moved her body and displayed it, but he sensed came from the essence of who she was.

In another era she would have embodied the romantic idea of a courtesan. A woman who required a great deal of money to keep the shine on her silky curls, the glow in her honeyed skin and her eyes from straying to the next main chance.

Yeah—another time and another place this could go down a lot differently.

A man like him…a woman like her…

But not today.

Not now.

And it didn't have a lot to do with the car.

With a media circus about to start up around him again, this smouldering blonde had a little bit too much attitude to burn. He might as well slap a big no-go sticker on that shapely ass of hers. She fairly neon-glowed with sex of a crazy, messy kind, and tempted as he was he couldn't afford to be indiscriminate—not this close to race-start. He'd do well to remember that.

Although his first impression of this woman had been of something quite different. When she'd first emerged for a timeless instant he'd seen only a tall, delicately built girl as graceful and hesitant as a mountain deer. She'd given him pause. For a moment there he hadn't wanted to shift a muscle in case he scared her off.

Then she'd looked right at him and headed for the Bugatti.

And right now her hands were on her hips and the glamour-girl in her was in full flow. Which was when he noticed something rather more down to earth. She wasn't wearing much. Or rather what she *was* wearing was advertising the lack of anything else.

Trying to be a gentleman, he dragged his attention upwards. But he needn't have bothered. She was clearly unfazed, and his cynicism about who she was and the price she put on herself lodged into place—because, despite his initial impression of something better, blondie was pure South of France glamour. If he upended her she probably had "Made on the Riviera" stamped on the soles of her pretty bare feet.

For a moment she'd looked a little thrown. He didn't know if she was embarrassed to be caught out or simply defensive because she didn't like being in the wrong. Frankly, he didn't care.

He cared about the car.

He whipped out his cell, punched in a number.

'As far as I'm concerned, lady, you've committed a felony. That car is a work of art and a treasure, and *you've* trashed it.'

She dragged off the huge sunglasses and a pair of pale-lashed doe eyes regarded him with a fair degree of astonishment. As if he were massively overreacting.

Nash knew he was staring back, but after the clothes and the attitude he just hadn't expected amber-brown, slightly tip-tilted, lovely… The eyes of a gentle fawn.

'I haven't trashed anything,' she countered in that low, sexy voice of hers.

Nash folded his arms, still shaking off the effect of those eyes. Somehow she was going to try and take the moral high ground. This should be good.

'It might be a little scratched—that's all,' she conceded. 'I suppose there *are* only a couple of thousand in the world—'

'Eight,' he said grimly. 'There are eight left in the world.'

For a moment he fancied he saw her take a deep swallow, but she continued on blithely, like a pretty blonde lemming running over a cliff.

'Seven more than this one—not such a catastrophe, *non?*'

He stared at her.

'Besides, it's man-made.' She smoothed her hands over the gentle swell of her hips, drawing attention to the obvious fact that *she* wasn't.

'Nice move, doll,' he drawled, following the movement of her hands. 'You're very pretty, and I'm sure you've got men lining up down the drive, but conscienceless women do nothing for me.'

Her hands stilled on her hips. She looked slightly shocked, and for a moment he wondered if it was another ploy, then she lifted her chin and said coolly, 'Perhaps you can get the parts and fix it?'

He could fix it?

Despite his irritation Nash almost laughed. Was she serious?

'Yeah, that easy,' he drawled, losing his battle not to pay too much attention to her silk nightgown, or something resembling one, and its faithful adherence to the lines of her body.

In particular when she moved—as she was doing now—it became highly revealing. The silk clung to the long, slender length of her legs, the jut of streamlined hips and the delicate curve of her clearly braless breasts. His body shifted up to speed. She rivalled the Bugatti in terms of fine lines.

He'd lied. She *did* do something for him.

'Looking for something?' Her voice was suddenly sharp, and it had lost its sleepy sexiness.

Nash dragged his gaze from the view to find those amber eyes observing him rather shrewdly. She'd clearly ditched the princess-without-a-clue act.

'Yeah,' he responded dryly. 'A conscience.'

She folded her arms, as if discovering some long-lost modesty.

'Oh, it's there,' she drawled, 'you just have to rattle around for it a bit.'

It was one hell of a line.

Against Nash's will a smile ghosted across his mouth. Not such a dumb blonde after all.

'I'll take a pass.'

'Shame.' This was said with a little toss of those curls as she walked towards the scene of her crime: the rear end of the Bugatti. 'But I'm sure it can be fixed. It's only tipped into some roses bushes after all—a little scratched paint at most.' She looked at him over her shoulder. 'Nothing to get all worked up about.'

Was it his heated imagination or in that moment did she drop her gaze infinitesimally below his belt?

He could hear one of his people speaking on the other end of the phone. He lifted it momentarily and said, 'Give us a minute, mate.'

'Have you changed your mind?' She paused deliberately—it could only be deliberate with this woman. 'About the car?'

'Nothing's changed, sweetheart, except your fine day.'

He watched the confidence dip slightly out of her body, and oddly it didn't give him the satisfaction he would have anticipated.

'Expect a bill.'

She notched up her chin. 'Can I expect anything else?'

'Yeah—a lecture from your old man about why messing

around with another guy's wheels can get you into all sorts of trouble.'

For a moment she looked at him as if she was going to say something about that, and for some reason he found he was hanging on her answer.

Instead she pushed back her tousled hair, gave him a distracted smile, as if she knew something he didn't, and headed back the way she'd come.

He wouldn't have been a red-blooded man if his gaze hadn't moved inexorably to what he had noticed before: a very shapely behind. It was like a perfect peach, all high and perky under the clinging silk of whatever it was she was wearing—or not wearing.

Vaguely he became aware that the old Italian bloke was glaring at him, and he dragged his eyes off the view.

'The car is not so damaged you need to frighten her,' grumbled the older man, 'and you can keep your eyes to yourself. Miss St James is a nice woman. She does not ask for all this trouble.'

Nash could hear the disembodied voice coming from his cell, but he was slightly bemused by the lecture being delivered to him in hot, angry Italian. Who *was* this guy? Her father?

'I know your type, with the flashy car. You want to find some loose woman, you go into town.'

Loose woman? What was this? 1955?

'No, mate, I just want the car. Fixed.'

He was tempted to gun the Veyron and leave the Bugatti to its fate. But it went against the few principles he had left. The old girl was a treasure, and she deserved to be treated like the lady she was.

He settled the pick-up details and was strolling over to the Veyron when he was distracted by the very distinctive sound of high heels hitting flagstones.

'Miss St James' had re-emerged in silky white pants, which

were swishing around her long legs, some sort of floaty, shimmery silky green top, which barely skimmed the tops of her arms and left her shoulders bare, and she'd applied bright crimson lipstick to that smart mouth of hers. Although her eyes were impenetrable behind those ridiculously large sunglasses she had a faint smile on her lips as she headed over to a boat of a convertible parked by the garden wall. He watched her climb in.

He was done here. He still wanted the car, and he wanted it fixed. But first he'd deal with the thorny question of *why* the Bugatti was nose-down in a bunch of roses.

'Hold it, sweetheart.'

She paused from rummaging in her bag, pointed chin angled over her shoulder, shades lowered, eyes assessing. 'Is there something else?' she enquired civilly.

Yeah, too civil.

He knew how to get his point across—how to use leashed aggression as a weapon in the male-dominated industry in which he'd shouldered his way up to the top.

He was somewhat stymied by the fact that as he approached the car she smiled, and her whole face softened, became sensuously lovely, almost expectant.

'Before you rip out of here,' he drawled, leaning in, 'just a word of advice.'

'Advice?'

'Lawyer up.'

Her smile flickered and faded. But before he could read her expression she pushed the shades abruptly up her face.

'As much as I like being tumbled out of bed by a handsome man and lectured to,' she shot out rapidly, her words scrambling over one another, 'I *do* have an appointment and this is all getting rather complicated.' She gave him a haughty look. 'If there is any damage to the car, add it to the bill, why don't you?' She zipped up her bag and muttered something about it being just one more thing to add to the list.

She wasn't stupid, Nash thought, looking down at all those bright pretty curls, but her sense of self-preservation was clearly running on zero. Didn't she realise if she was a man he would have hauled her out of that car and done what was necessary?

Maybe she did. Maybe she was relying on her woman status to keep her out of harm's way.

He reached in and palmed her keys.

'Hey!'

He levelled her with a look and had the satisfaction of seeing her back up in her seat.

'Yeah, about that. The world doesn't run on your timetable, princess.'

Her expression was hidden behind those shades, but the pulse at the base of her slender throat was pounding and the old bloke's accusation about her being a nice woman and him frightening her returned full strength.

He dropped the keys into her lap.

'Just as a matter of interest—mine, not yours, doll—how *did* the car end up in the garden?'

She fumbled to start her engine and he frowned. He wanted her to understand the consequences of her carelessness, but he didn't bully women.

She started up the engine, not looking at him.

'I think that would be when I left the handbrake off,' she responded, and without another word reversed fast in a cloud of dust.

Douleur bonne, what did she think she was doing?

Lorelei held on tight to the wheel as she tore up the drive, her heart pounding out of her chest. She just had to get away before the handsome stranger wrecked everything.

Alors, she could have just offered up a standard apology and volunteered to pay for all repairs. A more prudent woman would have done just that. But prudence wasn't her forte lately…

She just wanted today to be a nice day.

One more day.

Was it too much to ask?

She licked her dry lips, dragged her bag over as she drove, fumbled for her lipstick.

Don't think about it, she told herself, swiping her lower lip with the crimson colour, making a mess of it.

She braked, dropped the lipstick, fished it from her lap and hooked off her sunglasses impatiently to restore her face with a tissue in the rear-vision mirror.

For a moment all she saw were her eyes, huge and dilated and vulnerable.

Taking a deep breath, she put herself back in order and forged onto the highway, determined to put this behind her. *Oui,* she'd had a bad start to the day, but that didn't mean anything, and it wasn't *that* bad. Despite the trembling of her hands on the wheel she'd had a little fun, hadn't she? She was sorry about the car, but it hadn't been intentional and it was only a little scratched. She was a good person, she'd never hurt anyone on purpose in her life, she wasn't careless with other people's property; she wasn't a criminal…

Her heart had started pounding again.

Best not to think about it.

She depressed the accelerator, the wind tugging at her hair. Perhaps if she drove a little harder it would help.

She was living harder, too. She'd really pushed the boat out last night. In fact thinking about it made her feel a little sick.

She had positively, absolutely drunk too much. She'd flirted with the wrong men and her attention had definitely not been on her borrowed adornment for the twenties-themed party. When someone had pointed out a couple of the younger partygoers, climbing all over it, she had moved it herself, parking the vehicle in the private courtyard. Clearly she hadn't put the handbrake on.

Why hadn't she remembered to put the handbrake on?

For that matter, why had she behaved so poorly this morning? Why hadn't she apologised and done her best to smooth things over? Perhaps the better question was, what was she trying to prove? Was she that desperate for attention? For somebody to realise she needed help?

Brought up short by the thought, Lorelei let her foot retreat from the accelerator.

Did she need help?

The notion buzzed just out of focus. Certainly she wouldn't be asking any of her friends, none of whom had offered even a word of sensible advice since this whole nightmare began. Could she even call any of those people at her home last night friends? Probably not.

It didn't matter. At the end of the day a party merely meant she wasn't alone. She hated being alone. You couldn't hide when you were alone…

In the rear vision mirror she caught a flash of red. Instinctively she depressed the accelerator. The car did nothing. She tried again and realised she was pumping her foot. Panicking slightly, although this had happened before, she gently stood on the brakes, bringing the car to a slow standstill on the roadside. She saw the sports car flash past in a blur of red and ignored the pinch in her chest because he hadn't even slowed down. Not that she could blame him.

Had she really expected him to stop?

There was nothing for it but to turn off the engine for five minutes before taking it easy going down into town. The Sunbeam Alpine had been playing up for weeks. This wasn't the first time it had happened, and it wouldn't be the last.

Laying her elbow on the door and pressing her head against her hand, she closed her eyes, allowing the sun on her face to soothe the surging anxiety that threatened to sweep everything before it.

Nash watched the Sunbeam drop speed, weave a little. The brake lights stayed on as it ground to a standstill in a cloud of dust at the roadside.

He sped past.

He didn't have time for this. For any of it. The banged-up car, the performance in the courtyard…the unreasonable desire to pull over, pluck those shades off her eyes and rattle around for that conscience of hers she'd assured him she had.

He only got a few hundred metres down the road before he was doing a screeching circle and slowly heading back.

She hadn't got out of the car She seemed to be just sitting there.

Nash already wanted to shake her.

He pulled the Veyron in behind and killed the engine. Shoving his aviators back through his thick brown hair, he advanced on her car. Still she hadn't shifted.

What did she expect? A valet service?

She was sitting with her head thrown back, as if the sun on her face was a sensual experience, her expression virtually obscured by those ridiculously large sunglasses. He noticed for the first time that she had a dappling of freckles over her bare shoulders. They seemed oddly girlish on such a sophisticated woman. He liked them.

His tread crunched on the gravel but she didn't shift an inch.

'Car trouble?'

She slowly lowered the glasses and angled up her face.

'What do you think?'

Those amber-brown eyes of hers locked on his.

'What I think is you need a few lessons in driving and personal responsibility.'

A smile, soft and subtle, drifted around the corners of her mouth. 'Really? And are you the man to give them to me?'

Nash almost returned the smile. She really was playing this out to the last gasp.

'How about getting out of the car?'

She gave him a speculative look and then slowly began unhooking her seatbelt. Her movements were slow, deliberate. She unlatched the door, hesitated only for a moment and then swung her long legs out. She shut the door with a click behind her and leaned back against it.

'How can I help you, Officer?'

The scent of her hit him, swarmed through his senses like a hive of pretty bees, all honey and flowers and female.

Expensive, a steadying voice intervened. *She smells and looks expensive.*

Like any other rich girl on this coast. A dime a dozen if you'd got a spare billion in the bank.

He folded his arms. 'Going to tell me what's going on?'

He actually saw the moment the flirtatious persona fell away.

She gave a little shrug. 'There seems to be a problem with the engine. I accelerate but I lose speed.'

He nodded and headed for the front of her car.

Lorelei found herself following him, hands on her hips. He got the bonnet up with no trouble—something she never could. He leaned in.

'It's the original,' he told her in that deep, male voice.

'Are you a mechanic?'

'Near enough.'

Lorelei looked down the road as a couple of cars swished past, then back at the man leaning into the business end of her car.

Her eyes dwelt on the tail of an intricate dragon tattoo running down his flexed left arm, on his muscled shoulders, shifting under the fit of his close-weave black T-shirt, broad and imposing as he bent low, drawing attention to the strong, lean length of his torso and tapering to a hall-of-fame behind—all muscle. Prime male.

She snagged her bottom lip contemplatively, stroking him up and down with her eyes. She couldn't get over how thick and silky his dark brown hair looked, the wavy ends caressing his broad neck. She wondered how they would feel tangled between her fingers. She wondered what he would say if she apologised, if she told him she wasn't always this out of control…

'Whoever looks after it deserves a medal.'

Lorelei wondered a little hopelessly if he was ever going to look up—look at *her.* She gave a little inner sigh. Probably not. She'd burnt her bridges with this man.

'What was it?' he prompted. 'A gift?' When she didn't reply he straightened up and gave her a speculative look. 'I'd say from a guy who knows his engines.'

Lorelei cleared her throat, aware she'd been staring at him and that he was probably aware of it. 'I bought it myself. At auction.'

He looked so sceptical her hands twitched all over again on her hips.

'You need a specialist to run some tests on the engine.' He was looking at her steadily, as if he expected her to be writing this down. 'It's in good nick, so I assume you've got a specialist mechanic.'

She found herself recalled to her usual good sense. '*Oui.* I'll call him.'

'Everything else looks to be in order.'

As he spoke he set the bonnet down carefully, checked it was locked in place. His movements were assured and methodical and, oddly, Lorelei felt soothed by them. He treated her car with respect. Which was more than she had done with his employer's Bugatti, a little voice of conscience niggled.

'What will happen with the Bugatti?' she found herself asking.

'I expect the man who owns her will have some questions for you.'

Lorelei shoulders subsided.

'Do you want me to follow you back?'

No, most definitely not. Because she wasn't going back. She'd been running the Sunbeam like this for weeks, but she got the impression her handsome stranger would not be best pleased. He might not think much of her, but he was clearly in love with her car.

'*Mais non.* You stopped.' She pushed back a rogue curl dangling over the left side of her face. 'It's more than most people would have done. *Merci beaucoup.*'

Nash hesitated. He hadn't seen her like this before—calm, almost subdued—and it suited her. She wasn't quite as young as he'd first assumed—maybe thirty—and there was a maturity about her that he'd missed in all the glamour-girl theatrics.

'Right. Take care of her. She's a beauty.'

He ran his hand lightly over the paintwork and for the life of him couldn't work out why getting back into his car was so hard. Except she was just standing there, looking a little uncertain.

He sat in the Veyron, waiting, watching as she climbed into the sapphire-blue roadster, waiting for her to start the engine, waiting for her to pull out, all the while waiting to feel relief that she was off his hands. She gave him a simple wave and drove slowly back down the road.

Telling himself he was satisfied, he pulled out and took off.

Lorelei watched until she couldn't see him any more in her mirror, then ignored the pinch in her chest because she wasn't going to see him again, before turning the big car around and heading back the way he was going. Into town.

CHAPTER FOUR

'LORELEI, good morning.' The girl behind the desk beamed. 'You're early!'

'No, I have a client at midday, so I'm running late, *chère*. Can you be an angel and put a call through to the arena to let them know I'm on my way?'

As she reached her locker Lorelei finished keying her successful morning's tally into her cell: *Smashed up a Bugatti. Met a man.* Then she hesitated, because 'met a man' implied she would be meeting him again. Monaco was a postage stamp of geography, but person per square foot it was the most densely populated postage stamp in the world, making it highly unlikely…

She sighed, pressed Send to her best friend's number and dropped the cell into her bag, placing that in her locker. Her love life was fairly, well, non-existent these days. Getting close to a man in her current situation just meant another person to hide things from.

She stripped, pulled on jodhpurs and a white shirt, and crouched down to yank on her riding boots. It was only when she stood up to don the regulation jacket and caught sight of her reflection that she paused to enjoy the little moment when she stepped into this world.

It was almost a moment of relief. She understood this world. There were rules and regulations and they were satisfying. It was what she had always loved about dressage and showjumping. She had had so little structure growing up, and the sport had provided for the lack. Ironically it was fulfilling the same function now.

She smiled wanly as she buttoned herself up. The jacket hung a little on her, but so did everything. She'd lost weight during her father's trial and somehow never regained it.

Gathering up her clipboard, Lorelei made her way out into the stands to wait for her student.

Once this had been her dream, until a bad fall had put paid to her ambitions. Nowadays she trained up-and-coming equestrians on a freelance basis. It didn't pay spectacularly well, but it was work for her soul. After the accident she hadn't thought she would ever saddle up again. Two years of rehabilitation had taught her both patience and determination, and she brought them to her work. It made her a good trainer.

In a couple of years, when she was financially back on her feet again, she hoped to set up her own stables on a property she had her eye on outside Nice. For now, she trained and kept two horses at the nearby Allard Stables, where she also volunteered.

She brought her focus to bear as a glorious bay gelding entered the arena, carrying a long-legged teenager. Lorelei had been working with her for a month. She watched as horse and rider trotted round the perimeter and then came out of the circle, performing a shoulder-in. Her practised gaze narrowed. The rider was using the inside rein to create the bend, rather than her leg, and was pulling the horse off-track.

Too much neck-bend, no angle, she noted on the clipboard propped up on one knee.

Some of the best equine flesh in the world was on view here most days, ridden by the best of the best, but on Fridays the arena belonged to students such as young Gina, who was making a hash of the most fundamental lesson in advanced dressage. She would improve—Lorelei was confident on her behalf. These were skills that could be learnt. The rest was about your relationship with the horse, and Gina was a natural.

For the next half hour she took notes, then joined Gina and the bay gelding's regular handler in the arena. She was working with Gina on top of her usual student load as a favour to another trainer, but she didn't mind taking on the extra work. It was good to take her head out of her financial troubles and focus on something she could control, and fulfilling to see the progress Gina had made in little over a month.

She worked with both girl and horse for the rest of their session, then joined Gina and her mother to talk about her progress. It was important, so although she was running late for her appointment at the Hotel de Paris she made the time. It was on half one when she leapt into the Sunbeam, starting her engine as she checked her cell.

It was never a pleasant experience. So many messages—so few people she actually wanted to talk to. There were several from her solicitor, a raft from legal firms she'd never heard of and one from the agent through whom she was leasing the villa out to strangers. She had a vague hope that the income could be channelled back into the upkeep of the house and grounds. But she wouldn't think about that right now. She wasn't ready.

Maybe tomorrow.

Unexpectedly the stranger's comment that she expected the world to run on her timetable flashed to mind. But before she had time to dwell unhappily on the truth of that, and aware that her damn hands were shaking again, she keyed in her best friend Simone's number and attached ear buds to enable her to drive and talk.

'You had a car accident? *Mon Dieu,* Lorelei, are you all right?'

'No, not an accident.' She hesitated, knowing how lame

it was going to sound. 'I borrowed it for a theme party and parked it and left the handbrake off.'

There was a pause before Simone said with a suspicion of laughter in her voice, 'You know I love you, Lorelei, but I would never let you drive my car.'

'Then perhaps you should talk to the guy I dealt with—this big Australian. He seemed to think I was a disaster waiting to happen.'

'Poor *bébé*. I'm sure you charmed him in the end.'

'He was a little steamed about the car.'

'I bet.'

'I don't think he liked me very much.'

Simone snorted. 'Men always like you, Lorelei. You wouldn't be so good at milking them of euros for that charity of yours if they didn't.'

Lorelei acknowledged the truth of this with a little shrug. 'I guess this one was the exception. He was different—I don't know...capable. Manly. He looked over my car.'

'And—?'

'I think I liked him.'

Simone was silent. Testimony to the state of Lorelei's romantic life.

'I know. I must be crazy, right?'

'Is he employed?'

'Oh, honestly.'

'The last one I heard about didn't have a sou to his name.'

'Rupert was an installation artist.'

'Is that what he called it? I know you're touchy about this, but for the life of me I can't work out why you don't date those guys you schmooze for your grandmother's charity.'

Lorelei's heart sank a little. The nature of her charity work meant she was often seen in social situations with powerful men, but she never dated them. Being the daughter of one of the most infamous gigolos on the Riviera had left her wary of men who could pay her bills. She gravitated towards a type: struggling artist—whether it be painter or musician or poet—often in need of propping up, usually with *her* money. And that was where everything came unstuck.

Well, she didn't have that problem any more…

'So no name, no number—?'

'No hope,' finished Lorelei, and their laughter mingled over the old joke. 'I'm on my way as we speak to the Hotel de Paris.'

'*Ooh, la la,* tell me you're going to use their wonderful spa!'

'Not today. I'm being Antoinette St James's granddaughter and fronting for the foundation.'

'Your *grandmaman*'s charity?'

'*Oui.* They're doing a vintage car rally to raise funds for children with cancer. That's why I had the Bugatti on loan for last night's party. As an adjunct a racing driver here in Monaco has a private track a few miles inland, and he's going to run the kids around it for the day.'

'Which driver? Do you have a name?'

'I don't know. Let me see.' Lorelei braked at a pedestrian crossing and fumbled with the shiny folder she'd picked up from the Aviary office yesterday. 'Nash Blue. The name is vaguely familiar…'

The line went quiet.

'Simone?'

'I'm here. I'm just taking it in. Nash Blue. *Cherie,* how can you live in Monaco and not know anything about the Grand Prix?'

Lorelei rumpled her curls distractedly. 'I'm not very sporty, Simone.'

'You might want to keep quiet about that when you meet him.' Simone sounded arch. 'You didn't do *any* research, did you?'

'I haven't had time. It was dumped on me yesterday.'

'You *do* know Nash Blue is a racing legend?'

'Really?' Lorelei asked without interest, concentrating on weighting the folder down on the passenger seat with her handbag.

'He's a rock star of the racing world. He's broken all sorts of records. He retired a few years ago at the height of his career and—listen to this, *cherie*—he was earning close to fifty million a year. And I'm not talking euros. He was one of the highest paid sportsmen in the world.'

Must be nice, Lorelei thought vaguely.

'He gave up the track to design supercars—whatever *they* are. I think the consensus is he's some kind of genius. But, putting that aside for a moment, he's utterly gorgeous, Lorelei. I confess I'm a little envious.'

Unexpectedly Lorelei pictured a pair of intense blue eyes and wished she had this morning to do over again.

'I'm sure I'll do something to annoy him. I'm on a roll with that, Simone.'

'He rarely gives interviews. The few times he has he's been famously monosyllabic.'

Lorelei's heart sank. So she was going to have to do all the talking?

'But be *en garde, cherie*. He has a reputation with the ladies.'

'Oh, please. If he doesn't talk how does that even work?'

'I don't think much talking is involved.'

Lorelei rolled her eyes. 'I think I'm quite safe, Simone. You forget—I grew up watching Raymond ply his trade. I have no illusions left.'

'Not all men are rascals, *cherie*.'

'No, you married the one who wasn't.' It was said fondly. Lorelei found solace in Simone's happy marriage, her family life. But it wasn't something she ever envisaged for herself. Apart from Simone, her longest relationship had been with her twelve-year-old horses.

'All I'm saying is Nash Blue was a bit of a player in his racing days, and given his profile I doubt anything has changed.'

'*Oui, oui.* I'll keep that in mind.'

'All the parties and famous people you meet—you are one lucky girl, *cherie.*' Simone sounded quite wistful.

'I guess.'

And now she was lying to her best friend.

For a glancing moment Lorelei wanted to tell Simone about all the unreturned phone calls, the unopened emails…

But she couldn't tell her. She was so ashamed she had let it get to this point.

The villa was a money pit she couldn't afford to keep up, and the charity was an ongoing responsibility that took time away from paid work. Her father's legal fees and creditors had basically stripped her of everything else.

She'd lost so much in the last two years, first Grandy to illness and then her faith in Raymond. Right now the only thing that felt certain in her world was the home she had grown up in, and she was holding on to it by the skin of her teeth.

'Keep me updated, *cherie.*'

'*Absolutement. Je t'aime.*'

Lorelei was still thinking about the call as she turned into the Place du Casino and began thinking about where she was going to leave her car. She was running late, and thoughts of what awaited her at home were proving a distraction despite her best efforts to pretend to the contrary. Yet the sun was shining, which lifted her spirits, and she told herself she deserved to cut herself a little slack. Tomorrow she'd deal with all those intrusive emails. She might even front up at her solicitor's office—although perhaps that was going overboard.

She stilled as she caught sight of a familiar red Veyron parked right outside the hotel entrance. Brakes squealing, she came to a standstill midtraffic. The adrenalin levels spiked in her body, but it wasn't anything to do with thoughts of bills and creditors. Her heart pounded.

Behind her horns blared. She made a wide go-around-me gesture with her arm, scanning for a spot. She found one and cut across the flow of traffic, wincing at the blare of horns, but it was worth it to back up into the nice wide space. Perfect. All she needed now was to hand over the folder, smile at the racing-car driver and then she could go and find her stranger and apologise, offer to buy him a drink or two and hope her charm would do the trick.

She reapplied her lipstick with a steady hand, unravelled the blue scarf she wore to protect her hair from the wind and stepped out onto the road.

This time a car horn gave an appreciative little beep as she sashayed across the Place du Casino towards the maharajah's jewel box that was the hotel. That was more like it.

The day was looking up.

He was late.

Nash didn't give it much thought. The publicist would wait. Cullinan would wait. Everyone waited. It was one of the few useful by-products of fame and perversely frustrating. Nash was only too aware of the contradiction. It would be interesting if for once he was stood up.

But another benefit was being able to help out where he could for a worthy cause, and a kids' cancer charity was pretty high on that list.

That was why he had ridden down from the top floor in the middle of negotiations and now strolled across the lobby into Le Bar Américain. Five minutes of face-time and this charity rep would be keen to get going, given he'd held her up for… Nash glanced at his watch…thirty-five minutes.

He scanned the downlit warm ambience of the bar. John Cullinan was on a stool, leaning into both drink and cell as he cut some throats. He was the best in the business at what he did—as he should be, given what he was paid, Nash reflected. But you got what you paid for. Cullinan was worth every penny.

He killed the call the second he saw Nash. 'She's a no-show.'

Nash shrugged. It was of no importance, just a formality.

'I'll get onto the foundation—'

'Just forward the details to the guys at the track and let me know a time and we'll give the kids something to smile about.'

He was about to move off when he saw her. She had paused in the doorway to speak to the maître d'. Her head was slightly bent, exposing the lovely length of her neck and making those bare shoulders look impossibly seductive. He hadn't stopped thinking about those delicately boned shoulders, the fine stemmed length of her throat ever since he'd left her up on the highway.

Nash found himself unable to look away.

Was she meeting someone here? For some reason the muscles tightened all through his body as he cast an inclusive once-over across the room, hunting down the guy. No one had moved towards her, although she had pulled a lot of attention, and he knew in that instant she was alone.

For the first time since he'd quit racing professionally Nash felt the same competitive tension he'd used to before a race.

She turned to look across the room, pushing back a rogue curl with that gesture he remembered, and her eyes met his.

Even at this distance he could see her bow lips tighten. She didn't look happy to see him.

Irritation sparked as a dozen reasons why he should walk on by and forget about her waved themselves like red flags. Yet as every male head in the room turned as she headed his way he knew he wasn't going anywhere.

Lorelei found herself unable to look away.

He stood by the bar, stripped to a crisp white shirt stylishly taut along his torso and dark tailored trousers. His shoulders were impossibly broad, and he radiated confidence and money and power.

Lorelei removed her sunglasses and just stood there, trying to make the connection.

But even as she turned to the maître d' and gave his name she knew what the answer would be.

A shiver ran through her. In this setting it was obvious he was the most powerful man in the room. He was certainly the most attractive, and the chasm between mechanic and the man standing before her was immense. It couldn't be leapt.

She'd been had.

Lorelei stiffened as his gaze landed on her.

She'd also been seen.

His eyes locked onto her and for a moment he looked as poleaxed as she felt. Then he frowned.

She straightened, determined that not by an inflection in her voice or the blink of an eyelash should he see how angry she was—although she wasn't quite sure with who, nor how foolish she felt. She headed over.

Men were looking at her. Men always looked at her. She was tall and blonde and for some guys she was a prize. What they didn't know was that she wasn't available to be won.

She did the prize-keeping and the awarding.

'Mr Blue, I presume?' She offered her hand unsmilingly.

He wasn't smiling either, but he took her extended hand with common courtesy.

Lorelei told herself to relax. So they'd had a little moment this morning? He was a professional and she was…well, volunteering her time. Surely this could be polite and…oh…

His hand closed around hers, warm and dry and secure, and she melted just a little behind the knees. Was he holding on a little longer than necessary? Lorelei felt the colour mounting her cheeks. As he released her hand his thumb shifted and gently brushed over the hardened skin at the base of her palm.

A faint look of surprise lit those blue eyes and Lorelei snatched her hand back, feeling exposed. She could hear her grandmother's voice. 'Lorelei, a lady is known by the softness of her hands.'

Silly, old-fashioned, not true, and yet…

Another man stepped between them. 'You'll deal with *me,* Miss…St James.' He read her name off an email printout that Lorelei could clearly see had the Aviary Foundation's logo.

Lorelei wanted to take a step back but she held her ground. She knew a cut-them-down-to-size gesture when she was on the receiving end of one. She'd experienced enough of them over the weeks when she'd attended her father's trial in Paris. Nobody wanted her to be the unrattled loyal daughter, especially the media, but that was exactly what she had been. Even if it had meant sitting in the shower every night, crying her heart out.

'Lorelei St James,' she said coolly, drawing on the self-control she had perfected during that awful period. 'Let me guess—you must be Mr Cullinan, the *delightful* man who spoke to our foundation's receptionist yesterday and left her in tears.'

The guy bristled, but Nash's cool, deep voice brushed him aside.

'It goes with the territory, Ms St James. Sometimes John doesn't know when to turn it off. Do you have paperwork?'

A little thrown by finding herself under the intent scrutiny of those blue eyes again, for a moment Lorelei had to think. *What paperwork?* Then she pulled herself together and unclasped her handbag, producing the small glossy folder. Nash handed it over, sight unseen, to the scowling Cullinan.

'You can go, John. I'll handle this.'

Lorelei tried not to appear startled.

'Don't you want to discuss it?' She indicated the folder being carried away by Mr Cullinan. The foundation's president had been very clear: she was expected to go over the schedule with Blue's management.

'No,' he said simply.

To the point. Direct. Like any woman, Lorelei liked decisiveness in a man, but it also left her on the back foot. He'd taken away her reason for being here in a single gesture.

Now they were alone she felt even more exposed. Would he think she had some hand in this? That she'd known exactly who she'd been dealing with up at the house?

She decided to come right to the point. 'Mr Blue, was there a reason why you didn't introduce yourself this morning?'

Although she already knew the answer…

'At the time names didn't seem relevant.' His eyes moved with interest over her face. 'And it's Nash.'

Because he wasn't going to be seeing her again. Lorelei remembered how obvious she had made her interest in him and found herself cringing. What was it he'd said about not wanting to discuss it? *He can't make it any more clear, Lorelei,* a little voice of self-preservation whispered. *He's not interested. He's seen you at your worst. Nobody wants to be around that…*

She was pulled up short. What was that he'd said about calling him Nash?

'Tell me, Ms St James, have you eaten?'

Suddenly they seemed to be standing so close. Certainly too close for her to think clearly. His blue eyes moved broodingly over her. Lorelei could feel her body actually quivering in response.

'Are you offering to feed me, Mr Blue?'

A look of amusement flickered unmistakably in those intense blue eyes. 'It would seem that way.' He indicated the bar. 'What's your poison?'

Fortunately the answer to that question was always there, even as she scrambled to process the fact he was asking her to lunch with him.

He murmured, 'Champagne cocktail,' to the bartender and then quite casually slid his broad hand around her bare elbow.

His touch sent a shiver through her erogenous zones and Lorelei found she was wobbling a little on her heels as he began to walk her out of the bar.

'Should I ask where we're going?' Was that appallingly breathless sound her own voice?

His mouth twitched. 'Why ruin the surprise?'

It was silly to feel trepidatious but their history had been a little rocky today, and that hand on her elbow was a tad possessive for their short acquaintance. He was a take-charge guy, but she was a little apprehensive about what form that might take. She told herself not to be silly. After all, he was hardly going to throw her into a river with crocodiles. Was he? She'd scratched a car he clearly valued, and she'd apologised for that. *Had* she apologised?

Lorelei glanced up at him. He wasn't smiling, but she had yet to see him smile. Other guests and patrons were staring at them but Nash appeared oblivious. Simone's phrase…*a rock star of the racing world*...bumped into her consciousness. She was with a famous man. She guessed he was used to being stared at. Except the Hotel de Paris wasn't a place people usually stared…

For the first time in her life Lorelei realised *she* wasn't the main event.

The man she was with was.

He led her into the Jardin restaurant. It was impossible just to walk in and get a table—she'd tried once or twice before—but Nash did just that. As he seated her at the best table on the terrace, with the Mediterranean as a backdrop, her cocktail arrived. Hand delivered by the bartender.

This was a new experience.

'Merci,' she murmured.

A menu was placed into her hands and a waiter hovered as Nash chose the wine.

French sparkling.

How did he know?

Lorelei glanced at her cocktail and smiled a little at her own foolishness.

Mon Dieu, she was being positively girlish. Anyone would think she'd never sat down across from…a rock star.

She met those intense blue eyes and time trickled to a stop. She knew that look in his eyes. He hadn't looked at her that way when she'd been playing out her theatrics this morning—or perhaps she'd been too self-absorbed to notice.

No, she would have noticed *this*.

He was looking at her as if she was worth his time.

A flutter of feminine satisfaction winged through her chest even as her ego reminded her she was worth any man's time.

But this man wasn't any man, and he was interested and making no secret of it.

She felt hot and tingly and aware of her body in ways she hadn't been in such a long time.

Then she remembered what Simone had said about him being a player and she stood on the brakes. She lifted the menu.

'Did you plan to have lunch with the charity's representative, Mr Blue?' she enquired, pleased that her voice continued to be cool and play-by-my-rules.

'It's Nash.' His voice was low and lazy, 'And no, Lori, it wasn't on the programme.'

'It's Lorelei.' She didn't lift her eyes from the menu she was pretending to read. 'And I wouldn't want to hold up your important day.'

There was a pause and from the corner of her eye she caught the movement of his arm as he reached into his jacket. 'Excuse me one moment.'

She lowered the menu. He was keying a number on his cell.

'Luc, I won't be back.' His tone of voice was abrupt and to the point—nothing like the easy male drawl he used with her. 'Have them send the contracts straight over to Blue. I'll deal with them tomorrow.'

Lorelei put the menu down.

He pocketed the cell.

'I take it that was for me,' she observed, lifting a finely arched brow.

The wine had arrived. He poured her a glass himself, then lifted his tall glass of sparkling wine and touched the flute in her hand.

He didn't smile, but his eyes caught and held the part of her fighting to get free, and in that instant Lorelei stopped struggling.

His voice was deep and affectingly roughened, as if coming from a part of himself he usually held in check.

'Consider me all yours for the afternoon.'

CHAPTER FIVE

WITH the Bugatti long dismissed from his mind as a fake and the over-the-top theatrics she had engaged in difficult to reconcile with the poised woman sitting opposite him, Nash found himself entertaining what would have seemed outrageous a mere couple of hours ago.

She was a huge distraction, but he would make the time.

As he had led her to their table he'd appreciated for the second time today the graceful dip of her long, slender back before it gave way to the small curve of her hips, and the subtle sway of those hips as she walked with ease on deathtrap heels. She possessed an innate old-style grace and a hint of athleticism he couldn't quite link up with the sybaritic lifestyle she seemed to embrace.

She intrigued him.

He hadn't been able to get her out of his head since he'd left her on the highway. In the past if he'd wanted something he'd gone after it. But this something had turned up at exactly the wrong moment.

In a week's time his re-entry into racing was going to hit the media like a virus. Everything he did would be scrutinized—the places he went, the parties he attended, the women on his arm. Crazy drama-queen blondes were not part of the package. He intended to keep a low profile and wait out the blood in the water period until the media moved on to the next high-profile sportsman and hounded *his* private life.

Any woman he was seen with now needed to be low-key, and preferably without her own media circus. He'd broken off an on again/off again sexual relationship with a well-known British actress earlier in the year for just that reason. He knew the press would dig something out and air it in the months to come, but he also knew she was soon going to be announcing her engagement and that should put paid to any rumours. He wanted his re-entry into the sport to be as low-key as possible—the opposite of the media circus he'd been caught up in during his twenties.

The woman sitting across from him was *exactly* what a PR team would order. Cool, classy, understated. Not that he had any interest in involving anyone else in his decision. This was between him and his libido…and the lovely Ms St James. Although he didn't intend to give her much say. Action, in his experience, was a far more direct method.

His gaze lingered on her uncovered shoulders.

There was something about the delicacy of her throat and collarbone and the quiver of those bare shoulders that made him think about her naked under a sheet.

'All mine?' She echoed his words. 'You should be careful what you promise, Nash.'

It was the first time she had used his name and her accent curled enticingly around it. His body tightened.

But those amber eyes were direct.

'Are you planning a long lunch?' she enquired sweetly.

Quiet amusement tugged at his mouth. 'Isn't that a requirement of your job description?'

'Pardon?'

'Public relations.'

She looked genuinely surprised. '*Mais, non,* I am not in public relations.'

He leaned back in his chair, enjoying looking at her, enjoying the game. After spending the last two hours fine-tuning contracts this was a nice reward. Lorelei was certainly easier on the eye.

'What do you call it, then?'

'A favour.'

He lifted a brow.

'I'm on the board of the Aviary Foundation,' she explained. 'The usual publicist broke her ankle and I was deputised as her stand-in.'

It fitted. Yet he was disappointed. The idea that she actually worked, held down a career, had weighted those glamorous blonde looks of hers in something concrete. He studied her fine boned face, looking for something else beyond the undeniable beauty.

'It's an influential charity,' he said finally. 'How did you get involved?'

'My *grandmaman* set up the foundation some years ago. I have her seat on the board.'

In other words she came from money. She hadn't lifted a pretty manicured fingertip to earn it. He glanced down at those hands, checked for a ring, then looked again. Her nails were unvarnished and worn down.

But a seat on the board? She'd merely stepped into the niche carved out for her. Broken nails aside, perhaps there wasn't anything here beyond the eyes and the smile and the sexy accent.

He shifted in his chair.

'Do you do a lot of charity work?'

'I do my share. If one is in a position to do so I think there's no excuse not to.'

'Agreed.'

'About this morning…' she said slowly.

He shook his head. 'I think we've moved on from that, don't you?'

Lorelei picked up her champagne and sipped it. Had they?

She was grateful not to have to apologise or explain, because, really, how *did* she explain? She didn't want to look too closely at how out of control things had become.

He had that lazy, contented male look about him—as if he had her exactly where he wanted her and was sizing up his options with her. It was time to do a little sizing up of her own.

'I did some research on you,' she said, knowing it was only half a white lie—because couldn't Simone be counted as research?

He didn't look disturbed.

'You've got quite a reputation.'

Those blue eyes glimmered.

'As a competitor,' she added with a little smile.

He drummed the fingers of his left hand on the table. 'I don't like to lose.'

'It must make you hard to live with.'

'I wouldn't know.' He almost smiled. 'Not having to live with me.'

'I guess it's a question to ask your girlfriend—or wife.'

She didn't know why she'd phrased it that way. It was hardly subtle.

'There isn't a woman in my life.'

Lorelei knew she'd be a fool to believe that. Look at him—big, rugged, rich, sex appeal to burn.

'Oh, really? I heard you were quite busy in that department.'

'Did this come up in all that research?'

Lorelei ran her thumb over the stem of her glass. She realised he was watching her hand and that her gesture might be interpreted as quite provocative. She picked up her glass, intending to drink, then put it down again.

She'd had quite enough to drink last night.

'And you?' he prompted. 'Easy to live with?'

'Me?' She was no longer entirely sure what they were talking about. 'I'm a pussycat.'

'According to your husband?'

'No husband.' She met his eyes and saw satisfaction with her answer.

This time she did take a sip of her drink, and another.

She didn't get involved with men like this. Yet here she was, walking straight on in.

Whatever he said, he was probably seeing someone. Maybe not today, but certainly yesterday, and probably tomorrow. Girls were probably lining up around the block.

Her father in his heyday had always had two or three women on the go. One to pay the bills, another in reserve and a third he actually enjoyed sleeping with. Some young starlet or tourist passing through.

Lorelei frowned. She didn't like to think about that side of Raymond.

She preferred the side he'd thought she saw. He'd made an effort for her to see. The charming *bon vivant,* lavish with money and affection, especially with his darling daughter.

But she'd always been aware he romanced older women up and down the coast to keep the wolf from the door.

Her *grandmaman* had been the one with the real money, doled out sparingly.

Raymond had never complained, and his phone calls from the low-security prison where he was currently serving out the last months of a two-year gaol term were always full of jokes and cheer. She loved him for it, but she wished sometimes she could speak seriously to him.

She never had been able to breach that gleaming surface. Raymond didn't want to hear about the difficulties of life. And under the current circumstances she felt guilty even raising the subject of the villa.

Alors, she was back to thinking about the villa.

'Lorelei.' A deep voice said her name almost gently.

'Oui?' She blinked, took a breath.

Nash was watching her with an intensity that hadn't been there before, as if he knew something had changed.

'Sorry.' She made a forgetful gesture with one hand. 'You were saying?'

'Nothing that won't keep.'

He continued to watch her, a quiet smile conveying so much more than words. In that moment Lorelei knew she was in trouble.

Oh, she knew how to deflect a man, how to make it clear that despite sitting across from him, sharing a meal with him, she was not on the menu.

But right now she felt she was every dish he might like…

Finally Nash spoke.

'We've got a lot in common.' He settled back, angled in his chair, all shoulders and lean, muscular grace.

He seemed to be saying, *Take a good long look. It could all be yours.*

But for how long? she wondered.

'How do you gauge that?' she asked aloud.

'I like to compete. You're a serious trophy.'

'Pardon me?'

He gave her a lazy once-over she should have found insulting after the "trophy" description. Instead she felt it like a direct hit to her sleeping libido.

'You're smart and seriously sexy and I haven't been bored since I sat down with you. Like I said, you're a serious trophy.'

Lorelei inhaled sharply.

She knew this was how some men saw an attractive woman. She had just never met a man who had the nerve to say it to her in so many words.

'Nash, a trophy is an inanimate object you sit on a shelf.'

'A trophy can be anything you want to win,' he countered, sitting forward.

Lorelei had to remind herself not to edge back. He fairly emanated thumping male entitlement.

'I don't get in the race, Lorelei, unless I'm fairly confident of the outcome.'

For a breathless moment she considered asking him exactly how confident he was of her. But deep down she feared the answer.

Another Lorelei—the one who could hold men off with a death stare at a hundred paces—would have stood up and thrown the contents of her drink all over him. This Lorelei—the one clutching her glass like a life jacket and breathing in the spicy, earthy scent of him like oxygen—found herself asking, 'Is that a problem for you? Women boring you?'

He sat back, his hand resuming its drumming action. 'On occasion.' His head dropped a little to the side, as if he were considering her. He smiled slowly. 'Most of the time.'

Arrogant bastard.

She couldn't help smiling back.

'Perhaps the better question is, do you think you'll bore *me?*' she asked sweetly.

'How am I doing so far?'

Lorelei paused long enough to take another sip of her drink.

'Oh, I think you're in the race.'

Nash weighed up two options: dinner and dancing here in Monaco, or would he fly them to Paris? He was leaning towards the latter, because something about this woman made him want to impress her. She was beautiful, but she was also clearly highly intelligent…and wasn't that a turn-up for the books? He hadn't exaggerated when he'd told her he hadn't stopped thinking about her. But what if she hadn't turned up this afternoon? On the strength of her undeniable physical appeal would he have hunted her down? Until now he hadn't seen her like this—elegant, restrained…witty. Good company. Yet deep down he knew he would have gone looking, asked around, put in the legwork. There *had* been something about her from the beginning.

But this…the woman in full…was a revelation that made his body's unreasonable attraction to her no longer a betrayal of his common sense.

The chemistry between them was pretty much a flame to an oily rag, and if in the end she proved not much more than a spoilt rich girl it would be a disappointment, but it wouldn't stop him bedding her.

'Ms St James?'

Lorelei looked up. It was one of the waiters. She recognised him from the several other occasions she had dined here this year. He glanced nervously at Nash.

'I thought you should know your car is being towed away.'

'Pardon?'

'Your beautiful car, Ms St James. The authorities are taking it away.'

For a moment Lorelei didn't know what to do. Towed? Her lovely Sunbeam was being towed? But why…? This time she'd paid all the insurance and registration and…

She looked at Nash.

'I'm so sorry. I have to handle this.'

She scrambled to her feet, scooping up her handbag. Nash was getting to his feet too, frowning.

She wanted to see him again, but in that moment she knew it wouldn't work. She'd forgotten for a time just how bad things were for her out there. If circumstances were different in her world… But they weren't, and they seemed to be getting worse every day.

Without counting the cost of her actions, only knowing she would regret it if she didn't do it, Lorelei stepped up to him, put her hand gently to his jaw and lifted to kiss him. She inhaled man and aftershave, felt the heat of him and the surprising gentleness of his mouth because he hadn't expected this.

His momentary hesitation gave way to the sudden surge of his body against her own and his hand spread possessively across the back of her head. She tasted him fully as he moved to take over the kiss, giving her a moment's glimpse of exactly how overwhelming his sensual expertise could be.

Mon Dieu, this was what she was giving up…

But she was already pulling free, turning away, because she'd allowed herself to be seduced by the solidity and masculine certainty of this man when there was nothing here for her in the long run. All the while she was sitting here her problems were still out there, mounting up, waiting for her return, and now she had to deal once more with the chaos in her life.

She took off across the restaurant, as fast as her ridiculous heels would let her, knowing only one thing: she *had* to save the car. She wouldn't be letting anyone take away the last damn thing she owned.

Lorelei was across the Place du Casino and about to cross the road when a heavy hand curled possessively over her shoulder. She swung around, hitting out reflexively with her handbag, eyes wild with anxiety.

'Let me go. I've got to get to my car.'

Nash steadied her with both hands. 'I want you to wait here. Are you listening, Lorelei? Let me handle it.'

Responding to the authority in his voice, she blinked up at him. He was going to help? There was a scraping of metal on asphalt and, confused, she whirled around to see what was happening across the road. She saw the tow truck backing up in front of her car and automatically stepped out onto the road.

Nash swore and reached to grab her.

Of all the suicidal…

She took off across two lanes of traffic.

He wouldn't have believed it if he hadn't seen it, yet somehow she made it across unharmed.

His heartbeat slowly resumed normal strength.

Amidst the blare of car horns her high-decibel wishes were being made very clear in vitriolic French.

'Get away from my car!' she shrieked. 'What do you think you're doing?'

Nash was not often left speechless, but at that moment he might still have been in the courtyard at the old villa this morning. The sophisticated, sexy woman he had pushed back a busy afternoon's schedule for was gone. In her place was a reckless wild woman who was clearly out of control.

Adrenalin levels surging, he crossed the street more circumspectly, all the while watching as Lorelei stormed up to the guy supervising the removal of her car. She was waving her hands about as she remonstrated with him in typical Gallic fashion, but the guy was pretty much ignoring her.

Hell, for all he knew they were on a first-name basis and that car of hers was towed every day of the week…

Lorelei had her hands on her hips and was gathering quite a crowd. Ice-queen blondes losing their cool on a lazy afternoon in Monte Carlo had pulling power, and now Lorelei was… Was she taking off her shoes? She was taking off her goddamned shoes! What in the hell?

She slung first one and then the other stiletto heel at the guy. The first one missed but the second one caught him in the groin.

The bloke said something crude and headed for her, and Nash dropped amusement and swapped it for street-level aggression. He made a direct line for the problem, collared the ape so fast the guy didn't see it coming and shoved him hard up against the side of the truck.

'You want someone to lay into, mate,' he said, low and with deadly menace, 'try me.'

The man's face fell, then turned an apoplectic red. Nash realised he had him in a chokehold. He eased off. But Lorelei was suddenly right up beside him, stabbing her slender index finger within inches of the guy's face.

'You listen to him and you listen to me. I want my car back. *Pronto!*'

Nash growled. 'Hand in my back pocket.'

'Quoi?'

'Keys,' he snarled.

Fumbling, Lorelei retrieved them.

'Get in my car.'

'But—'

'Do it. Now.'

She backed up, limped a little to the roadside, spotted the red Veyron across the street. She could only see one of her shoes. The other one seemed to have rolled under the truck. The red haze had shifted and she was beginning to think clearly again. What on earth had she done?

People were standing on the pavement, watching.

Let them watch, she thought miserably, casting a longing look back at her car…and then at Nash, who had let the guy go and was using his phone.

Possibly to call in the men with the straightjacket for her before he made excuses to reverse right out of her life. She'd pretty much made a fool of herself, and from experience she knew that whilst men enjoyed the effort she put into her pretty packaging they didn't have much patience for her more high-octane behaviour. Not that she made a practice of causing scenes in public streets—no, that was a little more to do with the stress she was under at the moment. But Nash wasn't going to buy that. All he'd seen was crazy.

Serves you right, Lorelei St James, she thought as she picked her way across the road in bare feet.

She let herself into the car and forced herself to sit up dead straight, not slide down the seat and hide. She'd been doing enough hiding of late. It was an uncomfortable thought she quickly shoved out of her mind. But this was pretty bad. She'd behaved like a lunatic…

But, oh, her car.

Nobody would understand, but it was all she had left in her own name. It was the one thing she hadn't sold off to pay all the creditors. It was ridiculous, running a gas-guzzling monster like that, but when she drove it she felt like a queen in her castle—important, invincible…

All the things she had discovered recently she wasn't.

She watched Nash coming across the road. He looked so calm and in control. More things she wasn't.

He slid in alongside her, slamming the door, belting up, checking the lights as he fired up the quiet engine.

Lorelei fumbled for her cell.

'You don't need to make a call.'

She forced herself to look at him. Stupidly, her eyes went to his mouth and she relived the moment she had impulsively kissed him. '*Au contraire.* I need to track my car. They'll impound it, and last time it took over a week to get it back.'

'Last time?' His eyes flicked over her.

Lorelei assumed a facsimile of a haughty expression but her heart just wasn't in it.

'I admit it has happened before,' she said wearily.

He didn't respond.

'It's such a large car,' she found herself explaining. 'I find it difficult to park.'

'You parked in a loading zone,' he inserted dryly.

Lorelei worked some invisible creases out of her silken lap. 'Yes, perhaps. I'm a little short-sighted when it comes to parking. It does happen.'

'Yeah, to you I'm guessing a lot.'

Lorelei didn't answer. What could she say? *Oui, I'm a mess on heels.* Oh, her Louboutins. Could she ask him to…?

She glanced sidewards. *Non...*

'Nash,' she said slowly, 'could you be a darling and fetch my shoes…?'

He shifted around in the seat, his expression not encouraging.

'They're very expensive,' she murmured with a hopeful upwards look. Would it help if she fluttered her eyelashes? Showed him the receipt from the shop in Paris?

Without a word he swung the sports car out into the traffic and Lorelei shrieked as he did an abrupt U-turn. She grabbed her seat, holding on for dear life.

He braked with a screech.

'Don't move,' he uttered, punching open the door.

No, she wouldn't be doing that. Although she might just have lost a couple of years off her life…

He returned with both shoes, dropping them into her lap. He didn't even look at her, just pulled the Veyron into the light traffic and drove away from the scene of her crime. Lorelei craned her neck to try and work out what was going on with her car.

'You'll have it back in the morning,' he informed her abruptly.

She stared at him stupidly.

'It's not being impounded. A mechanic is going to have a look at that stop-start engine of yours. They'll run it up to you tomorrow.'

Lorelei plucked at her shoes, too stunned even to check for damage.

'Merci,' she said inadequately, wondering how she was going to begin to apologise and thank him. It had been so long since someone had done something just for her.

But what did it mean? This went beyond some silly flirtatious nonsense about a race and a trophy and him being out to win. He'd just done something very nice for her, and she couldn't enjoy it because she knew she had probably put the kybosh on this going any further.

As if sensing her disquiet, he turned those stunning eyes momentarily in her direction.

'I'll run you home,' was all he said.

She forced herself to shrug.

'Comme vous le souhaitez.' As you wish.

CHAPTER SIX

COULD he be a darling and fetch her shoes...?

As the traffic eased to a halt at a pedestrian crossing Nash snapped and did the only thing a man in his circumstances could be expected to do, given the series of events, the surging adrenaline and hot blood being pushed through his body, and the proximity of this unpredictable wild creature he had somehow become involved with.

He leaned across, slid a hand around the back of Lorelei's head, meshing his fingers slightly in the silky weight of her hair and releasing more of the fragrance of honey and flowers he could fast become addicted to, angled her astonished face and took her tender mouth with his.

The faint hint of champagne still clung to her lips. The warm sweetness of her breath as she gasped and sighed and made a little moaning noise before kissing him back made him want more. The feel of her, the rise of her response beneath him, suddenly stirred a much more primal urge to take what belonged to him, what was his. To mark her. He'd only known her a handful of hours and yet he felt as if he'd been waiting much longer to kiss her.

He deepened the kiss, invaded her mouth, tasting her, driving into her. He told himself it was sexual chemistry; it would burn itself out fast enough. But right now...he wanted her.

He couldn't get enough of her. Yeah, he'd fetched her shoes for her...she could wear them while he—

The blare of a car horn and Lorelei jerking in response had Nash releasing her. For a second he was caught in the headlights of her eyes, and the analogy of having something not quite tame within his grasp was suddenly very real.

Who was this woman?

'This isn't a good idea,' he imparted roughly.

'Non?'

Her rather unhappy interrogative took him by surprise and he almost smiled.

He couldn't believe what he was thinking. He needed to take her where she wanted to go and then forget the whole thing. He was damn lucky someone hadn't been filming the entire incident in the street—although that was a possibility, given the crowd she'd drawn.

She was running her fingers through her hair, rubbing the spot where he'd had his hand...

He was under time constraints. In a couple of weeks he'd be going into lockdown.

He had to be out of his mind...

But he could see her home.

She seemed to realise what she was doing and pulled her hands back into her lap. The gesture made him smile. Yeah, he could see her home.

For a breathless moment all Lorelei had been able to do was hold still, drowning under the skilled pressure of his lips, but she'd never been a passive woman and with a little moan she had kissed him back.

Apparently women who caused scenes in the street didn't scare all guys away. Well, not this guy, at least, whose mouth needed a contract for insurance purposes. Lorelei guessed not much would scare him. Confidence and certainty didn't seem to be a problem for Nash.

He hadn't even asked. He just took.

Lorelei was quite certain his not asking was adding to the outrageously good feelings still slip-sliding through her body. *Mon Dieu,* the man knew what to do with his mouth—and those fingers, lightly, firmly palpating the sensitive tendons and hollows at the top of her neck, tugging so pleasurably on her hair, were equally skilled. What could they do elsewhere on her body?

When his mouth had released hers she'd been panting slightly, and she hadn't been able to take her eyes off him as his gaze had drifted over her face, down across her bare shoulders.

'This isn't a good idea,' he'd said, in a flatteringly roughened voice.

A cold drop of uncertainty had hit the top of Lorelei's spine. *'Non?'*

He had smiled then, the charisma of it almost shocking. His blue eyes had filled her line of vision but the light honk of a horn had had her shaking off the spell and indicating vaguely at the windscreen.

'I think we can go.'

Nash moved lazily back to his side of the car, as if he had all the time in the world, and they shifted forwards, his hands on the gears as assured as they had been when splaying long, strong fingers through her hair. He hadn't pulled, like a less skilled man might. He'd tugged. And the little answering darts of response had shot like arrows from a quiver through her body.

She threaded her own fingers through her hair and then realised she was trying to recreate the feelings he'd evoked in her. She snatched her hand back, pressing it in her lap.

Feeling as if she might be slumping unattractively, Lorelei tried to sit up a little straighter, assume a more ladylike posture—only to find she was actually still upright. There had been no slippage…only a complete and utter inner landslide…

It was all about how she felt inside, she realized. All loose and relaxed and devil-may-care. The stake of anxiety she'd been tied to all day had gone. *Mon Dieu*—she ran an unsteady hand through her curls—the man was a miracle-worker. What on earth would it be like if…?

Nash gave her a slashing smile as if he understood exactly how it would be.

The courtyard was in full afternoon sun when the Veyron idled to a stop.

Nash killed the engine and without a word to her—not that they had exchanged many words driving up, at least not any important ones, as to what they were doing, if he'd be staying, where this was going—he was out of the car and coming around, lifting her door.

Lorelei tried to think fast. She was more than a little worried about inviting him inside. Most of the rooms in the villa were emptied of furniture, and the general air of neglect that hung over the place was worse on the inside. She hadn't minded having people in last night, with all the lights and champagne flowing and the rooms thick with people, but in the harsh light of day she knew how bad it looked. And after this morning's series of disasters she suddenly wanted Nash to think well of her.

But Nash wasn't paying any attention to the house.

He was looking down at her.

She hadn't quite appreciated just how big he was until this moment. She'd had a taste of it this morning, but in her heels some of the height discrepancy had been dealt with. Right now, Louboutins dangling from one hand, handbag from the other, she was only too aware of his powerful shoulders, the strength of his arms and how easily he could overpower her.

It was a jolting thought. Not that he had given her any reason to think he was a threat to her safety—on the contrary. But she was a woman who lived alone and he was…

A famous man who was hardly going to turn into Jack the Ripper.

He shut the car door behind her. 'Shall we go inside?'

'*Ah, oui.* Of course.' She picked her way across the gravel, thinking there was no *of course* about it.

At the front door he held out his hand.

'Key?'

'It's open,' she said, struck by his old-fashioned attitude, and pushed open the heavy front door.

Nash shoved his hand against the panelling, holding it wide for her.

'Anyone else home?'

'*Non.* I live alone.'

His eyes found hers. They were so close she could see the unusual darker rim around the blue iris. Suddenly she knew why those eyes gave the impression of such an intense blue.

'You shouldn't live alone,' was all he said.

Her gaze dropped helplessly to the firm line of his mouth.

'That's why I throw a lot of parties.'

He didn't smile as she wanted him to. Nor did he kiss her. But she'd already worked out that Nash wasn't going to do much of what she wanted him to. He was his own man in ways she hadn't quite encountered before and it was in equal measures confusing and unbearably exciting.

His heavy tread rang out on the stone floor and the cool emptiness of the house closed in around them. Lorelei shivered slightly as her mood did its usual dip. Almost as if he was reading her, Nash stepped up behind her and she had an odd sensation of his strength and solidity. She rather liked it.

She liked it a lot. And all of a sudden she realised this man didn't feel like a threat to her. He was making her feel safe. And safety had been the most elusive of conditions in her life.

Her father had taught her to live with risk; her *grandmaman* had constantly moved the goalposts to keep her forever striving to do her best. Past boyfriends had relied on her to keep the wolf from the door with her inheritance, her network of social contacts.

None of them had ever made her feel safe.

It was probably illusory. He was a big, take-charge guy and he'd been sweet to her all along the line. No wonder she was having rescue fantasies.

She took him through to the kitchen. It was one of the few rooms still fully furnished, for which Lorelei was silently grateful. But unfortunately, like her bedroom, it was a shambles. The caterers had taken away most of their debris, but there were still empty bottles and plates and overturned furniture.

'I had a party last night,' she felt obliged to explain. She didn't want him to think she lived in squalor.

'I'm guessing that's pretty standard for you.'

It was. It was standard for her role with The Aviary. 'Not at all,' she replied smoothly. 'I'm quite the homebody.'

He gave her a sceptical look. 'Yeah, the party comes to you.'

Lorelei didn't know why but there was an edge to what Nash was saying that had her cooling. *He* should try entertaining eighty people on the budget The Aviary Foundation gave her.

Nash was surveying the room. He wandered over to the counter. Lorelei followed his long muscled back with her eyes.

'Coffee pot?'

'My, my—you are domestic.'

Nash shrugged. He had a housekeeping service at all his homes, which made it unnecessary for him to ever approach a kitchen, but he'd grown up regular. As regular as a kid with a drunk for a father and only an older brother to care for him. He'd learned young how to wash his own dishes and scrub a floor and unplug a drainpipe.

Not to mention how to get himself off to school.

'Yeah, I'm a regular boy scout.'

He looked around. Lorelei had a kitchen and a half. Although he doubted she ever spent any quality time with a dishmop.

Not a domestic bone in that lithe, lovely body, he thought with satisfaction.

Lorelei began opening cupboards, retrieving ground coffee beans, switching on the kettle, pulling out the coffee maker.

'Cups?' he asked.

Lorelei indicated one of the cupboards.

'You're very practised at this,' she said.

He appraised her. 'I know how to make a cup of coffee.'

'Your *maman* brought you up right.'

'Mum walked out when I was nine.'

Nash caught himself. *Where in the hell had that come from?*

Lorelei's gaze moved to his. 'Parents,' she said carefully. 'They do muck us up.'

'Yeah.'

Lorelei noticed he spoke matter-of-factly, but there were hard emotions playing over his face and she kept her attention on the job at hand.

Unavoidably, she began thinking about her own *maman*—Britt, who had flickered in and out of her life. The mother she'd only known fractionally as a child, on those rare visits to New York and her apartment high above Central Park. A glorious blonde Valkyrie who sang to her Swedish folk songs and let her play dress-up in the *ateliers* of the best couturiers in Paris and Rome; a mother of sorts, who'd stalked the catwalks with Lorelei sitting front and centre at the shows, dressed up like a little doll to be cooed over by her glamorous, sweet-smelling friends. A mother who had been no mother at all, and was now a sort of friend she spoke to irregularly.

'I gather someone in your family owns a bank, given the real estate you're sitting on.' Nash was leaning back against the counter, muscular arms folded across his chest, displaying the tail of the dragon tattoo down his left arm.

'Not a bank.' Lorelei repressed a wry smile. *If only.* 'This house belonged to my *grandpère.* He had a successful import business. When he died it passed to my *grandmaman,* Antoinette St James, and I inherited it on her death.'

'I gather you were close? She left you her house.'

Lorelei wanted to say, *It's complicated.* 'She looked after me. Taught me right from wrong. Gave me standards.'

'And a house?'

'Oui.' She sighed. A white elephant.

'I imagine it's a burden, given its size?'

He understood. It didn't surprise her as much as it ought. He gave the impression of being quietly observant. What had Simone said? Monosyllabic? She imagined this was as chatty as Nash got, and it was quite a compliment to her.

She gestured at the ceiling. 'You don't need to be kind. It's clearly falling down around my ears.'

She waited for him to ask her why she didn't sell it. It was the obvious question.

'Did you grow up here?'

'In part. I spent my breaks between school terms with Grandy.'

He nodded. He was examining her as if she were something he was thinking of buying. Lorelei took the burbling coffee jug over to the counter.

'I take it your parents are gone, given you got this house?'

'*Non,* both living. My *grandmaman* didn't quite approve of my mother.'

'But she approved of you?'

'*Ah, oui,* in her way. Cream? Sugar?'

'Black.'

'Raymond, my father, did not meet with her approval, either.'

'You call your dad by his given name?'

Lorelei gave a little Gallic shrug. ‘He’s that sort of father. What do you call your *papa?*’

‘Not much. He’s dead.’

‘I’m sorry.’

He watched her pour. ‘Don’t be.’

‘Do you have siblings?’

‘An older brother.’

‘That must be nice. I’m an only child. Are you close?’

He looked down at her. ‘Want to trade family horror stories, Lorelei?’

She froze. For a moment she thought… But, no, he didn’t know. He would have said something. Lorelei lowered her gaze. She didn’t have anything to be ashamed of. She hadn’t broken the law. She was a good person….

‘I don’t have any.’ She spoke too quickly.

Nash watched a tide of faint pink colour move across the surface of her high tilting cheekbones. She suddenly looked a whole lot less certain of herself.

He wondered wryly when his decision to come inside and see where this led had turned into a download of family stories over coffee. Probably about the time she’d climbed out of the car outside and looked up at him with those uncertain eyes. For some reason what had flashed through his head was not an image of her naked on a bed upstairs in this shambles of a house, but a vision of her stepping in front of those two lanes of traffic and the two minutes it had taken off his life.

There was something about this girl that told him she didn’t have much of a clue about looking after herself.

He suspected the little stunt in the street today was the tip of the iceberg. It should be sending him in the opposite direction. With the media circus about to start up around him, his every move monitored, he’d be insane to bring something like this into his life, even for a night.

‘Nash, is this your usual modus operandi with women?’ she enquired, tipping up her chin, all signs of uncertainty gone. 'Rescue them, drive them home and get them drunk on coffee?'

She'd read his mind.

He'd be a busy boy for the next eight months and he wasn't looking for a long-term lover. He was looking for what most men wanted but didn't own up to: a hot blonde who disappeared in the morning. He remembered that over that restaurant table he'd seriously considered Lorelei might be that woman.

He considered it again.

She could make arrangements, pack an overnight bag. He'd sort the plane, show her the nightlife of Paris, acquaint himself with the sweet, sensual weight of what he'd held in his arms momentarily inside the restaurant…

He watched her sashay over to the kitchen table, prop that pert little ass of hers up on the distressed oak surface and dangle a long, lithe leg.

Caution be damned—why the hell not?

He'd suggest dinner, mention the restaurant, wait for her to pack a little bag.

She was sipping her coffee, twining a glossy curl around a finger, amber eyes busy on him. It might have been his imagination but she seemed to sit a little straighter, and those eyes grew a little warier the closer he came. Yeah, those eyes did all the speaking for her, and if he sensed a raft-load of secrets was lurking behind them it didn't concern him. He wasn't interested in uncovering her secrets. He just wanted to know what she was doing tonight.

He stopped in front of her.

'I've been giving tonight some thought.'

'Ah, oui.'

He'd actually been thinking about some fine dining at a famous first arrondissement hotel, but something a little more cutting edge might be a better setting for Lorelei.

'If you're not engaged?'

Lorelei put down her coffee. *'Mais, non.'*

He reached for her hands, turned them over in his. She let him.

'Dinner?'

'Oui.'

To his surprise her lashes swept down and for a moment she looked almost demure, rather old-fashioned.

'Paris?' He cleared his suddenly husky throat. 'There's a restaurant in the fifth arrondissement.' He named a legendary chef.

Her lashes swept up in surprise. 'Can you get a table at such short notice?'

He shrugged.

Lorelei was impressed. She'd forgotten. Not only did he have money to burn, he was famous. She wished he would stop stroking her hands. She didn't want him turning over her palms, finding those calluses again.

She also wished he hadn't said those words to her in the restaurant: *I don't get in the race if I'm not sure of the outcome.* Although forewarned was forearmed.

She tugged her hands away. 'I'm afraid not tonight, *non.* Not Paris.'

She didn't want to wake up tomorrow morning in a hotel room on her own, or with a man who had taken his fill and was only going to transport her home.

He had clearly set the tone of what this was all about for him. This was a race and she was the trophy. No doubt he'd collected a lot of trophies—possibly had a shelf for them, she thought snappishly.

Lorelei had no intention of sitting on a shelf. She had seen too much of it growing up with Raymond. Womanisers left her cold. If Nash wanted to pursue her, he was going to have to do just that.

No? Nash looked long and hard at that unexpected negative. *No?*

'Can I ask if it's personal, or Paris?'

'I'm fond of Paris,' she demurred. 'But not tonight.'

Nash regarded her bright curls, her glossy slightly parted lips, her guarded eyes watching him.

'I'd be happy to go to dinner with you here in Monaco,' she suggested slowly.

So much for the disappearing hot blonde.

He almost smiled. Almost.

For some reason he didn't really mind.

She had the brakes on. He could almost see the marks on the road.

He didn't have to think about it. Any intention he'd had of fast-forwarding this evening suddenly seemed crass, and in his mind's eye he'd already put it aside in favour of a long, slow build-up. Lorelei, clearly, would be worth it. Given the slightly haughty look on her face, she set a high value on herself—and who was he to argue with that?

'Monaco it is,' he said. 'I'll pick you up at eight.'

CHAPTER SEVEN

'THAT woman, she's got a media profile.'

John Cullinan's voice came stridently over the speakerphone.

Nash strolled naked across the bedroom of his penthouse apartment, towelling his hair dry.

He had left Lorelei's home only a few hours before and felt comfortable that he'd dealt with his unlooked-for attraction to her. He was old-style enough to appreciate her definite *No, not tonight, not Paris.* It showed her to be discriminating, which pleased him, but he was confident a few dates would suffice and she'd let him into her bed. It was the primary goal.

He liked to set goals.

At his non-response Cullinan continued, 'Her da's banged up in one of those low-security places out in the countryside. There was a celebrity trial a couple of years back. He defrauded a washed-up French actress out of her savings. But the star turn was the daughter. She turned up every day at the trial in a different outfit, stole the show. Seemed to enjoy the limelight.'

Nash threw down the towel and checked the time by his watch sitting on the bedside table.

'She doesn't even work for that goddamned charity.'

Nash stilled.

'Who doesn't work for the charity?' he asked, nice and low.

'Lorelei St James. And, get this: there's a string of high-profile men she's been linked to. That dot-com billionaire who dropped a fortune on the casino last year, a Hollywood producer, the financier Damiano Massena—pretty much any guy with a bit of a name and she's there. She targeted you today, boyo.'

Nash was caught off guard.

'You've got an overactive imagination, John.'

'Just doing my job. You can't afford the press. This woman likes the press.'

'Don't they all?' Nash muttered under his breath. 'The press conference is all you need to worry about, mate. Are we clear?'

'Clear.'

Nash cut the connection, running a hand through his damp hair.

He didn't want this information. But now he had it, what was he going to do with it?

There was one option, he thought. He didn't have to do anything about it. So she had a crim for an old man? Big deal. So did he. She had a past. Again, big deal. So did he. She was a beautiful grown-up woman who had lived in the world just like him, not a boring ingénue. Part of what attracted him to her was that life experience, her maturity.

It would be highly suspicious if she *didn't* have a past.

She had a past with *'a string of high-profile men.'*

He stood over his suit, laid out over the back of a chair—the suit he'd pictured Lorelei pressing her long, lithe body against, with him in it, as he danced with her, resting his hand on that sweet place at the bottom of her spine.

He laid that same hand on the back of his neck, where the tension seemed to be gathering at a rate of knots.

He pictured Lorelei in the arms of another man, and another. The woman in the backless gown remained the same, the suit was the same, but different guys. He frowned and dismissed it.

He reasoned that Cullinan didn't like her because she'd shown him up in the American Bar. The recollection of which had a bit of a smile tugging on his lips.

Relaxing, he retreated into the bathroom, palmed his electric razor and went to work on a beard that would be back in the morning.

Besides, if she was after some limelight wouldn't she have jumped at Paris?

How many media-savvy socialite blondes had he walked out of restaurants and into a posse of click-happy paparazzi who'd just *happened* to get a clue as to where he was dining and with whom?

He was accustomed to women with agendas. Years ago, when he'd still been green about the limelight, a young banking heiress had decided she wanted a racing-car driver. He'd been twenty-four, idealistic and he'd put a ring on her finger. Not an engagement ring—he hadn't been *that* naive—but he'd imagined that was what it took to assure her fidelity. She'd slept around on him from the beginning, and when they'd broken up she'd hit the media with the credentials of a seasoned campaigner.

It was the origin of all the stories about him. His heiress had turned him into a legend of infidelity, citing women he had never known. Her public profile had assured that she'd gone on to a career as consort to a series of high-profile men.

He'd gone on to a legendary driving career and a reputation for moving through women faster than he sped around any track. The media had been insatiable for stories about him. He had fed them with his policy of never lingering with one particular woman too long, there was no getting away from that, but he had never courted public attention. It had come after him, and consequently he had no illusions left about the negative side of publicity, about its effect on his attempts to lead a semi-normal life, and especially about the women who hustled their way into that life.

Yet here he was, deluding himself…

The razor dropped into the basin and he let it buzz there uselessly, leaning the heels of his hands on the sink and eyeing himself in the mirror.

Did he really need to give himself the lecture? At this stage in his life? Hadn't he already been here before?

If Cullinan was right, this was a woman who liked the limelight, who liked famous men, and she'd turned up at that hotel today and lied to his face that she had no idea who he was.

He vented a dry laugh. He'd been here so many times it was like a stuck record. In former days he would have just taken what was on offer and ignored the fallout. But he had more to protect this time around. Because right now, with his racing career once again poised in the wings, he was going to do things differently.

His expression hardened.

He knew what he had to do. He just didn't want to do it. But he couldn't in good conscience sleep with a woman and then dump her. He could be ruthless in his personal relationships, but he wasn't a bastard.

He snagged his cell before he could change his mind and put through a call.

She answered after several rings. '*Bonjour,* Nash.'

Her voice was lilting, husky…inviting him in.

For a second he forgot all his misgivings and he was back on the side of that highway, watching her standing uncertainly by her car. The difficulty he'd had in driving away…

Something about this wasn't familiar. None of this was familiar. This. Her.

No, he hadn't done this before…

Damn.

'I'm ringing to cancel,' he said bluntly.

There was a silence.

'It wasn't a good idea to begin with. I've got a lot of work on and I can't give you the time you deserve.' He knew these lines by heart. 'I apologise if I've messed up your evening's plans.'

He waited for the explosion. In his experience a woman on the make rarely remained neutral.

'You didn't know this earlier today?'

She didn't sound angry, she sounded genuinely at a loss, her voice almost uncertain, and for a moment it loosened his grip on all that life experience. He hesitated, because right now he was remembering he'd seen a lot of other things in Lorelei St James beneath the glossy exterior. Things he couldn't think about now or they'd undermine what was the right decision. The only decision.

'I did, but you're a beautiful girl, Lorelei. I let that distract me.' He paused to let it sink in. 'But, like I said, it's a busy time.'

'I distracted you?' Her tone had cooled to match his. 'Do you ask women to dinner who *don't* distract you, Nash?'

He released some of the tension in his chest. 'Okay, I'll lay it out for you.' He made his voice harder, grittier. 'The reality is you've got a media profile, Lori, and that's not going to work for me.'

There was a flat, astonished silence.

'Let me see if I understand this,' she said slowly. 'You no longer want to take me to dinner because you've read something about me in the newspaper?'

'No,' he said flatly. 'I don't want to take you to dinner because I don't want to read about *me* in the newspaper.'

He knew she'd taken his meaning because there was a pregnant pause.

'I'm sure that gets old for you quite fast,' she said, in a stiff little voice he didn't quite recognise as hers.

She paused but only to catch her breath.

'Is this about my father?'

He heard a note of that desperation she'd displayed on the street with her car, felt the give of his tightly leashed control and the threatened spill of emotions and desires he refused to give in to. Something about the way she kept going, revealing herself so openly, reminding him how unable to protect herself she had seemed this afternoon, made this intensely personal—and it was working against his usual detachment.

He focused on pulling it back. He was good at this. Reining it in. Being single-minded. He reminded himself it had been a long day, and this woman had contributed to some of that length with her theatrics.

'No, sweetheart, it's about you and your lack of visible support and me being flesh and blood. I made a mistake.'

He put finality in those four words. The conversation needed to end.

There was a sudden flash of silence.

His words echoed back at him, the harshness of the message he was giving her making him flinch even as he knew he'd given women the brush-off before. Blunt always worked, and the only casualty of this would probably be her ego.

'*Mais, oui,* you're a busy man.'

This time the heat in her voice was unmistakable and he relaxed a fraction. Angry was good. He could put an angry, indignant woman behind him.

'How inconvenient of me to distract you from what's important,' she bit out. 'Here was I, thinking you were a gentleman, but you're just a *man,* aren't you? Like all the rest.'

He heard the catch in her voice.

'And not a very nice one.'

The phone went dead.

He dumped the cell, frustrated. For a moment he felt her in his arms again, the warmth of her, the delicacy, saw the way her tilted eyes grew round when she was uncertain. It was that uncertainty he'd heard threaded through her voice just now, and for a moment he knew he'd hurt more than her ego. For a moment he considered the alternative that she might have been genuine. That the witty, surprisingly refreshing woman he'd talked to in her kitchen this afternoon was the genuine article.

Then he dismissed it.

She was right. He wasn't a very nice man and that had brought him a long way.

What remained was the fact he'd blown off two meetings to spend time with a woman he didn't know, and it was time to play catch up. He hadn't got anywhere without being single-minded. He needed to get his focus back where it belonged.

He dressed, made the calls necessary to bring the people who could make things happen together.

Santo's Bar. Half an hour.

It was a quick drive from his apartment to the waterside bar. Nash, however, found himself taking the scenic route, driving down the glittery Monaco boulevards, remembering the first time he'd raced here. The narrow grid, the excitement of the danger inherent in this course above all other road circuits... He'd won and his life had never been the same again.

It had been an extraordinary ride—that race and all the races that had come before and after it, building up his motor-design business, Blue, the journey to this town, to this moment. It had happened against the odds, given his beginnings. He'd come from a background of squanderers. Money, talent, opportunity—all squandered on drink and women and bad bets. And that was just his old man.

Success had come quickly to him. Probably too quickly. He'd had a raft-load of hangers-on at the beginning of his career whom he'd bailed out financially. His father, his brother, old friends... They'd all viewed him as a lucky bastard, but he knew different. He'd worked bloody hard to get where he was, and he had learned to hold on to what he'd earned. He damn well didn't need another person who wanted something from him…

And just like that he was thinking about Jack. His brother. He wasn't risking it again.

His expression hardened and he told himself if his gut was tied in knots it was only because Lorelei St James was clearly a premium lay and he wouldn't be having any. Animal attraction. It was why even now he swore the scent of her was still in the car, making him restless, angry, and making it hard to remember why he was denying himself.

Had she simply imagined it?

Had he really blown her off?

How had he phrased it? She had a *media profile.*

It was the trial. It could only be the trial.

Lorelei sank down onto the chaise in her bedroom and thought hard. What else could he have discovered? It wouldn't be difficult. She knew she had a social profile. She never Googled herself but she was aware that, like her friends, her name came up on different gossip websites.

She'd dated some known names in the past, but not seriously. She'd never been serious…or only once, when she was still a young girl and had thought a man telling you he loved you was reason enough to start planning a future—until you discovered he loved what he imagined was your trust fund. She'd never had one. Just a well-to-do *grandmaman* who'd kept her on a short leash and a small inheritance now gone.

Grandy had left most of her fortune to her charities. Lorelei knew she wouldn't have been human if she didn't sometimes think wistfully of how useful even a fraction of that money would be now, but she understood that Antoinette was punishing Raymond and not her. She had known one day Lorelei would be bailing him out.

Inevitably that day had come to pass. Unfortunately it had put the one thing Grandy had left her at risk: the villa.

But she wasn't thinking about that now. She needed to think about filling her evening, seeing as Nash Blue had changed his mind…

Possibly because he'd found a better option. A woman who was happy to go to Paris with him.

Lorelei's eyes narrowed. She snatched up her phone and began scrolling through the address book. Two could play at that game. She had simply masses of people she could call up…men who would break their necks tearing up the hill to take her to dinner. Her thumb hovered over names. Her heart fluttered hard in her throat. Why couldn't she just call?

Because… Because…

Fifi jumped up onto her lap, trying to climb her chest.

'Because I didn't want to be with anyone but him tonight,' she said, burying her face in her baby's warm fur. 'Dammit, Fifi, I was looking forward to tonight. I was… Oh, I'm being ridiculous. I'll make a call.'

She pressed Damiano Massena's number and he answered almost immediately. Clearly *he* didn't have a problem with her being a so-called distraction! But then, they had known each other for years on the party circuit. He was in town. He knew of an opening. It was always fun to go to an opening, and she knew he wouldn't press for anything more than her company. They'd sorted out that little crease in their friendship years ago. He was a womaniser and she was strictly hearts and flowers—not his type. He'd pick her up in an hour.

'Make it half an hour,' she insisted, pulling down the zipper on her dress. The last thing she wanted to do was sit around on her own.

She ended the call and let the dusky pink romantic confection she had chosen so carefully to wear tonight drop to her feet. She stepped out of it, leaving it puddled on the floor as she headed to the wardrobe. She'd put on something short and funky and guaranteed to get her all the male attention she could handle.

She tugged down a little gold party dress from its hanger. She'd go out, gossip, dance, amuse herself. Forget this had ever happened.

But she'd hold on to the fact he'd spoken so flatly, unemotionally, allowing nothing to alleviate his message: *I've changed my mind. You've got nothing I want.*

Turning around, she caught her reflection in the mirror—a tall, slender girl in an ivory slip and a simple string of pearls, who had dressed tonight with a particular man in mind. Her make-up understated, her hair smoothed carefully back into a deceptively simple knot.

The woman she actually was.

Unexpectedly a surge of sadness welled up from some place deep inside her. Was she never going to be allowed to be herself?

Lorelei inhaled sharply, ruthlessly dragging it all back in.

Irritated with her thoughts, and herself, she peeled off the slip and began the process of dressing as the woman she needed to be.

Santo's Bar was noisy, but it had shadowy corners where a couple of famous faces and the two founders of one of motor racing's more famous constructors could blend into the dark maroon leather and oak décor.

Nash sat on a light beer. He'd been off the hard stuff for almost four years. He didn't miss it, but every now and then a glass of single malt would have hit the spot. This was one of those nights.

He should be enjoying the company. It was all-male, and if they were a little loud and raucous, so was the bar. Antonio Abruzzi, Eagle's current star driver, was telling a story that had veered from off-colour to frankly pornographic. Nash had half an ear to it, but his attention kept wandering. He noticed a woman across from their table, winding a lock of dark hair idly around her finger as she talked, and instantly he was inhaling honey again, and flowers, and seeing the sun glinting off the sapphire-blue Sunbeam as Lorelei St James leaned back against it and smiled up at him with all the confidence of a very beautiful woman to whom a man had never said no.

Why in the hell *had* he said no?

He picked up his light beer and smiled grimly. He knew why. He was a goddamned expert on giving up what he liked for the sake of the bottom line.

It was just he was having trouble remembering what the particular bottom line was in this scenario. He'd swapped an evening with a blonde goddess for Abruzzi's stories and the watchful appraisal of the Eagle team who had signed him.

He stood up.

'Nash, man, where are you going?'

'Previous appointment.'

He shook hands with the Eagle guys, embraced Abruzzi and shouldered his way out of there.

He was going out as she was coming in.

Impossibly tall in vertiginous heels, she dwarfed the guy she was with—a thickset, strong-profiled Italian Nash recognised as the financier Damiano Massena. They'd crossed paths several times in both business and leisure.

Massena was dressed in a long black coat, suitable for the cooler evenings, and Lorelei was a living flame in a gold dress. In the overhead neon lights it was difficult to tell where the fabric ended and her long, lithe limbs took over. She looked every inch the trophy, and Nash found he'd ground to a halt. His gut clenched. Because Massena had her and he didn't, he reasoned brutally.

She brushed past him, didn't look up, but he saw she had made dark pools of her eyes and a glossy invitation of her mouth. She looked like sin. She looked like every good reason he didn't want to get involved with her.

And most of the reasons he did.

But he was noticing other things, too. The evening was cool and there was a visible quiver to her bare limbs.

Why in the hell hadn't Massena given her his coat?

He inclined his head slightly and her gaze moved fleetingly against his. Massena said something to her, gave Nash an amused, man-to-man look, and ushered her forward.

The aggression rushed up from nowhere and he brought his hand down on Massena's shoulder. The older man turned around in surprise, his expression hardening as he read Nash's expression.

What in the hell was he doing?

He jerked his head towards Lorelei, paused in the door with her bare arms wrapped around herself, avoiding his gaze.

'Get her inside,' he said uncomfortably. 'She's bloody well freezing.'

He kept walking. Yeah, being single-minded had brought him a long way.

Lorelei was aware she was talking a little too animatedly in the car, as if the flow of words would stem the rising tide of feeling behind it. Since running into Nash she'd been preoccupied and not much company. Damiano was bringing her home early.

'Are you seeing him?'

Lorelei didn't even bother to demur.

'We only met today,' she admitted in a low voice. 'We had arranged to go out to dinner. He cancelled and I—'

'You phoned me. I'm flattered,' he drawled.

Lorelei put her hand on his arm. 'I phoned you because you're one of my friends and I knew you would be good company.'

'Will you be seeing him again?'

'He's not interested.'

'For a man who isn't interested, *cara,* he has the eyes of a jealous husband.'

Lorelei swallowed, but couldn't ignore the flutter of excitement that observation engendered in her.

'A word of advice, Lorelei, from an old friend.' He gave her a wry look. 'Nash Blue is not a man for you to play with. He has been ruthless in the past with women a lot tougher than you, *cara.*'

'Ruthless?' Lorelei couldn't help the shiver that ran through her, although the limousine was climate-controlled.

'More so than me.' Damiano gave her a smile that reminded her where his own reputation with women had come from. 'And somewhat more effective with you, I am thinking.'

Lorelei didn't know what to say. She sat back and looked unseeingly through the dark window. She knew exactly how she felt about any man who was ruthless with women. She'd grown up with one. But she couldn't put aside all the sweet things Nash had done for her today. She was almost hugging them to herself.

In all the years since men had started following her with their eyes and making all sorts of empty promises no man had ever gone to so much trouble for her.

She could almost forgive him the cancelled date and the reasons he had given her.

Almost.

She had to ask. 'He's a womaniser, then?'

Damiano shrugged. '*Niente*—no more than any other rich and famous man, *cara.* I do know he's a man renowned for his self-control. He doesn't drink or smoke or brawl as far as I know. You say you met him just today?'

'Oui.'

Damiano threw back his head and laughed.

'I can't see what's so funny.'

'*Si,* I know, and that is what makes it even more amusing.'

Lorelei shook her head. She would never understand men. She relaxed a little, but as her turn-off grew closer she could feel the darkness edging in and a great unwillingness for the evening to end, for all the noise and activity to stop, to be alone. To think.

Yet when Damiano turned to her, all smooth Italian charm, and asked, 'Shall I see you inside?' she shook her head without giving it a second thought.

'I'm a big girl and I know where the lights are.'

But as she entered alone the cold, empty weight of the house bore down on her.

She made her way upstairs, trying not to think about her debts and those warning letters and threats and what it would all inevitably mean…and somehow what flashed to mind was, *What if Nash Blue followed her home?* And if he did—if he drew up in her courtyard in that smart car of his, if his heavy tread disturbed the gravel, if he stood there in the dark and called her name like a sober Marlon Brando—what would she do?

What would she do?

'Tip a bucket of water on him. That's what I'd do,' she told Fifi as she flooded her bedroom with light. It was the only fully furnished room in the place, an Art Deco boudoir worthy of the silent-film star who had built this Spanish villa back in 1919.

Fifi stirred from her place of residence on the bed and trotted underfoot as Lorelei washed her face and undressed and cursed a bit.

'He thinks I'm media happy and looking for a deep pocket,' she muttered. 'Well, we're neither of those things, Fifi.'

She went over to her escritoire and unlocked the deep drawer. Inside were months' worth of unanswered, unlooked-at correspondence from her solicitor and various legal firms who had handled Raymond's case.

As she settled herself down, pulling on her reading glasses and taking up a pen, she felt something akin to relief that she had finally started—until she began to read…

It was only when she was lying awake in the dark hours

later, resting her chin on top of Fifi's warm little head, that she realised it had taken someone like Nash to come along today and force her to see her behaviour through his eyes, this house through his eyes and for her to find the courage to face her problems.

She supposed she could thank him for that.

She shivered and drew the coverlet up a little closer to her chin. It was a cold night, and that was another problem with this house—it was drafty.

Get her inside. She's bloody well freezing.

Had he really said that, or was it wishful thinking?

The next morning she was walking barefoot along the back terrace when her Sunbeam rolled up.

She put down her freshly brewed coffee and hurried out to speak to the two men who had delivered it. The car had been given a certificate of good health, she read, noting a few key parts had been replaced and the car had been tuned.

There was no bill.

'I don't understand,' she said uneasily.

'Compliments of Nash Blue,' said the guy with a shrug. 'She's a beauty, madame, take good care of her.'

Lorelei's fingers crumpled the report in her hands slightly before she realised what she was doing. *Compliments of Nash Blue?* She wasn't a charity case. She didn't need to be rescued.

Five minutes later a van was drawing up on the gravel drive. Lorelei looked up from the mechanic's report, recognised the insignia on the side. A boy leapt out and came towards her, bearing a large bouquet of red roses.

She took them in both arms, burying her nose in the rich scent.

Damiano. How sweet of him—and unnecessary.

She plucked out the card and suddenly the blooms in her arms took on a whole different meaning.

Forgive me. Nash.

CHAPTER EIGHT

LORELEI parked and jumped out of the roadster.

The car was performing like a dream.

Which made staying angry with the man who'd fixed it and sent you flowers all in one morning extremely difficult.

This entire situation was difficult.

She wasn't sure what she was doing here, but she figured something would occur to her when they came face-to-face. She had a half-formed notion that she would pull out her chequebook and insist he take payment for the car. But Nash, being one of those masters of the universe, probably thought it was his responsibility to make sure all the women in his vicinity didn't have to lift a little finger to help themselves.

Which just made her eyes roll when she saw his name in big letters on the marquee. Who named their company after themselves anyway? It just proved the enormous size of his…ego.

She made her way through the crowd queuing on the perimeter of the fence. She gave her name at the gate and was handed her pass.

She'd dressed down in canvas top sneakers, skinny white jeans and a flirty gold lamé top that bared her arms and the backs of her shoulders. She'd pulled her hair back with a knotted blue scarf. But perhaps she was not dressed down enough.

People roamed about in windbreakers and casual gear, and

as she made her way across the concourse she could feel eyes on her—as if she were some exotic animal released from the zoo come wandering among them.

She didn't know any of the volunteers, either. This wasn't her branch of the organisation. She'd actually had to ring the foundation that morning to organise a pass.

Her work for The Aviary was strictly high-end, and consisted of schmoozing for the big bucks at parties and receptions throughout the year. It was how she had met Damiano Massena and cemented her reputation as being impossible to refuse.

Every year she attended The Aviary Foundation's annual ball with him and set the tongues wagging all over again. But there had never been anything between her and the men she fleeced on behalf of the charity. She didn't mix business and pleasure.

No, there was no reason for her to be here—yet here she was, making her way through the crowd at a motor-racing track, soaking in the carnival atmosphere…honing in on the cars, the cluster of media, the excited children and their parents…

It wasn't hard to pick out Nash when he emerged through one of the gates from the track offices. It wasn't just his height but the way he moved—heavy, purposeful and a little intimidating.

There was a flutter of female speculation and Lorelei saw women literally pushing their way up to the barrier next to the track to get a better look. Fortunately big macho sportsmen had never done much for her.

Nevertheless, she fumbled in her handbag and touched up her lipstick with her compact, removed her scarf, knotted it around her neck and shook out her hair. A woman needed all her weapons about her, entering *this* arena.

Weaving her way through the crowd, she caught glimpses of Nash with the kids. He wore a black overall with white and green stripes and lettering and carried a bunch of helmets which he was handing out. The parents looked as starstruck as their offspring. The crew were crawling all over the cars in preparation, and there was a faintly vivifying smell of petrol fumes in the air.

She vaguely recognised another racing driver, Antonio Abruzzi, but only because she'd scanned the charity's internet site on the subject of today this morning, to avoid walking in blind. The lanky Italian was saying something to the media crew set up trackside.

Lorelei found she was quite close to the barrier and a little space had opened up. She slipped in and looked out across the track.

Nash had his back to her and was hunkering down to fit a helmet over the head of a young girl of about ten or so, with long dark hair. She had that po-faced look on her face Lorelei recognised from her young students when they were about to mount up for the first time.

He said something to her and she smiled, let him settle the helmet over her small dark head, and even from this distance Lorelei could see the care with which he buckled up the strap under her chin.

Something fluttered strangely in her chest, and she found herself unconsciously touching the back of her neck where he'd stroked it yesterday.

He straightened and put his hand lightly behind the child's shoulders, ushering her towards the crew who were going to strap her in. Almost casually Nash glanced over his shoulder and their eyes met, locked.

Time seemed to slow down. The noise and jostling died away and Lorelei faced the undeniable truth that wild horses couldn't have stopped her coming down here today. As she ate him up with her eyes he turned around, those wide shoulders thrown into relief by his arms hanging at his sides—a typical masculine pose.

Vaguely Lorelei was aware of cameras going off around her as people lifted their phones to frame what anyone with an eye could see was a great shot. A male athlete at the top of his game, with the racing car just over to the right and Nash filling the foreground with his presence. Bigger, stronger, more impressive than just about any other athlete on the world stage.

His eyes were on her.

Lorelei lifted her chin. Now she knew what Simone was talking about.

He was a legend.

She'd just been distracted by the man.

Nash saw the defiance in her fine-boned chin as it poked in the air and thought, *No, you don't, mate. That little number is off the menu.*

She wasn't supposed to be here. After the incident with Massena last night he'd figured he had her pretty much read. She was a beautiful, privileged woman used to being pursued by wealthy men. Cullinan's tacky information had got her wrong. He'd been looking at the bottom of the survival chain when it came to women living by their wits. Lorelei St James was very definitely at the top.

He would have expected her to have moved on. Yet here she was, poised like a lily of the field behind the safety barrier, amidst a crowd of onlookers, looking as if she'd stepped out of *Vogue.*

In jeans.

But very expensive couture jeans, wrapped around a pair of impossibly long slender legs, lithe hips and a perfect peach of a derrière. She had a jaunty short blue scarf tied around her neck.

Despite the American accent he could hear underlying her voice she was every inch the Frenchwoman this afternoon.

She'd dressed for a day at the marina, not a racetrack. This was probably as far inland as she'd ever been.

A golden girl in every sense of the word.

And she was gazing at him as if she expected him to stroll on over, swing her up into his arms and carry her off like the prize she was.

He couldn't say it hadn't crossed his mind.

She was so long and lovely, taller than most of the women standing around her, and possessing a fine-boned elegance that drew a man. Made him want to protect her, shelter her… do a great deal for her.

But he'd been down that road with this girl.

He'd spent yesterday mopping up her messes. Last night contributing to one of his own.

No more. Even if he had to take fifty cold showers, no more.

Let Massena or whoever take care of her.

He had some kids to run around the track, some photos to pose for and then he was taking off up the highway to his house in the Cap d'Ail for some well-deserved R'n'R before he flew out to Mauritius for meetings, then lockdown for training.

He was about to turn away when she raised her hand. It was just a little gesture, a half wave arrested by uncertainty, and it was the uncertainty that stilled him. His body suddenly felt tight, the blood in his veins heavy, his muscles tensing one by one in anticipation.

He was vaguely conscious that the crowd had surged forward as he headed over. This was an insanely public gesture to make. He conned himself it was a small event. Everyone was here by invitation. He doubted him chatting up a random blonde at a practice track was even going to make the internet despite all the phones madly going off.

Her expression had frozen. She looked like a mountain

deer caught in a spotlight. She looked as if she didn't know what to expect. Something twisted in his chest.

He hadn't planned what he was going to say to her. He looked her right in the eye and she gazed unblinkingly back. And then he knew.

His tone was soft, low, deep. 'I'll talk to you later.'

Those amber eyes widened fractionally and she gave a slight nod.

He winked at the pair of gawping teenage girls standing next to her and strode off.

Most of the crowd had dispersed. Only the volunteers were cleaning up, the track crew coming and going. Nobody had questioned her wandering onto the track, walking alongside the cars, peering in.

It was getting late. Another half hour and it would be dusk. She glanced back towards the buildings. It was growing cooler and she only had her light cotton jacket. Maybe he'd forgotten what he'd said. Or maybe he'd been caught up. Or maybe he'd never intended to come in the first place.

She had put herself in this precarious position. She didn't chase after men. They chased *her.* Growing up watching Raymond work the female sex like a one-armed bandit had taught her that powerful lesson. To be the object of desire, not the one caught by desire. Therein lay hurt, abandonment and shame.

She knew she should go and get in her car and drive home. This had been a bad idea… Her idea of waving her chequebook at him and forcing him to accept payment for the Sunbeam seemed impossibly naive.

'Fancy a ride?'

His deep voice wrapped around her, every bit as delicious as the first time she'd heard it.

She turned around and found him a few feet away, dressed in jeans and a black T-shirt—so similar to the first time she'd seen him. All that thick dark hair was rumpled and a faint five o'clock shadow etched his strong jaw. His intense blue eyes gleamed in the fading light, watchful as a stealthy animal of prey. He was holding the straps of two helmets in one hand.

'Careful, Nash, what if someone sees us together?'

'Sweetheart, about fifty cell-phone cameras went off at once around us this afternoon. I think caution at this point is overrated.'

That wasn't the answer she wanted. She wanted him to say he didn't care and put her in his car anyhow.

'Come on,' he said abruptly.

He had opened a door. She stepped back. 'This one?' She looked doubtfully at the low-slung car.

'Blue 16. It won't bite.' His eyes were on hers, and why the expression in them reminded her of the wolf's paw reaching for Red Riding Hood she couldn't have said.

'Much,' she added dryly, reaching out a hand for the helmet.

He grinned.

Oui, the wolf.

He laid his helmet on the top of the car and moved in with hers.

Lorelei reached up to free her hair from the scarf but he was tangling his hand in it, tugging it away. Memory of the other time he'd touched her like this made her unbearably conscious of his big hard body only a hand-span from her own.

He must have felt it, too. 'Your hair,' he said, leaning in to inhale.

She felt his lips momentarily against the warm top of her head.

'Silky, soft… It smells like you.'

Breathless, Lorelei barely had time to react before the helmet was coming down, obscuring her pink cheeks, her questioning eyes.

He buckled the strap under her chin and Lorelei realised

she'd been waiting for this ever since she saw him helping the little girl.

She'd wanted him to help *her* with the same attention to detail, deliberateness, care…

She felt like an alien in the helmet. It made her smile.

Nash held the door. 'Get in.'

Possession was nine tenths of the law, Nash figured. Once he had her in Blue 16 she was pretty much his. A court of law might argue the toss, but he wasn't much interested in anyone else's opinion other than the girl sliding into the high-performance car.

He hadn't planned any of this, but when he'd seen her standing over here by the cars, just waiting for him, everything male and predatory in him had fired up. If he was going to do this, he might as well do it right.

He couldn't help tracking her legs in those leave-nothing-to-the-imagination jeans, the curve of her peachy derrière as she slid into place, her small breasts pushing up against the disco-dolly top. Everything about her was lithe, delicate, incredibly sexy. Feminine. Everything about that, about *her,* got him going.

This was hardly the first time he'd used a touring car and high speed to get a woman in the mood, but it was over ten years since he'd felt it necessary and right now it felt new. It felt like the first time.

It felt incredibly right.

He swung in beside her.

He adjusted his own helmet and ran a soundcheck.

'How do you feel about a bit of speed?' he asked through the mike.

'Exactly how fast are we going to be travelling?'

'Fast enough.'

She made an I'm-in-your-hands gesture.

How right she was.

He accelerated off down the track, keeping it simple, hugging the edges. Then he ramped it up. He loved this—those first moments when the car leapt from routine into supersonic and then there was just the rush.

The velocity shoved Lorelei back against the seat. She was grabbing the leather under her knees. He was going to scare the bejesus out of the little princess and then take full advantage of the results.

As the car flew down the track he could hear her panting breaths through the amplified mike. He could sense her tiny movements, her shakes and shudders. This was what he wanted. Her response, her subjection to his desires.

'Are you okay?' He spoke into the mike above the roar.

'Mon Dieu!' she panted.

And he knew, without taking his eyes off the track, that she was loving it. Every minute. And in that moment he wanted to give her the ride of her life.

She gave a shout as he rode the corner hard and tore down the strait. She squealed again, shoulders thrown back by the velocity, and he knew exactly what she was feeling because he'd felt it, too. The first time. Every time after.

This was why he raced.

It didn't explain why, with her, it felt new.

As he pulled back the speed and gradually rolled the car to a stop he could hear her breathing, her little murmurs of, 'Oh, my…oh, my…oh, my.' He knew he had her. What he didn't understand was why this felt so important.

They got out in silence.

He had his helmet off, but she was still unbuckling hers.

She threw her head forwards and back to release her flattened curls. They fell about her head in a messy tangle she didn't even try to smooth down as she lifted sparkling eyes to meet his. She was absolutely how he wanted her: messy, confident, excited.

Her lips parted and she was breathing hard and laughing.

He knew exactly how she was feeling. The blood was surging through his body but it had nothing to do with speed or the adrenalin rush. She stepped towards him and he found himself making the same move.

Neither of them spoke.

All Nash could think was that he wanted her so badly he would have thrown her across the bonnet of Blue 16 if half a dozen other guys hadn't been within gawking distance.

Lorelei was looking up at him as if she shared every one of his thoughts.

'Wow,' she said softly. 'Thank you.'

'You're welcome,' he said just as softly.

Lorelei felt herself drift towards him and suddenly Nash was there, in her space, and the atmosphere between them was on fire.

'Come on,' was all he said, and she allowed him to take her hand. She knew what he meant.

He put her in his civilian car, drove the highway just on the limit.

Lorelei didn't ask him where he was taking her. She was too busy asking herself what she thought she was doing.

He'd barely touched her but her body was literally humming, and the tension in the car was doing her head in.

What was he thinking? Where was this going? Did it really matter?

He'd made it pretty clear he was in charge.

She watched the capable pull and push of his big hand on the gears, his long, strong arm, the cut of musculature running under the high sleeve of his T-shirt, the faint press of his chest as he breathed in and out, the way his jaw settled with precision as he concentrated on his driving. He was driving fast, but he was driving safely. He had made her feel safe since the moment she met him.

They were coming up to the turn-off.

'Your place or mine?'

It was the first time he'd spoken.

It was a question she couldn't hide behind, pretending this wasn't about sex. *I came to the track to find you, to let you know I was available to you...*

This never happened to her. Never. She was always cautious. She didn't meet a man and climb into his car and go home with him... Her breath hitched because she realised they'd come to a stop at the turn-off and she still hadn't answered him.

Nash cupped her chin, lowered his mouth to hers. Kissed her so sweetly she wanted to cling to this moment.

He did let her go. To decide for her.

'My place. It's closer.'

CHAPTER NINE

IT WAS the longest drive known to man, although practically Nash knew it was barely twenty-five minutes.

Lorelei's soft, sexy eyes on him driving were about as close to actually being skin to skin without taking their clothes off.

Her quiet bothered him, though.

Was she thinking about Massena? Did he need to go there, ask those questions?

He didn't share.

He was very, very possessive.

Okay, up until now that hadn't been the case with other women, but it appeared to be the case with *this* woman.

He'd been up all night thinking about her, visualising her with another man's hand on her waist, another man seeing her home. It was unreasonable. He'd blown her off. He'd been the one to call a halt. Everything he knew about her meant this was playing with fire.

The traffic in town was heavy. The light was leaving the sky and the boulevards were twinkling.

Nash shot the Veyron in and out of snags until they were mercifully prowling into the garage under his apartment complex.

Lorelei's chest was visibly rising and falling as they sank into the spotlit gloom, the darkness making the space between them more intimate and strangely tense. The excitement and adrenalin rush of the track had been infiltrated by reality. Nash remembered the things he'd said to her, virtually accusing her of being a media-whore, and yet here she was, despite all of that.

'About my car—' she said suddenly, her voice low and husky.

'All taken care of.'

'I know, but—'

'Why bother your head about those things?' He cut her off. 'It's nothing—a trifle.'

He could sense in her the need to say more, but all of a sudden she just subsided, looking down at her hands in her lap.

'The flowers were lovely,' she said instead.

Nash suspected she was trying to tell him something, but he didn't want to hear it. This wasn't about him fixing things for her in her no doubt chaotic life. Nor her eminently female desire to turn their liaison into something prettified with flowers and romantic gestures. He was here for one purpose and one purpose only: to work through this unholy desire to have this woman any way he could get her. All. Night. Long. They'd deal with the morning and where they went from there tomorrow.

For a guy who liked to plan, he was certainly enjoying making it up as he went along.

Which somehow was making this hotter.

'This is where you live?' Lorelei said a little breathlessly as they pulled up.

'Penthouse.'

She looked around. 'Must be nice being in the centre of everything.'

'It has its compensations.' Like now.

'At least you can park somewhere. So we're safe from the public ordinance.'

He liked her turn of phrase. He also liked that she was betraying a little feminine nervousness. *No, sweetheart, you're definitely not safe.*

'Nash?' She put her hand on his knee and for a moment he had the thought she was going to climb over and straddle him in the goddamn sports car. But then he realised that was his fantasy and she was just looking at him with a question in her eyes.

He didn't want to answer those questions. Except he was remembering something she'd said to him. *Here was I, thinking you were a gentleman, but you're just a man...like all the rest.*

He winged the door. 'Stay there. I'm coming to get you.'

'No, Nash—'

'Yes, Nash.' He gave her a slashing smile and in a fluid movement was out and around to her side of the car.

She looked up as he winged her door and hesitated a moment. He liked that hesitation. It made him want to reach in and scoop her out, to take instead of ask, but Lorelei seemed only to need a moment to make up her mind. She swung her lithe legs out, never taking her eyes from his, reminding him in every movement of her class and her poise and why he needed to be a gentleman… She literally stepped out of the car and into his arms.

He felt the delicacy of her bones, the softness of her bare arms as they wound themselves around his neck, the scent of blossoms and honey bees from her hair or her skin or simply the way she was. She brought her lips to his, confident and sure, before his mouth slanted over hers and his plans for tonight disintegrated.

He had intended to thrust deep, to make sure they both got the message that this was about dealing with a problem—sexual attraction—and overturn any idea this was a romantic scenario. They were both grown-ups. They'd both been here before. It wasn't going to go beyond that. Yeah, he was going to make her understand…

Until now, with her in his arms, one hand curled against his cheek, her lips soft and responsive beneath his, when the kiss turned tender and romantic and deeply fulfilling on some atavistic level he didn't want to explore. Not now.

Not when he had this.

He heard her sigh his name.

Obeying primal instinct, he tucked his hands under her bottom, shaping the incredible contours, and lifted her until she was sitting on the bonnet of the Veyron. Thinking he needed to get her sky-high and they were currently below ground, he wondered what in the hell he thought he was doing. But he needed to kiss her more.

One more taste, he promised himself, pulling her in tight, feeling the warm skin of her waist as his hands delved under the silky fabric of her top. She wrapped her arms around his neck, her fingers tangling in his hair, making soft, satisfied little noises in the back of her throat that warned him this was quickly going to move out of control if he didn't get her off the car and somewhere private.

But it was Lorelei who broke the kiss, pulling back, eyes wide, breath coming fast, her whole body quivering. She looked around, not yet past caring.

Nash found himself bringing a hand to her cheek. 'There's just us. You and me.'

Her eyes softened. She touched his hand with her fingertips. It was a small gesture but he couldn't help entangling his fingers with hers, taking that small rough palm in his own.

'Inside?' she said a touch anxiously.

'Inside,' he agreed.

Nash lifted her from the bonnet and, taking her hand, strode to the elevator. He swiped the pass key and the doors closed. Even as Lorelei turned into his arms, pressing her face to the hard solidity of his chest, she felt the ground give way beneath her as they were hurled skywards.

She was breathing him in—heady, musky, spicy, hot male and, faintly, soap. The kind of plain soap she liked, not fancy. He was all kinds of good things, and even as her mind was running ahead, fantasising wild and wonderful, she wanted to cling to this moment, when it was just her, burrowing into the strength and solidity of him, and him tightening his hold on her.

She was vaguely conscious of a slight ping, the doors sliding open.

He lifted her as if she weighed nothing and carried her into his apartment.

As he kicked shut the door she took in the downlit expanse of modern masculine interior design. Smooth parquet floors, oyster walls and carpeting, and floor-to-ceiling windows that gave onto a multimillion-euro view of the velvety star-scaped vista of Monaco's famous marina. Lorelei had been in some fancy homes in this town for parties and receptions, but she'd never made love in one. Faintly she thought there was something to be said for a sky-high room with a view when it came to romancing a woman.

There was also something to be said for being literally swept off her feet.

'Nash?' She brought her palm hesitantly to his cheek.

He caught her hand, kissed her palm fiercely and kept going. He kicked open a door and Lorelei could see two dressers, a huge eastern rug, a vast bed. A man's bed—so different from her own ice-blue silk Art Deco double. She registered chocolate-brown linens and a neatness and uniformity to everything that made her smile a little. But that smile faded as he released her, and she slowly slid down his body until she was standing on her own two feet before him.

She instantly felt a little dwarfed. His shoulders were impossibly wide, and the power of his sheer masculine dominance over her physically and, she suspected, sexually in this encounter gave her a moment of pause.

To even things up it would probably be best for her to step into his arms, initiate what she wanted, make her own demands… And yet as she waited to find her own rhythm in this dance all she felt was longing. For him to kiss her again, to be tender with her, for this to be somehow different from what she'd ever known before. She didn't know why this man, why…

'Let me see you,' was all he said, in a voice so soft it was velvet over her sensitised skin.

Obediently she toed off her canvas lace-ups, but Nash was already enclosing her in his arms, as if he couldn't help himself, his hands at the back of her neck, tugging at the ribbon that held her top in place.

'Let me,' was all he said.

So she let him. He was having trouble with it, and so close against him she could feel his tension. She could offer to help…

But when she lifted her hands he shook his head, bent his head, and his hot breath whispered against her ear. 'Let me.'

The ribbon gave and with infinite care Nash was peeling off her top, bending down as it fell away to press his mouth to the gentle swells of her breasts above the delicate floral pattern of lace just screening her nipples. He unfastened her fragile gold bra and it drifted to the floor, a cobweb of silk and lace. Lorelei registered the spike in heat between them as Nash viewed her bared breasts in the soft light, felt the splay of his large hands beneath the slight under curves, closed her eyes as his thumbs dragged across her nipples.

'You are so beautiful,' he told her.

She opened her eyes to find his expression first intent upon her own and then dropping down. She followed his gaze, drinking in the intensely intimate sight of his big tanned hands cupping the curves of her breasts.

'I want to see all of you,' he told her in a roughened voice.

Lorelei unzipped her jeans and his hands joined hers to

slide them over her neat hips, to peel them down, helping her carefully to step out. His hands were slightly clumsy as they settled on her waist, and he was clearly drinking her in as she stood naked except for the tiny scrap of white silk that made up what passed for her panties.

'God, you are more than beautiful,' he said, almost reverently, and Lorelei, who had been praised for her looks by too many men, and had thought those words had long lost their ability to move her, let alone hold an ounce of truth, believed him.

She stepped against him and began pushing his T-shirt up, baring an abdomen packed with muscle, a wide, hard chest lightly covered in dark hair. The feel of his skin under her hands was remarkably smooth and hot. His body was like a generator for heat. She ran her hands up over his deltoids as he lifted his arms to reef the cotton off, and she had her first proper look at what had been filling out those clothes.

He had a simply magnificent body—all height and large frame, which were the gifts of the gene gods. Although what he'd done with it, Lorelei thought a little light-headedly, the stripped, lean muscle and the grace with which he moved, wasn't to be overlooked.

No, she wasn't overlooking anything—including an erection she wanted to explore pressing against denim. But Nash didn't give her the opportunity to do anything about that as he dipped his head and began kissing her, lifting her so that her toes barely touched the carpet, his hands on her buttocks, moulding her against him. until she felt the long, thick ridge of that impressive erection pressed against her belly.

He released her slowly and dropped to his knees on the rug, his hands cupping her hips. She swayed in against him, shivering as he placed a hot kiss on her belly, and another, and another lower down. He was touching her there, through the silk, and then the silk was sliding down her legs and there was just his mouth, and Lorelei slammed her hands down on the back of his head, tangling her fingers through his silky thick dark brown hair, clutching as the muscles in her thighs convulsed. The faint ache in her hips that was always there after a long day on her feet was nullified by the almost painfully sensitive pitch he brought her to, until pleasure began streaking through her.

Her soft cries came unbidden as the dam burst and the waves of pleasure went on and on. Nash's tongue moved almost reticently as he gauged just how much she could take as her body convulsed. Just as she thought she was coming down he brought her up again, and again she peaked. When she was weak and clutching at his shoulders, swaying on her feet, he rose up like some kind of victorious sea god emerging from the deep. He gathered her in his arms and Lorelei, a little weakened and blurry from her orgasms, saw his eyes were wild, his tongue swiping a lower lip wet with her essence. He gave her a slow smile full of sexual promise and she just stared helplessly at him.

What had just happened? *Alors,* she knew what had happened, but it had never happened to her before more than once at one time…and he had been so understanding of what she needed…

He lowered her onto smooth, cool sheets and her skin prickled not with cold but with anticipation as Nash stood over her. Slowly he began to unbutton his jeans with one hand, the other palming a square foil wrapper.

'Such a boy scout,' she approved a little unsteadily as the condom wrapper crackled.

'Always.' His eyes never once left hers and Lorelei watched as the denim parted, revealing his taut pelvic cradle, the cut marks of his abdominals, the deep grooves alongside his lean hips.

He shoved down his jeans and briefs in a single movement and gave her a slow smile as he saw the look on her face.

'I'm an engineer by trade, Lorelei,' he assured her with a wink. 'It's my job to make sure things fit.'

Lorelei watched him roll on the latex. She knew she ought to be taking the initiative, climbing into his arms and at least setting the pace, but somehow none of that happened.

Nash came over her, so big and dominant she should have taken pause. He dwarfed her, yet her shiver had nothing to do with reluctance.

'Are you going to kiss me, Lorelei?' His deep voice teased her.

'Oui.' She put a hand to his chest, but instead of giving him a kiss she reached up instinctively and stroked his jaw with the backs of her fingers, wanting to stay the moment.

Nash stilled. The blue of his eyes darkened almost to black as he caught her hand and pressed a hard kiss to her knuckles, then he brought his mouth down on hers. A hot, passionate stamp of possession. He wanted her.

Everything Lorelei had decided, conjured, felt about Nash Blue did a somersault. Everything she'd been holding up to protect herself tumbled away. She had wanted him from the moment she saw him, which was a first for her, but she wanted something else and she wasn't sure what that was yet…

As his mouth roamed over her face, her throat, her shoulders, she inhaled the scent of spices and soap and man, splaying her fingers in his thick dark brown hair. She reached lower, spreading her hands over his broad back.

Feeling oddly vulnerable, she let her thoughts flicker back to all the female interest in him today. She wondered what would have happened if she wasn't here. Was this what he did? Found the prettiest girl, scooped her up in his fast car and took her off somewhere…?

'Nash,' she said, perturbed by the anxiety she could hear in her own voice, 'what are we doing here?'

He smiled—a slow, unbelievably beautiful smile she had never seen before. There was an expectant tension in his hard muscled frame as he came over her, and instinctively she lifted her hand to his shoulder. His skin was so warm, his body so solid. She felt as if she could be anything, do anything, if she had this solidity behind her. It was a silly girlhood fantasy, long robbed from her by life and experience, but she was allowed it, wasn't she? Just for tonight? Tomorrow was soon enough to face cold reality, where she was on her own, but in the moment she had this.

She suddenly didn't care about all the other women, didn't care that she'd offered herself up to him at that racetrack. She didn't care about anything but the feeling of rightness having him here with her gave her.

'I believe we're making love,' he said, in that deep, rich voice that flowed like warm honey through her limbs and made her pliant as she drew his face down to hers.

'Nash…' She said his name, pressing her lips to the base of his throat. 'Nash…' She said his name as she placed kisses along his jaw, nuzzled him. Wanted him.

She reached down and stroked his erect, heavy penis with her hand. His face so close to hers grew heavy with sensual pleasure, and his eyes beneath those sinfully thick black lashes were hot and sexual. He was so beautiful and so male Lorelei couldn't stop looking at him. She didn't want to stop. She felt powerful but also vulnerable at the same time, and never so female.

He took her hand and helped her guide the hard silken length of him to the entrance of the wet, hot heart of her body, his eyes never leaving hers. The head of his penis probed gently, and then he moved into her with one long, slow thrust.

Lorelei moaned, trying to accustom herself to the unfamiliar feeling of fullness.

'How is it?' His glittering blue eyes were close to her own as he brought their temples together.

'Wonderful,' she whispered, and in that instant she believed him about making love.

Filled by him, she wrapped her legs around him, taking him deeper. The passionate kissing, his mouth riding against hers as he surged inside her, the careful way he held her even as the pressure built for him—all coalesced into an intense emotional experience as she began the steady climb towards a blissful fall.

CHAPTER TEN

LORELEI lay in his arms, her face obscured by the cascade of her pale curls, her delicate beige-tipped breasts rising and falling rapidly as she slept. Faint tear-marks still glistened on her cheeks.

She had wept. She had pressed her face into the curve of his shoulder and wept after the first time they'd come together. Her whole body had quaked in his arms. He told himself sometimes that could happen for a woman, and he felt in Lorelei that her emotions were very close to the surface. But what didn't happen were the emotions *he* had felt…

Protective. Passionate. And stirred to action. Because those tears, he sensed, were not just a physical reaction to the intensity of what had happened in this bed.

So he had held her as she cried, and soothed her with his body, until somehow he was inside her again—and this time everything was so much slower, as if time itself had altered to fit the rhythm of their entwined bodies and he was giving her what she needed.

Sex he understood. Physical pleasure was one of the necessities of life—like water and sunlight and racing at high speeds around a track.

He wasn't entirely sure he understood this. What had happened in this bed.

It was nearing dawn. The first fingers of light had come

creeping through the shadeless windows and there were pale shadows across the covers. The day was approaching and he didn't want it to come. He wanted to still time a little longer.

Watching her sleep, he felt almost as if he had captured some wild nymph from the woods and brought her to capitulation in his bed. She was so delicate, almost fey, he realised with a faint smile at the direction of his thoughts. She needed to be handled with care…and that should be sending warning bells off in his head, he thought, even as he stroked the silken curve of her bent arm.

His smile faded. Only hours ago he'd told himself this was merely the slaking of an appetite. He'd reasonably assumed his interest in her was powered by his sexual attraction to her body, as it had been with dozens of other women over the years.

But something else was at play here.

Even now he wanted to mark her so that other men would know she was his and wouldn't lay claim to her.

What am I doing here?

He didn't know.

Apart from the obvious, which was pressed against her hip and demanding his attention—or actually hers. It would be too easy to stroke her body to wakefulness and bury himself inside her, allow mindless pleasure to provide answers. But they had been doing that all night and his own stamina in itself had been a surprise. He'd never doubted his sexual prowess, but last night had been…rare.

Like the woman…

Nash touched the cluster of curls falling over one eye, hooking the silky weight behind her small ear, and she smiled sleepily, slowly opening her eyes. She lay there just looking at him and he was happy to let her look her fill. Her smile faded a little as she connected with his eyes, and she reached up and ran her index finger down the sweep of his jaw as if, like him, she was a little baffled by what had occurred.

'Is it morning yet?'

'Not yet.' His voice was rougher than usual, stripped back and raw. He needed coffee to lubricate it, but right now he wasn't thinking about breakfast.

Yeah, he could just about hammer nails with his erection but for a moment he wanted just to look at her.

Her hair lay about her head on the pillow like a bright halo. Her tip-tilted eyes were sleepy soft, her mouth swollen from his kisses. She appeared so delicate he would be a brute to initiate anything…

She sat up slowly, dislodging his heavy arm, which he obligingly lifted, a little surprised. But she was pushing back the covers, uncovering them both, still smiling, her eyes twinkling at him.

'Good,' she said.

Then slowly, silkily, she began to lead a trail of fiery little kisses down the centre of his chest, over his abdomen and lower, until he was gripping the sheet and forgetting everything but this.

Lorelei examined her reflection in the bathroom mirror. She'd done her best with the comb in her purse, warm water and a fresh toothbrush Nash had on hand in his cabinet. She hesitated as she held her lipstick up to her mouth, because the woman gazing back at her didn't need any make-up.

She had a glow.

Soft pink colour in her cheeks, a gleam in her eyes. Almost wonderingly she touched her lips. Her mouth looked frankly sensual.

She looked like a woman who had had a very good time indeed.

Smiling softly to herself, she dropped the lipstick back into her handbag and closed it, taking a longer look at the rest of her appearance. There was nothing worse than wearing clothes from the day before, but that couldn't be helped—and at least she wasn't in an evening gown.

Lorelei met her own gaze again, this time a little less confidently. This was a first for her, just to go off with a man and spend the night with him outside of a relationship. She knew he probably thought, given the chaos going on around her yesterday, that the walk of shame was hardly a first for her, but it was. She was careful in her romantic life to an almost fanatical degree. Men had to jump endless fences before they landed in her bed. She'd seen too much bed-hopping and sad, needy women growing up as Raymond St James's daughter to do anything else.

Ça va. She steadied her chin. She didn't have to worry. Even if she wasn't entirely sure what she was doing she didn't regret last night.

The tears, yes. She wished she hadn't cried. But that couldn't be helped.

She emerged to find Nash was talking into a cell phone on the balcony, the wind ruffling his hair. She was slightly taken aback by the sight of him in an Italian suit that lay close and faithful to the proportions of his fit body. He looked every inch the powerful and successful sportsman gone corporate, and here she was with damp hair, wearing yesterday's casual clothes. Talk about heading into the morning after with a disadvantage.

Sighing, Lorelei joined him, her desire to slide her arms under that expensive crease-free jacket, to encircle his hard, lean torso and enjoy the closeness of the moment held in check by the memory that, although last night had been intimate, she was old enough and wise enough in the ways of the world to realise they hadn't really done any talking of consequence. She didn't have a clue where she stood with him.

She wasn't entirely clear on where he stood with her, either. She'd gone into last night telling herself she had her eyes wide open, except this morning that pragmatism was curdled with a lot of fuzzy emotions she couldn't quite sort out.

So she settled for lifting onto her toes and pressing her lips to his freshly shaven jaw. Nash smiled, but he didn't make a move to end his conversation.

When he did it was to say, 'Ready? I'll run you home.'

Lorelei couldn't account for the cold trickle of disappointment that ran through her veins. It was perfectly reasonable that he'd be keen to get a move on this morning. It was after eight o'clock. He probably had a busy working day ahead—hence the phone call. She had to be at the equestrian centre at ten herself. They were adults. There were lives to get on with…

Dinner? *Oui,* dinner tonight, and then more…of this. *This* was making her tremble behind the knees and other places where she was tender. But also conversation. They would talk and clear the air and…

But perhaps this was it.

'Bien.' She injected a breeziness she suddenly wasn't feeling into her voice. It wasn't that difficult—she did it all the time in social situations. 'Can I drive?'

He pocketed his cell, gave her a wink. 'No.'

It wasn't until they were driving out that she fully appreciated she had made a mistake. On their trip last night she had been the centre of his attention. If a meteor had hit the road he would have merely hung a left and driven on, intent only on their mutual destination.

This morning he looked what he was: a busy man with a schedule and not a lot of downtime. Preoccupied, a little tense, blocking her out. She was very clearly being driven home. This was it.

She told herself she was a grown-up. Neither of them had made any promises, and she wasn't really in any condition to be opening up her life to anyone at the moment…

They were on the corniche when he said, almost casually,

'I've got meetings today and tomorrow. In fact I'll be held up for the next few days.' He glanced over at her. 'How about I call you next week? We can spend some time together.'

Light exploded behind Lorelei's eyes. It was one thing to tell herself this was the way of the world. It was another to hear him speaking so lightly about the intimacy they had shared… *Spend some time together.*

For a moment she didn't know what to say. What was she supposed to say? *I thought I could handle one night, but I was wrong. Last night overwhelmed me. I'm feeling emotions I know have no place between us and now you're telling me you'll call me... It's not enough.*

Her mouth suddenly felt dry, her throat tight.

'I know it's not ideal after last night, but—'

No, not ideal. Nothing about this was ideal.

He looked over at her. 'I've got a lot going on, Lorelei. I didn't expect this.'

No, neither had she.

He sounded annoyed, but also faintly bemused. Memories of him kissing her so slowly and thoroughly, as if the pleasure of it was all he'd wanted in that moment, assailed her unmercifully. Unconsciously she found herself running the tip of her tongue along the rim of her bottom lip.

Nash shifted restlessly beside her.

Why had she thought she could do this and not be hurt?

'Or you could call me.'

His voice was almost gruff and she glanced over.

No, she couldn't call him. How could he possibly think she would call him?

'Will I?'

Nash looked at her sharply. 'What's the problem?'

'Rien.' Her voice sounded like a rusty gate. 'What could possibly be the problem?'

He had the temerity to glance at that big silver rock of a watch clinging to his left forearm. 'Okay,' he said slowly, like a man navigating a floor suddenly covered in glass shards, 'I will call you.'

'You do that.' She stared stonily out of the window, a thousand angry words jostling for some sort of order of merit on her tongue.

'What am I missing here?' he said, probably not unreasonably.

Bastard! What do you think? I'm just going to vanish out of your life?

She'd grown up hearing those sentiments. Every woman her father had disappointed had flung something similar at him—as if he'd cared.

Douleur bonne, she might never have had a one-night stand before, but she certainly wasn't going to make a fool of herself by airing her messy female emotions now.

Non, she was a St James.

She lifted her chin. It had happened. Best to move on. She wasn't going to create a scene. From the tense silence emanating from Nash he was clearly expecting one.

The turn-off to her villa couldn't come quickly enough.

Nash barely had the Veyron at a standstill when she was fumbling for the door.

She swore, knowing that if she didn't get out of there fast she was going to embarrass herself. The door gave and she shot out.

'Lorelei.'

Nash's voice was peremptory—the voice she imagined he used on the track, with his pit crew, not a tone you used with a woman you had held in your arms and made love to.

Made love? It had been sex. What else could it be? They didn't know one another. She was a fool for expecting anything else…

She gave him his moment, not really expecting anything at this point, her hand still on the door.

'Do you want me to come in with you?' He actually sounded concerned—which was a joke.

She shook her head in disbelief. 'What's the point?'

Lorelei slammed the car door, and then wished she hadn't as she strode as fast as she could around to the front of the house. She rarely used the front entrance, but anger had blurred her thoughts. It had also blinded her, so she'd almost reached for the lion's paw front door handle before she saw the large padlock.

What on earth?

She gave it a tug. Was this some sort of joke? She seized hold of it with both hands and rattled. Then she banged even as she knew it was no use. She slammed her palms against the doors and then let them slide down and lowered her head, because it had finally happened.

Almost as an afterthought she noticed the large vellum envelope wedged under the door. She knelt down and picked it up, tore it open. She read slowly, the words like sticky toffee in her head. Was this even legal? The fact she didn't know was all the more damning. She should have known. She should have researched these possibilities. She should have been *aware*.

What had she been doing for the past months? *Rien.* Running around, blocking out reality, not making herself available to the people who could have helped her. Her solicitor, her accountant…her friends. And where had she been yesterday when this was happening? Pursuing a man. *Sleeping with a man who didn't care a jot for her.* She should have known!

Lorelei found she was trembling.

Non, she could deal with this on her own. She just needed to think logically.

Terese and Giorgio.

They would have some understanding as to what had happened here.

Fumbling in her bag, she dug out her phone.

The phone she'd been ignoring for days.

Sure enough there were several missed calls from the Verrucis and a message from Terese, she had rescued Fifi. Dialling, she got Terese's voicemail.

Fine—she'd ring for a taxi. Except she didn't do that. She dropped her cell into her bag and sank down onto the flags, her back pressed up against the door now bolted against her.

Strangely, she just felt like laughing. But she knew if she started it would end in tears, and crying wasn't going to change anything.

The worst had finally happened, and it was her own decision to delay and prevaricate that had brought her to this point. This was rock-bottom.

Until she heard the crunch of gravel, the tread of footsteps and slowly looked up.

Nash.

Mon Dieu, it just got worse. Could she just once have a personal disaster and not have this man witness it?

Yet something instinctive leapt in her body the moment she saw him.

'Lorelei?'

She clambered ungracefully to her feet, brushing herself down.

'What's going on here?'

'Rien.' She walked towards him, trying to divert him from the door.

Those blue eyes narrowed on her. 'Clearly. I don't respond well to games.'

'Fine,' she said, her voice high and airless. 'No more games. We had our fun. I need you to go.'

He was frowning down at her, and for a moment something about his anger penetrated the fog that seemed to have dropped around her. He was pounding out big, frustrated male and apparently *she* was the cause.

Gesturing at the drive, she repeated, 'Please go.'

'Why are you trembling?' He put his hand on her upper arm, his fingers closing firmly, as if he knew she would try to pull away.

'I'm not. I—' But it was too late. She was shivering so hard she thought she'd fall down. Wordlessly he pulled her into his arms and she was enveloped by all that strength and the lovely, familiar scent of him. *This is why,* she thought a little desperately, even as she struggled to be free. *This is why I'm a little crazy for him...*

'What in the hell?'

She knew he'd spotted the padlock.

He went still against her.

His voice was very low and resonant when he spoke. 'What's going on, Lorelei?'

When she refused to answer he released her and strode over to the doors, gave them a rattle.

'I've been locked out,' she said redundantly. 'The bank has foreclosed on my mortgage. I believe it happens if you don't meet your payments.'

Nash was silent. His hands rested on his lean hips as he regarded her. Lorelei made herself meet his eyes. She wasn't going to be ashamed. She wasn't.

'A mortgage? You said you inherited this house from your grandmother.'

'I've had some debts,' she said, lifting her chin defensively. 'I had to raise the money somehow.'

She saw the moment he noticed the envelope beside her bag, and before she could move he had it open. Her stomach plummeted. He didn't say a word, just started scanning it. Lorelei turned away, facing out to the sea view she had come to know so well over the years.

'You haven't met your payments in over six months,' he said flatly.

'Non.'

There was a long pause. 'Do you have somewhere to go?'

Lorelei pulled herself together. '*Ah, oui*—of course.'

She turned around and her insides trembled.

Why did he make her feel like this? She hadn't wanted to get involved with anyone. Once you let another person in you were vulnerable, and she couldn't afford to let her defences down.

She looked into his eyes and saw his frustration and disbelief and she knew it was better to let him go.

Her chest began to hurt.

He picked up her handbag and strode towards her. He tossed it and she caught it reflexively.

'Get in the car.'

'*Pourquoi?* Why?'

He gave her an old-fashioned look and kept walking. Lorelei hesitated, but only for a moment, because she didn't know what else to do. He held the door for her, his expression grim.

'You don't have to do this,' she said stiffly.

'Consider it me being a gentleman,' he responded, looking faintly exasperated. 'Get in.'

She slid into the passenger seat, her fingers like pincers around her handbag. At the moment it was all she possessed. Nash still had hold of the envelope. He was standing at the front of the car, making a call on his cell. He looked tense. She couldn't blame him. This wasn't his problem.

Minutes later he jumped in beside her.

'If you could drop me in town—' she began.

'Yeah, I suppose I could.' He gave her a hard look, gunning the engine. 'Tell me, Lorelei, does all the drama ever get old for you?'

It was not the moment to lose her composure, but the line between keeping it together and unravelling completely frayed a bit.

'I don't know, Nash,' she flashed back, wanting to slap him. 'How about you? Do one-night stands ever get old for *you?*'

She knew it was unfair. She'd gone into last night with her eyes open. Except she was hurting and her pride was currently being stomped all over.

He braked and shifted around. For a moment she wasn't sure what he was going to do and she backed up a little.

'Right…' he said slowly.

Right, what? Lorelei wanted to ask him what he thought he was doing when he threw the Veyron into First and she was flung back in her seat as he tore down the drive, sending stones and dust flying.

At the highway he swung right.

'This isn't the way into town.'

'No, this is the way to the airport.'

'Why are we going to the airport?'

'Sweetheart, those meetings I told you about aren't going to happen without me. I've got a flight to make, and as of…' he consulted his watch '…half an hour ago, the plane is fuelled and waiting.'

For a moment Lorelei actually thought he was saying he was going to dump her at the airport…until her brain caught up with her emotions.

'You're taking me with you?'

'Got it in one.'

'But I can't just leave. I've got to do something about *this.*' She shook the envelope, which had assumed gigantic proportions in her mind.

'It's pretty clear you haven't been doing anything about it for a long time,' he observed, giving a couple of the buttons on the console a flick. Music filled the cabin with a heavy bass line. 'A few more days isn't going to change a damn thing.'

Lorelei wanted to strike back at him—not just because he was imposing his wishes on her, but because he was right. She hadn't been looking after herself. The Scarlett O'Hara 'tomorrow is another day' shtick wasn't working for her any more, and this was the price she paid. Just as she hadn't thought through last night. She'd gone into his bed like a kamikaze pilot and wondered why she'd crashed and burned.

There was no way she was going to Paris with him…she wasn't some little sex doll he could just carry around with him, picking her up and putting her down…

Her thoughts came staggering to a halt. Simone was in Paris. She could find shelter with her best friend, ride out this storm.

'Very well,' she said stiffly. 'I agree to come to Paris with you.'

He shot her an amused look. 'Paris? Who said anything about Paris?'

She was a little taken aback—by that glimpse of humour more than his words. Did he think this was *funny?*

'Where are you taking me? You said meetings. Blue has offices in Paris. I assumed…'

'Mauritius,' he said flatly, his expression firming.

Sun, white sand, turquoise-green sea. Bliss.

Oh. *Oh…*

'But I don't have any luggage, my passport, clothes.' Even as she protested she was rummaging around in her bag. '*Ah, oui,* I do have my passport,' she said faintly. Was she really going to fly to Mauritius?

He gave her a look she recognised from last night. 'You don't need luggage. You don't need clothes. You won't be getting out of bed.'

Lorelei narrowed her eyes. 'Is that so?'

Nash smiled wryly, his eyes back on the road.

'And just in case that isn't clear enough for you, Lorelei,' he drawled, 'last night wasn't a one-night stand.'

CHAPTER ELEVEN

LORELEI was stunned by the natural beauty of the island below as their seaplane coasted in over turquoise water. Mountains rose up against a pale sky and the forest beneath looked thick and mysterious.

She turned to Nash and asked, 'what are they growing down there?'

'Sugar-cane plantations. It's a big part of the economy—apart from tourism.'

'I take it you haven't come to harvest sugar?' she commented, a little smartly.

He hadn't told her much of anything over their long flight. He'd buried himself in work and she had watched in-flight films and tried to avoid thinking about the mess she'd left behind her at home.

Right now she noticed his expression cooling both in regard to her *and* the view. His arm around the back of her seat told her she was still a welcome addition on this trip, but his eyes were those of a man who didn't share private or working details of his life with anyone.

Apparently being in his bed for one night didn't give her the right to ask any questions.

Which also begged the question whether he expected a second, and whether she would grant it.

'My meetings have nothing to do with us,' he commented, as if that was all that needed to be said.

The resentment she had been trying to suppress since he'd high-handedly made a pretty big decision for her and run roughshod over her wishes reared up. What made it worse was the fact she knew she'd brought this all on herself by burying her head in the sand all these months. Except it wasn't only about that, was it? It was to do with intimacy, and having this knowledge of him now, and realising for him it wasn't the same.

Suddenly angry with herself for being so boringly *female* and needy, she jerked around. 'Damn you, Nash Blue. I don't need to be rescued—by you or anyone.'

Nash had removed his jacket when the heat had hit them on landing on the African coast, and he had looked more relaxed over the last half hour, with his shirtsleeves rolled up, than he had on the plane when he'd worked, taking calls, scrolling through documents, preoccupied.

Now he sat forward, tension in every line of his body.

'Is that what you think this is?'

'What else could it be?'

Her entire body was quivering.

'How about me ensuring this isn't a one-night stand… which I assumed was upsetting you. Something, I might add, that was never my intention to begin with.'

'*Bonne chance* with that, as I have no intention of sharing your bed.' She stuck her nose in the air. She knew she was being ridiculous as she did it, but everything about this situation was making her feel diminished.

He regarded her as if she was speaking nonsense. 'I'm beginning to suspect this is not about me, Lorelei, but you. Am I to take it those guys you've dated in the past haven't treated you all that well?'

Lorelei froze, feeling hunted and cornered.

'My affairs are not your business,' she said shortly. 'I do

not ask you about other women…of whom I'm sure there have been far too many.'

'Possibly,' he responded, unruffled.

She snorted. She didn't want to think about his track record.

Hers was pretty tame, although he didn't have to know that. Her handful of boyfriends consisted of a visual artist, a poet, a writer and a classical musician…the last breaking up with her over two years ago, just as the perfect storm of Grandy's death and Raymond's arrest had broken over her. Truth told, she was rather grateful he had, as she couldn't possibly have supported him emotionally through the crisis. That was her role in all her relationships. She provided material support and emotional strength. She was, in effect, what she had always been with her father…the grown-up. And in the end every last one of them had foundered on the rocks because deep down what she craved…a man who could match her in strength of purpose…was the very thing she avoided like the plague.

She had seen enough unequal relationships paraded before her. It was a trap for a woman. She would always call the shots, hold the purse strings. She would keep herself independent—and strong.

Which was making all of this so very scary.

Because this man beside her, looking at her as if she were a puzzle he was determined to solve, was everything she should be running from. Dominant, wealthy, definitely calling the shots, and right now he had hold of those purse strings. None of that would really matter, except he filled her thoughts and took over her body and made her feel in a way she never had before.

She was vulnerable to him.

She had been from the moment she'd set eyes on him.

Why else had she slid into his car last night and abandoned her inhibitions in his bed? She wasn't being free with her favours. She was being optimistic with her heart.

Not that he would understand. She doubted Nash had ever been vulnerable to anything.

'I have some rules,' she said, smoothing back her curls. 'I expect you to abide by them.'

'This should be good,' he drawled.

'Don't patronise me, Nash. I want separate rooms.'

He regarded her as if she'd sprouted wings.

'I just feel there's too much inequality at play here.'

Oui, Lorelei, that's putting it mildly.

She didn't want to be one of his shiny toys, like the Veyron or the penthouse apartment in La Condamine. She had seen too much of it growing up…a price tag attached to love. It was why she kept her charity work for the Aviary Foundation separate from the rest of her life. She had never dated any of the men whose parties and functions she attended on a regular basis, and it hadn't been through lack of being pursued. She just didn't want to blur those lines between spruiking for the charity and spruiking herself. The idea terrified her.

'I'm not a toy for you to play with, Nash.'

Her whole body quivered as she spoke.

'In what way have I treated you like a toy?'

'I don't need luggage. I don't need clothes. I won't be getting out of bed,' she imitated sourly.

Nash's expression of pure male bafflement would have made her laugh in any other frame of mind. Right now she just wanted to hit him.

'It was a joke!'

She looked away, staring blindly through the plane porthole at the same view that only minutes ago had held her spellbound.

'Just don't call me doll any more,' she muttered.

'Sorry?'

She jerked her head around. 'I don't like being called *doll.* A doll is something you put in a box when you finish playing with it, or put on a shelf like a trophy.'

Nash was silent. He was examining her face as if translating Sanskrit.

'Have you finished?'

'*Non.* I didn't in a million years imagine when I went to your apartment last night I'd be ending the next day with you in Mauritius.'

'As I hadn't told you I was flying out to Mauritius, I'm sure you didn't,' he observed dryly.

He was being deliberately obtuse.

'I'm not that sort of person.'

'*What* sort of person, dare I ask?'

'One who freeloads.'

Nash threw back his head and laughed, the sound rich and warm.

'I'm glad you find it so funny,' she said stiffly. 'I can assure you nothing about this situation amuses *me*.'

Fed up, Lorelei folded her arms and averted her face. Still in yesterday's clothes, she felt creased and wilted and distinctly at a disadvantage. Whilst he found it funny and had it all under control.

'Lorelei.' He spoke patiently, the amusement still in his voice. 'I apologise for not telling you last night I was going away.'

She hated this—him being the cool, calm male and her being the hot, hysterical female. She'd been a witness to this scenario before and vowed she'd never play this role.

But who was forcing her into the role? Didn't she have a choice here? She was letting the inequalities of the situation play with her deepest insecurities and it wasn't serving her. The fact she was in this seaplane with him, coasting towards the runway, was proof enough that last night hadn't been all on her side.

'Apology accepted,' she said stiffly, wondering if they could start this all over again, with her being sexy and playing hard to get, instead of frustrated and sulky because she was in yesterday's clothes and he hadn't kissed her *once* since she'd slipped from his bed this morning.

'And I do not consider you a freeloader.'

She made a dismissive gesture with one hand, keeping her eyes averted.

'Is this about your father?' he said, cutting right through to the heart of the matter.

She raised her eyes to his. Grim.

'I don't talk about my father. Ever.'

He looked at her for a moment and then inclined his head. 'If that's what you wish.'

No, it wasn't. She wanted to wail and thump with her fists and bemoan Raymond and the fix he'd left her in, but none of that was Nash's concern and she wasn't laying more of her troubles at his feet. She'd dealt with this on her own thus far. She would continue to do so.

'Except you're not dealing with it, are you, Lorelei?' whispered a niggly little voice. *'You're winging over the coast of Africa with a man who delights and terrifies you in equal measure because he's seen what a mess you've got yourself into and he's trying to help.'*

All of a sudden she was beginning to feel ungrateful and childish.

She suspected a big part of her was trying to find something to take her attention off what she was trying resolutely *not* to think about—the mess she'd left behind her at home.

A mess that wasn't hers to begin with.

Those defence measures against the impossible weight of debt and the expectations she had laid upon herself to keep her family legacy intact were barely holding up any more and so she was lashing out. She also knew one of the reasons those defence mechanisms were no longer working had something to do with the man sitting beside her. He'd opened up vulnerabilities in her she was having trouble overcoming. Hence last night's tears.

She'd seen puzzlement and frustration in him several times as he'd come face-to-face with her issues back in the Principality, and it was getting harder to hide them from him.

She suspected it was one of the big reasons she hadn't had a relationship since Raymond's arrest. Why she had put distance between herself and her friends.

She should be putting distance between herself and Nash—especially when he was being so mysterious about exactly what they were doing here. The problem was, she couldn't separate mind and body. Her emotions were involved, as last night attested. If she slept with him again she was going to open more of herself up and there would be consequences.

'So these mysterious meetings—are they going to take up all of your time?' She tried to change the subject.

'Not entirely.' He smiled at her, as if he understood she was finding this difficult. 'I can, however, assure you you won't be bored, Lorelei.'

'Non?' she said snippily, knowing exactly what he was implying. 'I'm sure the island offers many attractions for tourists.'

Unexpectedly he tugged gently at the rogue curl she could never keep out of her eye, sliding it carefully behind her ear.

'Still fighting me, Lorelei?'

She looked away, out of the window at the land coming ever closer, and thought, no, she *wasn't* fighting him—and that was the problem.

'I can't get over how gorgeous it all is,' Lorelei confided as they drove the beachfront road in a Jeep. She'd teased him when he'd dumped their driver on the tarmac, telling him Freud had a few theories about his need to call the shots.

'Yeah, and I've got a few theories about Freud,' he'd responded, lifting her into the Jeep, enjoying her shriek and subsequent laughter. It was as if she'd decided all on her own to stop fighting him. It was impossible not to take in the scenery through her eyes as she chattered and pointed out landmarks that in the past he'd taken for granted.

Tall latania palms swayed along the roadside, and tropical flowers flashed out of the undergrowth as they sped past.

'You've brought me to paradise.'

Nash smiled to himself, finally comfortable with where this was going.

Lorelei had shied a little on the seaplane, and put on a bit of a performance, but he wouldn't have expected any less from the show pony she most definitely was. He realised he enjoyed that about her—the unpredictability. His life was usually so ordered. He didn't mind accommodating Lorelei's eccentricities. Outside in the late-day sunshine, with the fresh air whipping her curls into a frenzy, she seemed to have shrugged off her insecurities and was now embracing what he had to offer.

'Consider it part of the service,' he responded easily.

She flashed a smile at him and he was surprised at how good it made him feel.

He wanted her to be happy, he realised. He didn't like seeing that weight in her eyes as if the load she was carrying had been with her for too long. He suspected it was to do with that gaol bird father of hers. He could suggest to her cutting the cords that bind, as he'd done years ago with his own, but he doubted Lorelei would thank him for it.

He'd known since last night that she wasn't quite the hard-headed little mover and shaker those reports he'd initially paid attention to had painted her to be.

As they drove the leafy road circling the resort Nash watched some of the animation leave her. It wasn't his favourite place. A world-famous destination, sure enough, but they might as well not have left Monaco. The place dripped glamour and elitism, with groups of women in couture beachwear and jewellery, and men driving low-slung ego-extension cars.

'If you'd prefer we can stay here,' he commented as they

cruised past the ostentatious entrance, 'but I've got a place on the beach. It's a lot more private.'

'Naturellement.' She gave him a small smile. 'I would much prefer that.'

Unable to credit how good he felt, Nash increased speed and they shot down the beach road, heading up and over a rise. He heard Lorelei catch her breath as they plunged into tropical rainforest.

'Oh, this is beautiful,' she gasped, and as if to verify her words a brightly plumed bird swooped through the canopy of tree branches above them.

His bungalow was down on the shore—one of several private homes along this exclusive stretch of east coast beachfront. He had designed it himself with a local architect, the focus being on bringing the tropical forest right up to the doorstep and the ocean into the west-facing rooms.

Lorelei was quiet as she looked around, before turning to him and saying, 'This is most lovely, Nash. You're very lucky to have something so fine.'

'Not too modern for you, Lorelei?'

'Let me tell you I would kill to live in something so cutting-edge.'

'Then why the Spanish villa?'

Some of the animation slid away from her face. 'My *grand-maman* wanted me to have it.'

'You could always sell it.'

Lorelei turned away. He followed her through the dining area and out to the rear of the house, where windows gave way to the ocean, telling himself he didn't want to look any closer, dig any deeper.

He closed a hand around her lithe waist and she started, as if she'd already become unused to his touch. It made him more possessive. He found himself surrounding her, wanting to put himself front and centre in her life. He put it down to never accepting second place.

She removed his hands, walked away.

'Why don't you sell it?' he asked abruptly.

Lorelei shrugged her delicate shoulders.

Frustration rippled through him.

He thought about the fact that in a couple of hours he'd be sitting down to dinner with the Eagle reps, who also happened to be long-time mates.

His rather brutal earlier thoughts on the subject had been that she could entertain herself, and he'd get away as soon as he could.

But the guys would be bringing their wives. Her remark—*I'm not a toy for you to play with*—nudged him.

The problem was if he took Lorelei she'd be privy to his story before it broke in the press. He tried to picture her as a media leak but all he could see were her sleepy, sexy eyes when she'd climbed on top of him in the early hours of this morning and taken him almost shyly into her slippery hot body. Those little cries of completion as she'd reached her peak had made him feel like a god, and how sweetly she'd curled in his arms afterwards and fallen asleep, still holding on to him.

He groaned in frustration and ran a hand through his thick hair.

'We're meeting some friends of mine for dinner at eight,' he said gruffly. 'I had some clothes sent up for you. I guess you'll find them in the wardrobe.'

She turned and smiled at him. '*Merci beaucoup,* that's very good of you.'

He almost laughed. *This* she didn't fight him on.

Except she'd been fighting him ever since she'd climbed out of his bed.

He didn't understand her.

He didn't understand himself when he was around her. When he'd put her in Blue 16 on the track he'd only been thinking about a night, but this morning all he'd been thinking about was how soon they could be together again. He came up behind her at the glass doors leading onto the deck.

Today had been a long one for her. Even now he could see the faint mauve shadows under her eyes, a certainty fragility hovering over her. It was possibly the wisest course to leave her here. To go to dinner with the Eagle reps and give Lorelei some space. But it wasn't just about giving her space, he acknowledged. He cared about her feelings.

Frankly, he didn't want to make things any harder for her.

'Nash, the ocean is right on the doorstep!'

'It's a matter of perspective. There's a good twenty feet between the foundations and the surf, and this stretch of water is effectively a lagoon. It won't rise.'

'It's beautiful,' she said, looking up at him with an open face, and he smiled a little because she clearly cared nothing for the logistics and everything for the magic.

And wasn't that how she seemed to live her life?

He couldn't resist stroking her silken hair. Everything about her was touchable and soft and…yeah, he wanted to know her better.

But she wasn't an ingénue, and he wasn't a man looking for dependants. This was about her being a reward before he hit lockdown for training and him being her man of the moment. If he kept it that way this should work out for both of them.

If there was something beguiling about Lorelei's smile as she looked up at him it was to do with the tropical light and the promise of the night ahead. So he decided to follow her lead for once and just accept the magic.

'Yeah, it is beautiful,' he responded a little huskily, and framed her face with one hand. At last she opened up enough to let him kiss her. 'Second only to you.'

He tasted her—the softness of her lips, the sweetness of her breath—and the magic happened all over again. He knew he'd be taking her to dinner.

* * *

'So I'm to be your sex doll?'

Nash schooled his expression into something neutral as Lorelei emerged from the master bedroom, a tiny scrap of lace nothing dangling from her little finger.

He'd rung his housekeeper here at the bungalow and told her to organise some clothes through several boutiques at the resort, giving a vague approximation of size and stressing *sexy.* The helpful women at the boutiques had clearly interpreted this as less being more. He wasn't complaining.

Lorelei stood in the doorway looking unimpressed, although he did detect a tiny quiver about her mouth that told him she was trying not to laugh.

She looked sensational in an ankle-length orange pleated silk chiffon dress, embroidered with tiny crystals at its plunging neckline. It was the neckline that had his attention. His mouth was suddenly dry.

Belatedly he noticed she had swept her hair up into one of those sophisticated knots that took lesser women hours, and wore delicate crystal earrings. The juxtaposition between the ice goddess standing before him, her short sharp nose in the air and the little bit of erotica hooked over her finger finally dragged his eyes away from her braless breasts.

'You can be whatever you want to be,' he corrected, coming towards her. 'You could try being yourself.'

Lorelei's lips parted slightly.

'I am being myself.'

He plucked the bit of lace from her hand. 'Then there's no problem. I've seen your lingerie, Lorelei. You wear a great deal less than this.'

'Currently I'm not wearing any, but I would have preferred the choice.'

Nash's mind went blank.

'You look very smart,' she said with an arch lift of her brows.

Endeavouring to get himself under control, he rasped, 'It's the tailoring.'

A little smile sat at the corner of her mouth, as if she was very well aware of something else. 'Shall we go?'

The restaurant was open-air, on the beach, and the rhythm of local Sega music thrummed as a backdrop. Lorelei sipped her iced water, too nervous to risk a glass of champagne.

On the charity circuit she was always working to get people to like her, to respond to her, to open their chequebooks. Tonight she wasn't sure of the rules.

The large table was peopled with several couples: various identities from the motor-racing world, and one retired driver, Marco Delarosa, so famous even Lorelei recognised his face instantly.

This was Nash's world, both corporate and competitive, with the glamorous edge provided by sport. She wasn't quite sure what was going on, but amidst the thumping testosterone-fuelled talk about commercial deals and television rights she became conscious that Nash was talking about racing again.

This was confirmed when Nicolette Delarosa leaned over and murmured, girl to girl, 'We need to form our own team—at least then we might be a viable part of this conversation.'

A team.

One by one the pieces fell into place.

He was staging a comeback.

With Eagle.

This was why he was so media-shy. This was why he'd cancelled their date. Yet here she was, at this table, privy to the big secret.

She couldn't understand why, but Lorelei felt a frisson of unease.

Seeking reassurance, she flashed her gaze up to Nash beside her. His body language was relaxed—shoulders loose, open. He was fully himself because he was among friends.

This was nothing like what she had built up in her mind. He wasn't treating her like a rich man's arm candy, as she had feared, those were her own insecurities.

It was clear in this company that when Nash was private it was because he needed to be—monosyllabic, as Simone called it, because everything he said publicly was weighed and measured. With his friends he was this relaxed and good-humoured man.

His thick black lashes were screening the full impact of his eyes, but although he was listening to Delarosa she knew his attention was on her. Had been on her all evening.

As if sensing the shift in her thoughts he lifted his lashes and there were his intense blue eyes. Lorelei found her pulse was fluttering wildly out of control. He was looking at her as if she was naked under him in bed.

Mon Dieu, other people would see…they would know…

The hum of conversation died away and there was only an incredible stillness. It seemed to happen between them again and again—his eyes and her heartbeat and that elemental force that shook her when she was in his arms. Only his arms. *Only him.*

What was going on? She couldn't fall so far and so fast for this man.

Almost to rip herself free from the spell he'd cast, she reminded herself that Nash was a public figure because of his sport, and he was about to enter that arena again. Did she really want to be the woman on his arm? To face that sort of intrusion into her personal life?

'Lorelei St James,' said one of the women, her voice a little too loud. 'I *knew* that name was familiar.'

All of a sudden her musings ground to a halt. In that instant she felt Nash's hand close over hers under the table.

'Pardon?'

'It has to be over a decade ago now, but I remember seeing you at the World Equestrian Games.'

Lorelei released a hurried breath. '*Ah, oui*—many years ago.'

'I jump myself. My family breed Arabians.'

She felt Nash's hand turning hers over, his fingers finding those calluses on her palm. All of a sudden she felt horribly exposed, and she didn't quite know why, but to pull her hand away would be the first step to getting up and walking out, and she was done with that sort of reactive behaviour. It didn't serve her. So she mastered her nerves and continued to smile at the woman. To answer questions. To discuss the relative merits of each breed.

Couples were dancing to an old Cole Porter tune outside, and Nash suddenly pushed back his chair, interrupting the woman's flow. He got up, offered Lorelei his hand.

'What a brilliant idea,' said another of the women.

Lorelei followed him out, and the moment she was in his arms he caught one of her hands and turned it palm-side up. She didn't want to struggle to free herself so she let him.

He rubbed his thumb over the calluses.

'Why didn't you tell me about these?'

He didn't sound accusing, just genuinely surprised.

'You never asked.'

'You're right. I haven't asked. But I'm asking now.'

She tugged her hand away. He let her.

'They bother you? The calluses?'

'They're not very feminine,' she said tightly.

'I disagree.' He put his hands around her waist, drew her close. 'You've got capable hands.'

Lorelei leaned in against him. 'They used to be my gift,' she said unthinkingly, seduced by the sudden proximity of his size and strength.

'Your gift?' he prompted

'I evented. Rode horses in dressage and show trials. I was quite good.'

'How good?'

'Good enough.' She felt slightly awkward. 'International standard.'

Nash stopped swaying her in his arms. He was looking down at her as if she'd said she once had two heads.

'I've surprised you,' she said, a little more crisply.

'You've impressed me,' he said slowly. 'But you said you rode, in the past tense. Why did you give it up?'

'I had an accident. It's made any sustained time in the saddle difficult.' She hated this part. It was the reason she never talked about it. People either felt sorry for her or dismissed it as a minor disappointment. Both rankled. Almost in sympathy she felt the echo of phantom pains in her hip flexors.

'How did it happen?'

His voice was low, and it was easy to forget they were on a dance floor. It was as if they were in their own private little world.

'I was twenty-two. I came down over a jump, and so did the horse. He landed on me.'

Nash stilled.

'I survived—obviously. It took several surgeries and a lot of physio, but I'm able to ride recreationally again.'

'How long were you in recovery?'

'Two years.'

She saw him absorb that information.

'Those marks on your hips?' he said a little roughly.

Her eyes darted to his. He'd noticed. They were so faint. Did he find them unattractive?

'We all have scars, don't we?' she said slowly. 'It's a part of life.'

Nash surprised her by sliding his hands subtly onto her hips. 'You hide yours very well,' he said.

'What about you?' she challenged. 'Where are your scars?'

He looked her in the eye. 'I wear them for the world to see,' he answered. 'Every time I race.'

Race, present tense.

She wanted to ask him about it but Nash bent down and said in her ear, 'And your old man? Is he really a gigolo?'

Lorelei pulled her arms free and went to walk away, but Nash had her tightly around the waist.

'Touchy, aren't we?'

She flashed active dislike at him and said tightly, 'He's the best on the Riviera.'

'There you go,' he said lightly. 'Not so hard talking about it, was it?'

'Have you finished?'

'I'm just wondering,' he said, continuing to sway her lightly, 'how many other secrets you're hiding.'

Lorelei looked away. 'Nothing that could possibly interest you.'

'On the contrary, Lorelei, I have a feeling it's all going to interest me. Come on—we'll get your wrap.'

'I don't understand. Where are we going?'

'Where do you think?'

CHAPTER TWELVE

FROGMARCHING her across the sand in heels only got him so far. Lorelei ground to a halt and swiped off her shoes, then threw them at him. He'd seen her aim before. He had the sense to sidestep and duck.

'You worked the crowd well tonight,' he called after her.

'I wasn't working,' she responded. 'I was just being myself—not that you would know anything about that.'

Nash caught up with her.

'Hard work, is it? Prising open those wallets?'

She stopped dead. 'Why are you making it sound underhand, as if I have other motives?'

'I'm sure when you were on Andrei Yurovsky's yacht last summer you had the best interests of the charity at heart,' he responded. 'And when you were in New York with Damiano Massena earlier this year it was purely a charitable impulse.'

Lorelei blinked rapidly. 'You're jealous,' she said as if this were a wonder.

'No, sweetheart, not jealous. Territorial. There's a difference.'

'I'm not a country, Nash,' she said coolly, but he could tell he'd rattled her. 'You can't invade me and stick up your flag.'

'I can do whatever I damn well please.'

He had hold of her wrist. He wasn't sure how that had happened. He just wanted answers. Despite everything he'd convinced himself about not wanting to dig any deeper, all of those possessive feelings had roared into life as she'd so casually admitted to a professional equestrian career.

She hid everything—and he'd thought *he* was the expert at keeping his private feelings under wraps. Lorelei could give him lessons.

'You're implying I sleep with men for money,' she said icily. 'I really don't think we'll be going any further, do you? Now, take your hands off me. I'm going home to bed.'

Nash shook his head.

'Are you going to release me?'

Her voice was very calm but he could see the betraying uncertainty in her expression. He was taken back to the first time he had seen her eyes—a little mountain deer quivering at his approach.

'Explain to me that party you had the other night.'

Lorelei frowned, shaking her head. 'Why do you care? What do you want from me, Nash? What is this about?'

'I want to understand you.' The words were almost prised from him. He couldn't understand where this seething frustration had come from but he needed answers.

The urge to rip her dress off her and have this out skin to skin in the sand, coupled with the need to protect her from herself, had him in a vortex of desire and self-loathing.

'Work!' she almost shouted at him. 'Just like you. Work!'

Her shoulders rose and fell.

'The CEO of the charity often asks me to host things,' she said jerkily. 'His wife finds it too oppressive. I was brought up to do these things.' She added the last almost wearily, 'By my *grandmaman.*'

'Who's dead?'

'Yes, she's dead!' Lorelei's voice lifted almost on a wail. 'She's been dead two years, three months, five days!'

Nash stilled. There were tears behind Lorelei's eyes. She suddenly looked much younger and a little lost. Two years…

It had to be around the time of her father's arrest. And she was still grieving.

She'd lost both her father and her grandmother.

'Is that why you still do it even though you can't afford it? Is that where the debts have sprung from?' He kept his voice low, not wanting to trigger those tears. He didn't know what he'd do if she began to cry.

Lorelei lowered her head. He could almost literally see her heart hammering. Her bare chest was so delicate—almost like a baby bird's. Guilt took a bite out of him. But he had to know if he was going to help her.

'Does this CEO bloke know about your problems with money?'

'I don't have a problem with money. I have a problem with paying my bills,' she said, lifting her chin a little aggressively. Baby bird or not, she was spitting like a cat. 'And, *non,* I don't care to share my private business with the world and his wife. Or you.'

She spun around and ran. He loped after her, hitting the automatic door release on the car.

The ten-minute drive back to the bungalow was tense, but it gave Nash time to think over all she'd said. His little eventer who couldn't manage her chequebook.

As they entered the dark house he asked, 'How long did you think you could hide it?'

'I wasn't hiding anything,' she rapped out, staccato-fashion. 'I was dealing with it. In my own way.'

'And how's that been working for you?'

'Well, pardon me,' she said, reeling around, 'but we're all not big, capable genius designers who can fix everything with the snap of our fingers!'

Nash stared down at her. 'What did you call me?'

'You heard—and I think your ego's big enough for me not to repeat it.'

He wanted to kiss her. Frame her lovely frustrated face and kiss her until she was his again.

'*Do* you want me to fix this for you?'

She frowned.

'Do you?' he repeated.

'You really don't know me at all, do you? You haven't even bothered to scratch the surface.'

Nash made a low sound of frustration. Didn't she understand he was going out on a limb for her here? He never pried too deeply into his lovers' lives. To do so invited intimacy, and he didn't do that. He did sex.

'How is it, Nash, that I know so much about you and you seem to know so little about me?'

'Sweetheart, only you know what you've read in the media—and most of that's crap.'

She narrowed her eyes at him like a cat, spun around and headed for the bedroom—then seemed to change her mind and bowled right back to him. 'Here's what I know. You're amazing. You're hardworking and driven and you have this shell that you need because you're in the public eye. But when you're with your friends you're different. You don't push your opinions or need other people to agree with you. You're just certain in a way I'll never be. I admire all those things about you.'

She was breathing hard, her eyes bright with repressed feeling. Nash tried not to engage but there she was, in his face.

'But all you admire about *me* is my world-class ass—and don't even think about smiling, because as far as I'm concerned you can kiss it, Mr Racing Car Driver. I'm not waiting around for you to wake up to yourself.'

She really should have stopped after *amazing,* thought Nash as he stepped up to her, meshed his hand through her hair and brought his mouth down possessively on hers.

As if he'd lit a match next to an open petrol tank Lorelei ignited, surging against him, aggressive as he'd never felt her before. Even the first time she'd kissed him, when she'd taken the initiative, there had been a feminine reticence in her as if she needed to keep her protective barriers in place.

There were no barriers up now. The feel of her mouth moving desperately against his own made him crazy. Kissing her, hauling her with him, he staggered to the nearest flat surface—which happened to be one of the guest bedrooms. Nash would have laughed if he could at how eager he was—like a damn teenager, reefing down his trousers, with Lorelei making desperate noises as she cleaved to him, making it more difficult to actually shed any layers of clothing.

He slid his hands up her thighs, pooling her long silken skirt, and remembered as his hand touched bare skin that she'd gone commando.

Thank God.

She whimpered and drew him to her, clamping her thighs around his lean hips. Her eyes were wide and what he saw there wasn't simply desire, it was anxiety.

'Lorelei?' He was so close to the edge, and yet she was looking at him as if she wasn't quite sure what was going on.

'Nash, I'm scared.' The words were almost wrenched from her. Her fingers were digging into his shoulders as if she was dangling off a cliff face, her bright troubled eyes fixed on his.

'Don't be.' He suddenly didn't feel all that secure himself, and that was a new experience. The words he found for her came from a deeper place inside him. 'I've got you.'

As if that were enough for her she lifted her mouth to his, shaking, a little wild, and her body came alive beneath his own in a way it never had before, coaxing him to take her. He only just remembered the condom. Deep inside her, he held on to his control by receding increments as she seemed unable or unwilling to let go. He felt her resistance not as a challenge but as a desperate uncertainty on her part. Her words came back at him. *You're just certain in a way I'll never be.*

He pressed his forehead to hers. 'Look at you,' he said,

grazing her cheek, her mouth, her throat with his lips, moving slowly now. 'So strong, so wild. Do you remember when you threw that shoe at the traffic inspector?'

Lorelei gave a little start under him.

He brushed against her clitoris and she bucked. He did it again.

'Both shoes. I knew it then.'

'What—what did you know?'

'I'd never keep up.' He shifted his hips.

She made a sound—part murmur of approval, part moan.

'You stuck your finger in his face and read him the Riot Act.' He cupped her bottom. 'I thought you were going to get us arrested.'

She quaked against him. 'Sorry… I'm sorry.'

'No, no, don't be sorry,' he urged, moving harder inside her. 'Never be sorry. Do you remember when I took you back to the villa?' He angled his thrusts to reach higher. 'This—is what—I wanted—to do. Right there. In the Veyron.'

'Why?' she cried. 'Why didn't you?'

But she was already there.

'Stick shift,' he groaned as Lorelei's inner muscles clamped around him. He was grabbed and thrown down again and again, until his body convulsed uncontrollably against her and she clutched at him, riding out her own pleasure. It seemed as much his as hers, making sounds he only half recognised.

As he subsided heavily on top of her the chemical high kicked in and for several minutes he just held her, his chest pumping. He was conscious only of her trembling, responsive body cleaved to his—until he became aware something else was at play here. This wasn't just the euphoria of great sex. He could feel the connection with her still and didn't want to break it. He really didn't want to move, but he knew there was a risk if he didn't pull out of her, dispose of the condom.

It was as he began to sit up that he became aware she was making soft, helpless sounds. Insidious recognition reached down into his gut and grabbed hold of something he hadn't had to acknowledge in years.

The voice of his old man, telling him it was his fault, always his fault. To be a man and not a snivelling four-year-old boy.

He needed to hold her. That part of him that told him it was weakness that was at war with the man in him, who curved his hands around her slight, quaking shoulders, gathered her up in his arms and held her.

She turned her face into his shoulder and he experienced a surge of tenderness that threatened to further undo him. He was not accustomed to being gentle, but somehow he was, stroking the curls tumbling down the back of her neck, using his broad thumb to trace the curve of her ear, kissing her there because he needed to.

Except the face she lifted to his was not tear-streaked. Her amber eyes glowed; her cheeks were hot and flushed. She had never looked quite so beautiful, and she was smiling at him, softly laughing, her face haloed by all those silky fair curls.

'Stick shift.' She giggled as if she'd never heard anything funnier.

As he'd lost control he'd been listening not to Lorelei's tears but to her helpless, happy laughter as she came and came, and like a bolt of lightning it hit him hard. With this woman, only with Lorelei, he felt like a conquering king.

Lorelei leaned across and gave Nash a lick of her ice cream.

She was sitting on the high sea wall and he was leaning against it between her legs, his back to her, his head just above her knees.

Beyond, fishermen were casting nets in the sea and local children ran splashing in the shoals, their happy voices punctuating the shriek of gulls, the occasional backfiring of a scooter, which seemed to be a popular method of transport, and the general hum of tourists and locals as the summer season ran out its course.

They had been exploring the tiny fishing village of Trou d'Eau Douce here on the east coast all morning, and lunch lay ahead, but Lorelei would have been perfectly content to stay exactly where they were. In the moment.

'This tourist route must be boring for you,' she said cheerfully, not sounding at all sorry.

'Yeah, I'm bored out of my mind,' Nash responded, giving her the benefit of a relaxed grin.

Lorelei didn't think she'd ever seen him this relaxed. They were supposed to be on a yacht with his friends, but this morning Nash had cancelled.

'Don't you have meetings? You haven't been going to them. Isn't that the point of why we're here?' She had felt obliged to ask those questions, but her heart had been beating like hummingbird wings.

'The point is spending time with you,' he'd responded as if it were natural, and Lorelei had suddenly felt the world opening up around her into a thousand possibilities, all of them leading back to Nash.

He had forced secrets from her the other night, pushed past her fears and something important had cracked open in her, and instead of darkness only light had poured out.

He had made love to her all through the night until her body had felt like a map of Nash's voyages, each one leaving her feeling weightless and oddly free.

It was as if being here with him these last few days had unlocked those shackles of family and the past she'd been dragging around for so long. The thought of going back to how she had been seemed impossible now.

She was falling in love with him, and there could be no coming back from that. And if love was a voyage they were sailing into uncharted waters this morning.

Last night he had taken her hands and shown her the secrets of his body, almost intimidating in its muscular perfection but, like hers, telling stories.

He was marked all over with nicks and cuts, old scars from his years on the track that weren't always obvious until she touched him, ran her palms and fingertips over his back and hip, the long developed muscle of his quadriceps, and right there she had felt the groove in his flesh where he'd told her he'd had cartilage removed after a smash in Italy.

'Got adventurous on a corner and ended up upside down,' as he'd casually put it, 'with some wreckage in my leg.'

Yet last night on the beach outside a restaurant, when she had tried to ask him about himself, what drove him, he'd diverted her by hitting her most touchy subject: Raymond. In bed he had diverted again, by leading her directly to his physical scars, deftly hiding what lay beneath.

She wondered if he was always like this with women—stripping them bare of their secrets but managing to keep his own wound up nice and tight.

But she found she didn't want to think about other women, his past, because it didn't matter to her. She wanted only to be in the moment, because she could trust that. Looking beyond, not knowing what was coming, instinctively frightened her.

'My *grandmaman* never let me buy ice creams when I was a little girl,' she confessed, licking the final scrap off the inner rim of the cone. 'She said ice cream should be eaten in a bowl with a spoon at a table. Preferably without your elbows touching any surfaces.'

'She sounds like an old dragon.'

'*Non,* she was always very sweet, just set in her ways. She raised me, you know, from when I was thirteen and started boarding school. I always came home to her in the holidays. She made it her mission in life to improve me.'

'What needed improving?'

'My manners. I was a total barbarian—you have no idea.'

She crunched the cone between her teeth.

Nash grinned and she offered him his own bite.

'Clearly still a barbarian.' She laughed, covering her mouth. 'I had to learn early how to behave myself in public. Grandmaman was quite well-known in our parts. She was photographed by Cecil Beaton in her day, you know. She was an amazing beauty.'

'I see where it comes from,' said Nash, those blue eyes scanning her face.

Lorelei shrugged off the compliment. 'Looks fade. She would have preferred to be an artist herself, but she was a wonderful patron. She drew artists, writers, musicians to our house. Quite a circle. Her third husband, my *grandpère,* left her a fortune and she set up the Aviary Foundation, a gallery in town and a charity to raise money for various causes. When the accident put paid to any hopes I had of a riding career she gave me new purpose, put me on the board of the Aviary where I've been ever since.'

'Your career, in effect?'

'*Ah, oui,* sometimes it feels that way. Although I've tried to keep the charity separate from my everyday life. It's not always easy.'

She paused, realising she'd gone wading into deeper waters. But she wanted to talk about this. She hadn't forgotten what he'd accused her of last night, or what he'd said back in Monaco when he'd cancelled their date.

'Despite what you think, Nash, I don't date the men I deal with through the charity. I don't blur those lines.'

'Yeah…about that, Lorelei…'

He looked gratifyingly uncomfortable and it pleased a hurt little part of her.

'About that, Nash…?' she prompted.

'I was out of line. I apologise.'

'Do you?' Suddenly their easy camaraderie seemed forced. Her insecurities backed up in her throat.

She so wanted this man's understanding and approval,

and it left her wide open to being hurt. All of a sudden she wasn't sure she could do that. But nor was she sure she had a choice any more.

Last night everything had changed for her.

'I was trying to work out how you lived your life. I was—' He broke off, as if he knew the more he said the deeper he'd be digging himself a hole.

Lorelei made a gesture of cessation.. 'Perhaps we should just leave it at the apology.'

But his eyes flashed up and darkened on hers. 'I was jealous,' he said flatly.

Her heartbeat sped up. *'Ah, oui?'*

'Thinking about you with another man kills me.'

He said it as if it was being ripped out of him without anaesthetic, but he looked her in the eye and Lorelei found she was swaying a little with the impact of his words.

She lowered her lashes.

'Nothing to say, Lorelei?'

'Why, Nash, don't think about it, then.' She lifted her gaze and gave him a little smile.

'Not exactly what I was looking for,' he responded, but his eyes were warm.

Feeling a little breathless, she reached out and ran her fingers through his hair. 'That is nice to hear, Nash. Some not very nice things were intimated about me in the papers around the time of Raymond's trial. I think the journalists were just looking for dirt.'

'It sells papers,' said Nash grimly.

Oui, he would know. She was talking to a man who had spent more than a decade dodging the paparazzi.

'I hope I never have to go through that again. Five weeks in Paris for the trial, and every morning I opened the paper there would be another story.' Lorelei shuddered delicately.

Nash was frowning. She wondered what he was thinking. Had he read any of those stories? She didn't want to ask. She didn't want to think about it any more. But she did want to clear the air.

'All of these men I was supposed to be involved with—I was on Yurovsky's yacht last summer with at least fifteen other women, one of them his girlfriend at the time, and as for Damiano, I've known him since I was a teenager. It's never been romantic.'

'You don't need to explain your past to me,' he said roughly, but she could see the satisfaction curling like smoke in his eyes.

He was *jealous?*

'*Au contraire,* Nash, I've told you a great deal about my past and you've told me so little. I think you have a habit of privacy.'

'You want to hear about other women?'

Lorelei made a dismissive gesture. '*Eh, bien,* you will not be serious about this! Why don't you keep your important secrets, then?'

He leaned in and pushed her rogue curl behind her ear.

'What do you want to know, Lorelei?'

She brightened. 'We could start with something I asked you about last night—about your scars. You said you show them every time you race. What did you mean?'

The amusement dropped away from his expression and he rocked back on his heels.

'I know it's probably very complicated,' she persevered, 'but I'd like to know why you do what you do…'

'Complicated?' he said with a humourless smile. 'No, sweetheart, it's incredibly simple. It's in the blood. My old man, John Blue, worked in pit crews around the world and dragged us with him.'

'Ah, an international childhood.'

'Yeah, you could say that.'

He was quiet for a moment, but Lorelei waited. She sensed she'd just glimpsed the tip of an almighty iceberg.

'Mum walked out when I was barely more than a baby. Couldn't take the lifestyle, couldn't take the old man. Can't blame her.'

He turned away from her, shoving his hands into his pockets, bunching his shoulders.

'She left us boys with Dad,' he said, looking away down the beach as if scanning for something. 'He was a drunk and a bully and he made our lives a living hell. Until one day when Jack—my older brother—was big enough to climb behind the wheel of a car and he started us both rally driving. Jack was good, but I was better.'

She didn't quite understand. 'You raced for your *papa?*'

'No, I raced in spite of my old man.' His voice was taut and stripped of emotion. 'He had world-class dreams and I was going to fulfil them for him. The minute I signed with Ferrari I cut contact with him.'

Lorelei suppressed a shiver. He hadn't shown this side to her. She imagined it was this single mindedness that had made him so very good at what he did and a very wealthy man.

'You took your revenge?' she said quietly, uncertain as to how she felt about that.

'No, I survived.'

It was a terse statement, to the point, and it chilled her to the bone.

'You didn't abandon your old man,' he said suddenly, meeting her eyes, and she could see he'd shut down again, 'I admire that.'

'Non.' The negative was pushed from her instinctively. She rejected his statement with her entire body. 'Don't admire me. My mother wasn't there for me either, but my father didn't drink or make my life hell—at least not on purpose. He loved me. How could I abandon him? I couldn't abandon someone I love.'

Nash was watching her as if her words were flicks of a knife.

'Good,' he said with finality, and she knew the subject was closed, 'I'm glad he loves you. You deserve that, Lorelei.'

Meaning he didn't? Lorelei wanted to offer him something, but she had a strong feeling whatever she did in this moment would be rejected. He was a man driven by demons and it was all too possible she had come too late into his life to make any difference at all.

With a sudden movement Nash bounded up onto the sea wall beside her, offering her his hand. Standing over her, he was once more the solid, take-charge guy who made the world seem a less chaotic, threatening place when she was with him.

'Enough of the past. I want to show you the mountains this afternoon. We'll take the Jeep up.'

Later that evening over dinner she asked him the question that had been bothering her most. 'That accident you were in, in Italy, is that why you got out of the sport?'

Nash shook his head. 'You'd think so, but no.' His voice was quiet and deep and sure. The rose candlelight cut into the restaurant walls, lining his dark head in gold. 'My take on it is I don't have any dependants. If I killed myself racing at least I'd leave the world doing something I loved.'

Lorelei almost choked on her mouthful of wine, a little stunned by his matter-of-factness. 'That's a terrible thing to say.'

'I'm not planning on careening off the track any time soon, Lorelei.'

'No, but—' She broke off helplessly, wondering if he actually knew how empty he had made his life sound. 'What about your brother Jack?' she prompted.

Nash said nothing, began cutting into his steak.

'What about me?' The moment the words passed her lips she couldn't believe she'd been so gauche. 'What I mean to say is, if anything happened to you I'd be heartbroken.' She gave him a small smile to lighten the impact.

He reached for his iced water. 'I'll keep that in mind.'

Lorelei had the urge to rub the spot in her chest that had gone suddenly cold.

'Something must have made you stop,' she said, her voice a lot less confident.

He put down his glass. 'My brother Jack is an alcoholic, like the old man. He let his business slide, lost his wife, gambled away his life. He thought he had nothing more to live for. Six years ago I walked into a hospital room in Sydney and I barely recognised him. I'd been racing professionally for eight years, and I'd been back once.'

Nash met her eyes. 'His ex-wife told me I was to blame. Jack always wanted the career, but I was the one who got the talent. So I quit racing. I moved back to Sydney and I lived with him for a year. Got his business back on its feet, went every day to AA with him and made sure he was okay. I owed it to him. He got me to university. He's my brother. And he hates me.'

'But why?'

'The talent and the luck. To my old man I was a meal ticket, and my brother was convinced I stole what should have been his. In my family nobody works. The joke is I've worked hard all my life to get where I am. That's what I do. I work. I came back to Europe and I sold the design for Blue 11, and part of the reason I did it was because I wanted to show them it was more than luck, more than being able to hold a car on the road at speed.'

His expression was grim. 'It should have been enough for me, but it wasn't. I love to race. And now I don't have to prove anything. To the old man, to Jack, even to myself. I don't want to lose it a second time.'

Lorelei was quiet. Finally she said, 'Hence the comeback?'

'You picked up on that the other night at dinner?'

'It was hard not to. I was at the table, Nash.'

He put his hands palm-down on the table, giving her a

wry smile. 'Have I ever told you, you do have a world-class ass, Ms St James?'

'Several times,' she replied dryly, dabbing at the tears in the corners of her eyes, then offering up her most beguiling smile. He deserved it after that. 'I think you should take me home and I'll show it to you.'

Nash pushed back his chair, raised his hand for the cheque.

Lorelei lay with her head on his chest, her mind full of the story he had told her. She knew it was selfish, but she couldn't help wishing he wasn't staging this comeback—because it was going to have repercussions on their fledgling relationship.

'Why now, Nash? Why race now?'

His voice was heavy, relaxed. 'Like I told you, I started out racing in spite of my father. Now I race for myself.'

'But why now in particular?' she pursued.

'I don't know.' He yawned. 'At the risk of sounding New Agey, I've been feeling a lack in my life and I know racing will fill that.'

'What sort of lack?'

Nash chuckled. 'Not the sort you're imagining, Lorelei.'

A little frustrated, she lifted her chin. 'You don't know what I'm thinking.'

'Yeah…' his smile was lazy '…I do. I'm thirty-four. All anyone's going to be asking over the coming months before I start winning any flags is whether it's an early midlife crisis.'

'You're confident of winning?'

He gave her that very male look she was already familiar with. It was a redundant question. He was confident about everything, and he always won.

She sat up. 'During the early months of my rehabilitation the thing that got me out of bed was the desire to get back in the saddle. It was only when I realised I couldn't go back to competitive riding that I found the emptiness resided not in the fulfilment of a dream but in the absence of anything else in my life.'

There was a long silence.

'So what's in your life now?' he asked, his voice deceptively lazy.

But Lorelei knew him well enough to catch the watchfulness in those blue eyes viewing her from beneath heavy lids.

You.

The rush of feeling overwhelmed her. She wanted to be enough for him.

She wanted to stand in for racing.

She wanted him to realise what an extraordinary man he was, and for once to stop pushing himself.

She wanted a great deal she probably couldn't have.

'I have my work,' she said diffidently.

'Yeah, the charity.'

'No, my horses…' she began with a little frown.

'You have horses?'

'*Oui,* two, I stable them at Allards.'

'So you still ride?'

'Whenever I can.' She hesitated, then went on the offensive. 'So what are you lacking in *your* life, Nash?'

'Me?' He looked amused. 'I'm just easily bored.'

'I'll have to come up with some ways of keeping you from being bored, then,' she said softly, and slid forward over him, her curls falling down to brush over his chest in the way he liked. His eyes met hers, and all that banked heat made the blood pool in her thighs and pelvis. 'I've got a few ideas.'

She knew how to make a man want her, trip over his feet to get to her, but it had never been about that with Nash. From the moment he had put his hand on her shoulder outside the hotel and told her he would handle it, rushed to her rescue like a valiant knight, she'd been off-centre with him. She had always looked after herself, knowing all too well how unreliable men could be. She had given Nash access to the vulnerable heart of hers and made him her lover, and right now she knew there should be more.

For the first time in her life she wanted more.

'Isn't this comeback supposed to be hush-hush?' she asked

He cupped her bottom. 'I think I'm safe.'

Lorelei kissed him. He was telling her he trusted her, that he accepted her right to know and she had his respect.

'Besides,' he said complacently as she kissed her way down his body, her bare bottom resting back on his thighs, 'we're releasing a timed leak on Monday. By Wednesday the media will be all over it.'

Lorelei felt as if he'd yanked a rug out from under her.

Her head came up. He wasn't saying he trusted her at all. He was just saying the timing made it irrelevant. She tried to ignore the crumpling in her chest.

'What's happening Wednesday?' she asked, feeling a little sidelined.

'A press conference,' he replied calmly, stroking her thighs, 'and then lockdown.'

'What's lockdown?'

'Training.'

'And then what?'

'The circuit.'

'A lot of travel?'

'For the next year.'

He sat up, and she gave a gasp as he flipped her onto her belly and began placing hot kisses down her spine, over the rounded curves of her bottom.

'Perhaps I can fly in?' she suggested, feeling a little stunned.

'I'd enjoy that,' he said, tracing one quivering buttock.

'Would you?' she said a little sharply.

Nash put his mouth to her ear. 'Your visits would be most welcome.'

She waited for him to ask her to go with him.

He didn't.

Nash took the steps by threes, coming out of the darkness into the bright light spilling down the front of the bungalow. He was impatient to get back to Lorelei.

This afternoon they'd driven back to the bungalow around dusk. Nash had never felt less like a boys' night, but he knew he'd been fairly difficult to pin down, given he was spending all his time with Lorelei, and there were ends to tie up and other people involved in this. He had responsibilities.

'Two hours, tops,' he'd told her, 'and then I take you out to dinner.'

She had smiled softly, a little sad, he knew, because of what he'd told her last night. He had his reasons, and it had not been easy, but she needed to understand racing came first.

He found the bungalow empty and for a strange moment his insides hollowed out.

She was gone….

This was how it would feel next week, and the week after that, and after that.

He made a frustrated sound, slamming the door. He was behaving like a green kid. There was no reason why he couldn't keep seeing her on a casual basis. A few nights here and there when he was in town, perhaps flying her out when he was working. He was capable of cleaning this up, keeping everything locked down.

Then he noticed the doors onto the deck were wide open. He relaxed. This at least was familiar. She was outside—probably on the beach. Then he spotted it: a piece of white paper weighted under a rock at the top of the steps leading down to the beach. There was another one on the bottom step. He hesitated, then smiled to himself.

He had found four paper signals when he caught sight of her on the shore. He stood at the edge of the clearing. She was clearly waiting for him, because the moment she saw him she lifted her sheer kaftan.

He stopped dead.

She was wearing one of those tiny bikinis the boutique had interpreted as adequate beachwear. Adequate, Nash countered, if the beach was private and no other man was going to see her in it.

She reached behind her and untied the strap of the top.

A sudden surge of instinct had him doing a quick scan of their surroundings, aware his might not be the only pair of eyes on this little show. There was nothing but the private beach, the rustle of the wind in the palms and tropical undergrowth and the murmur of the water on the shore.

Lorelei was peeling off the bikini bottoms, utterly unselfconscious. He watched as she lifted her arms above her head, moving with lithe grace as she stretched sinuously, seeming to be enjoying the warm breeze moving over her skin. There was a full moon and at this angle she looked to be reaching for it with both hands.

She spun around, her head sank back and she began to dance.

Nash swore his heart stopped. He knew her body—he'd explored every inch of her firm, tanned flesh—but in this moment he almost didn't recognise her. Because he saw something more—the instinctive sensuality that was a part of her, her incredible naturalness and her acceptance not only of her body but of the cards life had dealt her.

Why had he not seen this before? The answer was there. He'd been blind.

His desire for her was suddenly a living flame inside him.

He strode down the beach towards her.

She continued to turn and glide, and when he was mere feet from her she slipped away with a soft laugh, running nimbly down to the surf.

Nash didn't hesitate. He stripped off his shoes, shirt, trousers, boxers and strode down to plunge recklessly into the cool draw of the ocean. The water was inky, but the moonlight cast enough light for him to see Lorelei, still now, as gentle waves broke at her hips.

She laughed as he caught her around the waist, dragged her down into the water with him.

A wave smacked against his back and he caught her mouth with his and tasted salt and woman. *His* woman. Lorelei.

She licked her way into his mouth, winding those slim arms around his neck, her slick body riding against his in the water. Her long legs wound around his, and he lifted her, his sex nudging hers. She was wet and hot and welcoming, and he was surprised the water around them didn't sizzle with the heat they were generating between them.

She was like some pagan priestess, initiating him into this rite, uninhibited and demanding as a great goddess should be, taking and offering in equal measure.

He rode deep into her body, the sway of the tide pulling them this way and that, making achieving a rhythm almost impossible. Yet the ocean held their bodies aloft and his climax eventually pulled him into a vortex of perfect symmetry with her. Lorelei pulsed around him, and if he was a fanciful man—which he was not—he would have said it was like flying.

He eventually carried her out of the water and up to the beach, where he wrapped her in a towel and took her inside. She was shivering and laughing as he dumped them both under the shower, with warm water cascading down. He washed her hair and then rubbed some of the lemon-scented liquid into his own.

She leaned against him as he rinsed her off, and he was

struck all over again by how delicate she was. That feeling of possession he'd been nurturing this week roared into life. He didn't want to let her go.

It was never supposed to have been more than a few days out of time—a last indulgence before the weeks of intensive training that lay ahead. He couldn't have known she would get under his skin. Women came and went. Yet as he tumbled her into their bed he knew part of Lorelei would always stay with him.

His chest felt tight, but he knew he would get past this. He had life lessons to draw on in how to master his own emotions and make them serve him. Painful lessons, learned by a small boy too young to really understand what was happening in his life, always looking for someone to cling to, always being punished for it. The constant cycle of confusion.

There was nothing confusing about the life he had grown up to lead. Everything was compartmentalised. Everything had its place.

Including this. Including Lorelei.

Tomorrow he would be flying back to Monaco and straight into the press conference, a show race for Eagle in Lyon, and then training. He wasn't ready. He had been doing too much thinking about this beguiling woman in his arms and not enough about the job.

The irony was, if he was given another week he'd spend it all with her.

But he'd never put a woman before the job.

Like his parents, he knew how to be ruthless to achieve his ends.

Lorelei was dreaming. In her dream she was walking down a long corridor. There were doors on either side of her, stretching as far as she could see.

As she passed they would open.

There was her mother. She was young—as Lorelei recalled her in her earliest years—holding out a doll with long golden curls that bore a marked resemblance to the child she had been before she cut off her hair. Another door opened on her father, Raymond, as she had last seen him, rigid in a suit, his back to her. Finally there was *Grandmaman,* holding out money in one hand and a tiny miniature of the villa in the other.

Lorelei could feel the constriction growing in her body. She was moving faster. Hands were coming out to snatch at her skirt, her ankles, demanding things of her until she thought she would go crazy. And then she heard a deep, certain voice saying her name. 'Lorelei.' She stepped into his arms and the walls of the dream fell away. She was held poised in midair in the strongest pair of arms imaginable.

'Nash.' She clung to him and knew she was home, would always be safe.

He wouldn't let go. Which meant she *could* let go…

Lorelei gasped, coming awake in a bath of perspiration. Nash was leaning over her in the dark. He gently stroked the hair back from her eyes.

'Go to sleep. His voice was deep and sleep roughened. 'It was just a nightmare.'

'Oui,' she murmured croakily, and closed her eyes.

For a long while she lay awake, with Nash's arm pinning her, his body curved around hers like a bulwark against uncertainty.

She felt a little *triste.* It could have been because of the fast-fading dream but was probably because they were going back to Monaco tomorrow.

But it wasn't the villa or her debts that filled her horizon, it was the man beside her, who appeared not to be sleeping either, although his chest rose and fell steadily.

She burrowed in a little closer.

I've fallen in love with this man, she thought, framing it like a statement and waiting to feel the panic it should open up inside her.

All those fears of dependency, of being left behind, of not being loved back.

None came.

She curved her body trustingly into his and closed her eyes. She was back in the ocean with him, certain of this one thing: *this has been as close to flying as I've ever come.*

CHAPTER THIRTEEN

'LORELEI, we need to talk.'

According to the flight screen they were twenty minutes out of Nice.

Lorelei removed her ear buds and looked up. Nash had been hooked into a laptop for the better part of an hour, which was why they hadn't been sitting together.

Or at least she told herself that was why, but she had been telling herself a great many things since boarding his plane. If he was being a little distant this morning she assumed he was thinking about what he was flying back into. She certainly was.

He was a famous man, about to reignite that fame, and there were consequences for her. She would be foolish to discount them.

But when she looked at him everything fell away, leaving only what she felt for him: a tremulous sort of tenderness mingled with a longing to have this in her life.

He dropped into the seat beside her, stretching out his long legs, but there was nothing casual about the expression on his face.

'You look ominous,' she said lightly.

'Do I?' He looked at her, his eyes cool. 'I'm going into lockdown tomorrow. That's going to have ramifications on my personal life.'

His personal life? She guessed that meant her. She moistened her lips.

'I see.'

Did she see? Lorelei curled the fingers of one hand around her music device instead of around his hand.

Why, all of a sudden, couldn't she reach for his hand?

Yesterday she wouldn't even have thought about it. She wouldn't have had to. Whenever he was beside her he held her hand.

'I gather it will limit the time we can spend together?' Her voice held none of the turmoil suddenly swirling in her belly.

'I'll be training intensively and then I hit the circuit.' Nash spoke matter-of-factly. 'This hasn't happened at a propitious time. I wish it could be different, but it can't.'

Lorelei had never thought about what it would be like to jump from a plane without a parachute. She imagined the landing would feel something like this.

There were so many things she could say. *I don't understand. Please explain yourself more clearly. Don't do this. Please don't do this....*

But he was doing it. She looked into his hard eyes and knew beyond a shadow of a doubt he would do this to her.

'I don't want you to feel tied to me in any way.'

Lorelei tried to sit up but every bone in her body felt broken. Still, she had to get up. She couldn't just sit here, stunned.

'It wouldn't be fair to you.'

From a long way away she was hearing an echo from the past. It was her father, explaining why she couldn't live with him any more, that she was to go to her grandmother. She'd been thirteen years old. She hadn't understood then. She had cried until she threw up.

But she understood now. She was a grown woman. She had lived in the world, had been swept away by feelings that fed her soul, and he had enjoyed some recreational sex.

'How good of you to explain it all to me,' she said, her

voice more throaty than usual. 'I suppose there is a reason we didn't have this conversation several days ago?'

He was watching her stone-faced. 'Things have changed. Several days ago I didn't know we would need to.'

'I see—and what has changed for you?'

'I didn't realise we'd be going any further than Mauritius.'

She knew he was right. She hadn't thought beyond Mauritius, either. She'd just assumed everything would fall into place.

'Lorelei, I know you've invested some emotions in our time together,' he said almost carefully. 'When we flew out I made some assumptions.'

'Ah, oui.' She clutched her music device and in that moment wished it were a weapon. 'All the men I was supposed to have fleeced.' The words stuck to the roof of her mouth.

'Assumptions about myself,' he growled.

For the first time she looked at him properly. He didn't look like a man feeding her a line. He looked like Nash. Tense, brooding, not wanting to hurt her, but tearing her apart all the same.

After all, Lorelei, it's not his fault he's not in love with you. You made that little bed all on your own.

But he had been there with her. All the way.

'You're an extraordinary woman, Lorelei, and you deserve a lot better than a man like me.'

And just like that it was over.

'Apparently I do,' she said woodenly, hearing her voice as if it were coming from a long way off. 'I really don't know what to say.'

For the first time since he'd sat down beside her Nash looked unsure, as if they had taken a wrong turn somewhere and he was looking for the best way to circumvent the route.

'I don't necessarily want to end it, Lorelei. All I am saying is there are difficulties involved. I'll be gone for long periods and my focus will be on the job.'

All the cold inside her chest pushed its way up into her mind. She welcomed it.

'I'm saying I wouldn't want you to feel committed to me.'

Lorelei blinked. Her eyes were the only part of her face she could move.

'You really are a complete bastard, aren't you?'

Those intense blue eyes flashed up, hard as agate, but his voice was soft as he acknowledged heavily, 'Yeah.'

What more was there to say?

She didn't know how to fight for this. How did you fight for something that had to be given freely? She didn't understand him. She'd thought she did. She had seen in him from the very first such solidity. He had seemed impervious to the turmoil in her life, a strong hand she could hold as she righted herself.

So she had opened up her heart to him, had thought she understood him, but it was clear she knew nothing at all.

Anger and rage and sorrow all rolled through her in an almighty wave and she thought if it crashed now the emotions would drag her under.

She had to be strong. *Stronger than him.*

'What happened to you? Who did this to you?'

He actually flinched as she said the words. He stood up, those big shoulders that held up the world suddenly a little heavier, his expression almost remote.

'I've got a job to do, Lorelei, and relationships have never been my strong suit.'

No, me neither....

She actually felt too stunned to fully process what had happened. It was only when they landed on the tarmac and she spotted the limo that confusion set in.

What was she supposed to do? Was he taking her back to town? To the villa? Oh, *Dieu,* she couldn't get into the villa. She gulped a deep, sustaining breath. She needed to calm down. She needed to stop standing around waiting for him to call the shots.

Taxi. She needed a taxi.

Nash said, almost formally, 'The car is for you. It will take you into town. I'll take the Veyron.'

For a moment she considered refusing, but what was the point?

'Ainsi soit-il.' So be it.

'The car will take you back to my apartment. You can stay there until you get back on your feet.'

He had to be kidding.

As if anticipating her reaction, he said, 'You need a roof over your head.'

'I do not think that is your concern any longer, Mr Blue.' Her voice was croaky, as if she'd been yelling for a very long time.

'Let me do this for you,' he said quietly.

The bastard.

She stepped up to him, looked him in the eye. 'Why on earth didn't you just leave me on the doorstep that morning after? If all you wanted was a one-night stand you could have left it there. I didn't ask for you to take me to Mauritius. But I damn well deserve better than being dumped fifteen minutes after we land.'

It was good to say it, and to say it with some control, but she knew she wasn't just raging at Nash. She was raging at her dear, feckless father, who had rescued her from her absent mother's apartment in New York all those years ago, only to neglect her and dump her on his mother, who for all her good intentions had been a difficult and somctimes ferocious taskmaster.

She deserved to be loved and accepted for who she was, not what others expected her to be.

Nash looked her in the eye and said, 'Yeah, you do.'

It was that resigned acceptance of her anger and his role

in her pain that left her with nowhere to go. He was behaving as if it was all inevitable.

As if he didn't have a choice.

But he did. Couldn't he see that? Surely he could see that?

She'd fought like a tiger to regain full mobility after her accident, she'd stood by Raymond through his trial and all the scathing publicity, and she'd struggled like a fish in a net to hold on to the villa these past months.

But she couldn't make this man fight for her.

Turning away, she said softly, 'Nash, do you have any feelings for me at all?'

'Lorelei, of course I do.' He jaw was so rigid it was a wonder he could speak.

She took a deep breath.

'Bon,' she said forcefully, and pushed past him. 'In that case I don't ever want to see you again.'

She stepped into the limo.

'Take her wherever she wants to go,' she heard him say to the driver.

In the car Lorelei blocked the oncoming truckload of pain by opening her cell and regrouping.

She checked her client list for next week and sent off a text to Gina's mother to bump up her appointment for this afternoon. Work, rules and structure. She had never needed it so much as right now. She sent a text to her solicitor, asking for an appointment, which gave her a vague feeling of asserting a little control over events. Finally she scrolled through her address book, turning over in her mind which one of her friends she could ask for a bed.

In the end she sent a text to Simone. A million miles away in Paris.

Please come. I need you.

Then she closed her eyes and decided the tears that were building inside her really had no place right now. She would hold them until she was alone. And with that she realised for the first time in two years she was once more in complete control of her actions.

Nash was about to throw the keys for valet parking outside the hotel when suddenly he knew he wouldn't be going inside. It had only taken a couple of phone calls on the way down to have information regarding the lien on Lorelei's loan sent through, and in an hour the locks would be taken off her house. But somehow it wasn't enough.

He reached into his pocket and palmed his cell, dialled the limo. 'Where did you drop her, mate?'

He had a press conference. He had a training schedule ahead. He needed to let her go. Instead he leapt back in the car and gunned the engine.

He'd driven past, but never been inside the equestrian centre. There had never been a reason. He gave her name at the desk and the wide-eyed girl told him Lorelei should be in the arena and asked did he need an escort? She was free.

'I'm sure I can find it,' he replied with a slight smile, and followed the arrows.

What in the hell did he think he was doing? Better question: why had she come here? Straight here? Who was she meeting? He couldn't fathom the growing jealousy in him.

The first thing that hit him was the odour of manure and horse. So far, so expected. He jogged lightly down the steps of the stadium seating, scanning as he went. There were horses being worked in the domed arena. He recognised Lorelei. She was unmistakable, leaping a bay gelding over barriers. It was a breathtaking sight. Her grace and ability was fully on show.

He sank down slowly onto one of the bench seats.

Presently she drew alongside another rider, and that was when he noticed something else. The young girl on the smaller horse had a prosthesis on both her right arm and leg. Lorelei was showing her how to guide her horse.

An arrow-backed middle-aged woman sitting nearby looked at him with interest. She was the only other person within earshot.

She leaned back. 'Lorelei runs our programme here for disabled young people. She's a superb trainer. If you're interested I can set up an appointment, but I have to warn you she's in demand. There's a waiting list.'

Nash gave the woman a polite nod and settled back.

He didn't know what he was feeling.

But, my God, she was magnificent.

She looked like a queen in the saddle.

He remembered what she had told him about her two years of rehabilitation. He'd just assumed she'd given up. When he knew better than most what made someone a gifted athlete was that drive. Why hadn't he realised she would take that same drive and rechannel it?

It was what he had done.

The trappings of fame and success for him had become the bells and whistles people paid attention to. But he'd earned it with hard work and focus. Yet he'd completely discounted that when he'd looked at Lorelei. He'd just seen bells and whistles, a beautiful blonde bauble. Why?

Feelings shifted like tectonic plates in his chest. Why hadn't he asked more questions? Why hadn't he seen this in her? She wasn't weak. She was strong. It made sense that she would pick herself up and start all over again. And she'd do the same with that bloody house of hers.

However she'd accumulated those debts, there would be a good reason.

And he intended to find out.

Nash wasn't sure how long he sat and watched. He only knew when he emerged into the late afternoon he wanted to smash something. When he returned to his car his cell was throwing up a volley of messages.

The press conference.

He hit redial. 'John, I'm on my way.'

He walked into a conclave of cameras and the relief of his Eagle teammates. He sat down, put his hands either side of the mike and said calmly, 'Ladies, gentlemen—sorry to keep you waiting. I'm driving for Eagle next year.'

A volley of questions came at him. He took a few, then fielded the rest, scrolling through his phone.

He knew tomorrow there'd be copy on how Nash Blue had been so bored at his own press conference he'd seemed more interested in playing with his phone. At another time it would have amused him. But right now he didn't care about the press, the public or even the Eagle reps, who seemed more than adequately able to handle this without him.

He got up and walked out into the empty carpeted corridor.

'Mike,' he said with deceptive casualness to his genius PA, 'I've got a few leads I need chased up.' He asked for all the pertinent information about Raymond St James's trial and his creditors.

John Cullinan stepped into the hall. 'Nash, man, are you in this or not?'

'Yeah.' Nash pocketed his cell. He'd done all he could for the moment. 'I'm in.'

Sitting on the little red couch in a twin room at the Hotel de Paris, Lorelei shook her head over the paperwork the bank had given her.

'So let me get this straight,' said Simone, mixing coffee. 'He's opened up negotiations with the bank for you, covered your outstanding mortgage payments and is acting as guarantor for the next six months?'

'*Oui,* it appears so.'

'Is that legal?'

'If I give the bank my signature.'

Simone stopped stirring. 'If? *If?*'

'I can't accept this, Simone. Not now.'

'You're going to accept it, *chère,* if I have to tie you up and carry you down there myself. He must be feeling a cartload of guilt to be doing this.'

'*Non,* it's just Nash—the way he is.' Generous. Always so generous with his time and his money…and his brother. He'd given up everything for a year for his brother. He'd given up his racing career for his brother.

He deserved to have another chance.

Lorelei found her breathing had become scratchy.

Like Simone. Who had flown down immediately from Paris, leaving her children with her husband and taking a leave of absence from her high-powered job. To make coffee, offer a kind shoulder and listen.

You did those things for the people you loved.

But he didn't love her or he wouldn't have let her go.

Simone came and set a mug down in front of her.

'He's racing tomorrow in Lyon. We could go. You could speak to him about this.'

Lorelei shook her head vigorously.

Simone gave her an old-fashioned look. 'Do you know what I think, *chère?* This man loves you. He's just having a few problems working out how to show it.'

'Don't, Simone. You have no idea how many times I heard all my stepmothers and their girlfriends talking like this. *He's this way because he's a man. He's this way because you make him like this.* In the end he's this way because it's who he is. It's who he wants to be. Nash wants to race cars, he wants to win and he puts work above everything.'

Lorelei released a huge sob of a breath.

'All my life that's how it's been. *Papa* put his women ahead of me. *Grandmaman* put the charity ahead of me. I'm not mooning over a man who thinks oil and grease and speed outweigh my love.'

'You're in love with him.' Simone sat down beside her.

'That's what you got out of my little speech?'

Simone shook her head with a smile. 'Isn't it all that matters in the end, *cherie?*'

Was it all that mattered?

Lorelei lay awake, staring out at the night.

Her father would say, *Oui, but of course. L'amour is everything.*

But Raymond had never really loved anybody in his life but himself, with a little corner of his heart reserved for her.

She deserved so much more. Everyone deserved to be loved wholeheartedly and for themselves. A sob made its way up through her body, leaving her shaken, but still she couldn't cry.

She loved Nash, really loved him, but she felt battered. He had left her behind, he didn't love her back, and here she was—so very, very dependent on him.

Except for one thing.

The villa.

He could have gifted it to her. The meaningless gesture of an excessively wealthy man. He hadn't. He had chosen instead to take the pressure off her with the gift of time. Time to think. Time to make a decision about what she really wanted to do. It also enabled her to envisage a time when she could pay him back.

He knew her well enough to know it was the only gift she wouldn't throw back in his face.

Lorelei rolled onto her back.

Mon Dieu, he hadn't made her dependent. He had made her strong again.

In every way.

Lorelei bolted up in bed.

She flung open the other bedroom door and the little bedside light flickered on as Simone sat up groggily.

'How long will it take me to drive to Lyon?'

'Three hours, give or take.' Simone yawned. 'Why?'

Lorelei bit her lip. 'I'm going to do what I should have done on that plane. Fight for him.'

Simone gave her a wavery smile. 'Should I expect to see you on the news tomorrow night, throwing punches at track girls?'

It was a gentle reminder not to overreact.

Except what had Nash told her? Not to be sorry, never to be sorry.

'It's always a possibility.'

CHAPTER FOURTEEN

IT WAS race day.

Nash continued to scan the documents emailed to his smartphone. Raymond St James had quite a list of creditors.

Lifting his eyes from the bright screen, for a moment all Nash could see was Lorelei, locked out of her beloved home, trying desperately to steer him away, to hide the truth of her situation, only admitting, when forced, 'I have had some debts.'

Some debts.

'Nash, man, you're cutting it fine.'

He dumped the phone and dragged up the zipper on his fire-retardant suit, pulled the face mask on and reached for his helmet.

The sound of the crowd, the smell of gasoline fumes, the whir of his car being readied usually pushed up his adrenaline levels. But this afternoon he didn't need any help with that.

His heart was pounding, he was sweating inside the hot suit, but he knew how to switch off and do his job.

He'd raced all over the globe for a decade.

He'd won; he'd lost. Mostly he'd won.

He usually knew the outcome before he got in the car. He studied the field, he knew his car and he applied logic and ability and allowed for that two per cent of unpredictability that lay in any race.

It was that two per cent that was on his mind—and it had nothing to do with the race.

As he ripped across the finish line outside Lyon the fact that he took little pleasure in the win didn't detract from the roar of the crowd. Slinging himself out of the car, he embraced Alain Demarche and Antonio Abruzzi in turn. Shook hands with a couple of guys from the pit crew and mounted the podium.

He was stepping off amidst champagne and track girls when he saw her.

She was standing with Nicolette Delarosa. She was wearing blue jeans and a simple green shirt and her hair was a halo around her piquant face. But, most tellingly, a lanyard dangled around her neck.

He focused on the lanyard, knowing then that this wasn't some fantasy apparition. She was real. Heart thumping, he moved away from the podium but the crowd had already swallowed her up.

He shouldered his way through and grabbed one of the security guards forming a phalanx around him.

'There'll be a '55 Sunbeam Alpine in the VIP car park. Can you hold on to it until I get out?'

'Sure thing.'

'The woman who owns it will kick up a fuss. Make sure she's treated with respect.'

'Absolutely. Great race, man.'

'Thanks.'

Let her be there. If she wasn't he'd grab a car and drive every mile back to Monaco and fetch her.

He hadn't wanted to race today. All he had wanted to do was go and fetch her back. But he had a job to do. A lot of people were relying on him—as always. You couldn't escape responsibility for others. Lorelei had never tried. Her compassionate humanity humbled him.

She had hidden so much behind those charming mannerisms. What he had read as light-heartedness and frivolity were her coping mechanisms. He'd got it all wrong.

How in the hell had he got it so wrong?

In the bungalow the night he'd confronted her about hiding things she'd accused him of not knowing her at all, of not trying to know her.

She'd been right.

He hadn't wanted to look at what was shouting in his face. He'd been so damned determined to keep to his single-minded plan to race that he'd been willing to sacrifice this extraordinary chance he'd been given to love and be loved to his own selfish need to prove himself. To prove his old man was wrong. He wasn't weak, a snivelling kid who drove people away with his demands for love and attention, the innocent child who had reached instinctively for love and been denied it. So he'd learned to deride his own needs, and when Lorelei had come along, he hadn't had a clue how to even *begin* loving her.

Yet he did. Her compassion and her humanity had torn into those barriers he'd raised, yet still he'd gone back for more.

It had always been there when they made love, from the very first night, and he'd seen it when she danced on the beach—the acceptance in her body of who she was.

Her acceptance of *him*.

Come be with me. Let me show you how to love me, how to love yourself.

He closed his eyes, took a deep, sustaining breath, and knew his life had just taken a sudden irrevocable turn. For the better.

He was in his civvies and to his surprise Lorelei was just sitting on the bonnet of her car. Not kicking, not scratching, not a thrown shoe in sight. She was chatting casually with three security guys, who stood around looking more interested in making an impression than doing their job.

The guys evaporated with polite nods as Nash approached. Lorelei leaned back, angling her body at him. The old playful pose dragged him back to the first time he'd met her, when she'd put on that little show and he'd lost his head over her.

'I thought I dreamed you up,' he said, his voice suddenly rather hoarse.

'Are you in the habit of doing that?'

'Lately? Yeah. All the time.'

She slid off the bonnet of the car and stood before him, suddenly not so sure of herself, her face solemn.

'I'm not Jack,' she said.

He went still.

'And I'm grateful for the time with the villa, but I'm not your rescue package, Nash Blue.'

He bowed his head.

'I know that, Lorelei,' he said in a thickened voice. 'I saw you at the equestrian centre. The day we got back I followed you.'

'You followed me? I didn't see you.'

'You were training a young girl with a prosthesis. I had no idea.' He stepped towards her, aching to take her in his arms. 'Why didn't you tell me?'

Lorelei hesitated. 'I don't know. I could say it was because it didn't come up, but the truth is…' Her voice died away. She shook her head. 'I'm not proud of it, but I wanted to hold something back from you because I sensed you were holding so much back from me.'

He nodded slowly. 'Fair enough. But you have to know when I got the big picture everything I'd told myself about my feelings for you came crashing down. I didn't want to love you, Lorelei, and so I told myself you could never be anything but another person I'd have to bail out.'

'In the end you did,' she said in a strangled voice.

'No.' He shook his head with a soft smile. 'I gave myself time.'

'You gave *me* time,' she corrected.

His smile grew. 'Oh, sweetheart, you're no rescue package. I did it for both of us.'

Lorelei stood there for a timeless moment.

'Then why couldn't you love me?'

It was a plea from her heart.

'God, Lorelei.' It was wrenched from him. 'I was afraid I'd love you too much.'

Time stood still.

'I was a clingy kid,' he said, almost tonelessly. 'Dad had a stream of women in the early days, and whichever woman picked me up she'd be mum. But they'd always leave. Dad would drive them away with his drinking.'

Lorelei didn't shift an inch, afraid if she did he would stop. She so desperately wanted to hear it all, even as her mind turned in horror from the picture he was painting.

'The old man used to say they left because of me.' He shook his head at her expression. 'It's bull, I know. But when you're a kid you believe your dad.'

'Nash—' She reached up and stroked his face, unable not to touch him.

'When I went back to Sydney and saw the shape Jack was in his ex-wife said the same thing. *He's this way because of you.* And in a way she was right. I succeeded. I got the career, the money, the accolades. Jack couldn't cope.' He looked her in the eye. 'I looked at you, Lorelei, and all I saw was a fragile girl who'd run up debts and was living like there was no tomorrow.'

'C'est vrai,' she said softly. It was true. She had been.

'I knew you'd been through the wringer with that trial and all the nasty publicity, and I thought if I put you in the public eye it would be as if I'd turned a hunter's spotlight on you. All the stuff about your father would come out. For all those reasons I couldn't do it to you. I thought I'd break you. Just like I broke Jack.'

Lorelei shook her head.

'Then I saw you at the equestrian centre and I knew I'd got it wrong.'

She waited.

'All my life people have put my success down to natural gifts, and, yeah, I've got some talent. But I've worked damn hard to get where I am. When you told me about your accident I knew we were alike. I understood you'd worked hard at your sport. I assumed you'd given it up. But when I saw you'd turned your dream into something better—something outward, for other people—I recognised what I already knew. You're a special woman, Lorelei St James. Then I did some phoning around. Why in the hell didn't you tell me those debts were your father's legal fees?'

Lorelei swallowed. 'I didn't tell anyone. I was ashamed.'

'You should be bloody proud. Your father is a lucky man. I kept telling myself you were like Jack—I'd overwhelm you, wreck your life—but the truth is you're strong. You're the strongest person I've ever met. Stronger than me. You overwhelm me.'

Stunned by this outpouring, Lorelei didn't know what to say. Nash, who never said more than he had to, hadn't stopped talking, and he was calling her special and strong and all the things she'd always wanted to be to someone but somehow never had been.

But all of this praise, all of this putting her on a pedestal, frightened her.

'Please don't turn me into a trophy. I'm flesh and blood—prone to mistakes, to overreacting…'

'No.' He shook his head vigorously, taking hold of her. 'No, I've never seen you as a trophy, Lorelei. I only said that because I didn't want it to be any different than what I'd known before. But it already was. From the moment we met. And that passion of yours—I never want you to lose it.'

'You broke our date!' She knew it was a small thing, but suddenly it assumed the huge dimensions it had always held inside her head and heart. Because she hadn't completely trusted him after that, and when he'd let her down she'd been half expecting it.

She needed to know why.

'Call it a last-ditch attempt to throw myself across the track. I knew even then I would love you to distraction. That night when I was coming out of that bar, and you were going in, I was on my way to see you.'

He loved her *to distraction?*

'You were?' Lorelei felt a rush of warmth dispelling the last of the coldness that had been dwelling within her these last two days. 'I wish you'd told me. I wish this had all been different….'

'It *is* different. God, Lorelei, I can't lose you. Nothing matters to me if you're not there to share it with me. It was never so clear to me as it was today. That race—I was numb. And then I saw you, and suddenly it was clear as light.'

Her heart thrummed and started beating to a slower, truer beat.

'You were right—what you said that night in Mauritius. The racing was never the point, I was empty, and I found you, and the emptiness went away. I knew I loved you. Deep down I knew it. Every which way I tried to figure it, I kept coming back to this selfish need I had to keep you with me. I kept telling myself you wouldn't cope, but it was *me*.'

He lowered his voice. 'I was so afraid of building a life around you and you walking away. I wasn't prepared to risk it.'

Lorelei laid her hand over his heart.

'All I want is to love you,' she said softly, sincerely. 'If you'll let me.'

He caught her up fiercely in his arms and for a long time just held on to her. Lorelei thought about the little boy who had craved love, the man he had grown into who had avoided it and its painful associations, and the man standing before her now, holding her so tightly, as if she were as vital to him as the blood in his veins, the air he breathed.

As he was to her.

He loved her for who she was, not who he wanted her to be.

It was a miracle.

Suddenly sobbing for breath, she framed his face tightly with her hands. 'Wherever you go, wherever you are, that's where I'll be. I won't leave you, I won't betray you and I won't stop loving you.'

Nash wrapped her in his arms and kissed her. She could feel him shaking slightly, feel the groundswell of feeling behind the sensual motion of his mouth against hers.

He rested his temple on hers.

'Just let me love you,' he said simply, his deep voice shaking with the force of his emotion.

'Ah, oui,' she whispered. 'I can do that, too.'

It was on a rare sunbathed morning in April when Lorelei stepped out into the gardens of the villa.

A great deal had changed in these parts in six months. A ridiculous amount of money had been poured into restoring the Spanish villa to its original grandeur, and its gardens once more lay in variegated parterres. The fountains sprang to life as the bride joined her father at the top of the steps. Lorelei held one section of her long ivory skirts aloft as she laid her other hand in the crook of her father's arm.

'Are you certain, *ma chère?* Nothing is set in stone.'

Lorelei smiled. 'But it is, *Papa.* It was the moment I set eyes on him.'

Raymond sighed. 'I suspected as much. So it is *l'amour* and I gain a very rich son-in-law.'

Lorelei's laughter sang them down the steps. She paused only to pluck a spray of her grandmother's lavender and tuck it into Raymond's lapel.

He had been released from prison shortly before Christmas, and was living quietly in Fiesole with wife number five—an older Italian widow with far too much money and a very good accountant. Lorelei was fairly sure Raymond was safe from his own light-fingered proclivities.

Nash waited restlessly with a small congregation of friends and family on the lawn of the old villa. Beyond was the view of Monaco made famous the world over in a much-loved film and the blue curve of the Mediterranean sea.

For the first time in months he hadn't slept in their bed here at home. He'd been relegated to a suite at the Hotel de Paris, which held special memories for them both.

This morning he'd dressed in a cutaway coat and striped tie, and had had his shoes polished whilst his brother Jack ribbed him about those who stood tallest falling hardest. At ten o'clock he'd climbed into the vintage Bugatti and took off up the hill.

This was the most important date of his life, and after every stumbling block he'd faced getting her here the sight of Lorelei coming towards him beneath a fine veil of valenciennes lace almost overwhelmed him.

Nash felt Jack's hand grip his arm briefly.

He nodded and blew out a deep breath.

He reached out his hand as Lorelei approached and she took it. Her fingers were trembling, but his were sure.

The officiant took them through the vows, pronounced them man and wife, and as he took Lorelei in his arms he knew exactly what all the fuss was about.

'Why, Nash, you're trembling,' she said with a little smile just for him.

'Just wait until I get you alone, Mrs Blue,' he replied.

'I can hardly wait,' she whispered.

Nash grinned. Yeah, that was one way of putting it.

And that was when the kissing started.

* * * * *

PROJECT: RUNAWAY HEIRESS

BY
HEIDI BETTS

An avid romance reader since junior high, *USA TODAY* bestselling author **Heidi Betts** knew early on that she wanted to write these wonderful stories of love and adventure. It wasn't until her freshman year of college, however, when she spent the entire night before finals reading a romance novel instead of studying, that she decided to take the road less traveled and follow her dream.

Soon after Heidi joined Romance Writers of America, her writing began to garner attention, including placing in the esteemed Golden Heart competition three years in a row. The recipient of numerous awards and stellar reviews, Heidi's books combine believable characters with compelling plotlines, and are consistently described as "delightful," "sizzling" and "wonderfully witty."

For news, fun and information about upcoming books, be sure to visit Heidi online at www.HeidiBetts.com.

A huge American thank you
to UK reader Amanda Jane Ward, who read much of this story and troubleshot details for me all the way to the end to help ensure that my British hero came across as authentic and, well, you know. . .British.

Any mistakes are my own—
due entirely, I'm sure, to the fact that Jason Statham still refuses to accept my phone calls.

Thank you, Manda! If I couldn't use Jason for my research, you were definitely the next best thing. ;)

One

Impossible. This was impossible.

Lily Zaccaro maximized her browser window, leaning in even more closely to study the photo on her laptop screen. With angry taps at the keyboard, she minimized that window and opened another.

Dammit.

Screen after screen, window after window, her blood pressure continued to climb.

More angry keystrokes set the printer kicking out each and every picture. Or as she was starting to think of them: The Evidence.

Pulling the full-color photos from the paper tray, she carried them to one of the long, wide, currently empty cutting tables and laid them out side by side, row by row.

Inside her chest, her heart was pounding as though she'd just run a seven-minute mile. Right there, before her very eyes, was proof that someone was stealing her designs.

How had this happened?

She tapped her foot in agitation, twisted the oversize dinner ring on her right middle finger, even rubbed her eyes and blinked before studying the pictures again.

The fabric choices were different, of course, as were some of the lines and cuts, making them just distinctive enough not to be carbon copies. But there was no mistaking *her* original sketches in the competing designs.

To reassure herself she wasn't imagining things or going completely crazy, Lily moved to one of the hip-high file cabinet drawers where she kept all of her records and design sketches. Old, new, implemented and scratched. Riffling through them, she found the portfolio she was looking for, dragged it out and carried it back to the table.

One after another, she drew out the sketches she'd been working on last spring. The very ones they'd been prepared to work with, manufacture and put out for the following fall's line.

After a short game of mix-and-match, she had each sketch placed beside its counterpart from her rival. The similarities made her ill, almost literally sick to her stomach.

She leaned against the edge of the table while the images swam in front of her eyes, sending a dizzying array of colors and charcoal lines into the mix of emotions that were already leaving her light-headed and nauseated.

How could this happen? she wondered again. How could this possibly have happened?

Wracking her brain, she tried to think of who else might have seen her sketches while she was working. How many people had been in and out of this studio? There couldn't have been that many.

Zoe and Juliet, of course, but she trusted them with her life. She and her sisters shared this work space. The three of them rented the entire New York apartment building, using one of the lofts as a shared living space and the other as a work space for their company, Zaccaro Fashions.

Although there were times when they got on each other's nerves or their work schedules overlapped, their partnership was actually working out surprisingly well. And Lily showed her sisters all of her design ideas, sometimes even soliciting their opinions, the same as they shared their thoughts and sketches with her.

But neither of them—not even slightly flighty party girl, Zoe—would ever steal or sell her designs or betray her in any way. Of that, she was absolutely, one hundred percent certain.

So who else could it have been? They occasionally had others over to the studio, but not very often. Most times when they had business to conduct, they did it at Zaccaro Fashions, their official, public location in Manhattan's Fashion District, where they had more sewing machines set up, with employees to produce items on a larger, faster scale; offices for each of the sisters; and a small boutique set up out front. Something they hoped to expand upon very soon.

Of course, *that* particular dream would be nearly impossible to realize if their creations continued to get stolen and put on the market before they could release them.

She collected all of the papers from the cutting table, being sure to keep each of the printed pictures with its corresponding sketch. Then she began to pace, worrying a thumbnail between her teeth and wearing out the soles of her one-of-a-kind Zoe-designed pumps while she wondered what to do next.

What *could* she do?

If she had any idea who was responsible for this, then she might know what to do. Bludgeoning them with a sharp object or having them drawn and quartered in the middle of Times Square sounded infinitely satisfying. But even going to the police would work for her, as long as the theft and replication of her clothes stopped, and the culprit was punished or fired or chased out of town by a mob of angry fashion designers wielding very sharp scissors.

Without a clue of who was behind this, though, she didn't even know where to begin. Wasn't sure she had any options at all.

Her sisters might have some suggestions, but she *so* didn't want to involve them in this.

She'd been the one to go to design school, then ask their parents for a loan to start her own business. Because—even though they were quite wealthy and had offered to simply *give* her the money, since she was already in line for a substantial inheritance—she'd wanted to do this herself, to build something rather than having it handed to her.

She'd been the one to come to New York and struggle to make a name for herself, Zoe and Juliet following along later. Zoe had been interested in the New York party scene more than anything else, and Juliet had quit her job as a moderately successful, fledgling real-estate agent back in Connecticut to join Lily's company.

Without a doubt, they had both added exponentially to Zaccaro Fashions. Lily's clothing designs were fabulous, of course, but Zoe's shoes and Juliet's handbags and accessories were what truly made the Zaccaro label a well-rounded and successful collection.

Accessories like that tended to be where the most money was made, too. Women loved to find not only a new outfit, but all the bells and whistles to go with it. The fact that they could walk into Zaccaro Fashions and walk back out with everything necessary to dress themselves up from head to toe in a single shopping bag was what had customers coming back time and time again. And recommending the store to their friends. Thank God.

But it wasn't her sisters' designs being ripped off, her sisters' stakes in the business being threatened, and she didn't want them to worry—about her or the security of their own futures.

No, she needed to handle this on her own. At least until she had a better idea of what was going on.

Returning to the laptop, she hopped up on the nearest stool and straightened her skirt, tucking her feet beneath her on one of the lower rungs. Her fingers hesitated over the keys, then she just started tapping, not sure she was doing the right thing, but deciding to follow her gut.

Two minutes later, she had the phone number of a corporate-investigation firm uptown, and five minutes after that, she had an appointment for the following week with their top investigator. She wasn't certain yet *exactly* what she would ask him to do, but once he heard her dilemma, maybe he would have some ideas.

Then she continued searching online, deciding to dig up everything she could on her newest, scheming rival, Ashdown Abbey.

The London-based clothing company had been founded more than a hundred years ago by Arthur Statham. Their fashions ranged from sportswear to business attire and had been featured in any number of magazines, from *Seventeen* to *Vogue*. They owned fifty stores worldwide, earning over ten million dollars in revenue annually.

So why in heaven's name would they need to steal ideas from her?

Zaccaro Fashions was still in its infancy, earning barely enough to cover the overhead, make monthly payments to Lily's parents toward the loan and allow Juliet, Zoe and herself to continue living comfortably in the loft and working in the adjoining studio. Ashdown Abbey might as well have been the Hope Diamond sitting beside a chunk of cubic zirconium in comparison.

The hijacked fashions in question had originated from

Ashdown Abbey's Los Angeles branch, so she dug a little deeper into that particular division. According to the company's website, it was run by Nigel Statham, CEO and direct descendant of Arthur Statham himself.

But the Los Angeles offices had only been open for a year and a half and were apparently working somewhat independently of the rest of the British company, putting out a couple of exclusive lines and holding their own runway shows geared more toward an American—and specifically Hollywood—customer base.

Which meant it wasn't all of Ashdown Abbey out to ruin Lily's life, just the Los Angeles faction.

Lily narrowed her eyes, leaning closer to the laptop screen and focusing on a photo of Nigel Statham. Public Enemy Number One.

He was a good-looking man, she'd give him that much. Grudgingly. Short, light brown hair with a bit of curl at the ends. High cheekbones and a strong jaw. Lips that were full, but not too full. And eyes that looked to be a deep shade of green, though that was difficult to tell from a picture on the internet.

She wanted to despise him on sight, but in one photo, he was smiling. A sexy, charming smile that went all the way to his eyes and threatened to turn her knees to jelly.

Of course, she was sitting and she was made of sterner stuff than that, so *that* wasn't going to happen. But at first glance, she certainly wouldn't have pegged him as a thief.

She continued to scroll through pictures and articles and company information, but much of it was for the U.K. division and the other European stores. The Los Angeles branch still seemed to be finding its footing and working to establish itself as a British clothing company on American soil.

Deciding there wasn't much more she could do until she met with the investigator except seethe in silence, Lily began to close up shop. She checked her watch. She was supposed to meet her sisters for dinner in twenty minutes, anyway.

But as she was shutting down browser windows, something caught her eye. A page filled with "job opportunities at Ashdown Abbey—U.S.A." She'd been perusing the list just to get a better idea of how the company operated.

Now, though, she expanded the window, clicked on the link for "more information" and hit Print.

It was crazy, what she was suddenly thinking. Worse yet that she was contemplating actually going through with it.

Her sisters would try to talk her out of it for sure, if she even mentioned the possibility. The investigator would undoubtedly warn her against it, then likely try to convince her to let *him* handle it at—what?—one hundred…two hundred and fifty…five hundred dollars an hour.

It would be so much easier for her to slip in and poke around herself. She knew the design world inside and out, so she would certainly fit in. And if she made herself sound smart and qualified enough, surely she would be a shoo-in.

A tiny shiver of anxiety rolled down her spine. Okay, so it was dangerous. A lot could go wrong, and she probably stood to get herself into a heap of trouble if anyone—or the *wrong* someone, at any rate—found out.

But it was too good an opportunity to pass up. Almost as though she was meant to go through with this, fate bending its bony finger to point the way. Otherwise, what were the chances *this* particular position would open up just when she most needed the inside scoop on Ashdown Abbey?

No, she had to do this. She had to find out what was going on, *how* it had happened and get it to stop. And going to work for Ashdown Abbey seemed like a good way to do exactly that.

Not just good—perfect.

Because Nigel Statham needed a personal assistant, and she was just the right woman for the job.

Two

Nigel Statham muttered an unflattering curse, slapping the company's quarterly financial report down on top of his father's latest missive. The one that made him feel like a child in short trousers being scolded for some minor transgression or another.

Handwritten on personal stationery and posted all the way from England—because that's how his parents had always done it, and email was too commonplace for their refined breeding—the letter outlined the U.S. division's disappointing returns and Nigel's failure to make it yet another jewel in the Ashdown Abbey crown since he'd been appointed CEO eighteen months ago.

Disappointment clung to the words as though his father was standing in the room, delivering them face-to-face: hands behind his back, bushy white brows drawn down in a frown of displeasure. Just like when he'd been a boy.

His parents had always expected perfection—an aim he

had fallen short of time and time again. But he hardly thought a year and a half was long enough to ascertain the success or failure of a new branch of the business in an entirely new country when it had taken nearly a century for Ashdown Abbey to reach its current level of success in the U.K. alone.

He thought perhaps his father's expectations for this new venture had been set a bit too high. But try telling the senior Statham that.

With a sigh, Nigel leaned back and wondered how long he could put off responding to the letter before his father sent a second. Or worse yet, decided to fly all the way to Los Angeles to check in on his son in person.

Another day, certainly. Especially since he was currently dreading the job of training a brand-new personal assistant.

He'd been through three so far. Three attractive but very young ladies who had been competent enough but hardly dedicated.

The problem with hiring personal assistants in the heart of Los Angeles, he decided, was that they tended to be either aspiring actresses who grew bored easily or quit as soon as they landed a part in a hand-lotion commercial; or they were aspiring fashion designers who grew bored when they didn't make it to the top with their own line in under six months.

And each time one of them moved on, he had to start all over training a new girl. It was enough to make him consider hiring an assistant to be on hand to train his next assistant.

Human resources had hired the latest in his stead, then sent him a memo with her name and a bit of background information, both personal and professional. It probably wasn't even worth remembering the woman's name, but then he'd never been *that* kind of boss.

Before he had the chance to review her résumé once more, there was a tap on his office door. Less than half a second later, it swung open and his new assistant—he deduced she was his new assistant, at any rate—strode across the carpeted floor.

She was prettier than her photo depicted. Her hair teetered somewhere between light brown and dark blond, pulled back in a loose but smoothly twisted bun at the back of her head. Her face was lightly made up, the lines classic and delicate, almost Romanesque.

A pair of dark-rimmed, oval-lensed glasses sat perched high on her nose. Small gold hoops graced her earlobes. She wore a simple white blouse tucked into the waistband of a black pencil skirt that hit midcalf, concealing three-quarters of what he suspected could prove to be extraordinary legs. And on her feet, a pair of patent-leather pumps, color-blocked in black and white with three-inch heels.

Being in fashion, he took note more than he might have otherwise. But as a man, there were certain aspects of her appearance he would have noticed regardless.

Like her alabaster skin or the way her breasts pressed against the front of her shirt. The bronze-kiss shade of her lips and rose-red tips of her perfectly manicured nails.

"Mr. Statham," she said in a voice that matched the rest of the package. "I'm Lillian, your new personal assistant. Here's your coffee and this morning's mail."

She set the steaming mug stamped with the Ashdown Abbey logo on the leather coaster on his desk. It looked as though she'd added a touch of cream, just the way he liked it.

She placed the pile of envelopes directly in front of him, and he flipped through, noticing that it seemed to be all business correspondence, no fluff to waste his time sorting out.

As first impressions went, she was making a rather positive one.

"Is there anything else I can get you?"

"No, thank you," he replied slowly.

With a nod, she turned on her heel and started back toward the door.

"Lillian." He stopped her just before she reached the doorway.

Spine straight, she returned her attention to him. "Yes, sir?"

"Are those Ashdown Abbey designs you're wearing?" he asked. "The blouse and skirt?"

She offered him a small smile. "Of course."

He considered that for a moment, almost afraid to believe that his luck in the personal-assistant department might actually be changing for the better.

Clearing his throat, he said carefully, "You wouldn't happen to be an actress, would you?" He resisted the urge to use the term *aspiring,* but only barely.

A slight frown drew her light brows together. "No, sir."

"What about modeling? Any interest in that?"

That question brought out a short chuckle. "Definitely not."

He thought back to some of the bullet points from her résumé. She hadn't simply wandered in from the street, that was for certain. Her background was in both business *and* design, with a degree in the former and a few very strong courses in the latter.

On paper she was rather ideal, but he knew as well as anyone that everybody became a bit of a fiction writer when it came to cooking up a résumé.

"And your interest in the fashion industry is..." He trailed off, leaving her to fill in the blank on her own.

For the blink of an eye, she seemed to consider what response he might be looking for. Then she replied in a firm tone, "Strictly business. And the opportunity to get my hands on fresh designs sooner than the rest of the world. I'm a bit of a clotheshorse, I'm afraid." She ended with a guileless half grin that brought out the tiniest hint of dimple in the center of her right cheek.

Almost in spite of himself, he caught his own lips turning upward. "Well, then, you've certainly come to the right place. Employees get a discount at our company store, you know."

"Yes, I know," she said slowly, and he could have sworn he saw a sparkle of devilment in her eye.

"Excellent," he murmured, feeling better about her employment already.

He hadn't exactly seen her in action, but she had, as they say, passed the first hurdle. At the very least, she hadn't walked in with a wide smile and an IQ equal to her age.

"If you haven't already, please familiarize yourself with my daily schedule and appointments for the week. There may be a few meetings and events to which I'll need you to accompany me, so watch for those notations. And be sure to review the schedule frequently, as I tend to change or update it regularly and without warning."

Picking up his coffee, he took a sip, surprised to find it quite tasty. Almost the exact ratio of cream to coffee that he preferred.

"Yes, sir. Not a problem."

"Thank you. That will be all for now," he told her.

Once again, she turned for the door. And once again, he stopped her just before she stepped out of his office.

"Oh, and, Lillian?"

"Yes, sir?" she intoned, tipping her head in his direction.

"Excellent coffee. I hope you can make an equally satisfying cup of tea."

"I'll certainly try."

With that, she closed the door behind her, leaving Nigel with a strangely unexpected smile on his face.

As soon as the door to Nigel Statham's stately, expansive office clicked shut and she was alone—blessedly, blissfully alone—Lily rushed on weak legs to the plush office chair behind her large, executive secretary's desk and dropped into it like a sack of lead.

She was shaking from head to toe, her heart both racing and pounding at the same time. It felt as though an angry gorilla was trapped inside her chest, rattling her rib cage to get out.

And her stomach…her stomach was pitching and rolling so badly, she thought she must surely know how it felt to be on a ship that was going down in a storm-tossed sea. If she *didn't* lose her quickly scarfed-down breakfast in the next ten seconds, it would be a miracle.

To keep that from happening, she leaned forward, tucking her head over her knees. Over them, because it was nearly impossible to get between them in the slim, tailored skirt she'd chosen for her first day of working undercover and with a false identity.

Lillian. *Blech.* It was the best name she'd been able to come up with that she thought she would answer to naturally, the blending of her first and middle names—Lily and Ann.

And as a last name, she'd gone with something simple and also easily identifiable, at least to her. George—what she and her sisters had called their first pet. A lazy, good-natured basset hound their father had found wandering around the parking lot where he worked.

Her mother had been furious right up until the moment she'd realized George woofed at the top of his lungs the minute anyone stepped foot on their property. From that point on, he'd been her "very best guard dog" and had gotten his own place setting of people food on the floor beside the dining-room table whenever they sat down to eat.

So Lillian George it was. Even though being referred to as Lillian made her feel like a matronly, middle-aged librarian.

Then again, she sort of looked like a librarian.

Her usual style, and definitely her own designs, leaned very strongly toward the bright, bold and carefree. She loved color and prints, anything vibrant and flirty and fun.

But for her position at Ashdown Abbey, she'd needed to be much more prim and proper. Not to mention doing as much as she could to disguise her identity and avoid being recognized or linked in any way to Zaccaro Fashions.

She could only hope that the change of name and switch to a wardrobe drawn entirely from Ashdown Abbey's own line of business attire, coupled with the glasses and darkening of her normally light blond hair would be enough to keep anyone at the company from figuring out who she really was.

It helped, too, that Zaccaro Fashions was only moderately successful. She and her sisters weren't exactly media darlings. They'd been photographed here or there, appeared in magazines or society pages upon occasion, but mostly in relation to their father and their family's monetary worth. But she would be surprised if most people—even those familiar with the industry—would recognize any one of them if they passed on the street. Although Zoe was doing her level best to change that by going out on the town and getting caught behaving badly on a more and more regular basis.

After a couple of minutes, Lily's pulse, the spinning of her head and the lurching in her stomach all began to slow. She'd made it this far. She'd made it past human resources with her creatively worded but fairly accurate résumé and her apparently not-so-rusty-after-all interview skills. Then she'd stood in front of corporate CEO Nigel Statham himself without being found out or dragged away in handcuffs.

He also hadn't followed her out of his office, shaking a finger at her deceit, or instructed security to meet her at her desk. Everything was quiet, calm, completely normal, as far as she could tell.

Ashdown Abbey certainly didn't have the hum of voices

and sewing machines in the background the way the Zaccaro Fashions offices did. But, then, Zaccaro Fashions wasn't a major, multimillion-dollar operation the way Ashdown Abbey was, either. They hadn't yet reached the point where their corporate offices and manufacturing area were two separate entities.

Frankly, Lily thought she could use the mechanical buzz of a sewing machine or her sisters' laughter as she worked with her cell phone pressed to her ear right about now. Sometimes silence was entirely overrated. Times like these, when all she could hear was her own rapid breathing and the panicked voices in her head telling her she was crazy and sure to get caught.

To keep those voices from getting any louder and leading her in the wrong direction, she started to recite one of the simple, meaningless poems she'd been forced to memorize in grade school, then slowly sat up.

Tiny stars flashed in front of her eyes, but only for a second. She blinked and they were gone, leaving her with clear vision and a clear—or clearer, anyway—head.

Nigel Statham believed she was his new personal assistant, so maybe she should go back to acting like one.

Rolling her chair up to the desk, she pulled out her computer's keyboard and mouse, and started clicking away. She'd familiarized herself with the computer's operating system just a bit before going into Nigel's office, but was sure there was much more to learn.

His daily schedule, for instance. Something she was apparently going to have to stay on top of or risk not knowing what she was supposed to be doing from one hour to the next.

She felt a small stab of guilt as she bypassed the email program, wondering if her sisters had found her note yet and honored her wishes by *not* telling anyone about her sudden disappearance or trying to track her down themselves.

She'd told them she had some personal business to attend to. Something she couldn't discuss just yet, but needed some time away to deal with. She assured them she would be fine and wasn't in any danger, and asked them to trust her to get in touch as soon as she could.

She didn't want them to worry about her, but she wasn't ready to tell them what was really going on, either. One day… one day she would fill them in on everything. She would tell them the entire story over a bottle of wine, and chances were they would have a good laugh about it.

But not until it was resolved and there was a happily-ever-after to report. When the threat to their company was gone and there were no fears or rumors left to spread like wildfire if anyone else got wind of it.

Before she left, she'd also met with Reid McCormack of McCormack Investigations about running comprehensive background checks on everyone under Zaccaro Fashions' employ. Lily honestly didn't believe he would find anything incriminating, but better safe than sorry.

And she'd informed him that she would be out of town for a while, so she would call in weekly for updates. It seemed easier than having him leave messages at the apartment, where her sisters might overhear or access them, or having him call her on her cell phone at an inconvenient moment while she was still in Los Angeles.

Frankly, she hoped he never had anything negative to report, or that if he did, it would turn out to be completely unrelated to Zaccaro Fashions—an employee with an unpaid speeding ticket or college-age drunk-and-disorderly charges that had eventually been dropped.

But until her first scheduled check-in, she needed all of her energy and brain power focused on her new job and attempts at stealth investigations.

Studying Nigel's schedule for the day, she was somewhat

relieved to see that it didn't seem to be a—quote, unquote—*heavy* day for him. It looked as though he would be in his office most of the time. He had a lunch appointment and a conference call in the afternoon, but nothing so far that would require her to go out with him—and hope not to be recognized or to do something she wasn't ready or properly trained for.

She glanced at the schedule for the rest of the week, making a mental note to check again in a couple of hours. Just to be safe until it all became second nature to her for as long as she was here.

She took a few minutes to investigate some of the other programs and files on the system, but hoped she wouldn't be expected to do too much with them too soon. Either that, or that the company provided tutorials for the seriously lost and computer illiterate.

What she did understand, though, was design. She knew the vocabulary, the process and what was needed to go from point A to point B. So she did recognize and know how to use some of the items already installed on the PA's computer.

The question was: Could she use them to access the information she needed to track down the design thief?

Maybe yes, maybe no. It depended on whether or not Nigel knew about the thefts.

Was he involved? she wondered.

Had he sent a mole from Ashdown Abbey into her company? Or maybe on a less despicable level, had he recognized her designs within his company's latest collection and ignored them? Looked the other way because it was easier and could advance Ashdown Abbey's sales and brand recognition?

A part of her hoped not. She didn't want to think that there were business executives out there who would stoop to such levels just to get ahead. Not when they had a bevy of talented designers on staff already and didn't *need* to stoop to those levels. Or that someone so handsome, with that deep, toe-curling British accent, could be capable of something so heinous. Although more attractive people had been guilty of much worse, she was sure.

It happened every day, and she wasn't naive enough to believe that just because a man was sinfully attractive and already a millionaire he wouldn't steal from someone else to make another million or two.

Not that any of her designs had earned a million dollars yet, Lily thought wryly, but the potential was there. If she could keep other companies and designers from scooping her.

Tapping a few keys, she brought up what she could find on the California Collection—the Ashdown Abbey collection that included so many of her own works, only with minor detail alterations and in entirely different textiles. Just the thought sent her blood pressure climbing all over again.

A few clicks of the mouse and the entire portfolio was on the screen in front of her, scrolling in a slow left-to-right slideshow. The flowy, lightweight summer looks were lovely. Not as beautiful as *Lily's* designs would have been, if she'd had the chance to release them, of course, but they were quite impressive.

She studied each one for as long as she could, taking in the cuts and lines. The collection mostly consisted of dresses, perfect for California's year-round sunny and warm weather. Short one-pieces, a couple of maxi dresses, and even some two-piece garments consisting of a top and skirt or a top and linen slacks.

Not all of them were drawn directly from Lily's proposed sketches. Small comfort. And it might actually work against her if she ever tried to prove larceny in a court of law.

A good defense attorney could argue that there might be *similarities* between the Ashdown Abbey and Zaccaro Fashions designs, but since the Ashdown Abbey line also included designs *without* similarities, it was obviously a mere case of creative serendipity.

Hmph.

Closing down the slideshow, Lily dug around in the other documents within the file folder. She found another graphics slideshow, this time the sketches for the final pieces that made up the California Collection.

They were full color and digital, done on one of the many art and design computer programs that were becoming more and more popular. Even Lily had one of them on her tablet, but she still preferred pencil and paper, charcoal and a sketch pad, and actual fabric swatches pinned to her hand-drawn designs over filling in small squares of space with predetermined colors or material samples on a digitized screen.

But what caught her attention with these designs wasn't *how* they were done, it was the fact that they were signed. Ashdown Abbey apparently had design teams on the payroll rather than one designer in charge of his or her own collection.

Moving from the graphics files to the text files, she found a list of the California Collection's entire design team, complete with job titles and past projects they'd worked on for Ashdown Abbey. A jolt of adrenaline zipped through her, and she hurried to send the list to the printer.

The zip-zip of the machine filled the quiet of the cavernous outer office. It rang all the louder in her ears for the fact that she didn't want to get caught.

When a buzz interrupted the sound of the printer, Lily jumped. Then she looked around, searching for the source of the noise. Finally, she realized it was coming from the phone, one of the lights on the multiline panel blinking in time with the call of the intercom.

Chest tight, she took a deep breath and pressed the button for Nigel Statham's direct line.

"Yes, sir?" she answered.

"Could I see you for a moment?"

The abrupt request was followed by total silence, and she realized he'd hung up without waiting for a reply.

Grabbing the list of designers from the printer tray, she folded it over and over into a small square and stuffed it into the front pocket of her skirt. Patting the spot to make sure it was well concealed, she strode to the door of Nigel's office, unsure of what she would encounter on the other side. She didn't even know if she should bring a pad and pencil with her to take notes.

What did personal assistants automatically pick up when summoned by the boss? Paper and pen? A more modern electronic tablet? She hadn't even had a chance to poke around and find out what was provided for Nigel Statham's executive secretary.

So she walked in empty-handed after giving one quick tap on the door to announce her arrival.

Nigel turned from typing something into his own computer to jot a note on the papers in front of him before lifting his attention to Lily. She stood just behind one of the guest chairs, awaiting his every request.

"What are you doing for dinner this evening?" he asked.

The question was so far from anything she might have expected him to say, her mind went blank. She was quite sure her face did, too.

"I'll take that to mean you don't have plans," he remarked.

When she still didn't respond, he continued, "I'm having dinner with a potential designer and thought you might like to join us. Having you there will help to keep things on a business track, as well as better familiarize you with your position."

For lack of anything more inspired to say, she replied with a simple, "All right."

Nigel gave an almost imperceptible nod. "I'll be leaving

from the office, but you're welcome to go home and change, or take a bit of a rest, if you like. I'll come round for you at eight. Be sure to leave your address before you finish for the day."

He returned his attention to his work, giving Lily the impression that plans for the evening had been decided and she'd been dismissed.

"Yes, sir," she said, because she thought it was respectful and some sort of acquiescence was needed. Then she tacked on a short "Thank you" for good measure before hurrying back out to the reception area.

Taking a seat behind her desk, she tried to decide how she felt about this latest turn of events.

On the one hand, she already had a list of designers for the Ashdown Abbey collection based on her work. She considered that quite a coup for her first day in the enemy's camp.

On the other, her most fervent prayer had been merely to get through the day without being found out. She'd never imagined she would be asked to put in extra time outside the office. Especially not *alone* with the boss.

Of course, she wouldn't really be *alone* with him. It was a business dinner, so at least one other person would be there. But it was still an after-hours situation in much-too-close proximity to the man who held her future in his hands.

Her professional future and possibly her very freedom.

Because if he ever learned who she really was and why she was working incognito within his company, she'd likely find herself behind bars. No amount of crying "he was mean to me first" would save her then.

Three

At five minutes to eight, Lily was still racing around her apartment, trying to be ready before Nigel arrived.

It didn't help that she'd just moved in and had brought very little with her from New York. Or that this was supposed to be merely a place to sleep. Nothing fancy. Nothing expensive—at least by Los Angeles standards. Simply somewhere to rest and hunker down with her suspicions and evidence while she worked days at Ashdown Abbey.

Never had she imagined that her boss—CEO of the entire company—would decide to "drop by" and pick her up for dinner.

And then there was the fact that she hadn't planned for after-hours job requirements. Once she'd arrived, she'd filled her closet with Ashdown Abbey business attire, not only to fit in, but to subconsciously give Nigel Statham and everyone else the impression that she absolutely belonged there. But she hadn't purchased a single item for an evening out.

Granted, she could probably get away with wearing the same skirt and blouse that she'd worn that day. If she was attending this meal as Nigel's personal assistant, then it couldn't hurt for her to look like one.

But she suspected Nigel's choice of restaurant might be of the highly upscale variety, and she didn't want to stand out. Or worse, blend in with the servers.

So she'd done the best she could with what her limited current wardrobe had to offer.

Another black skirt, shorter this time, with a sexy—but not too sexy—slit up the back. A sheer, nearly diaphanous sapphire-blue blouse that she'd intended to wear as a shell over a more modest chemise top. Now, though, she wore it over only a bra.

She'd checked and double-checked in the mirror to be sure the effect wasn't trashy. Thankfully, the bra was barely visible, even though in certain light, flashes of skin could be seen beneath the top.

To dazzle it up even more, she added sparkling chandelier earrings, a matching *Y* necklace, and open-toed four-inch heels that—now that she was wearing them—might be a bit too suggestive for nine-to-five. They were more than appropriate for a night out on the town, though, professional or otherwise.

She threw a few items like her wallet, a lipstick, keys and her cell phone—just in case—in a small, plain-black clutch, and *finally* thought she was ready enough to jump when Nigel arrived.

She'd just taken a deep, stabilizing breath and was contemplating one last visit to the restroom when the doorbell rang.

Whatever calm she'd managed to find with that long inhalation evaporated at the shrill, mechanical sound, and a lump of dread began to grow in the pit of her stomach.

Fingers curled around her purse, she swallowed hard and

moved to the door. Because she didn't want Nigel peeking inside and seeing that there were no personal touches to the apartment to affirm her claims of having lived in the city for several years, she opened it only a crack, using her body to block his view.

As quickly and smoothly as she could, she slipped out into the hallway, pulling the door closed and locked behind her. Leaning back, she used the doorjamb to prop herself up, feeling suddenly overwhelmed and overly scrutinized.

Nigel's hazel eyes studied her from head to toe. He was standing so close, she could see the specks of green dotting his irises and smell his spicy-with-a-hint-of-citrus cologne.

She inhaled, drawing the scent deeper into her lungs, then realized what she was doing and stopped, holding her breath in hopes that he wouldn't notice her small indiscretion.

It was not a good idea to start thinking her boss smelled good. She already found him attractive, simply because he was. Anyone, female or male, would have to agree based on his physical attributes alone. Much the way everyone knew the sky was blue, a handsome man was a handsome man.

That didn't mean she should be building on that initial assessment by adding "smells really good" to the tally.

He was a good-looking man with exceptional taste in cologne, that's all. Lily hoped that others might consider her on the pretty side with good taste in perfume, as well. Especially after how much time she'd put into her appearance tonight.

Nigel—her boss, her attractive and well-scented *boss*—returned his gaze to her face.

"You look lovely," he commented. "Ready to go?"

"Yes."

To her surprise, he offered his arm. There was nothing romantic in the gesture, only politeness. After a short hesitation, she slipped her hand around his elbow and let him lead her down the well-lit, utilitarian hallway of the apartment building.

Would an American man have acted so gentlemanly, or was it just Nigel's British upbringing? Whatever the case, she liked it. Maybe a little too much.

They walked down the three short flights of stairs rather than waiting for the elevator. Outside, the early evening air was fresh and cool, but not cold. A long, silver Bentley Mulsanne waited at the curb, and Nigel opened the rear door, holding it while she got in.

She'd intended to slide across so he could climb in behind her, but there was a rather large console turned down between the two rear seats, as well as fold-out trays on the back of the front seats. The one on his side was down, with an open laptop resting on it.

While she was still marveling at the awesome interior of the luxury vehicle, Nigel opened the door opposite hers and took his place, quickly closing the computer and tray.

"Sorry about that," he said, moving the laptop out of the way on the floor beside his briefcase.

When she didn't respond—she was apparently sitting there frozen, like a raccoon caught rummaging through household garbage—he returned the center console to its upright position, then leaned past her to pluck the seat belt, stretch it across her motionless form and click it into place.

As he stretched to reach, his arm brushed her waist, terribly close to the underside of her breasts. A shiver of something very un-employee-like skated through her, warming places that had no business growing warm. She swallowed and tried to remain very still until the sensation passed.

Nigel, of course, had no idea of the response he'd caused by such an innocent action. And with luck, he never would.

Licking her lips, she tamped down on whatever was rolling around under her skin and made sure her lips were turned up in at least an imitation of a smile.

"Thank you," she said, tugging at the safety belt to show that she was, indeed, alive and well and capable of simple human functions. "It looks like you're working overtime," she added, relieved that her voice continued to sound steady and normal.

He leaned back in the seat, running his hands along his thighs and letting out a breath as he relaxed a fraction. "There doesn't seem to be overtime with this position. It's round-the-clock."

Lily certainly knew what he meant by that. She'd worked twenty-four/seven to establish the Zaccaro label. Then when her sisters had joined in, the three of them had given all they had to get the company truly up and running.

Even now that they had their boutique open and were producing items on more than a one-off basis, life was no less stressful or busy. They'd simply exchanged one set of problems for another. And having an office-slash-studio at home only kept the work closer at hand.

"For tonight's dinner," Nigel began in that accent that would be charming even if the looks and personality didn't match—at least to her unaccustomed American ears, "we're meeting with a designer who's looking to move from Vincenze to a higher position at Ashdown Abbey."

Lily's eyes widened a second before she schooled her expression. Vincenze was a huge, multimillion-dollar design enterprise. A household name and very big deal. If she wasn't busy running her own fashion-design business, she would have been ecstatic over the possibility of going to work for them.

Yet tonight they were meeting with someone who wanted to *leave* Vincenze for Ashdown Abbey.

Which wasn't to say Ashdown Abbey was a lesser label.

Far from it. If anything, Ashdown Abbey and Vincenze were similar when it came to levels of success. But their design aesthetics were entirely different, and it would definitely take some doing—at least in her experience—for a designer to go from one to the other without traversing a sharp learning curve.

Fighting to keep her mind on the job she was *supposed* to be doing rather than the one that came more naturally to her, Lily said, "I'm not sure exactly what my role is this evening."

"Just listen," he replied casually. "It will be a good way for you to learn the ropes, so to speak."

He turned a little more in her direction and offered a warm smile. "Frankly, I asked you to join me so I wouldn't have to be alone with this fellow. These so-called business dinners can sometimes drone on, especially if the potential employee attempts to regale me with a long list of his or her talents and abilities."

Lily returned his grin. She knew what he meant; the fashion industry was filled with big mouths and bigger egos. She liked to think she wasn't one of them, but there was a certain amount of self-aggrandizing required to promote oneself and one's line.

"Maybe we should work out a signal and some prearranged topics of discussion," she offered. "That way if things get out of hand and your eyes begin to glaze over, you can give me a sign and I'll launch into a speech about global warming or some such."

Nigel's smile widened, showing a row of straight, sparkling-white teeth. "Global warming?" he asked, the amusement evident in his tone.

"It's a very important issue," she said, adopting a prim-and-proper expression. "I'm sure I could fill a good hour or two on the subject, if necessary."

He nodded a few times, very slowly and thoughtfully, his

lips twitching with suppressed humor. "That could certainly prove useful."

"I thought so," she agreed.

"What would you suggest we use as a signal?"

She thought about it for a minute. "You could tug at your earlobe," she said. "Or kick me under the table. Or perhaps we could have a code word."

"A code word," he repeated, one brow lifting with interest. "This is all starting to sound very...double-oh-seven-ish."

Appropriate, she supposed, since he reminded her a little of James Bond. It was the accent, she was sure. Her stomach tightened briefly.

Feigning a nonchalant attitude she didn't entirely feel, she shrugged. "Spies are good at what they do for a reason. But if you'd prefer to be trapped for hours by a potential employee you can't get away from, be my guest."

Silence filled the rear of the car, only the sound of the tires rotating beneath them audible as the seconds ticked by and Lily's anxiety grew.

She might have overstepped her bounds. After all, she'd only been in this man's employ for twelve hours. That might have been a bit too early to start voicing her opinions and telling him what to do.

Worse, she probably shouldn't have jumped on his mention of James Bond movies and followed the spy thread. Because technically, *she* was a spy within his organization, and she didn't want him spending too much time wondering how she knew so much about the business of espionage.

"I definitely agree that an escape plan is in order," Nigel said, finally breaking the nerve-inducing quiet. "How would it be if I inquired about your headache from earlier? You can say that it's come back and you'd really like to get home so you can rest."

"All right." It sounded as good as anything else they might

come up with, and she certainly knew more about headaches than she did about global warming.

"And if *you* grow bored," he continued, "you can ask me if I'd like another martini. I'll decline and say that we should get going, as I have an early appointment in the morning, anyway."

"Will you be drinking martinis?" she asked.

"Tonight, I will," he said, a spark of mischief lighting his eyes. "It will bolster our story, if we make an excuse to leave the restaurant early."

"We haven't even arrived at dinner yet, and already we're thinking of ways to get away as soon as we've finished eating," she remarked.

"That's because it's a boring, uptight business dinner. If this were a dinner date, I would already be considering options for drawing things out. Excuses to keep you there well past dessert."

Lily's heart skipped a beat, her palms growing damp even as a wave of unexpected heat washed over her. That was not the sort of thing she expected to hear from her boss. It didn't *feel* like a benign, employer-to-employee comment, either. It felt much too…suggestive.

And on top of that, she was suddenly picturing it: a dinner date with Nigel rather than a business dinner. Sitting across from him at a candlelit table for two. Leaning into each other as they spoke in soft tones. Flirting, teasing, building toward something much more serious and intimate.

The warmth grew, spreading through her body like a fever. And when she imagined him reaching out, touching her hand where it rested on the pristine white linen of the tablecloth, she nearly jumped, it seemed so real.

Thankfully, Nigel didn't notice because the car was slowing, and he was busy readjusting his tie and cuff links.

Lily licked her lips and smoothed her hands over her own

blouse and skirt, making sure she was as well put together as he was.

When the car came to a complete stop, he looked at her again and offered an encouraging half smile. "Ready?" he asked.

She nodded just as Nigel's door was opened from the outside. He stepped out, then turned and reached back for her.

Purse in hand, she slid across the wide seat and let Nigel take her arm as she stepped out. His driver nodded politely before closing the door and moving back around the hood of the car to the driver's seat.

Looking around, Lily realized they were standing outside of Trattoria. She wasn't from Los Angeles, but even she recognized the name of the elegant five-star restaurant. To her knowledge, the waiting list for reservations was three to four months long.

Unless, she supposed, you were someone like Nigel. The Statham name—and bank account—carried a lot of weight. Not only in L.A. or England, either, but likely anywhere in the world.

She was no stranger to fine dining, of course. She'd grown up at country clubs and taken international vacations with her parents. She even knew a few world-renowned master chefs and restaurateurs personally.

But she wasn't with her family now, and hadn't lived that way for several years; she'd been too busy working her fingers to the bone and building her own company the old-fashioned way.

She was also supposed to be from more of a blue-collar upbringing, not a secret, runaway heiress. Which meant she shouldn't be familiar with seven-course meals, real silverware or places like this, where appetizers started at fifty dollars a plate.

The good news was that she wouldn't embarrass herself

by not knowing which fork to use. The bad news was that she needed to act awed and out of her element enough not to draw suspicion. From anyone, but especially Nigel.

Passing beneath the dark green awning lined with sparkling lights, he led her past potted topiaries and through the wide French doors at the restaurant's entrance.

A tuxedoed maître d' met them immediately, and as soon as Nigel gave his name, they were led across the main dining area, weaving around tables filled with other well-dressed customers who were talking and laughing and seemed to be thoroughly enjoying their expensive meals.

At the rear of the restaurant, the maître d' paused, waving to a medium-size table set for four where another man was already seated.

Rounding the table, Nigel held a chair out for her while the other man rose. He was young—mid to late twenties, Lily would guess—with dark hair and an expensive suit. Most likely a Vincenze, even one of his own designs, since that's where he was currently working.

"Mr. Statham," the designer greeted Nigel, holding out his hand.

Nigel waited until she was seated to reach across the table and shake.

"Thank you for meeting with me."

Nigel inclined his head and introduced them. "Lillian, this is Harrison Klein. Mr. Klein, this is my assistant, Lillian George."

"Pleased to meet you," Harrison said, taking her hand next.

When they were all seated, a waiter brought leather-bound menus and took their drink orders. True to his word, Nigel ordered a dry martini. He even made a point of asking for it "shaken, not stirred," then turned to her with a humorous and entirely too distracting wink.

Soon after they placed the rest of their orders, their salads and entrées arrived, and they made general small talk while they ate. Nigel asked questions about Klein's schooling and experience and his time at Vincenze.

It was odd to be sitting at a table with another designer and the CEO of one of the biggest labels in the United Kingdom—and soon possibly the United States—without adding to the discussion. So many times, she had to bite her tongue to keep from asking questions of her own or inserting her two cents here and there into the conversation.

In order to avoid saying something she shouldn't, she stayed busy sipping her wine, toying with the stem of her glass, studying the lines of each of their outfits. Mentally she deconstructed them, laying out patterns, cutting material and sewing them back up.

Finally, they were finished with their meals and the table was cleared. Nigel declined the dessert menu for all of them, but asked for coffee.

And then he held out a hand to the other man. "Your portfolio?"

Harrison's Adam's apple bobbed as he swallowed nervously, but he leaned over and retrieved his portfolio from the floor beside his chair. He passed it to Nigel, then sat back and waited quietly.

Lily found her pulse kicking up just a fraction. This was such an important, nerve-racking moment for any designer. She still wondered why someone who already had a job at a successful design corporation would be interested in moving.

She had gone an entirely different route, striking out on her own to establish a personal label and company instead of taking a job elsewhere and working her way up the ladder.

In a lot of ways, that would have been easier. It might have taken her longer to form her own label and have her own storefront, but she certainly would have learned from the best and maybe avoided some of the pitfalls she'd encountered while barreling ahead with her one-woman—and then three-woman, thank goodness—show.

The tension at the table thickened as Nigel studied the portfolio carefully, page by page. Sitting beside him, Lily could see each design clearly, and couldn't resist drinking them in.

After several long minutes, Nigel closed the portfolio and passed it back. "Very nice, Harrison, thank you."

From the other man's expression, Lily could tell he'd been hoping for a far more exuberant response. She almost felt sorry for him.

"We'd best call it an evening," Nigel continued, "but we have your résumé and contact information, and will be in touch."

Klein's face fell, but he recovered quickly. "I appreciate that. Thank you very much," he said, holding out his hand.

The two men shook, putting a clear end to the dinner meeting. But Lily couldn't resist tossing in a quick, "Are you sure you wouldn't like another martini?"

Nigel raised a brow in her direction, one corner of his mouth twitching in mirth.

"No, thank you. I've had quite enough to drink. I think it would be best if we call it a night, especially considering our early morning meetings."

Biting back her personal amusement, she nodded. The three of them rose, said their goodbyes and headed out of the restaurant. It took a few minutes for Nigel's car to arrive, but they were silent until they were closed inside and the vehicle was slowly moving again.

"So," Nigel began, shifting on the wide leather seat to face her more fully. "What did you think?"

Somewhat startled by the question, Lily swallowed. "About what?"

"Klein," he intoned. "The interview. His designs."

What a loaded set of questions, she thought. She had opinions, to be sure. But as his personal assistant, should she be spouting them off? And what if she said too much, revealed herself as being too knowledgeable for such a low-level position?

"It's all right. You can speak freely," he said, almost as though he'd read her mind. "I want your honest opinion. It doesn't mean I'll listen, but I'm curious all the same. And it won't have an impact on your position at Ashdown Abbey one way or the other, I promise."

Hoping he was as good as his word, she gave a gentle shrug. "He's talented, that's for certain."

"But..."

"No buts," she corrected quickly. "He's clearly very talented."

Nigel kept his gaze locked on her, laser eyes drilling into her like those of a practiced interrogator.

"Fine," she breathed on a soft sigh. "He's very talented, *but*...I don't think his designs are at all suitable for Ashdown Abbey."

"Why not?" he asked in a low voice.

"Ashdown Abbey is known for its high-end business attire, even though you've recently branched out into casual and sportswear. But Klein's aesthetic leans more toward urban hip. I can see why he's done well at Vincenze—they've got a strong market in New York and Los Angeles with urban street and activewear. But Ashdown Abbey is a British company, known for clothes that are a bit more professional and clean-cut."

She paused for a moment, wondering if she'd said too much or maybe overstepped her bounds.

"Unless you're planning to move in that direction," she added, just to be safe.

Long seconds ticked by while Nigel simply stared at her,

not a single thought readable on his face. Then one side of his mouth lifted, the hazel-green of his eyes growing brighter.

"No, we have no plans to move in that direction for the time being," he agreed. "Your assessment is spot-on, you know. Exactly what I was thinking while I flipped through his designs."

For a moment, Lily sat in stunned silence, both surprised and delighted by his reaction. She so easily could have screwed up.

With a long mental sigh of relief, she reminded herself that she was supposed to be poised and self-assured. She'd lobbied for the job as his PA by making it clear she knew her stuff. As long as she didn't let anything slip about her true identity or reason for being there, why shouldn't she let a little of her background show?

"Maybe you'll be glad you hired me, after all," she quipped.

He gave her a look. A sharp, penetrating look that nearly made her shrink back inside her shell of insecurity.

And then he spoke, his deep voice and spine-tingling accent almost making her melt into the seams of the supple leather seat.

"I think I already am."

Four

Though she insisted it wasn't necessary, Nigel walked Lillian to the front door of her flat. It was the least he could do after eating up her evening with Ashdown Abbey business.

He hadn't actually needed her to accompany him to the restaurant this evening. Past personal assistants had certainly attended business functions such as that, but most had taken place during normal working hours. He'd never before requested that his assistant go to dinner with him—even a business dinner.

He wasn't entirely sure why he'd made the request of Lillian. Perhaps he'd hoped to test her mettle because she was so new on the job. They'd had a mere handful of hours together at the office, during which she'd impressed him very much. But he'd wanted to see her outside of the office, in a more critical corporate situation, to see how she handled herself in the real world, when faced with real Ashdown Abbey business associates.

But that was only what he was telling himself. Or what he'd tell others, should he be asked.

The truth lay somewhere closer to him simply not being ready to say goodbye to her company just yet.

She was quite attractive. Something he probably shouldn't have noticed...but then, he was human and male, and it was rather difficult to miss.

The package she put together intrigued him, and he'd decided to find a way to study her a bit more closely and for a while longer.

Coercing her into going to dinner with him might not have been the wisest decision he'd ever made as an employer toward an employee, but it had been quite enlightening.

Lillian George, it turned out, was not only beautiful but smart, as well. In the car, she'd been witty and charming. Though she'd started out nervous—at least by his impression—she'd quickly loosened up and even begun to tease him with her notion of creating a plan for their escape from a boring dinner meeting.

Then, at dinner itself, she'd been nearly the perfect companion. Quiet and unassuming, yet brilliant at making small talk and knowing when to speak and when to remain silent. Definitely an excellent performance from his personal assistant.

Not for the first time, though, he wondered what she might be like over a dinner that had nothing to do with business.

His mind shouldn't be wandering in that direction, he knew, but once the thought filled his head, he couldn't seem to be rid of it. It would have been nice to focus his full attention on her throughout the meal, and to feel the same from her. To talk about something other than Ashdown Abbey and potential new designs or designers, and to chat about the personal instead of business.

How long had it been since he'd taken a woman to dinner or out on the town?

Not since Caroline, for certain.

And a beautiful woman who had nothing to do with his family's company…?

Well, Caroline definitely didn't qualify there. She hadn't been involved with Ashdown Abbey when they'd first met, but she *had* been an American model eager to sleep her way to the lead in their runway shows and ad campaigns—preferably in the U.K. so that she could go "international."

And the random models he was often seen with at fashion-industry functions simply didn't count.

But then, neither did tonight. Not really. Though a part of him wished it could.

They made their way down the narrow hall of her building, coming to a stop in front of the door to her flat. She fit her key into the lock and turned it, but didn't open the door. Instead, she turned back round to face him, the knob still in her hand, one arm twisted behind her.

"Thank you," she said softly. "I had a very nice time tonight."

"Even though I forced you to come along as part of your role as my assistant?" he couldn't help but inquire.

She smiled gently at him. "Even though. I appreciated the chance to sit in on one of your meetings. I know how important something like that is. And I appreciate that you let me voice my opinion on Harrison Klein's work. You certainly didn't have to ask when I've only been working for you a single day."

"That's *why* I asked," he told her. "I wanted to know what you were made of, and that seemed a fast way to find out."

"So I passed your little test?" she asked, tipping her head slightly to one side.

"With flying colors," he said without hesitation.

"I guess that means I still have a job and should go ahead and show up in the morning."

"Most definitely. Keep up the good work, and I may just promote you to VP of the company."

"I'm sure the current vice president would be delighted to hear that."

Nigel shrugged. "Eh. It's my uncle. But he's a grumpy old sod and should probably be retiring soon, anyway."

Lillian laughed, the sound light with only a hint of nerves.

Were they the nerves of an executive secretary having a frank discussion with her new boss? Or of a woman standing much too close to a man in an empty hallway?

Knowing he was skating dangerously near the line that separated personal from professional, Nigel straightened and cleared his throat.

"Well," he murmured. "I should let you go inside and get to bed, since I know you have to be at work early tomorrow. Thank you again for your company this evening."

"Thank you for a delicious meal. It was a treat to be able to sit at Trattoria and order more than tap water with a slice of lemon."

He chuckled at that. It hadn't occurred to him that his restaurant of choice might be that far out of the realm of normalcy for Lillian. But now that he thought about it, Trattoria was almost certainly too pricey for an assistant's salary. Even an executive assistant's.

"I'm glad you enjoyed it. Good night, then."

Placing his hands on her upper arms, he leaned in and pressed a quick kiss to her cheek. Quick and entirely innocent…but one he found himself wishing could be longer and much *less* innocent.

Juliet Zaccaro paced the length of the living room in the loft apartment she shared with her two sisters.

"I don't know what you're so worried about," her youngest sister, Zoe, said from where she sat in the corner of the sofa.

She was curled up, nonchalant and bored. More concerned with her latest manicure than their middle sister's well-being.

"How can you say that?" Juliet all but snapped. "Lily has been missing for a week."

"She left a note," Zoe returned. "She told us not to worry about her, and not to look for her. Obviously, she knows what she's doing and needs some time away."

Zoe might have been speaking the truth, but that didn't mean Juliet had to like it. Or agree.

"I don't care," she said, crossing her arms beneath her breasts and pausing in her pacing to tap her foot angrily. "This isn't like her. What if something is wrong?"

"If something was wrong, Lily would tell us," was Zoe's bored and yet utterly confident reply. "She's never exactly been shy about asking for help before."

Juliet's brows pulled together in a frown. She really hated it when Zoe—the youngest, flightiest, most self-absorbed of the Zaccaro sisters—was also the sensible one.

"Well, it can't hurt to look for her. *Ask* her face-to-face if everything is okay."

Absently, she twisted the gold-and-diamond engagement ring on her left ring finger around and around. Where in heaven's name could Lily have gone? *Why* would she run off like this? It wasn't in her sister's nature at all to disappear without a word…or to disappear after leaving only a brief, cryptic note.

Juliet might have been the oldest of the Zaccaro girls and stereotypically the responsible one, taking her role as big sister seriously, but Lily was no empty-headed blonde slacker. She'd started her own fashion line that had evolved into her own company. She'd been successful enough and dogged enough to bring Juliet and Zoe in as partners to help her run the company with her.

These were not the actions of someone who would wake up one morning and decide she wanted to be a beachcomber instead. Not when there was so much going on at Zaccaro Fashions right now, so many balls in the air that Lily was juggling almost single-handedly.

Juliet and Zoe helped where they could, but…well, Zoe tended to be easily distracted, and they never knew if she would show up clearheaded and raring to go or call from Las Vegas to say she'd met a guy and would be back in a couple of weeks.

And Juliet was nearly ready to yank her hair out. In addition to overseeing handbag and accessory design for Zaccaro Fashions, she had her wedding to plan. And her moody, sometimes demanding fiancé to keep happy… She hadn't told her sister yet, but Paul had begun pressuring her—strongly—to move back to Connecticut after their honeymoon. He'd seemed fine with her life in New York when he'd proposed. She'd been here more than a year already, and he'd acted as though he was supportive of her new career direction and would be more than willing to move down to be closer to her.

Then she'd said yes, accepted his proposal and things had slowly started to change. It bothered her. Concerned her, even. But the date had been set, the venue reserved, a caterer hired, flowers chosen… How could she back out now just because her feet were getting a little chilly?

As she kept telling herself, multiple times a day, it would pass. Dragging her thoughts back to the matter at hand, she stalked across the hardwood floor to the kitchen island and slid open the drawer where they kept everyday odds and ends. Pencils and pens, paper clips, a pair of scissors and the thick borough of Manhattan phone directory.

She pulled it out and flipped to the yellow, paid-advertisement section, looking for listings for private detectives or investigators or whatever they were called. Maybe one of them could figure out what had happened to Lily, because she was sure staggering around in the dark. She had no idea where to begin looking for her sister, or even who to call to ask about her possible whereabouts.

As she got closer to the *P*s, the directory fell open, and she noticed a stiff business card stuck between the tissue-thin pages. Plucking it out, she turned it over and read the black print on a plain white background.

McCormack Investigations
Corporate. Private.

She had no idea where the card had come from, but judging by the corresponding ad on the page in front of her, it was probably one of the numbers she'd have called, anyway.

Taking the card with her, she marched back across the living room, casting an annoyed glance at Zoe, whose attention had been drawn to the latest issue of *Elle.*

"I'll be in my room," Juliet muttered through her teeth.

Tipping her head over the back of the sofa, Zoe watched her go. With an exaggerated sigh, she closed the magazine and tossed it on the coffee table.

"Okay. I think I'll go over to the studio to work for a while. Let me know if you want to go out for dinner."

Even if they made plans, chances were Zoe would change her mind and zip off to some club at the last minute, leaving Juliet to her own devices.

She waited until Zoe was gone and she was alone to pull out her cell phone and dial the number for McCormack Investigations. It took her a few minutes to convince the receptionist that her problem was a serious one and that time was of the essence, though she didn't go into a lot of detail.

The woman collected her name and contact information, promising to pass her message along and get back to her as soon as possible.

Juliet would have preferred being put on the phone with one of the company's investigators immediately or being told she could come in first thing in the morning to meet with someone in person. But she knew her dilemma wasn't exactly an emergency—at least not yet.

And please, God, don't let it become one. The idea of something happening to her sister made Juliet's blood run cold.

So she agreed to stay by the phone and told herself not to panic, not to let her imagination race out of control.

She should go over to the studio with Zoe and try to get some work done. Keep her mind off Lily and the phone in her hand that refused to ring, even after five whole minutes of waiting.

Instead, she resumed pacing a path through the middle of the living-room area. Which was much easier without Zoe in the way, distracting her with her sensible arguments and assurances that Lily was just fine.

Step. Step. Step.

Tick. Tick. Tick.

Turn.

Step. Step. Step.

Tick. Tick. Tick.

Five minutes turned into ten. Ten into twenty.

She stopped. Worried her thumbnail. Tapped her foot. Went back to pacing.

At thirty minutes and counting, she let out a huff of breath and dropped into the center of the sofa, the cushion wheezing at the sudden addition of her weight.

When her cell phone pealed, she jumped and let out a startled yip. She'd been concentrating so hard on making the stupid thing ring that when it finally did, it scared the bejesus out of her.

Heart pounding for more reasons than one, she brought it to her ear and whispered, "Hello?"

"Ms. Zaccaro?"

"Yes."

"This is Reid McCormack from McCormack Investigations. I have here that your sister is missing and you'd like help tracking her down."

"Yes," she said again.

"You understand, don't you, that she's an adult and is allowed to leave town without telling anyone where she's going," the man on the other end of the line intoned.

Through gritted teeth, Juliet responded, "Yes."

"And if she left a note…she did leave a note, correct?"

Hoping she didn't end up with a cracked molar after this conversation, she ground out yet another, "Yes."

"If she left a note, then she really can't be considered missing. The police would tell you to wait and hope you hear from her. And that you can't file a missing-persons report unless there are actual signs of foul play."

Feeling deflated and more frustrated than ever, Juliet dropped her head and murmured a dejected, "I understand."

A beat passed before Reid McCormack spoke again.

"So why don't you come by tomorrow around 11:00 a.m.? I can't promise anything. I may not even be able to look for your sister. But we'll talk. All right?"

His low-timbred, slowly spoken words had Juliet's head shooting up so fast, it left her dizzy.

Had she heard him correctly? Clearing her throat, she swallowed and forced out the only thing she could think of. "What?"

"Come by tomorrow," he repeated as patiently as a parent spoon-feeding a child, "and we'll talk."

"All right. Thank you." She hopped to her feet in excitement, though she knew perfectly well he couldn't see her.

"See you tomorrow, then," he murmured before they said their goodbyes and hung up.

Juliet slapped her phone down on the low coffee table, then headed back to her room. What did one wear to a meeting with a private investigator?

The only detectives she could picture were the television and pulp-fiction type—*Magnum, P.I.,* Sam Spade, *Columbo.* But somehow she couldn't imagine showing up in a hibiscus-covered blouse or '30s-style dress and wide-brim hat.

Thanks to her role at Zaccaro Fashions, her closet was bursting at the seams with clothes to choose from. Surely she could put something together by tomorrow morning.

As she fingered through hangers and studied her shoe choices, she found herself pushing aside Mr. McCormack's assertion that he might not be able to help her find Lily, letting herself believe that he not only could, but *would.*

Five

Lily arrived at Ashdown Abbey bright and early the next morning—but not without a struggle. She'd only gotten about four hours of sleep before her alarm had rudely awakened her and forced her back into the land of the living.

Gulping down her third cup of coffee since reaching the office, Lily sat at her desk and prayed she would be able to hold her composure when Nigel stepped off the elevator.

After saying good-night and slipping into her apartment, she'd gone to the bedroom and changed into a pair of simple cotton pajamas, then returned to the living room with all of the printouts and information she'd managed to sneak out of Ashdown Abbey earlier.

Her movements had been so calm and deliberate. Robotic. Because underneath it all, she was a beehive of confusing thoughts and conflicting emotions.

She was *not* in Los Angeles to have her hormones go haywire just because she was in close proximity to a handsome, charming Brit. He was supposed to be her *enemy,* for heaven's sake.

But her hormones *were* going wild, distracting her and throwing her off her well-planned-out path.

Not just because Nigel was an attractive man. She'd met handsome men before. Met them, worked with them, dated and even slept with a few.

Good looks were nice, but she wasn't so weak that they could push her over the edge into total stupidity. Nor could a thick British accent, no matter how toe-curling it might be.

No, there was something else about Nigel that had her pulse thrumming and her head spinning like a kaleidoscope.

She actually kind of liked him so far, despite her preconceived notions of who Nigel Statham must be—a rich, entitled CEO, not above stealing another designer's ideas to advance his own agenda.

But would a rich, entitled thief ask her opinion on something as important as hiring choices and then actually *listen* to her answer? Would he compliment her on her insight and walk her to her door at the end of the evening?

The worst part, though, was the kiss. A simple kiss on the cheek, not much different than she'd received a thousand times from older acquaintances, uncles, even her own father.

Then again, it was *so* not like a kiss from her father. Light and on the cheek, yes. To anyone who might have been watching, it would have seemed to be exactly what it was—a polite, friendly good-night kiss. A thanks-for-a-nice-evening, take-care, sleep-tight kiss from one friend to another. Or in this case, a man to a woman he'd only recently met.

But Lily knew differently. Or at least she *felt* differently. Never before had a simple kiss on the cheek caused her temperature to rise. Her heartbeat to kick into a gallop. Her stomach to launch into a series of somersaults that would put an Olympic gymnast to shame.

And that was all at only the first touch of his lips on her skin.

She'd expected him to pull away almost immediately. A quick peck, that's all. It was almost what she'd hoped for, because then her vitals would return to normal.

For some reason, though, he'd lingered. Not long enough for the moment to become awkward, but certainly long enough for everything in her to turn warm and liquid, and for her chest to tighten as she held her breath.

One-one thousand.

Two-one thousand.

Three-one thousand.

She'd begun to count silently, the way she and her sisters had when they were young, playing hide-and-seek. Until she worried that lack of oxygen might start to make her light-headed.

And then he'd pulled away. Straightening to his full height, and gazing at her with an intensity that sent a shiver down her spine.

Murmuring another quick, mumbled goodbye, he'd turned on his heel and marched away.

He'd gone, but the aftereffects of the kiss had remained. Through the rest of the night and into this morning.

She could swear she still felt the brush of his mouth against her cheek even now.

And wasn't that going to be a terrific way to go through the day? Imagining ghost lips dancing along her skin. Wondering if the look she'd seen in Nigel's eyes just before he'd walked away had been desire…or distaste.

Taking another long swig of coffee, she let the strong, hot brew slide down her throat and trickle into her system. A caffeine IV would be better. Then again, so would a nice shot of vodka. Or maybe a splash of whiskey to make the coffee both smoother and more potent.

Fingers flexing around the ceramic mug, Lily told herself to stop being so flighty. She wasn't here—in Los Angeles or at Ashdown Abbey—to daydream or wax poetic. And she certainly needed to get her act together before Nigel arrived.

Thoughts of that stupid kiss and what it might or might not mean had kept her up half the night. They didn't need to distract her all day, too. Especially since she had much more important things to focus on.

One was pretending to be the perfect personal assistant for Nigel.

The other was digging and snooping to see what else she could find concerning her stolen designs.

She'd gone through the California Collection design printouts as much as she could last night before finally succumbing to exhaustion and crawling into bed, but she could barely remember a thing about them now. A second and possibly even third run-through was definitely called for. Of course, she couldn't do that until tonight when she was home and alone again.

A few yards down the hall, she heard the hum of the elevator and the whoosh of the doors as they opened and closed. Rushing to set aside her coffee, Lily took a deep breath, straightened in her chair, and started typing nothing in particular in an effort to look busy.

Nigel spotted Lillian the minute he stepped off the lift onto his office floor. If it was possible, she looked even more lovely today than she had last evening, and she'd looked quite stunning then.

Perhaps because he'd always had a bit of a soft spot for the "sexy librarian" type. Her hair was pulled back in a sexy bun, bookish, dark-rimmed glasses resting on the bridge of her nose. Her jewelry was understated. She wore a red blouse that opened at the throat to reveal just enough pale flesh and shadowed cleavage to make a man's libido sit up and take notice.

She was seated behind her desk, so he couldn't tell what she was wearing from the waist down. What he imagined, though, was tight and formfitting, showing off her legs and posterior to perfection. On top of that, he imagined her perching on the edge of the desk, legs crossed, shoe dangling from the toe of one foot, nibbling seductively on the end of her pen.

Oh, yes—naughty librarian, indeed. Or more to the point, naughty secretary. Which was the thought that had plagued him all through last night.

An affair with his secretary was not only bad form, but an extremely bad idea in general. As was allowing himself to be distracted by ungentlemanly and very un-bosslike thoughts about her.

He'd spent an inordinate amount of time unable to sleep, kept awake by memories of their dinner together and that kiss at her door just before saying their good-nights.

For a kiss akin to one he might give his mother or a beloved aunt, it had rocked him back on his heels and made him sorry he had to walk away.

Worse, though, was that the thought of that one simple kiss on the cheek had snowballed into a thousand other thoughts and images he had no business thinking.

Lillian perched on the edge of her desk, shoe dangling from her toes was only the first of many. The wee hours of the night had also been filled with more erotic fantasies.

Pressing Lillian up against the door to her flat and kissing her for real. On the mouth, with lips and tongue and unbridled passion.

Walking her backward into her flat and taking her on whatever surface they bumped into first. Table, counter, sofa, coffee table…even the floor itself.

Bringing her home with him and making love to her in his

own bed. On satin sheets, with moonlight streaming across their naked bodies and bringing out the highlights in her dark blond hair.

The one that was bound to cause him the most trouble, however, was of watching her saunter into his office under the pretense of work, only to have him strip her of those sexy schoolmarm eyeglasses, pull the pins from her upswept hair and shag her brains out in the middle of his desk.

It was the single, red-hot thought spiraling through his mind and making it decidedly uncomfortable to walk the remaining distance to his office. She lifted her head as he approached, and he hoped to heaven she didn't notice the state of his arousal behind the zip of his otherwise pressed and pristine trousers.

"Good morning," she greeted him.

If her smile seemed a bit stiff or falsely bright, he pretended not to notice. She wasn't the only one feeling awkward and uncomfortable over whatever had passed between them last night.

"Good morning," he returned without inflection, studiously avoiding eye contact while he reached for the morning's post on the corner of her desk and flipped through.

"Coffee?" she asked.

"No, thank you."

Her smile slipped, uncertainty skating like clouds across the sky-blue of her eyes.

Nigel blew out a breath. He was being a bleeding sod, and he knew it. It wasn't her fault that he'd gotten very little sleep and woken up about ten feet to the left of the wrong side of the bed.

"I would love a cup of tea, though," he said in a much kinder voice.

She nodded quickly and rose, going around him and her

desk to the small pantry that was tucked away at the far side of the reception area.

He watched her cross the expanse, her long legs eating up the space in record time. The slant of her three-inch, open-toed shoes made those legs look even longer, more taut. And her skirt—which turned out to be short and black—encased her buttocks like a second skin.

Not exactly conducive to quelling his arousal. The only thing that might help with that was distance. And possibly being struck blind.

Since the latter wasn't likely to occur in the next few minutes, he opted for the former. Taking the stack of envelopes with him, he moved into his office and took a seat behind his desk.

He'd just logged on to check his email when Lillian appeared carrying a full tea service—the one he'd ordered when he'd first come to work in the States, but hadn't seen hide nor hair of since. When he'd requested a cup of tea from his previous assistants, they'd all brought him a big, clunky ceramic mug with a nondescript tea bag bobbing in a pool of lukewarm water.

Nigel sat back, waiting while she set the tray on the edge of his desk and proceeded to pour already steeped tea from a china pot into a china cup. Through a stainless-steel strainer and complete with matching saucer, no less.

"This is a surprise," he said.

She raised her head, meeting his gaze. The question was there in her eyes.

"I was expecting something much simpler," he explained. "Aren't you Americans fond of tea that comes in bags?"

"We are," she answered. "Very. Probably because it's a lot easier than all of this." She waved a hand to encompass the tray and its accoutrements. "But I've heard you Brits are much more particular about your tea. And that you don't think we Americans could brew a decent cup to save our lives."

His lips quirked with the urge to grin. "We sound like a demanding lot with sticks up our bums."

Lillian chuckled, returning her attention to the tea service. "You said it, I didn't," she replied, handing him the cup and saucer.

"To be safe, I went online and researched how to make a cup of *true* English tea. I make absolutely no promises that I've done it right, but I do hope you'll at least give me points for trying."

Gesturing to the other items on the tray, she said, "Milk, sugar and lemon."

The real thing, he noticed. Milk—not cream, which so many Americans assumed should be added just because they used it in their coffee—the sugar cubed and the lemon cut into wedges.

"I wasn't sure which, if any, you preferred."

"If this tastes as good as it looks, I may even give you a bonus," he told her. "For future reference, though, I take it black, so all the rest isn't really necessary."

She blinked, looking at him as though he'd said he wasn't actually British, it was all just a cruel hoax.

"Then *why* do you have a full tea service in the kitchenette? I bought all of this specifically so you could have tea just the way you like it and wouldn't be disappointed."

He bit back a grin, but had the dignity to flush at her chastisement. "Truthfully, it came that way, as a set. My mother has used a full tea service from the time I was a lad, so I suppose it never occurred to me that I really only needed the pot, cups and saucers."

With a huff, she dropped into one of the soft leather chairs opposite his desk and crossed one leg over the other. Her skirt shifted, revealing inches more of stocking-clad skin that he shouldn't be staring at. But he couldn't seem to drag his gaze away until he'd looked his fill.

Licking suddenly dry lips, he swallowed and drew his attention—reluctantly—to her face.

"I apologize for misleading you."

"But I worked really hard on getting this right, and now I find out I could have just dropped a tea bag into a cup of hot water and been done with it," she said, still sounding put out.

He inclined his head, acknowledging her upset. "I understand. My fault entirely. Feel free to do exactly that from now on. It may not be my preference, but it's no less than I deserve."

She studied him for a moment, blue eyes locked on his. Then she leaned back, almost deflating into her chair.

"You're not what I expected, you know," she said finally, surprising him with her boldness.

He cocked a brow. "Oh? How so?"

"I thought you would be a bit more demanding. Dictatorial, even. Like that chef on the cooking show who yells all the time and calls the contestants names."

Nigel couldn't help but chuckle. He knew exactly who she was talking about. "Actually, I believe he's Scottish, not British. And I don't recall ever calling anyone a donkey, no matter how angry I might have been."

"Good thing," she replied matter-of-factly. "I don't think you'd appreciate my reaction if you used a term like that with me."

"I can imagine." He could, and it wasn't pretty. Of course, he'd never been one to get red in the face and start slinging invectives when he lost his temper, so she had nothing to worry about on that score.

"You're not at all what I expected, either," he confessed.

He regretted the words as soon as they passed his lips. It

was a bit too much sharing for their short acquaintance, not to mention entirely out of character for him.

Of course, she'd heard him, so it wasn't as though he could pretend he hadn't said it.

She tipped her head to one side, glancing at him curiously. "You mean you thought I'd be quieter, more tractable, eager to please."

Nigel chuckled aloud at that description. Despite the fact that she had, indeed, seemed eager to please her new boss in the two days she'd been in his employ, something told him that wasn't entirely usual for her, and that the rest didn't suit her by half.

Quiet? Not if by that she meant meek.

Tractable? He couldn't imagine any such thing.

"No," he answered, giving his head a rather decisive shake. "Not at all. Given the past assistants I've had here in the U.S., I was expecting you to be…a few biscuits short of a tin, if you understand my meaning."

"You're in the habit of hiring mentally unstable personal assistants?" she teased, brow raised.

"Not unstable, thank goodness," he responded, "but young, and not a lot going on above the neck, other than good grooming and dreams of becoming either a supermodel or the next fashion designer to become an overnight success. Not only could they not make a decent cup of tea, but they couldn't keep their minds on their responsibilities long enough to accomplish what they'd actually been hired to do."

She thought about that for a moment, then inclined her head and her gaze toward the cup still resting on the desk in front of him.

"You haven't even tasted the tea yet. How do you know *I* can make a decent cup?"

He didn't bother to answer, simply lifted the cup to his mouth and took a long, hearty swallow. Setting the cup back down, he said, “Excellent. It would have been better if I’d started drinking it while it was still piping hot, but really—quite excellent.”

“Well, you have only yourself to blame for that, don’t you?” she quipped.

Without a hint of remorse or fear of speaking in such a manner to her employer. And not just any employer, but the CEO of the whole bloody company.

Why did that amuse him so damn much? Amuse, as well as arouse.

The sight of her, the thought of her, the knowledge that she would be seated just outside his office door for eight hours each day, was enough to send his blood to the boiling point.

Even now, he wanted to stand up, round his desk, lean down and kiss her just for the hell of it.

Well, for the hell of it, and also to discover if she tasted as good as he thought she would. That was something he suddenly wanted to know. Very, very badly.

In an attempt to cool the heat rising in his body and bringing small beads of perspiration to dot his brow, he raised the tea back to his lips and drained the cup dry. It didn’t cool him off as much as he’d hoped.

“So,” he commented to fill the increasingly awkward silence. “You can make a fine cup of tea, and you know your way about the design business—at least judging by last night’s conversation. I think it’s safe to say you’ve already surpassed the skills of all of my other assistants here in the States put together.”

“I’ll take that as a compliment,” she replied, giving him a bright smile that Nigel believed could only be genuine.

So he responded with one of his own. “As you should. It was intended as one.”

“I can expect that bonus to be reflected in my first paycheck, then?”

She made it a question. Loaded and dangerous.

Narrowing his eyes, he answered carefully. "We'll see. Keep up the good work, and I'll have no problem rewarding your efforts monetarily. But you've only been here two days. I need to see you in action awhile longer than that before I make any promises."

She shrugged one slim shoulder. "Can't blame a girl for trying."

With a laugh, Nigel emptied the rest of the tea into his cup, then sat back, linking his hands in front of him. "Certainly not. And you may just earn yourself some extra perks yet. Especially if you bring me another pot of tea before running down to the fourth floor to see how things are going. We've got a special runway show coming up in two weeks, and I want to be sure we're on track."

Lillian sat up in a suddenly more serious, alert manner. "I'll be happy to, but isn't that something you should do yourself? I'm not sure I'll know enough to judge how well things are going."

"You'll do fine," Nigel assured her. "The head of the design team should be able to tell you what's been done so far and what still needs to be taken care of. Then you can report to me, and if I think anything is out of sorts, I'll go down and put the fear of unemployment into them."

"Very stealthy of you," she said. Then, taking a deep breath, she pushed to her feet. "I'll do my best. It will be fun to visit the design-room floor. I've never been on one before."

Her gaze darted away and she shifted from one leg to the other. Peculiar, to say the least.

Ignoring the odd behavior, Nigel said, "Take your time down there. It really is quite fascinating to watch the designers work."

She nodded, collecting the china cup from the center of

the desk and adding it to the other items on the tea-service tray. Gathering it all, she headed for the door.

"Tea first," she said over her shoulder, "then I'll go down and spy on your happy little elves."

He watched her disappear out into the reception area, enjoying the sway of her hips and straight line of her back. It wasn't until he heard her returning with a second cup of tea several minutes later that he realized he hadn't moved a muscle since she'd walked away.

Which was not a good sign. Not good at all.

Six

Lily knew better than to make rash judgments about people. First impressions often made you think somebody was wonderful, friendly, trustworthy…and then later you discovered they were none of those things. Other times, the opposite was true. You met someone and didn't care for them at all, only to discover hidden aspects of their personality later that caused you to end up becoming close friends.

So the fact that she was finding Nigel Statham more handsome, more charming and more enticing the longer she knew him—even after only two short days—could go either way. She'd started out certain he was a thief with questionable business ethics. Could she have been completely and totally wrong about that? Or was she letting his intense good looks and honeyed accent blind her to the truth?

She'd expected to come to Los Angeles, go to work for the big, bad CEO of the U.S. branch of his family's company and immediately begin finding evidence to shore up her arguments about his involvement in the theft of her designs.

Instead, she'd found nothing. None of her poking around in his files—or his former personal assistants' files, at any rate—had turned up a single thing or question mark. If anything, she was less convinced of his involvement.

But the theft *had* occurred, so there had to be evidence somewhere. A thread she could find, pick at and follow back to its source.

The elevator she was riding down to the fourth floor stopped with a small jolt and she straightened, pushing away from the rear wall where she'd been leaning to wait for the doors to open.

She'd lied to Nigel when she'd told him she'd never visited a design-room floor before. Sometimes she felt as though she lived on one, especially when she and both of her sisters were in their home studio together, all working in tandem.

Which was probably why she was so looking forward to visiting the one here. Not only was she curious to see how things worked at a company of this size, but it would be comforting to be back in the thick of the creative side of the fashion business again. Even temporarily.

As she stepped off the elevator, the click of her heels on the slick polished floor mixed with the sound of voices and the hum of sewing machines. Not a dozen running all at once, but one here, one there, being used as needed, much the way they were in her shop.

She loved it. A noise that would probably grate on anyone else's nerves after a while soothed hers and helped her to take her first deep, comfortable breath since leaving New York.

She was smiling as she made her way down the main hall. This floor was made up of large, open-area rooms filled with long tables, dress forms, sewing equipment and plenty of fabrics and supplies. And most of the rooms she passed had their doors open so she could see the people working inside. Design teams, most likely, each assigned a different look or aspect of whatever collection they were currently putting together.

What Lily wouldn't give for this kind of setup. Not only the work space—which was like comparing a football field to a foosball table—but the employees. Extra creative minds, extra hands, twice or probably even quadruple the work accomplished in half the time.

Of course, in order to put something like this into effect, she would also need a lot more money. And that would mean either asking her parents for another, more substantial loan, or winning the lottery.

But a girl could dream, couldn't she? And one day, Zaccaro Fashions *would* be this big, this efficient. They would be a huge, world-renowned brand name in their own right, and she wouldn't need her future inheritance to make it happen.

She wanted to stop at each doorway and take a good, long peek inside. She wanted to know what everyone was making, see their work, listen in on their conversations. Especially since it was possible they were once again ripping off her designs.

There wasn't a lot of time for poking around, though. She was supposed to find a man named Michael Franklin, the head designer for this particular collection, and get a progress report for Nigel.

Despite his comment that she should take her time, she didn't trust him not to come looking for her. He was a big, corporate bigwig who didn't even make his own coffee or tea. What were the chances he could get through an hour or two without needing her for something?

And he was quite obviously a man who expected his assistant to come running the minute he called…even if she was three floors away. So the less time she spent away from her desk the better, at least until she'd been at the company a little longer and had a better handle on his routine.

Strolling down the hall, she took in the activities of each room peripherally as she passed, heading straight for the office at the end, where Nigel had told her she would most likely find Mr. Franklin. Or at least it was a place to start.

"Office" was a bit of a misnomer. It was actually a glass-fronted version of the other design areas, but in addition to equipment and a cutting table that doubled as a sketching and design surface, there was a cluttered desk and file cabinets.

Mr. Franklin's name was etched on the closed door, but no one was inside. Chewing the inside of her lip for a second, she tapped her foot and tried to decide what to do next. Her only option, she supposed, was to go back the way she'd come and pop her head into each room after all. Surely someone would have an idea of where she could find Mr. Franklin.

She was spinning on her heel to do just that when she nearly ran into another woman coming toward her.

"Oh, I'm so sorry."

Their simultaneous apologies were followed by amused chuckles.

"Sorry about that," the woman said again. "I saw you standing outside Mr. Franklin's office and was just coming to ask if I could help you with anything."

"I'm looking for Mr. Franklin, actually," Lily said. And then she stopped, tipping her head and narrowing her eyes as she concentrated more intently on the other woman.

"Wait a minute. Don't I know you?" She wracked her brain, positive the young woman looked familiar.

"Oh, my gosh," she exclaimed as it finally came to her. "You're Bella, aren't you? I'm sorry, I can't think of your last name off the top of my head, but you're Zoe's friend, aren't you? Her roommate from college."

"It's Landry," the other woman, who was a petite brunette,

supplied. And then she widened her cornflower-blue eyes. "Do you mean Zoe Zaccaro?"

Lily nodded.

"I haven't seen Zoe in ages, but we definitely spent our college years together. How do you know her?"

"I'm Lily, Zoe's sister. We met briefly the last time you visited Zoe in New York."

She wasn't surprised at Bella's lack of recognition. Normally, she and her sisters looked enough alike—with their long, blond hair and similar facial features—that they were often mistaken for one another. But with her hair both darkened and pulled up in an out-of-character twist, and unfamiliar glasses perched on the bridge of her nose, she'd done a pretty good job of muting all of the things that made her stand out as a Zaccaro by looks alone.

Not to mention that she hadn't seen Bella in years—and had only met her a couple of times before that, when they had visited Zoe on campus or Zoe had brought Bella home with her for the odd holiday break.

"Oh, yes. Wow, small world. It's great to see you again. And how is Zoe?" Bella asked.

"Great," Lily told her. "Same as usual."

They both laughed at that, aware of exactly what Zoe's "usual" was.

"So what are you doing here?" Bella wanted to know.

The question stopped Lily cold, slapping the smile right off her face. Uh-oh. Until then, she'd forgotten she was supposed to be keeping a low profile and *definitely* remaining anonymous to everyone who worked at Ashdown Abbey. She had forgotten while exchanging pleasantries with a friend of her sister's whom she'd run into out of the blue.

Mind racing, she tried to figure out how to cover her mistake and come up with a plausible reason for her presence here in Los Angeles.

"The three of us are, um…taking a little time off from designing, working to establish the store and brand as they are now. So while Zoe and Juliet are running things back home, I decided to come out here and intern with Ashdown Abbey for a while."

That sounded okay, didn't it? She very pointedly didn't mention that she was working as the big kahuna's assistant. And she hoped Bella didn't find out, because then she would have to explain why she was going by a different name and pray they never ran into one another while Nigel was around.

"Cool," Bella replied, apparently accepting Lily's explanation at face value.

"How about you?" Lily asked, eager to turn the younger woman's attention away from her and on to something, anything else.

"Oh, I'm, um…" Bella stammered, glancing down at the toes of her pointy, leopard-print shoes before returning her gaze to Lily, but not quite meeting her eyes. "I'm an associate designer for the company," she said finally. "I've been here for almost three years now."

"That's wonderful," Lily told her, meaning it. She didn't know Bella well, wasn't even sure how long she and Zoe had been friends, but she'd never heard her sister speak a bad word about her, and she seemed perfectly nice.

"You're working on the latest collection, then?" she asked, nodding her head to indicate all of the fourth-floor workrooms.

Bella gave a jerky nod, her gaze skating away again for the briefest of moments. "I don't really have much to do with it. I'm just sort of a cog in the wheel, doing a little here and a little there. Whatever needs to be done."

"Hey, you have to start somewhere," Lily said with a pleasant smile, knowing the truth of that better than anyone. "I'm sure it will be great. All of Ashdown Abbey's designs are exceptional. You should be proud to be a part of it."

That was true, too, even if it pained her to say so. Especially since she was still smarting from their use of *her* great designs for their California Collection.

She thought about trying to wheedle information from Bella—about the California Collection, or Nigel, or maybe just Ashdown Abbey itself. It was possible she knew something important without even being aware of it. But after blurting out her real identity when she was supposed to be undercover, she was afraid of coming across as too curious and giving herself away even further, so she kept her mouth shut. She could always come back later to pick Bella's brain if she needed to.

It also crossed her mind that—being a friend of Zoe's and having been in their studio in the past—Bella might have had something to do with the theft of her designs. She didn't want to believe that a friend of her sister's—especially one who'd roomed with Zoe for four years straight—would do such a thing, but made a mental note to look into it anyway. At least cursorily, just in case.

"Do you know where Mr. Franklin is?" she asked instead of beginning an impromptu interrogation right there in the hallway.

Bella glanced back over her shoulder. "Um…he should be here somewhere. Try workroom B. He's been working pretty closely with that team this week."

"Great, thank you."

"Do you want me to take you?" Bella offered, finally making eye contact.

"No, thanks. I can find it, and I'm sure you have work to do," Lily said. "It was nice to see you, though. I'll tell Zoe you said hi."

After saying their goodbyes, Bella headed in one direction

while Lily retraced her path toward the elevator. She went more slowly this time, figuring she had a valid excuse for poking her head into each room to see who was there and what was going on. So what if workroom B was one of the last rooms she'd pass?

She caught glimpses of the color palette and fabrics that were being used for this particular collection, as well as a few of the designs themselves being pieced together on dress forms. Lily liked what she saw, and so far, at least, she hadn't spotted anything that set off alarm bells in her head. Nothing that looked eerily similar to her own design aesthetic.

It was a relief, but also a touch disappointing, since it got her no closer to finding out how her designs had been stolen in the first place.

Since she didn't see anyone in the other workrooms who seemed to be in charge, she decided to wait until she reached workroom B to ask after Mr. Franklin. She could always backtrack later if she needed to.

Reaching workroom B, she stepped inside, taking in the two women bent over a cutting table, heads together in discussion, and another woman over by a dress form, talking with a short, squat man while they fingered pieces of a pattern already attached to the form, moving them around and trying to decide on the best placement.

She might have been jumping to conclusions, but Lily assumed the man was Mr. Franklin. Sidling just a few feet more into the room, she leaned against one of the cutting tables and studied some of the patterns and sketches laid out there while she waited for them to conclude their business so she could get Nigel's update and report back to him before he sent out a search party.

The next week went by in such a blur, Lily could barely keep up. Nigel kept her running, skipping and hopping nearly twenty-four/seven.

Even once she clocked out and dragged herself to her home away from home, she had enough energy only to wash her face, change into pajamas and fall into bed for as much sleep as she could manage before the alarm went off and demanded she start all over again. Which left very little time for snooping and research.

She was gaining a whole new respect for secretaries, receptionists and personal assistants, to be sure.

And even though she was often left scrambling or faking her way through certain tasks, Nigel seemed pleased with her performance. So she supposed if the "design thing"—as her father sometimes called it—didn't work out, she could always fall back on this.

But she wasn't here to work hard and see that Ashdown Abbey's CEO looked good so the company could advance. She was here to save and avenge *her* company, and she was becoming increasingly frustrated with her inability to do that.

More determined than ever to find a moment or two to poke around for her own benefit, Lily stalked out of the elevator first thing that Monday morning and went straight to her desk. She'd arrived a tad early, and with luck, Nigel would run late this morning so she could dig into the California Collection files without fear of getting caught.

There had to be something somewhere that would lead her to the culprit she sought. She was especially interested in finding the original sketches that the California Collection was based off of. They should give her more of an indication of what inspired the collection than the later, more cleaned-up versions she'd already printed. They might even give her some hint of how someone got ahold of her designs in the first place to mimic them.

Of course, her lack of progress with her private little investigation wasn't the only dilemma she was facing. She also had a real private investigator breathing down her neck.

Reid McCormack had called to ask where she was and what she was up to. She'd found the question and his tone of voice peculiar, since he was the one who was supposed to be working for her.

But while she'd hired him to see what he could find out about Ashdown Abbey's theft of Zaccaro Fashions' designs from his vantage point in New York, she hadn't told him that she was planning to head for Los Angeles to do a bit of investigating on her own. She doubted he would approve, and suspected he would only try to talk her out of it.

She was right about the disapproval part. He'd been as livid as a person could be over the phone when it wasn't his place to tell her what to do—or what not to do—and he knew it.

He'd wanted to know *exactly* where she was and *exactly* what she was doing. Then when she'd refused to tell him, he'd informed her that "whatever she was up to," she obviously wasn't doing a very good job of it because her sister—Juliet—had just come to his office asking him to track her down.

Lily had gotten the feeling he was more put out at having to lie to one sister because the other was already a client than anything else. And maybe that he'd been blindsided, not even knowing client number one had hied off on her own until potential client number two came along wanting her sister treated like a missing person.

Though she'd hoped Juliet and Zoe would trust her to go off on her own for a while without needing specifics, she apparently hadn't done as efficient a job as she'd thought of making excuses, assuring her sisters she was fine and would return home soon.

It had taken a long time and quite a bit of verbal tap dancing to finally convince Mr. McCormack to pretend to take Juliet's case. Lily offered to compensate him for his time on both issues, if he didn't feel comfortable taking money from Juliet for doing nothing and lying to her to boot. And it was only until she could figure out what to say to her sisters that wouldn't send them into a tailspin. She promised to call Juliet herself as soon as she could so her family wouldn't continue to think she was missing or in trouble.

It went against McCormack's personal code of ethics, she could tell. She could almost imagine him grinding his teeth, flexing his fingers over and over again, and generally fighting the urge to reach through the phone line to strangle her.

Eventually, though...*eventually*, he agreed. About as enthusiastically as one might say, "Oh, yes—please give me a root canal without anesthetic!"

So now that was hanging over her head, as well. She hated thinking that her sisters were worried about her, especially when she'd left a note with the sole purpose of making sure they didn't.

But if she called to reassure them again and let them know everything was okay, they—namely Juliet—would want to know where she was and what was going on. They would be more curious and demanding than ever. And she had no idea what to tell them.

With a sigh, she dropped down into the chair at her desk and punched the power button on the computer. While it was booting up, she stowed her purse and tried to figure out where to begin. The sooner she could get this mess cleaned up and the mystery solved, the sooner she could go home and tell her sisters everything.

She tapped at the keyboard, searching folder and file names, looking specifically for anything related to the California Collection while keeping one eye on the elevator down the hall.

Though she wasn't sure it would lead anywhere, she discovered a folder that seemed to have all kinds of documents in it related to the California Collection. As quickly as she could, she slipped a blank flash drive into the USB port and hit Copy.

The file had just finished loading, and she was dropping the flash drive into her purse, when the door to Nigel's office opened directly behind her.

Her heart stopped. Literally screeched to a halt inside her chest as a lump of pure panic formed in her throat.

"Good. You're here," Nigel murmured at her back.

She knew she should respond, at least turn around and face him, but she felt glued in place, as frozen as an ice cube.

Thankfully, rather than getting upset or reprimanding her for her seeming lack of respect, he came to the edge of her desk. When the dark blue pinstripe of his dress slacks came into her peripheral vision, she finally managed to swallow, turn her head and lift her gaze to that of her boss.

As always, the sight of him made her mouth go dry. She'd thought that after working with him for a while, getting used to his quiet confidence and startling good looks, it would get easier to be around him. That she would suffer less and less of a lurch to her solar plexus each time they came in contact—which was more often, even, than she caught her own reflection in the restroom mirror.

Heart beating again—though not in any pattern a cardiologist would approve of—she licked her lips and made herself meet his eyes.

"Good morning," she said, glad her voice sounded almost human. "I didn't think you were in yet."

Understatement. She'd been watching the elevator like a mouse on the lookout for the cat of the house. Meanwhile, he'd been in his office the entire time. If he'd been a cat and she a mouse, she was pretty sure she'd be lunch by now.

"I was waiting for you to arrive," he said by way of answer.

Pushing aside a few items on the corner of her desk, he sat

down, letting one leg dangle. A nicely muscled leg, encased in fabric that tightened across his upper thigh.

Once again dragging her gaze to his face, she tried to take slow, shallow breaths until her internal temperature stopped climbing toward heatstroke levels.

"We need to talk about next week's show," he continued.

"All right." He'd sent her down to speak with Michael Franklin several more times, but to the best of her knowledge, everything was still running smoothly and on schedule.

"As you know, the show is in Miami."

She had known that, though she hadn't paid much attention one way or the other to the show's location.

"I have to be there, of course," he said in that slow, calm British way of his. Whatever point he was trying to make, he was taking his time getting there.

"The runway show itself is for charity, but buyers for many of our biggest accounts will be there, and we'll be taking orders for the designs throughout the event."

She nodded in understanding.

"I was hoping you might be willing to go along, as well."

Lily's eyes widened and she sat back in her seat, more than a little surprised by the request. They'd been discussing the show on and off since her arrival, but he'd never once hinted that he might want her to travel across the country with him.

"Do your personal assistants normally travel with you for this sort of thing?" she wanted to know.

He inclined his head. "Quite often."

"Then you're *telling* me I'll be going along, not asking if I'd like to," she said, making it more of a statement than a question.

"Not at all," he replied quickly, shifting on the corner of her desk. "I'd very much like you to accompany me, and it will be work-related, but I'll certainly understand if you have other plans."

She thought about it, trying to weigh the pros and cons and mentally map out the best plan of action where her true purpose for working at Ashdown Abbey was concerned.

On the one hand, she would probably make more progress and have more privacy to really dig around if she stayed behind while Nigel flew to Miami.

On the other, she *really* wanted to go. The idea of traveling with Nigel—no doubt first-class all the way—was intriguing enough. But the true thrill would be the up-close-and-personal experience of a live show with numerous famous designers sending their latest creations down the runway.

She could really benefit from watching how the organizers pulled it together and getting to see how such a large-scale event worked behind the scenes. Watching the clothes walk down the runway on professional and likely very sought-after supermodels. Rubbing elbows with some of the biggest names in the business—designers, buyers and the media alike. People who might one day take an interest in her own designs and help Zaccaro Fashions go national and then international.

Granted, she wouldn't be able to let any of them know who she really was or talk up her own work, but still… The contacts she might make, even under the guise of acting as Nigel's personal assistant, could serve her well down the road.

"It will be an overnight stay," Nigel added, breaking into her thoughts to give her even more to consider. "Through the weekend, actually. We'd fly out Thursday and return late Sunday night."

It was a substantial amount of time to be away from the Ashdown Abbey offices and attempt to carry out her pretense in public, but was she really going to say no? Pass up such an amazing opportunity? She would never be able to live with herself if she did, despite the fact that it would set back her "investigation" by that much longer.

"I'd love to go," she said after a minute of deep thought,

relieved when the words came out normally instead of sounding like those of a kid standing outside a bouncy castle.

"Brilliant," he exclaimed, slapping the palms of his hands against the tops of both thighs.

Then he rose and headed back toward his office. "You can check my schedule for the specific itinerary and the promotional materials for the show to get an idea of what you might like to pack. We'll work out the rest of the details later."

With that, he disappeared behind the solid wooden door separating their two work areas, leaving her alone once again.

Knowing he was there meant she couldn't risk doing any more snooping. Especially since she'd learned the scary way that he could pop out at any moment rather than relying on the phone or intercom to address her.

She should have been annoyed, but was suddenly too excited. Now she had Miami to look forward to.

It was a detour, and would definitely put her behind on the whole find-the-thief-and-get-the-heck-back-to-New York thing. But it was *Miami,* for heaven's sake.

Not just Miami the city. She'd been there several times before, as well as Key West and one ill-fated trip to Daytona Beach that her parents still didn't know about. And with luck, they never, ever would.

No, it was Miami during the event of the season—at least one of them, as far as the fashion world was concerned. A number of labels, not just Ashdown Abbey, would be flaunting their latest designs during what had become a very high-profile annual show.

The show itself—Fashion for a Cause—raised money for a different charity each year. This time, it was for a children's hospital. But the one-of-a-kind fashions that were shown at the event were then mass-produced and began to show up in retail outlets across the country and even around the world, depending on orders received during and soon after their debuts at the show.

Lily and her sisters were nowhere near the level one needed to achieve to participate in this type of event. She'd never even attended, though it had always been a distant, hopeful dream.

Now she had the chance to go. Not just as a member of the audience twelve rows back, but as Nigel Statham's girl Friday.

It was kind of a thrill. One that could quickly turn into a nightmare, if her true identity was discovered, but she was pretty sure it was worth the risk. Even after bumping into Bella Landry, no one had looked at her differently or started asking pointed questions about her presence, so she still seemed to be safe.

In fact, during a bit of digging into Bella's association with Ashdown Abbey, she'd actually learned that the young woman had just requested a bit of personal time from work. Lily intended to look into that, see if there was any more to it than sick days or a short vacation, but hadn't yet had the chance.

But with luck, her obscurity at the company would continue.

And she was almost giddy with anticipation about the charity show, so…yeah, she was going to take the chance. Wear giant sunglasses, introduce herself under her assumed name and hope for the best.

Too excited to simply sit there, she accessed Nigel's daily schedule and zipped ahead to the dates of the Miami trip. It looked as though they would be gone four days and three nights. Flying on the corporate jet. Staying in the luxury suites of the Royal Crown Hotel, one of the most expensive hotel chains on the East Coast.

As excited as she was about the runway show itself, she wondered if there would be time to slip away for a massage and spa treatment. Lord knew the amenities at the Royal Crown had to be amazing.

Like any good PA, she needed to start making a list. Of everything she would need to pack for herself, but also whatever business-related items she—or more specifically, Nigel—might need.

Clothing-wise, she knew she should continue wearing garments exclusively from the Ashdown Abbey lines. But even though they did some very nice summer and activewear pieces, nothing that she'd seen so far was as ideal for the sun and surf atmosphere of Miami as her own designs.

Her lightweight fabrics, bright colors and floral prints would be perfect, absolutely perfect for such a trip. And she had several just-perfect pieces with her in California.

The question was: Did she have the courage to take them along and wear them in front of Nigel? Would he notice they weren't from the Ashdown Abbey collections and wonder about her sudden switch? Or would he write it off as simply a female thing, knowing that women tended to have overstuffed closets filled with every type of clothing for every type of occasion and very few were loyal to only one designer or label? If it looked good, fit well and—with luck—was on sale, a woman would buy it.

She sighed. It wasn't easy pretending to be a serious, buttoned-down executive secretary when all she wanted to do was rush home, kick off her shoes and blazer, let down her hair and run around packing sundresses and sandals for Miami as though it was a beach vacation rather than a short but significant business excursion.

Seven

The flight from Los Angeles to Miami was as long as it had ever been, but it passed by so smoothly, Lily couldn't have said whether it took three hours or thirty.

Nigel's—or rather, Ashdown Abbey's—corporate jet was incredible. She'd been on a Jet Stream before, but traveling with Nigel as his personal assistant was quite different from traveling with her parents and sisters for a business-slash-pleasure trip. Especially since that had been years ago, when she was much younger and harder to keep in her seat.

This time around, she was mature enough to appreciate the soft-as-butter leather seats, the interior that looked more like a *House Beautiful* living room than the inside of an airplane and the single flight attendant who appeared when she was needed, but was otherwise neither seen nor heard.

A car was waiting for them when they landed. The driver stood outside, ready to collect their bags and load them into the trunk after holding the rear door while they climbed inside the perfectly air-conditioned vehicle. Given Miami's balmy heat, Lily was grateful for the convenience.

Despite her continued misgivings, she'd opted for many of her own clothes for this particular excursion. She'd packed a couple of dark, formfitting suits, just in case, but had filled her luggage mostly with her own summer-inspired creations. Sleeveless maxi dresses that were feminine but elegant enough for the occasion, and a couple of linen skirts with light, flowy tops.

So far, Nigel didn't seem to mind her change of wardrobe, even though she'd been wearing a much darker, more subdued outfit the last time he'd seen her, and now she was sunflower bright in a short yellow dress and strappy cloth espadrilles.

The truth was, she felt much more like herself dressed this way. But since she needed to remember she wasn't *supposed* to be herself around Nigel Statham, that doing so could very well pose a problem.

She would have to be careful of what she said and how she acted—around everyone, not just Nigel—no matter what she was wearing.

When they arrived at the hotel, the driver pulled to a stop beneath the portico, then hurried around to open Nigel's door. Nigel stepped out and turned back to reach a hand in toward her.

Lily slid across the seat, putting her fingers in his as she climbed out, careful not to flash too much thigh as her dress rode up a few perilous inches.

The second they touched, a wave of heat washed over her, making the breath stutter in her chest just a bit. She tried to tell herself it was the heavy humidity hitting her as she stepped out of the air-conditioned interior of the car, but she didn't think that was true.

She'd been struck by too many unexpected hot flashes or zaps of electricity in his presence to believe they were geographical or weather-related. After all, she'd first noticed her reactions to his proximity in his office, and there had certainly been no natural humidity or direct sunlight beaming down on her there.

Avoiding Nigel's gaze in case he'd noticed the hitch in her breath, she moved away from the car while the driver and a bellman unloaded their luggage and stacked it on a waiting cart. When they finished, Nigel tipped the driver, then placed a hand at the small of her back as they followed the hotel employee inside.

Nigel had already given the bellman his name so that as they passed the registration desk, key cards were ready. All the bellman had to do was collect them, then lead the way directly to the bank of elevators that would take them to the presidential suites.

Before they'd left Los Angeles, Lily had told Nigel that just because he was staying in a luxury suite didn't mean she needed to. She could just as easily stay in a regular room, or perhaps a lower-level suite, then meet up with him whenever necessary.

Nigel wouldn't hear of it, however. He insisted that it would be more convenient to have her right next door. And besides, the reservations had already been made; no sense bothering with them now.

So even though she still thought it was an unnecessary expense, she was kind of looking forward to having an entire presidential suite to herself. It would be almost like having the entire loft back in New York to herself, which almost never happened.

The elevator carried them slowly upward, the doors opening with a quiet whoosh. The bellman stepped out with the rolling luggage cart and led them down the carpeted hallway.

At the end of it, he paused, slipped a key card into the coded lock, and let them into what was, indeed, a luxury suite.

The carpeting beneath their feet was thick and off-white, the furniture plush and chosen to match. French doors lined one entire length of the main room—facing the ocean, of course.

The view, even from across the room, was magnificent. Lily couldn't wait to get to her own suite so she could walk out onto the balcony and enjoy the soft breeze and salty sea air.

Remaining near the open door, Lily watched the bellman pull bags from the cart. When he reached for hers, though, she stepped forward and stopped him.

"Oh, no," she told him. "Those are mine. They go in my room."

The young man paused, hand still on the handle of her overnight bag. "Would you like me to carry them into the bedroom for you?" he asked, sounding slightly confused.

"No," she tried to clarify. "I'm staying in another suite. Next door, I believe."

Letting go of the bag, he checked the small paper envelope in his hand that had held the key card. "I'm sorry, ma'am, but I was only given the key to one room. Could your room be under another name?"

That drew her up short. Turning to Nigel, she cast him a questioning glance. His face was as blank as a sheet of paper.

Sensing the confusion in the room, the young man cleared his throat. "Let me call down to the front desk. I'm sure there was simply an oversight. We'll get it straightened out right away."

Crossing the room, he picked up the phone resting on the credenza beside a huge vase of freshly cut flowers. He spoke in low tones to whoever picked up on the other end.

A moment later, he hung up and turned back to them, his expression saying clearly that they weren't going to like whatever it was he had to say.

Lily's stomach tightened as she waited.

"I'm sorry, but the front desk only has one reservation under Mr. Statham's name, and none for you."

Lily exchanged another confused glance with Nigel. He shrugged a shoulder beneath the tailored lines of his charcoal suit coat.

"So we'll get a second room now. It's not a problem."

The bellman winced, and Lily knew what was coming even before he took a fortifying breath to speak. The fact that he refused to look either of them in the eye was another clear sign of impending doom.

"Unfortunately, we're fully booked. With the Fashion for a Cause event in town, just about all of the higher-end hotels are. I'm very sorry."

For several beats, no one in the room said a word, or moved a muscle for that matter. The bellman looked nervous. Nigel looked undecided. And Lily was pretty sure she looked plain old put-out.

But whatever mistake or misunderstanding had taken place, it certainly wasn't the poor hotel employee's fault.

With a sigh, Lily said, "It's all right. This suite is big enough for a family of twelve. I'm sure the two of us will be able to make do." She ended with what she hoped was a reassuring smile.

The bellman's chest dropped as he blew out a breath of relief. He thanked her profusely and finished taking their luggage off the cart, which he then rolled to the door.

Nigel followed behind, handing him what she hoped was a generous tip—hazard pay, and for nearly being sent into a panic attack—before he disappeared into the hallway.

"I'm sorry," Nigel said, strolling back to the center of the sitting area and stopping just a yard or so in front of her. "There must have been some sort of mix-up."

"I'd say so."

"My assistant normally makes these reservations for me."

She lifted a brow, silently asking if he seriously intended to blame this situation on her.

He almost—almost—cracked a smile.

"I don't usually invite my assistants to join me for these things, however, so when I asked you along, I apparently forgot to tell you we'd need to book a second room."

"Apparently," she replied drily.

Then, without another word, she turned and crossed to the large mahogany desk set against the far wall. Pulling open drawers, she found the phone book and started flipping through.

"What are you doing?" Nigel asked, moving a few feet closer.

"Looking for another hotel. A less ritzy one that might have a room available."

Reaching the desk, he leaned back against the corner nearest where she was standing, crossing his arms over his chest. "Why?"

She shot him a castigating glance. "I'm going to need somewhere to sleep. And as we've established, you only reserved one room, and this hotel is full up."

"I thought you said the suite was large enough for the both of us."

Lily kept her attention glued to the phone book, pretending her stomach hadn't just done a peculiar little somersault. In a low tone, she murmured, "I lied."

"Don't be silly," he said after a moment of tense silence.

Though she kept her gaze strictly on the yellow pages of the directory, his long, masculine fingers suddenly came into view, grasping the book at its center and plucking it from her hold.

Setting it flat on the desk behind him, he remained where he was, one palm flat on the phone book to hold it in place and stop her from snatching it back.

"There's no need for you to stay elsewhere when there's plenty of room here. Besides, as I told you before, having you at another hotel, possibly all the way across town, won't exactly be conducive to business. What if I need you for something?"

She narrowed her gaze, mimicking his earlier posture by folding her arms beneath her breasts and hitching back on one hip.

"You can call and I'll come over. I'm sure that all of the hotels in this area have working phone lines and taxis that travel in between," she told him flatly.

The specks of green in his hazel eyes flashed briefly, and Lily thought perhaps she'd gone too far. She was supposed to be his beck-and-call girl, after all, and should probably keep her sarcasm to a minimum.

"I'm afraid that's simply unacceptable," he told her, his already noticeable accent growing even thicker and more pronounced. "I don't pay you to show up when you can, I pay you to be there when I need you."

Score one for the prim-and-proper Brit, she thought.

Licking her lips, she said, "How much do you think you'll need me?" No sarcasm this time, just a straight-out question. "I was under the impression this trip would be on the light side, as far as work was concerned."

"Still," he responded without really addressing her question, "it would be better for us to stay in close proximity, just in case. Having you one door over would have been fine, but no farther than that."

Pushing away from the desk, he offered her an encouraging smile. "Don't worry, we'll make it work."

He returned to the pile of their combined luggage in the center of the room. Picking up his briefcase in one hand, laptop case in the other, he moved them to the coffee table in front of the sofa. It matched the eggshell hue of the carpet almost perfectly.

"I don't suppose this presidential suite has two bedrooms," she remarked, relaxing enough to take a few steps in his direction.

She kept her arms across her chest, though. Not tightly, but because she knew if she let her arms fall to her sides, she would only end up fidgeting.

Resigning herself to staying in the same suite as her boss was one thing. Staying in the same suite with this man, who just happened to be her temporary boss, but who also caused her mouth to go dry and other places to grow damp, was something else entirely. It made her nerves jump and dance beneath her skin.

"I don't believe so, though you're welcome to check."

More because it gave her a chance to put a little space between Nigel and herself than because she thought there was an actual chance at success, she strolled away to explore the rest of the suite.

For the most part, it had everything: a rather large kitchenette; dining and sitting areas; an entertainment area complete with television, DVD player, stereo and even a Wii; an officelike work area; and a balcony. There was a small bathroom in the main portion of the suite, but she assumed the bedroom had one of its own, as well.

And then there was the bedroom itself. Unless it somehow broke off into two separate sleeping quarters past the single doorway, there was only one. One spacious, beautiful, far-too-intimate bedroom.

Stepping over the threshold, she took in the totality of the room in a single glance. The enormous bed—a queen size, at least, but she suspected king—with the woven bamboo headboard. A low, matching bureau with an oval, almost seashell-shaped mirror attached. The small table and chair over by the sliding glass door leading to the balcony. And the open doorway that led to the master bath.

She'd been right about that, too. Apparently sparing no expense, the hotel had put in marble flooring, marble vanity, marble shower enclosure and marble tub surround. The bathtub and shower were also separate—one sunken, with jets that made her want to strip and climb in for a long, hot soak that very minute; the other the size of a compact car with an etched-glass enclosure and half a dozen nozzles arranged on the other three sides to send water spraying in all the right places.

Without a doubt, Nigel would be paying thousands of dollars a night for so many of these amazing amenities. And Lily was beginning to think they might just be worth it.

But the question remained—where was she supposed to sleep?

Nigel watched Lillian as she prowled around the suite, investigating the layout. He was afraid she would be disappointed by what she found—namely a single bed in a single bedroom off the main sitting area.

She stood in the doorway, studying the room. He tried to decipher her thought process by her body language—the line of her spine, set of her shoulders, the movements of her hands and fingers dangling at her sides. Unfortunately, she was giving nothing away.

After several long minutes, she turned back around. For a second, she stared at him, looking none too pleased. But then her gaze floated past him and her chest fell as she expelled a breath.

"I guess I can sleep on the sofa," she said, giving him a wide berth as she walked past him. "With luck, maybe it pulls out."

The sofa was long enough for a body to stretch out upon,

but didn't look comfortable enough that anyone would want to. Still, she started removing the cushions one by one, feeling around for a handle that would turn it into her bed for the night.

Nigel opened his mouth to stop her before the first cushion was even taken off, but found himself distracted by the sight of her shapely rear as she leaned over. He'd noticed her change in wardrobe this morning when he'd picked her up for their flight—from the dark, Ashdown Abbey business attire she'd been wearing around the office to a much lighter, brighter dress of unknown origins—but hadn't truly appreciated her current clothing choice until just now.

When she didn't find what she was looking for, she straightened with a huff, putting her hands on her hips. He could have gone on admiring the view all afternoon, but finally took pity on her.

"Nonsense," he said, causing her to spin around, cushions still askew. "There's no need for you to stay on the sofa."

She quirked a brow. "Do you expect me to sleep on the floor, then?"

He gave a snort of laughter. "Certainly not."

The quirked brow lowered as she narrowed both eyes, her mouth flattening into an angry slash. "If you say the bed is big enough for both of us," she all but growled, "I will not be responsible for my actions."

Her frown deepened when he chuckled at her obvious irritation.

"What kind of employer do you think I am?" he couldn't help but tease.

She didn't respond, simply waited, her expression still one of a woman who'd just unwittingly sucked on a lemon.

Crossing the space between them, he cupped her shoulders, giving her an encouraging "buck up" shake before letting his palms slide down her bare arms.

"Surely this suite is spacious enough for the two of us to manage without getting under each other's skin. And we can ask that a cot be brought up before nightfall, set it up out here. I'll use it," he added. "You can stay in the bedroom."

Some of the temper leached out of her features, softening the lines around her mouth and eyes.

"I can't make you do that. This is your suite. You should be able to enjoy the bed."

He had half a mind to inform her that he'd enjoy it best if she joined him there. He hadn't even seen the bed in question yet, but he'd stayed in enough luxury suites to have a pretty good idea of just how expansive and inviting it would be.

Surely enough room for two to sleep comfortably. And more than enough room for them to do much more than that.

Though he knew it was a bad idea all around, he indulged himself for a moment in fantasies of having her naked and in his arms. Of rolling around on slick satin sheets with her. Of having her beneath him, above him, plastered to him by their own perspiration and mutual passion.

His errant thoughts alone caused tiny beads of sweat to break out along his brow and upper lip. He could only imagine the physiological response he might suffer from full-on body-to-body contact of a carnal nature with her.

Which was a problem. A rather large, obvious problem, if she'd cared to glance down and notice as much. Thankfully, she didn't.

But hadn't he sat down just last week and given himself a stern talking-to? Hadn't he learned his lesson with Caroline?

Lessons, plural, he reminded himself now. Thanks to his ill-fated affair with Caroline, he'd learned not to get involved with women who were even loosely involved in the fashion industry, and certainly not one with whom he worked. His own personal assistant would be even worse.

He'd also learned that it was probably wise to avoid any

sort of romantic attachment to American women altogether. Especially when he was trying to get Ashdown Abbey firmly established here in the States. And when his father was breathing down his neck about the delay in that success.

For those reasons and probably hundreds more, Lillian needed to remain off-limits. He couldn't deny that he would enjoy a quick, lusty romp with her. No warm-blooded male could without being accused of lying through his teeth.

But better to lie on a too-short, too-narrow cot in the middle of the sitting room, picturing Lillian on the other side of the bedroom door, than to make one of the biggest mistakes of his life.

No amount of pleasure was worth the destruction crossing that line could bring. Or so he tried to convince himself.

"It's no problem, truly," he told her, wanting to move things away from the hazardous territory his thoughts were treading upon.

Not giving her a chance to protest further, he grabbed her bags and carted them into the other room, setting them at the foot of the bed. When he turned, she was behind him, watching his every move.

"Go ahead and unpack, settle in. I'll call down for a cot and ask them to have it delivered by nightfall. In the meantime, I have a business dinner at seven o'clock with the head of one of our most important accounts. I'd like you to come along, if you're feeling up to it."

After a short pause in which she didn't respond, he added, "I'll understand if you're tired from the flight and would prefer to stay in."

"No," she responded quickly, straightening in the doorway. "I'd love to go."

He gave a sharp nod. "Excellent. I'll leave you to freshen up and get ready. We'll leave in an hour, if that's all right."

"Of course."

They both started forward at the same time, she toward her luggage and he toward the bedroom door. Their arms brushed as they passed one another, a jolt of electricity, awareness, summer heat pouring through him. It made him catch his breath, swallow hard and wonder if she was suffering the same disturbing effect…or if he was the only one doomed to spend the weekend drenched in sexual frustrations thicker than the Miami heat.

Eight

Dinner their first night in Miami. Breakfast in the room—but set out so beautifully and served so elegantly that they might as well have been at a five-star restaurant. A business luncheon. And then, the evening before the Saturday morning fashion show, a cocktail party where a handful of those involved in the show—designers, buyers, planners, executives—could rub elbows and size up the competition in a friendly, noncompetitive atmosphere.

Lily had known the schedule ahead of time, but hadn't realized how busy or rushed it would actually be.

True to his word, Nigel slept on a cot in the middle of the sitting room of the luxury suite. The roll-away bed looked completely out of place and—to Lily, at least—flashed like a giant neon sign that spelled G-U-I-L-T every time she laid eyes on it.

She didn't have any other ideas or a better solution to their awkward one bed/two bodies predicament, but it still wasn't right that she'd kicked him out of the bedroom of his very own suite.

Guiltiness aside, however, she had to admit she was more than a little relieved to have a door to close and a separate room to escape to each time they returned from yet another business-related outing.

She didn't fear for her safety, exactly—at least not physically. She feared for her sanity and her best intentions.

The longer she was with Nigel, the more she admired him. The more attractive she found him. The more often she caught herself zoning out to simply stare at him, admiring the line of his jaw, the slight bow of his mouth, the way his lips quirked when he was amused or his brows rose when he was curious or intrigued.

What sent her skittering into the bedroom so often under one flimsy excuse or another, though, was the problem she was having regulating her temperature. Oh, how she wished she could blame it on the Florida heat and humidity. Such a nice, handy reason for the hot flashes that kept assailing her at the most inconvenient moments.

But it was hard to point fingers at the weather when the worst of her symptoms seemed to hit mostly indoors, when they were surrounded by comfortable-verging-on-chilly air conditioning.

Which led her to only one terrifying conclusion: it wasn't her current location causing her so many problems…it was Nigel himself.

It was her body, her hormones, her apparently too-long-dormant, ready-to-party-like-it-was-1999 libido kicking up and screaming for attention.

Why couldn't her sex drive have come out of hibernation while she was still in New York? There were men there. Handsome, funny, available men. Or so she'd been led to believe by her sister, who seemed to find a different one to go home with every other night.

But seriously, how hard would it have been to—in crude terms—get laid before flying to Los Angeles, where she was pretending to be someone else entirely? Why had she been living practically like a nun the past several months, only to meet Nigel and have her inner pole dancer wake up wanting to shake her moneymaker?

Oh, yes, she was in trouble. Pretending to be a mild-mannered personal assistant by day, tossing and turning and fighting the urge to throw open the door and invite Nigel to join her in the big lonely bed by night.

That was why she made herself scarce at every opportunity. That was why she turned the lock on the bedroom door each night before she climbed into the king-size bed.

Not to keep him out, but to keep herself in.

But with every tick of the clock, every sleepless hour that passed, Lily was losing the battle. The thoughts that spiraled through her head made her hot and restless and frustrated.

Then she would wake up still tired and out of sorts, doing her best to get her errant emotions under control while she dressed and got ready. Thinking she was back to normal and fully prepared to face Nigel again, she would open the bedroom door…and find him standing there, looking like the answer to the prayers of single women around the world. Or he would turn at the sound of the door opening and her heart would screech to a stop, leaving her chest empty and her throat burning.

She was amazed she managed to stumble her way through the day without doing something truly embarrassing like drooling, weeping or collapsing at his feet in a puddle of needy, pathetic female.

Nigel never showed signs of suspecting her inner turmoil,

so she must have been doing a decent job of hiding it. Thank goodness.

Now here she was, holed up once again in the suite bedroom that had caused all of her problems to begin with. And Nigel was out there, once again, waiting for her.

They had time yet before they needed to leave for the pre-show cocktail party, but as cowardly as she knew it was, she couldn't bring herself to spend their in-between time out in the main sitting area.

She'd tried, early on in their stay. They'd talked business, and Nigel had filled her in on what to expect from the weekend and various events they would be attending. But the longer they talked, the more they ran out of things to say, and the more awkward the lengthy pauses became.

Awkward and…tension-filled. As though the air was slowly being sucked out of the room, replaced by a growing electrical current. It would cause her chest to grow tighter by degrees and goose bumps to break out along her skin.

So over and over again, she retreated to the bedroom and relative safety.

She wondered if Nigel was beginning to get suspicious. But even more, she wondered if he felt any of the sizzling awareness, the building attraction that assailed her every time they were alone together.

A part of her hoped he did. After all, she shouldn't be the only one suffering and running for cover like a nervous squirrel.

A bigger part of her, though, hoped that he didn't. Uncontrollable lust and a passionate fling with the man who was supposed to be her boss but was really a possible archnemesis was something she so sincerely didn't need.

It would be much better to suffer in silence, even if her continued run-and-hide routine was becoming increasingly difficult to pull off, while he remained completely oblivious.

At least tonight they would be surrounded by other people. The party would keep them busy, talking and shaking hands, drinking and nibbling on hors d'oeuvres. By the time it was all over with and they made their way back to the hotel, they would both be exhausted and more than ready to go their separate ways for a good night's sleep. Or as many hours as they could squeeze in before having to get up and go to the fashion show, anyway.

She was walking around in one of the hotel's soft, fluffy terry-cloth robes, fresh from the shower and lining up her underthings before beginning to dress, when there was a light tap at the door. Her heart lurched, mouth going dry, because she knew it could only be Nigel.

Swallowing hard, she took a deep breath and tiptoed over, checking the front of her robe to be sure she wasn't flashing too much bare skin before pulling the door open a crack.

As expected, Nigel stood on the other side. He was still dressed in the clothes he'd been wearing all day, but had removed the suit jacket and tie and opened the first few buttons of his dress shirt, giving her a rather mouthwatering peek at the smooth chest beneath.

Through the crack of the door, he looked at her, his gaze starting at her still-damp hair and skating down the line of her terry-wrapped body to the tips of her painted toes, then back up. His eyes glittered as they met hers, sending ripples of desire to every dark nook and cranny of her being.

Her pulse kicked up and she tried to swallow again, but found that both her throat and her lungs refused to function.

Thankfully, he saved her from choking on her own words and sounding like a strangled crow by filling the uncomfortable silence and speaking first.

"Lillian," he began. "Sorry to disturb you, but I have a small request."

He sounded so serious, she immediately straightened,

shifting from vulnerable woman getting dressed to personal assistant on the alert in the blink of an eye.

"Of course," she responded. "What do you need?"

"Would it be too much to ask that you wear something special this evening?"

Her brow rose. Images of lacy teddies and garter belts with silken stockings filled her head. Surely he couldn't mean *that* sort of "special."

From out of nowhere, around the other side of the door-jamb, he revealed a long, hunter green garment bag with the Ashdown Abbey logo embroidered in the upper right-hand corner.

"This is one of the gowns from the line we'll be showing tomorrow. I was hoping I could talk you into wearing it to-night as a bit of a sneak peek for our competition."

He shot her a lopsided grin, accompanied by a wicked wink, and she couldn't help smiling in return.

"I'll be happy to try," she told him, reaching toward the top of the garment bag where he held it by a thick, satin-wrapped hanger. "But I'm not exactly a supermodel. It may not fit."

His gaze flitted down her fluffy white form once again, as though he could see straight through the robe to the body beneath.

"I think you'll be fine. We don't design for stick-thin women to begin with, even when it comes to runway shows, and this dress in particular is a very accommodating design."

"All right," she said with a small nod.

She'd brought one of her own elegant maxi dresses with her that would have been perfectly acceptable for a cocktail party, but she had to admit she was curious to see what Nigel wanted her to wear. And it was more than a little flattering to be asked to model one of Ashdown Abbey's brand-new, as-yet-unseen designs in front of other designers and associ-ates for the first time.

She would rather be showing off her *own* creations, of course, but since she wouldn't be able to reveal that they were her designs, anyway...well, beggars couldn't be choosers.

Still standing there, dress in hand, bedroom door open, she wasn't quite sure what else to say. It didn't seem right to simply slam the door in Nigel's face, even though she was eager to peel open the garment bag and see what lay inside.

Finally, he said, "I'll give you a few minutes. Let me know if you have any problems."

With that, he took a step back, but seemed reluctant to move away. And she was equally reluctant to close the door, shutting herself in again. But they did have a party to get to.

"I'll only be a few minutes," she murmured.

"Take your time. The limo won't be here to pick us up for an hour yet."

She disappeared back inside her luxurious little Girl Cave as he turned and headed off to get ready himself. Hanging the garment bag on the open armoire door, she slid the center zipper all the way down and peeled back the sides.

It was almost like scratching a lottery ticket. She held her breath, slowly revealing the gown beneath.

As lottery tickets *and* designer gowns went, it was a winner. Stunning. Gorgeous. Awe-inspiring. And for her, just a bit envy inducing.

The sheer, champagne-colored chiffon shimmered in the light and with every movement, no matter how slight.

The ruched bodice ran at an angle to the single beaded shoulder strap, about two inches wide, leaving the other shoulder entirely bare. A wide swath of the same jewels from the shoulder made up a belted waistline of sorts.

From the waist down, the chiffon flowed in angled layers over the same-colored charmeuse all the way to what she assumed would be the floor once she put it on.

Suddenly, she was both excited and nervous at the prospect of modeling it. Not surprisingly, the dress was beautiful. But she hadn't worn anything this fancy in a very, very long time. And now, not only was she being asked to dress up like she was attending a royal wedding, but she would be expected to "sell" another designer's work.

Knowing she didn't have a choice, she hurried back to the bathroom to finish with her hair and makeup, then returned to the main room and shrugged out of the terry-cloth robe. Even though she'd planned for a cocktail party and packed accordingly, the underthings she'd brought didn't quite suit the gown she would now be wearing.

If Nigel had shown her the dress ahead of time, she probably would have taken a quick shopping trip for something a bit sexier. Stockings instead of nylons, perhaps, and a bra and panty set the same color as the gown.

Luckily, some of the bras and panties she had with her were pale enough not to be seen through the champagne material. And though the bra wasn't strapless, the straps were able to be rearranged or removed completely. She would just have to hope it stayed up and in place all night.

Moments later, she was reaching for the gown, turning it around and searching for the narrow hidden zipper that ran the length of the back. Time to see if the design was as forgiving as Nigel claimed.

Stepping into the pool of material, she drew it up and slipped the single strap over her left shoulder. The bodice settled over her breasts and the cups of her bra, the rest of the gown falling into place from her midriff down.

Reaching around, she clutched the two sides of the dress at the back in one hand and held them together. The fit might be snug, but she thought it would work. Especially if she held her stomach in most of the time.

She looked okay, too, judging by her reflection in the bureau mirror. Provided the dress stayed in one piece once she got it zipped up. Which she couldn't quite manage on her own.

Butterflies unfurling at the base of her belly, she moved to the bedroom door and opened it, slowly and quietly. Venturing into the other room, she glanced around, searching for Nigel. She might not *want* to ask for his help, but she kind of needed it.

But the sitting room was empty.

Still holding the gown closed behind her with one hand, she strolled farther into the room, checking the balcony and wondering if he'd left the suite entirely for some reason.

Then she heard a click and turned just as he stepped out of the guest bath looking like a million bucks. Maybe one point eight.

He was wearing a tuxedo. Just a plain black tuxedo, the same as men had been wearing for decades.

And yet Lily would be willing to bet he looked better in it than any other man in the history of tuxedos. The word *scrumptious* came to mind. As well as *delectable* and—as Zoe might say—*hunkalicious.*

The midnight-black jacket and slacks fit him like a glove. If they hadn't been tailored specifically for him, it was the finest bit of off-the-rack sewing she'd ever seen.

His sandy-brown hair was combed back, slightly wavy, but every strand in place.

And the tie at his throat...well, there was something about that tight, classic bow and the gold cuff links at his wrists that made her want to drop her arm, let the gown drop to the floor, and stalk forward to start peeling him out of his own uptight party wear.

The thought stopped her cold. Made her give herself a mental shake and stern reminder that lusting after the boss was a bad, bad idea.

Of course, on the heels of that came the notion that she

wouldn't mind being a bad girl. Just for a little while. And only with Nigel.

His mind may have been wandering down the same wicked path, because his eyes snapped with flecks of green fire the minute he saw her. His gaze raked her from head to toe, and she could have sworn a tiny muscle flexed along his jaw.

She drew a deep breath, which caused the bodice of the not-yet-zipped dress to slide down a notch. Pinning it in place with her only remaining free hand, she cleared her throat and smiled weakly.

"I need a little help," she murmured.

He raised a brow, his attention still glued to her lower-than-intended décolletage.

By way of explanation, she turned, giving him her back and showing the long, open rear of the gown.

She felt rather than saw him move behind her and grasp the small tab of the zipper near the base of her spine. In a slow, gentle glide, he pulled it up.

When it was high enough, she dropped the arm that had been holding the two sides together and moved it instead to her nape, where she brushed aside her loose hair. The back of the dress only reached her shoulder blades, but better safe than sorry.

As he reached the top of the zipper, his knuckles brushed her bare skin, sending shivers rippling across her body in every direction. She braced herself and tried not to let that shiver show, but she felt it all the way to her toes.

Long seconds ticked by while she stood unmoving, not blinking, not even daring to breathe. And then Nigel stepped back, his hands falling away from her bare flesh.

Relief washed through her…but so did regret.

"There," he said, the single word coming out somewhat gruff.

Lily let go of her hair and turned again to face him. This time, his gaze seemed to be taking in the detail of the gown.

"Lovely," he told her with a nod of approval. "As I knew it would be."

Lifting his eyes to hers, he asked, "What do you think?"

"It's beautiful," she answered honestly, smoothing a hand over the front of the dress and then fluffing it a bit to show the ethereal layering of the skirt. It flowed and fell like angels' wings, almost as though it wasn't there at all.

"And how does it feel?" Nigel wanted to know. "Comfortable enough to wear for the evening?"

"I think so," she told him. It was rather nice of him to ask. Most employers—most men, for that matter—wouldn't bother.

"I'll need to find some jewelry and shoes that go with the dress," she added, "but it fits better than I would have expected."

"Ah," he said, holding up his index finger and offering a crooked grin. "I believe I can help with that."

Leading her over to the sofa in the middle of the room, he began opening boxes that had been stacked across its narrow length and pulling out bits of tissue paper from around whatever the boxes held.

"I had them send over some of the footwear for tomorrow's show. All of the shoes for the line are similar in style, and we always make sure to have extras on hand, but I wasn't sure of your size."

He stepped back, gesturing for her to take a look, pick out whatever she needed. Brushing past him in her bare feet, she peeked and found an array of gorgeous, very expensive footwear.

They were, indeed, all very similar, making her even more curious to see the entire line. She wanted to know what designs Ashdown Abbey had created to go with all of these shoes…or vice versa, actually.

Checking sizes, she chose a pair of strappy gold open-toed heels and balanced on the arm of the sofa to slip them on. Even before she stood up again and glanced down to see how they looked with the dress and her painted nails peeping out, she knew they would be perfect with the gown.

Lifting her head, she found Nigel's eyes on her. Intense. Blazing. The air caught in her lungs and refused to budge.

Seconds ticked by, then minutes. Finally, he cleared his throat and reached for something else amidst the boxes and loose tissue paper.

"This should complete the look nicely," he said, flipping open the lid of a large, flat, velvet-lined box.

Inside was a breathtaking necklace and earring set. Champagne diamonds in exquisite gold settings. And if they were real—which something told her they were—they had to be worth a small fortune.

Plucking the earrings from their bed of black velvet, he dropped them into her palm. Then he removed the necklace and stepped around her to stand at her back.

Lifting the sweep of loose, wavy curls she'd worked so hard on, she waited for him to finish with the fastener before dropping her hair and pressing her fingers to her throat to touch and straighten the main pendant and surrounding web of gems.

"This is a lot of expensive fashion. Are you sure you trust me to wear it out of the suite?" she asked somewhat shakily, only half teasing.

"You aren't planning to run off with it all at the stroke of midnight, are you? Like Cinderella," he teased in return.

She certainly felt like Cinderella. A young woman pretending to be someone other than who she really was, dressed to the nines to attend a grand ball with a man who definitely qualified as a Prince Charming.

She only hoped her true identity didn't become known as the clock struck midnight, as he said. That might possibly be worse than running off with thousands, maybe hundreds of thousands of dollars' worth of Ashdown Abbey property.

Since she had no intention of doing the latter, she knew she was safe on that count. It was the former she needed to worry about. But with luck, it wouldn't be an issue tonight or at any time on this trip.

She hoped not once they returned to Los Angeles, either, but one thing at a time. First she needed to get through this evening. Then tomorrow's fashion show…then the remainder of their short stay in Miami…then their return to Los Angeles… She would deal with the rest after that.

"I'm no Cinderella," she said by way of answer.

"No," Nigel responded.

The single word came out short and clipped, drawing her attention to his face and the hard glint of his hazel eyes.

"Cinderella could never look so lovely in this gown or these jewels," he added more softly.

Lily's heart stuttered in her chest. Okay, that was definitely more than a simple compliment. That was…a come-on. A warning. A promise of things to come.

She knew now, without a shadow of a doubt, that Nigel felt at least a fraction of the attraction to her that she felt toward him. The lust she'd been feeling, the shocks of static electricity whenever they were in the same room together, were *not* one-sided.

Which was good. It was nice to know she wasn't going crazy or nursing an awkward schoolgirl crush on the captain of the football team whom she would never in a million years have a shot with.

But it was bad, too. Because while she might be able to

keep a lid on her own out-of-control emotions and baser instincts, she couldn't be sure that lid wouldn't come flying off in the face of his pent-up passions if he decided to point them in her direction and throw caution to the wind.

Already her mouth was growing dry, her hands damp. Her pulse had kicked up to a near-arrhythmia pace. And every other portion of her body was heating at an alarming rate, sending a flush of inappropriate longing across her face and her upper body.

If Nigel noticed her state of distress, he didn't comment. Instead, he held an arm out, offering his elbow.

"Shall we?"

Saved by the RSVP and waiting limousine, she thought, releasing a small, relieved breath.

"Yes, thank you," she replied, wrapping her hand around his firm forcarm.

They glided to the door so smoothly their movements might have been choreographed. If they could keep up such astounding synchronicity, Lily thought they might, just *might,* be able to pull this off.

Not only her pretense of being someone she wasn't, but of hiding the sexual tension that—to her mind, at least—rolled off the pair of them in waves.

But while the outside world was likely to see merely a very handsome, rich and successful businessman escorting his fair-to-middling female assistant to an industry function, she was almost painfully conscious of the heat from Nigel's body burning through the fabric of his tuxedo jacket to all but scorch her fingertips. Of the rapid beat of her heart behind the bodice of her borrowed gown. Of every second that ticked by when she could think of nothing but being alone with Nigel in a very naked, nonprofessional capacity.

Nine

Hours later, the noise and crowd of the cocktail party behind them, Lily sat beside Nigel in the rear of the limo as it carried them back to the Royal Crown. Her eyes were closed, her head resting against the plush leather seat. To say she was tired would be a tremendous understatement.

As though reading her mind, Nigel's knuckles brushed her cheek, tucking a strand of hair behind her ear.

"Tired?" he asked.

His touch was featherlight and possibly one-hundred-percent innocent, but still it had her sucking in a breath and fighting to maintain her equilibrium.

Rolling her head to the side, she forced her eyes open, braced for the impact of meeting his gaze. It still hit her like a steamroller.

Knowing she wouldn't be able to form coherent words to respond to his query, she merely nodded.

One corner of his mouth tipped up in an understanding

smile. "You were incredible tonight," he told her in a soft voice that washed over her like warm honey.

"You look amazing," he continued. "Better than any model we could have hired to showcase this design. And the way you are with people…you're a natural. You had everyone at the party eating out of your hand. The men especially. Well, the straight ones, at any rate," he added with a teasing wink.

Despite her weariness, she couldn't help but return his grin of amusement. "I'm glad you approve. I don't mind telling you I was nervous about tonight. I didn't want to embarrass you *or* do anything in this beautiful gown to put a damper on tomorrow's show."

"Not possible," he said with a sharp shake of his head. "You were…extraordinary. As I knew you would be."

His heartfelt compliment made her blush and filled her with unexpected pleasure. She shouldn't be happy that he was so impressed with her performance tonight. She should be annoyed. Sorry that she'd helped to bolster his or Ashdown Abbey's reputation in any way.

But she *was* pleased. Both that she'd maintained her ruse as a personal assistant, and that she'd done well enough to earn Nigel's praise.

She was candid enough with herself to admit that the last didn't have as much to do with his standing as her "boss" as with him as a man.

"Thank you," she murmured, her throat surprisingly tight and slightly raw.

"No," he replied, once again brushing the back of his hand along her cheek. "Thank *you*."

And then, before she realized what he was about to do, he leaned in, pressing his mouth to hers.

For a moment, she remained lax, too stunned to move or respond. But his lips were so soft and inviting, and she'd been imagining what it would be like to kiss him for so long…

With a low mewl of longing, she shifted into his arms, bringing her own up to grasp his shoulders. She opened to him, letting her lips part, her body melt against his and everything in her turn liquid.

Nigel groaned, pulling her to him with even more force, his wide palm cupping the base of her spine while his tongue traced the line of her mouth, then delved inside at her clear invitation.

The world fell away while they ate at each other, devoured each other, groped each other like a couple of randy teenagers.

A million reasons why they shouldn't be doing this clamored through her head. But those doubts and fears were little more than a low-level hum behind the loud roar of desire, yearning, need.

Despite the regrets she might suffer later, right now she didn't care. She couldn't remember ever being kissed this way, ever wanting a man as much as she wanted Nigel Statham.

He was danger and sex and exotic intrigue on two legs, with a bone-tingling British accent to boot. How women didn't adhere themselves to him like dryer lint throughout the day she didn't know.

How amazing was it, then, that he seemed to be attracted to her? Seemed to want her?

Maybe he put the moves on all of his personal assistants. Maybe one of his goals while he was in the United States was to shag, as he might say, as many American girls as possible.

If that was the case, she expected to be really annoyed later on. At the moment, however, she was more than willing to be just another notch on this handsome Brit's bedpost.

While one hand kneaded the small of her back, his other swept up to the bodice of the couture gown, cupping her breast, stroking through the material. Despite the thick ruching and bra beneath, her nipples beaded, drawing a moan of desire from deep in her throat.

Nigel answered with a groan of his own, increasing the pressure of his mouth against her lips. There was barely a breath of air between them, but even that was too much. And as he thrust his tongue around hers over and over, she met him with equal ferocity, sucking, licking, drinking him in.

He smelled of the most wonderful cologne. Something fresh and clean, with a hint of spice. Whatever the brand, she was sure it was expensive. And worth every penny, since it made her want to lick him from clavicle to calf, inhale him in one shuddering gulp, absorb him into her own skin like sunshine on a warm summer day.

But if he smelled good, he tasted even better. Warm and rich, like the wine he'd been sipping all evening at the party, with a hint of the whiskey he'd downed toward the end. She didn't even particularly care for whiskey, but if it meant drinking it from his lips and the tip of his tongue, she could easily drown in the stuff on a regular basis.

Nigel's hand was trailing down her side, sweeping the curve of her breast, her waist, her hip and slowly inching the long skirt of the dress upward when the limousine came to a smooth but noticeable halt. A second later, the driver's side door opened and Nigel pulled back with a fiercely muttered, "Bollocks."

Quickly, before the fog of passion had even begun to clear from her brain, he straightened her gown and the lines of his own tuxedo, taking a moment to swipe lipstick from both her mouth and his just as the lock on the rear door of the limo clicked.

By the time the door swung all the way open to reveal the driver standing there waiting for them, everything looked completely normal. Professional, even. Nigel and Lily were sitting at least a foot apart, canted away from each other on the wide bench seat, as though they hadn't even been speaking, let alone groping one another like horny octopi.

Without a word, Nigel exited the car, then helped her out.

Nigel thanked the driver, passed him a generous tip and escorted Lily into the main entrance of the hotel. They passed through the lobby, her heels clicking on the marble floor until they reached the elevators. Inside, they were silent, facing the doors and standing inches apart, even though they were alone in the confined space.

When they reached their floor, Nigel gestured for her to step out ahead of him, then took her elbow as they moved quietly down the carpeted hallway. The perfect gentleman. The perfectly polite employer with no lascivious thoughts whatsoever about the assistant who was staying in his suite with him.

With some distance now from that amazing kiss in the limousine, Lily wasn't sure what to think or how to feel.

Did she want to pick up where they'd left off as soon as they got into the suite? A shiver assaulted her at the very thought.

Or did she want to put the kiss behind her? Chalk it up to the heat of the moment and go their separate ways once they got inside? That thought made her a little sad, which surprised her.

Reaching the door, she waited for Nigel to slide the key card through the lock and decided to play it by ear.

If he began to ravish her the minute the door closed behind them, she would go limp and let it happen. No doubt enjoying every step of the way.

If he returned to his usual quiet and respectfully reserved self, not coming anywhere near her again…she would do the same. It might even be for the best, regardless of how much she would mourn the loss of his lips, the taste of him on the tip of her tongue.

As she entered the suite ahead of him, her heartbeat picked up, the tempo echoing in her ears as her anticipation grew. But he didn't grab her the second the door closed behind them, didn't push her against the wall and begin the ravishment she'd been fantasizing about. They stepped into the sitting room. Perfectly polite. Perfectly civilized.

The sound of Nigel clearing his throat made her jump. She turned slowly to face him, disappointed when she didn't find him stalking toward her, desire burning in his hazel-green eyes.

"I feel as though I should apologize for what happened in the car," he murmured in a low, slow tone of voice.

Her heart plummeted. Well, she supposed that answered the question of what he thought about the kiss, didn't it? She tried not to be offended—hadn't she already admitted to herself that fooling around with her boss-slash-possible enemy was a bad idea?—but couldn't help being slightly hurt. After all, to her, the kiss had been one step away from spontaneous combustion.

"But quite frankly," he continued when she didn't respond, "I'm not that sorry."

Her eyes widened, locking with his. What she saw there was the same passion she'd experienced in the limo. The same need, the same longing…but banked to a slow burn rather than a blazing inferno.

"Which makes what I have to ask next rather awkward."

Lily swallowed, the blood in her veins going thick and hot.

"Would you mind stepping out of your gown?"

She blinked. That wasn't so bad. A little odd, yes, but only because she would have expected him to be closer when he made the request. Maybe whisper it in her ear or want to strip it from her body himself.

But if watching her disrobe was part of his fantasy, she could certainly comply.

And then he went and ruined whatever small thread of fantasy had been forming in *her* head.

"The dress and shoes need to be returned before tomorrow's show."

"Oh." Yes, of course. The fashion show. She was walking around in one of its borrowed designs.

"Sure," she said, fumbling for both words and clear thoughts. "Just...give me a minute."

Feeling unsure and uncoordinated, she turned toward the bedroom and crossed the distance with as much dignity as she could muster while kicking herself for being seven kinds of fool.

Closing the door behind her, she moved robotically, removing the necklace, earrings, bracelet and ring, and setting them on top of the bureau. Then she toed off the strappy ice-pick heels. And though she nearly dislocated her shoulder doing it, she managed to grasp the tab of the gown's zipper at her back and tug it all the way down. Stepping out of the dress, she returned it to its satin hanger inside the garment bag, then zipped that closed.

Since she couldn't go back out to the rest of the suite in her underwear, she covered herself with the same fluffy hotel robe as earlier, which she'd left lying at the foot of the bed.

Gathering all of Nigel's borrowed items, she strode back into the sitting room. He was standing exactly where she'd left him, but she refused to meet his gaze. She'd had quite enough humiliation and emotional up-and-down, back-and-forth for one night, thank you very much.

Walking to the sofa, she draped the garment bag over the arm, dropped the shoes back in their tissue-paper-lined box, and laid the collection of pricey jewelry on the low coffee table.

"There you go," she told him, her tone clipped, even to her own ears. And still she wouldn't look at him. "Thank you again for letting me wear them tonight. It was a privilege."

Truth. It *had* been a privilege...right up until the moment it became pain.

With that, she turned and marched back to the bedroom, spine straight, head held high. She remained that way until after she'd closed and locked the door. Until she'd shed the robe and her underthings, leaving them in a pile on the bathroom floor. Until she'd stepped into the hot spray of the shower, letting the sharp beads of water pummel her, pound her, drown her in mindless sensation.

Only then did she let go of her rigid control, let oxygen back into her lungs and the hurt into her soul.

Only then did she crumble.

Well, that didn't go quite as he'd planned. And he felt like a total prat.

The kiss in the limousine had been anything but forgettable. There had been moments when he'd thought he might implode from the sensations that assailed him at the mere touch of Lillian's lips against his own.

It had taken every ounce of self-control he possessed to pull away from her when the car stopped, and to get them both set to rights before their driver came around to open his door and got more than an eyeful. Thank goodness he'd retained enough of his senses to even notice the slowing of the vehicle.

The walk into the hotel and ride up in the lift had been another agonizing test of his control. He'd wanted nothing more than to turn on her once the doors slid closed, press her up against the wall, and continue from where they'd left off. Kissing, caressing, fogging the glass...or in this case, the mirrored walls.

Every step down the narrow pathway to their suite, he'd imagined what he would do to her as soon as they were shut safely inside. Alone and away from prying eyes.

But he couldn't very well pounce on her the minute the

door swung shut, could he? She might have thought him a sex-crazed maniac. Or worse, believed that whether or not she acquiesced might impact her job.

Nigel muttered a colorful oath. The *last* thing he needed was a sexual-harassment complaint brought against him or the company.

But more than that, he didn't want to be *that* fellow—the one who flirted with his secretary, made her believe that there might be recompense if she went along with his advances… and the unemployment line if she didn't.

And he *never* wanted Lillian to think that of him. Professional status and reputation be damned. His attraction to her was genuine—if ill conceived—and he wanted her to know that. He wanted her to be genuinely attracted to him, as well. Where was the fun in any of this if she wasn't?

He'd thought he was being witty and smooth by asking her to remove the dress for tomorrow's show. True, he did need to get it back so that it would be ready and waiting for its respective model by morning.

Inside his addled and obviously not very intelligent mind, however, he'd imagined her slinking out of the dress and shoes—either right there in front of him or in the privacy of the bedroom—and then him suavely murmuring that *now that she was naked, how would she feel about picking up where they'd left off?*

It had all sounded so bloody brilliant as he'd played it out over and over in his head. And then somehow he'd mucked it up. He'd said the wrong thing or said it the wrong way.

Something had gone cockeyed, because Lillian's face had transformed from soft and mistily content to shocked and hurt.

He'd missed the chance to apologize and set the matter straight before she disappeared into the bedroom. Then when she'd come out, he'd been too gobsmacked and tongue-tied by his own stupidity to rectify the situation before she ran off again.

Bloody hell. What was it about this woman that turned him into a complete wanker?

Regardless, he had to fix it. He might not be spending the rest of the evening exactly as he'd hoped—naked and writhing around with Lillian on that king-size bed he had yet to sleep in—but he couldn't let her storm off thinking he was a git. That the kiss they'd shared meant nothing or that getting Ashdown Abbey's dress back safe and sound was more important to him than what was blooming to life between them.

Long minutes passed while he tried to decide how to go about cleaning up the mess he'd made. The clock on the mantel counted them down, grating on his nerves even as he paced in time with the steady *tick-tick-tick* of the second hand going round.

After wearing a path in front of the sofa, he moved closer to the bedroom door. He could hear the faint sound of water running and assumed she was taking a shower.

The thought of her stripped bare, standing beneath the steaming jets, made it increasingly hard to concentrate. It made other things hard, as well. Especially when he pictured her working up a lather of soap and rubbing it all along her body. Stroking, smoothing, scrubbing. First her arms, then her breasts and torso and…lower.

A thin line of perspiration broke out along his upper lip and his muscles went tense. He'd never known that the act of getting clean could be so dirty. And he very much wanted to walk in there to assist with both.

Chances were he'd get his face slapped for his trouble. He had to *talk* to her first. Work on seducing her back into the shower second.

The water shut off suddenly. And he strained to listen for

movement on the other side of the door while bracing himself with both hands against the jamb on this one.

He didn't want to frighten her, and chances were he was the last person she wanted to see right now, but he needed to talk to her.

Waiting a few minutes until he thought she would be finished in the bathroom but not yet climbing into bed, he tapped lightly on the door.

His palms were damp. His chest was actually tight with anxiety.

This wasn't like him at all. He hadn't been riddled with nerves about facing a girl since… Had he ever been? At university he'd even been a bit of a ladies' man, if he said so himself.

And now he was sweating like David Beckham after a particularly rigorous football match at just the prospect of confronting Lillian once again. Especially when he knew it would mostly involve groveling and apologizing and begging her not to continue believing he was a total squit.

When long moments passed without her opening the door, he began to suspect she was avoiding him. Not that he blamed her. But he knew she was in there, knew she'd heard his knock and knew she couldn't possibly be asleep yet.

He cocked a brow. Well, now he was growing somewhat annoyed.

He knocked again, louder this time. If need be, he would go in there with or without her invitation—after all, it was his suite, and he'd been generous up to now allowing her to have the spacious bedroom and master bath all to herself. Though he'd much prefer she open the door voluntarily so he wouldn't have to add overbearing bullying to his list of crimes tonight.

Just when he was about to try the door himself, he heard a small snick and the knob began to turn. The door opened only a crack, the light from the sitting room illuminating just one eye and a narrow portion of Lillian's face. The rest was left in shadow by the darkness of the bedroom beyond.

"Yes?"

Her voice was low, flat and far from friendly when she said it.

"I'm sorry to disturb you," he began.

Which was so very close to simply *I'm sorry,* yet he managed to skirt a straight-out apology. Brilliant.

"Could I speak to you for a moment?" he tried again, still taking the coward's way out.

"It's late," she told him, keeping the door open no more than a single inch. "I'm tired. We can talk in the morning."

And with that, she closed the door. Soundly, firmly and with a clicking lock of finality.

Bugger. Nigel barely resisted the urge to smack his fist against the solid door frame.

Well, he'd mucked that up good and proper, hadn't he? Damn it all. The bloody dress that had started this debacle was on its way back to join the rest of the collection and await tomorrow's fashion show, while he was still trying to find a way to mop up the mess he'd made.

He took a deep breath, as frustrated with Lillian's refusal to speak to him as with his own bungled efforts.

Enough of this. It was going to be dealt with right here, right now and that was the end of it.

Raising his hand, he knocked again, hard enough that she couldn't help but hear the summons and know he meant business.

"Go away, Mr. Statham."

Oh, so it was back to Mr. Statham, was it? When she'd just begun to call him Nigel.

There was only one thing to be done about that.

Leaning close to the door, he lowered his voice and ordered, "Open this door, Lillian."

He could have sworn he heard a snort of derision, followed by a mumbled, "I don't think so."

His jaw locked, teeth grinding together until he thought they might snap.

Slowly, carefully, enunciating every word, he bit out, "Open this door, Lillian, right now."

He paused, listening for movement, but heard none. "You have until the count of three," he told her, sounding like every angry father in every movie he'd ever seen, "or I'll kick it in."

In truth, he wasn't certain he *could* kick the door in. He prided himself on staying in shape, playing at least a game or two of squash per week, in addition to his regular exercise routine. But nothing in his past led him to believe he would have either the strength or the martial-arts-like coordination necessary to actually break down a door.

And then there was the sturdiness of the door itself. Not to mention the lock, which—hotel quality or not—might just prove to be un-break-down-able. He rather hoped he didn't have to find out.

Stepping backward, he took a deep breath, steeled himself and got ready to follow through on his promise.

And then there came a click. And the muted turn of the knob.

He watched as the brass-plated handle inched around, letting the air seep from his lungs on a slow exhale and the tension leach from his tendons.

Once again, she opened the door only a crack, but at least this time it was a couple of inches instead of only one. Popping her head out, dark blond hair still damp from her shower, she glared at him.

"Are you threatening me?" she asked, eyes crackling like lapis. "Because that smacks of a threat. Or possibly even harassment. I've got a phone in herc with 9-1-1 on speed dial, and I'm not afraid to use it."

Nigel sighed, resisting the urge to rub a hand over his face in frustration. With her. With himself.

"Just a moment of your time," he said. "Please."

When she didn't immediately slam the door in his face, he soldiered on.

"I wanted to apologize for earlier."

Her lashes fluttered as she narrowed her eyes a pinch, but he ignored the warning. With luck she would hear him out and stop shooting daggers.

"It wasn't my intention to offend you by asking you to remove the dress so it could be returned for the show tomorrow. In retrospect, I might have worded my request a bit differently."

He watched her arch a brow, her grip on the edge of the door loosening slightly. She even let it drift open another fraction of an inch.

"For instance, I should have said that the sooner we got the dress off you and headed back for the show, the sooner we could return to what we were doing in the car. Or better yet, I should have ripped the dress off you as soon as we stepped into the suite and said to hell with the show. So we'd be short a look and a model would be sent home in tears...it would have been worth it to avoid hurting your feelings, as I obviously did. And to be making love to you right now instead of standing here having this conversation, hoping you won't slam the door in my face. Again."

There, he'd said it. It had pained him, especially in the region of his pride, which seemed to currently be residing near his solar plexus, making it feel as though a very heavy anvil were pressing down on his diaphragm.

Now to see if it had any impact on Lillian whatsoever, or if she would, indeed, slam the door in his face for a second time. He watched her carefully, trying to judge her response from the one eye, one cheek and half of her mouth that were visible.

Her lashes fluttered, and her tongue darted out to lick those lips nervously.

And then the door began to creak open—so slowly, he thought he might be imagining things.

But the door did open, all the way. And she stepped out, into the light of the sitting room. Behind her, he could see that one of the lamps beside the king-size bed was lit, but it wasn't bright enough to fill the entire room.

She was wearing one of the hotel robes, covered from neck to ankle by thick, white terry cloth. She should have looked shapeless and unattractive, but instead she looked adorable. Her hair hung past her shoulders in damp, wavy strands, her flesh pink from its recent scrubbing.

With the belt pulled tight, he could easily make out her feminine curves. The flare of her hips, the dip of her waist, the swell of her breasts. A V of skin and very slight shadow of cleavage were visible in the open neckline of the robe, making him want to linger, stare, nudge the soft lapels apart to reveal even more.

He was on extremely thin ice with her already, however, and didn't think it wise to press his luck. No matter how loudly his libido might be clamoring for him to do just that… and more.

Threading her arms across her chest, she watched him warily.

"So you don't…regret what happened in the limo?" she asked quietly.

Nigel's heart gave a thump of encouragement. If she was asking, that meant she'd been thinking about it. Thinking and worrying.

Taking a cautious step forward, he flexed his fingers to keep from reaching for her. But he answered clearly, honestly, consequences be damned.

"Not even if you call the authorities, as you threatened.

Or file a sexual-harassment complaint at Ashdown Abbey, as you have every right to do."

She seemed to consider that for a moment, and then the stiffness began to disappear from her rigid stance. Her expression lightened, her arms loosening to drop to her sides.

Taking a deep breath that lifted the front of the robe in a way that shouldn't have been seductive but was, she let it out on a long sigh.

"This is a bad idea," she murmured, letting her gaze skitter to the side so that he wasn't certain if she was speaking to him or more to herself.

"I'm working for you," she continued. "You could fire me or use me because I'm in your employ. Things could get ugly."

Nigel's shoulders fell almost imperceptibly, and he felt as though his entire bone structure slumped inside his skin. She was right, of course, but that wasn't at all the reaction he'd been hoping for.

"True," he acquiesced, albeit grudgingly. "Though I'm *not* using you, and I would never fire you over something… personal. Something that I would be equally responsible for and took equal part in."

Her eyes locked on his. "You're that noble, are you?"

His chin went up, every ounce of the pride and dignity driven into him from birth coming to the fore. "Yes. I am."

It was her turn to slump as she let out a breath. "I was afraid of that," she said, sounding almost resigned.

And then her voice dropped, but he had no trouble hearing her. No trouble making out both the words and the meaning.

"I'm not sorry, either. About what happened in the limo."

Ten

Lily knew she *should* be sorry about what had happened in the limo. She should also have graciously accepted Nigel's apology without saying anything more, then turned and locked herself back in the bedroom.

Oh, how smart that would have been.

Oh, how she wished she had that much strength of will.

But no matter how hurt and offended she'd been by Nigel's actions concerning the dress, she hadn't been able to stop thinking about *that kiss* the entire time she'd been in the shower. Even through her tears and ragged breathing, her body had hummed with unspent passion. With need and longing and plain old *want*.

Her thoughts had swirled with *what-if*s. What if they hadn't been interrupted by their arrival at the hotel? What if she hadn't been wearing one of the designs for tomorrow's fashion show? What if he'd kissed her in the elevator, then pounced on her like a cat on a mouse the minute they'd reached the room?

What if everything from the past forty minutes had happened far differently and they were in bed right now? Making love. Exploring each other to their hearts' content. Scratching the itch that had plagued her since the first moment she'd met him.

She shouldn't want any of that. She should be smart enough or even angry enough at his possible involvement in the theft of her designs to slam the door on all of it. To man up and stop letting her hormones do her thinking for her.

But she couldn't. Or at least none of her attempts so far had been successful.

So she was giving up. If you couldn't beat 'em, join 'em, right?

She knew now that Nigel was just as attracted to her as she was to him. That what she'd felt in the limo when they kissed hadn't been one-sided. And she just wanted to throw caution to the wind, to be with a man who made her toes curl and her insides feel like molten lava.

And so what if she did? Nigel didn't know who she really was, and she wasn't going to be around that much longer. A few weeks, maybe a month more. Just until she solved her mystery and could return home with information that would save and vindicate her company.

Nigel never even needed to know her true identity. She'd done a fairly good job as his personal assistant so far, if she did say so herself. And knowing it wasn't permanent employment, that he wasn't going to be her boss forever, made it even easier to justify a hot, steamy fling. She could let her hair down, have a good time, and walk away with no consequences. With a quick letter of resignation and excuse about getting another job elsewhere—preferably far away, but without hinting at her true residence in New York—she could wipe the slate clean.

So this was almost like a freebie. Casual, no-strings vacation sex.

Considering how long it had been for her, how long since she'd had a date or sex—casual or otherwise—all she could think was *yes, please.*

Which was why she'd come clean and told him that she didn't regret what had taken place between them after the party, either. She'd wanted him to tear her dress off her body and take her up against the nearest wall of the suite the minute they'd set foot inside.

Well, maybe not that dress, but *a* dress.

And she didn't want to spend the rest of the night alone in that immense bed, tossing and turning and unfulfilled.

Watching his eyes go dark and glinting at her softly spoken admission, she took a deep breath and decided to press on, letting him know in no uncertain terms *exactly* what she meant.

"As much as I enjoyed modeling one of Ashdown Abbey's newest designs, I wish I hadn't been wearing that dress tonight. Because I would have enjoyed having you rip my clothes off the second we walked through the door."

His eyes darkened even more, his jaw tightening until a muscle ticked near his ear.

"Be very certain of what you're saying, Lillian," he grated, the words sounding as though they were being dragged from the depths of his soul. "Because once we begin, there will be no stopping. No more noble gentleman. No more polite facade."

Shivers rocked her nerve endings at what he left unspoken. That once they stopped dancing around their need for each other, once they dropped all pretenses and got down to business, it would be raw, primal, unapologetic S-E-X.

Swallowing hard, she took a single step forward. Determined. Ready.

"I understand," she told him. "And I'm not slamming the door in your face."

Heat exploded across Nigel's face. Lighting up his eyes like emeralds, rolling off his body in waves and battering her like a storm front.

He closed the distance between them without a word, moving in almost a blur of motion. One minute he was over there, the next he was grabbing her by the arms and yanking her to him with such force, her feet nearly left the ground.

His mouth crashed down on hers, twining, mating, devouring. She met him kiss for kiss, thrust for thrust.

He tasted just as he had in the limo—only better, because this time she knew it wasn't a one-time-only, heat-of-the-moment thing. This time she knew he wanted her, she wanted him, and they were going all the way to the finish line, consequences be damned.

Her hands climbed the outside length of his arms to clutch his shoulders. They were broad and strong and welcoming. She kneaded them for a moment before trailing her fingers around to the front of his shirt.

She didn't need to open her eyes or look at what she was doing to loosen the knot in his tie, unbutton his collar, then open the entire front of his starched white and pleated tuxedo shirt. He groaned as she touched his bare chest, and she was close to groaning with him.

The pads of her fingers dusted across hard and flat pectorals, tickled by just a sprinkling of crisp hair. Blast-furnace heat radiated from his skin and seeped into hers.

Pushing the sides of his shirt and jacket apart, she continued to explore, to study the contours of his body as though she were reading Braille. Then she ventured down to the waist of his pants.

Her nails raked his stomach and he sucked in a breath. Though her own breathing was none too steady and she was gasping for air from their long, tortuous kiss, Lily grinned at the feel of his abdomen going rigid at her touch. She trailed her fingers through the path of hair leading down the center and disappearing into his slacks.

With a groan, he took her mouth again, cupping the back of her head with both hands, stabbing his fingers through her hair and against her scalp to anchor her in place.

She was only too happy to be there, to have him desperate for her, out of control, ravishing her. She only wished they'd started earlier instead of wasting all that time on arguments, hurt feelings, uncertainty and explanations.

Finding his belt buckle, she worked it free, pulled the two ends apart and dragged the long strip of leather through its loops in one fierce yank. It hit the floor with a thud a second before she went for the closure of his pants.

She could feel the heat of him, the hard, swollen length pressing against the back of her hand through his fly. She took a moment to run her knuckles up and down along the prominent bulge, making Nigel moan and nip her lower lip with his teeth.

She smiled against his mouth, then let out a low moan of her own when his hands slid down either side of her spine to her bottom, squeezing roughly and tugging her even more firmly against his blatant arousal.

Squirming in his grip, she rubbed all along the front of him while at the same time wiggling her fingers between them to undo the top of his pants and slowly ease down the zipper.

He let her work. Let her get as far as dipping her fingertips beneath the waistband of his briefs before lifting his lips from the pulse of her throat, setting her half a step away, and tearing at the belt of her robe. It took him a moment to deal with the knot, which got stuck from all his tugging. But then it was loose, the edges of the robe falling open and catching at the bends of her arms when he pushed the plush material over her shoulders.

She was naked beneath, her flesh flushed pink now from passion rather than the steam of her shower. When the cool air of the suite hit her bare skin, she shivered. But she didn't try to pull her robe back up for warmth or try to cover her nudity. Not with Nigel standing there, staring at her as though she was the most delectable morsel ever created.

Not when she'd been dreaming about this moment for far too long. Wanted it far too much to hide.

So she stood there. Half-naked. Half shivering, both from the cool interior and the need coursing through her veins. And she let him look his fill.

Of course, while he was looking at her, she was returning the favor, taking in his surprisingly tanned skin against the backdrop of the white shirt and black tuxedo. His amazingly muscular and well-formed physique. He could have been a model posing for some sexy cologne ad—and raking in the dough when women everywhere flocked to buy whatever he was selling.

Though it felt like minutes, she was sure it only took a few seconds for them both to drink each other in, then lose all patience for the five or six inches that separated them. Nigel's hazel-green eyes glittered, reflecting the same desire she knew filled her own.

Lowering his head, his eyes grew hooded, and he made a feral sound deep in his throat before stalking toward her. He reached her in a blink, sweeping one arm around her back and the other behind her knees.

Her heart gave a little flutter as he lifted her against his chest in one smooth movement that didn't seem to tax him in the least. She released a breath of laughter and clutched his neck as he hiked her even higher.

He returned her grin, then leaned up to press his lips to

hers. Never breaking the kiss, he carried her across the room and straight to the waiting bed.

Once there, he balanced her carefully with one arm while reaching out to turn back the covers with his other hand. Then he laid her near the center of the soft mattress, following her down until he covered her like a warm, heavy human blanket.

The fabric of his tuxedo rubbed along her bare skin except where it was open down the front. The heat of his chest pressed to hers, making her want to wiggle and worm even closer, if possible.

Wrapping her legs around him, she drove her hands inside his open shirt and tuxedo jacket, loosening it even further and pushing it jerkily over his shoulders and down his arms. He moved with her, aiding her efforts until he could shrug out of the garments and toss them aside.

Then he returned the favor, stroking her waist, her rib cage, the undersides of her breasts, but not lingering in any one spot, even though she writhed for his touch. Ignoring her whimpers of need, he finished removing her robe, lifting her when he needed to in order to tug the thick terry cloth out from under her. Then it, too, was gone, hitting the bureau with a *slap*.

His chest heaved as he stared down at her, his gaze raking from the top of her head to where her legs were still twined around his thighs. He took in her bare breasts, the slope of her belly, her triangle of feminine curls.

Everywhere he looked, she broke out in goose bumps. His nostrils flared, and his eyes flashed with a wolfish gleam.

Without taking his gaze from her, he kicked out of his pants and shoes and the rest of his clothes, dislodging her hold on him only when absolutely necessary. In seconds, he was naked and glorious, so beautiful he made her throat close with unexpected emotion. She swallowed it back as he moved over her. Reminded herself that this was just a casual fling, nothing more.

Lifting her arms, she wound them around his neck, drawing him to her even as he met her halfway. They kissed slowly, finally taking time to explore each other's mouths at a leisurely pace. The taste, the texture, likes and dislikes.

Of course, for her, it was all likes. And judging by the feel of him pressing against her inner thigh, he was liking everything just fine, as well.

His fingers tangled in her hair, angling her just the way he wanted while she raked his back, reveling in the play of muscle, the dip of his spine, the row of vertebrae leading down to the delectable swell of his ass.

His moan filled her mouth and his arms tightened around her. She arched into him, wanting to get close, even though they were already nearly as close as two people could be.

Dragging his lips across her cheek, he nipped at her throat, nibbled the lobe of her ear, trailed his mouth over her clavicle and toward her swollen, arched breasts.

Her breathing was choppy, her head getting fuzzier and fuzzier with longing as he teased her mercilessly and her temperature rose. But there were things that needed to be taken care of before they went much further. Before the fuzziness turned to full-blown mindlessness and she forgot everything but her own name.

"Nigel," she murmured, tightening her legs around his hips and moving her hands to his biceps while he nuzzled the side of her breast.

"Nigel," she said again when he didn't respond, resorting to tugging at his hair instead. "Condom. I don't have one—do you?"

It took a second for her words to sink in, for movements to slow and his mouth to halt mere centimeters from the center of her breast.

His head fell to the side and he groaned, the sound vibrating against her skin, making her shiver. With a particularly colorful-but-amusing curse of the British persuasion, he pushed himself up on his forearms to glare down at her.

Without waiting for her acquiescence, he peeled away from her and climbed out of the bed, flashing his sexy bare bottom as he hustled into the other room, where she assumed he had a stash of protection. Thank goodness, because she hadn't exactly packed for Los Angeles *or* Miami with hot, impulsive sex in mind.

Despite his command not to move a muscle, she pushed herself up on the bed, propping the pillows behind her and leaning against the bamboo headboard. She thought about tugging the sheet up to cover her stark nudity, then decided that if Nigel could stroll around the suite completely naked and unselfconscious, then she didn't have to be so modest, either.

He returned moments later, clutching a couple of distinctive plastic packets. Tossing one on the nightstand, he kept the other, tearing it open and quickly shaking out the contents.

Lily watched with barely suppressed eagerness as he sheathed himself in short, competent motions, then rejoined her on the bed, a dark, devilish gleam glinting in his eye as he closed in on her.

"I told you not to move."

His voice scraped like sandpaper, but still managed to pour over her in a rush of honeyed warmth.

She arched a brow, flashing him a wicked, unapologetic smile. "I guess I've been a bad girl. You may have to spank me."

Heat flared low in Nigel's belly, spreading outward until

it tingled in his limbs, pooled in his groin and flushed high across his cheekbones.

"Oh, I intend to do much more than that," he said in a voice gone arid with lust.

If he'd ever seen a more beautiful sight in his life than Lillian George sprawled naked in bed, waiting for him, he couldn't remember it. And now he didn't think he would ever forget.

As aroused as he was, as desperate as he was to be inside her, he couldn't seem to tear his gaze from the delightful picture she made. Her light brown hair falling loose around her shoulders, sexy and mussed from his fingers running through the long, silken strands. Her pale skin flushed with the rosy glow of desire.

Her breasts were small but perfect, their pale raspberry nipples puckered tight with arousal. And the rest of her was equally awe-inspiring—the slope of her waist, the triangle of blond curls at the apex of her thighs, the long, lean lines of her legs.

But what he loved most was her lack of inhibition. She didn't try to hide from him, didn't try to cover her nudity with her hands or a corner of the sheet. She was comfortable in her own skin. And more, she was comfortable with him, with what they were about to do with each other.

Feigning a patience and self-control he definitely didn't feel, he moved beside her, pulling her legs straight and tugging her into the cradle of his arms. She rolled against him, her breasts pressing flat to his chest, the arch of her foot rubbing lazily along his calf.

He brushed a loose curl away from her face, tucking it behind her ear. "In case I forget to mention it later, I'm awfully glad you agreed to come with me this weekend."

Her lips turned up at the corners, her blue eyes going soft and dewy. “Me, too.”

“And though I don’t mind sleeping in the other room, it will be nice to spend the night in this nice big bed, for a change.”

She lifted one dainty brow at him. “I didn’t say you could stay in bed with me.”

He narrowed his eyes, fighting the twitch of his lips that threatened to pull them into a grin. “Planning to use me, then relegate me back to that dreadful cot, are you? Let’s just see if I can change your mind about that.”

He watched her mouth curve into a smile just before he kissed her. Her arms wrapped around his neck and trailed down his back as he shifted his weight, bringing her more snugly beneath him.

He’d meant what he’d said—bringing her along on this trip really had been one of his better ideas, even if he hadn’t known at the time that they would end up here. He couldn’t deny, however, that he’d hoped.

Almost from the first moment she’d walked into his office, every fiber of his being had shot to attention and begun imagining scenarios in which they ended up much like this. He’d known such a thing was dangerous, though, and couldn’t—or shouldn’t—happen.

But now that it was…he couldn’t bring himself to be sorry. Or to worry about the consequences. All he wanted was to continue kissing her, caressing her, making love to her all night long.

And if she thought to send him back to that cramped, lumpy roll-away bed after she’d gained her satisfaction… Well, he would just have to keep her so busy and blinded by passion that she lost all track of the time. He would be spending the night in her bed before she even realized the sun was coming up.

He stroked the smooth roundness of her shoulders, her

arms, her back. Everywhere he could reach while their tongues continued to mate. He could kiss her forever and never grow bored. But there was so much more he wanted to do with her.

With a small groan of reluctance, he lightened the kiss, drawing away just enough to nibble at the corner of her mouth, trailing down her chin to her throat. She threw her head back, giving him even better access. He took his time licking his way down, pressing his lips to her pulse, dipping his tongue into the hollow at the very center, where he felt her swallow.

They rolled slightly so that he was lying over her again, and she welcomed him by hitching her legs high on his hips and locking her ankles at the small of his spine. It brought him flush with her feminine warmth, and brought a groan of longing snaking up from the depths of his diaphragm.

Her fingers kneaded his biceps while he turned his attention to her lovely, lovely breasts. The nipples called to him: tight little cherries atop perfectly shaped mounds of pillowy-soft flesh. He squeezed and stroked with his hands while his lips circled first one pert tip and then the other.

Beneath him, Lillian wiggled impatiently and made tiny mewling sounds while his mouth grew bolder. He kissed and licked and suckled, trying to give each breast equal consideration until the press of her moist heat against his nearly painful arousal grew too distracting to ignore.

Lifting his head, he pressed a quick, hard kiss to her mouth. "There's so much I want to do to you," he murmured, brushing her lips, her cheekbone, the curve of her brow with the pad of his thumb. "So much time I want to spend just touching you, learning every inch of your body. But we may have to wait until later for all of the slow, leisurely stuff. Right now I simply need you too much."

He canted his hips, nudging her with the tip of his erection to emphasize his point. Bowing into him, she brought them into even fuller, more excruciating contact. He hissed out a breath, closing his eyes and praying for the endurance to make it through this night and shag her properly without embarrassing himself.

To his shocked delight, she clutched his buttocks with both hands and leaned up to nip his chin with her teeth. “I’m all for fast first. Slow is overrated.”

Nigel chuckled, wondering how he’d gotten so bloody lucky. Hugging her to him, he kissed her again, melding their mouths the way he fully intended to meld their bodies.

Skating a palm down the outside of her thigh, he hitched her leg higher on his hip, opening her to him and settling his sheathed arousal directly against her cleft. He sucked in a breath as her moist heat engulfed him as though the thin layer of latex wasn’t even there.

If he was this affected, this close to the edge just by resting against her so intimately, what would happen once he began to penetrate her? Once he was seated to the hilt, with her tight, feminine walls constricted around him? He was almost afraid to find out, and imagined something along the lines of the top of his head flying off and consciousness deserting him entirely.

Lillian ran her fingers into his hair, raking his scalp and tugging his mouth down to hers. Impatiently, she writhed against him, inviting him in, making it more than clear what she wanted.

Peppering him with a series of biting kisses, she murmured, “Stop teasing, Nigel. Do it already.”

He would have chuckled at her less-than-eloquent demand if he wasn’t just as desperate for her. Sliding a hand between their bodies, he did tease her, enough to draw a ragged moan from deep in her throat. But only to test her readiness and be sure she could accommodate him.

Gritting his teeth, he found her center and pressed forward. She was tight and hot, but took him willingly, inch by tantalizing inch. Their panting breaths and staccato moans echoed through the room while he sank as far as he could go. Filling her, torturing himself.

She fit him like a glove—silken, warm, heavenly. It was a bliss he could have easily spent the rest of the night savoring. If only he hadn't been so desperate to move, the fire, the desire racing through his veins. Lillian's teeth at his earlobe, her softly whispered encouragement, and the way she spoke his name on such a breathy sigh let him know she felt the same.

His whole body taut with need, he drew back. Sliding forward. Slow, even motions that brought exquisite pleasure even as the impulse to thrust faster and harder grew.

Mewling in his ear, Lillian's arms tightened around his neck, her legs around his waist. Her breasts rubbed eagerly against his chest, spurring him on.

"Nigel," she murmured into his neck. The sound of his name on her lips, the feel of them on his skin sent pleasure skating down his spine.

"Please," she begged, slanting her hips, driving him deeper. It was a request, or possibly even a demand, for more.

With a growl he gripped her hips and began to move in earnest. Long, slow strokes followed by short, fast ones. Then the opposite—long and fast, short and slow.

He mixed it up, throwing off any semblance of gentlemanly behavior in an effort to increase pleasure and bring them both to a rocketing completion. With luck, he would be able to hold back his own orgasm long enough to see that Lillian was well-pleased first, though that was becoming more and more of a priority.

And then she started bucking beneath him, her nails raking his back as she cried out. His name, a plea, a litany of *yes, yes, yes, yes.*

Fever heated his blood to a boil while he silently joined in her chorus of need. His muscles tensed, grew rigid. Slipping a hand between them, he drifted his fingers through her downy curls and found the tiny bud of pleasure hidden there.

At the very first touch, Lillian threw her head back and screamed, convulsing around him. Nigel plunged deep, again and again, wanting to prolong the ecstasy, but having no control over millions of volts of electricity setting off fireworks beneath his skin and low, low in his gut.

With a heartfelt groan, he stiffened inside of her, thrusting one last time as ecstasy exploded behind his eyes and spread outward to every cell and nerve ending.

Long, silent moments passed while his heart pounded beneath his rib cage and they both tried to school their breathing. Sweat dotted their skin, sealing them together as he rolled them carefully to one side.

He kept an arm around her, one of her legs thrown over his hip. Her riot of wavy brown hair spilled across the pillow beneath her head, and he smiled, reaching out to pluck a stray strand from where it was stuck to her lips.

At the featherlight touch, she blinked dreamily and opened cornflower-blue eyes to stare up at him.

"Mmm," rolled from her lips in a throaty purr.

Nigel chuckled. "I'll take that as a sign that I left you moderately speechless."

Her mouth curved in contented acquiescence, her eyes fluttering closed again.

Assuming she'd drifted off to sleep, he extricated himself from their tangle of arms and legs and padded to the loo to dispose of the condom and clean up. Returning to the bed, he crawled in beside her, arranged the covers over their still-naked bodies and pulled her back into his arms once again.

She snuggled against him, resting her head on his shoulder and throwing one of her legs over his thigh. Amazingly, the close proximity had arousal stirring to life a second time. But more than mere desire, a warm wash of satisfaction seeped through him unlike anything he'd ever felt before after what was supposed to be only a casual, rushed sexual encounter.

He'd known Lillian George was different—special even—from the first time he'd seen her. He just hadn't known how special, and he wasn't certain even now. All he knew was that she evoked emotions in him he couldn't remember ever feeling before. And created thoughts in his head that he'd never before been tempted to consider.

Stirring beside him, Lillian turned her face up to his, letting her eyes fall open a crack. Her breath danced across his skin and she made a low humming sound deep in her throat before parting her lips to speak.

"I changed my mind," she said drowsily. "You can sleep in the bed with me, after all."

Considering that he was already quite near to doing that already, he couldn't help but chuckle.

"Why thank you," he said, doing his best to feign gratitude when what he really felt was amusement. "That's terribly generous of you."

"I'm a generous person," she mumbled, but he could tell she really was slipping off to sleep this time.

He pressed a kiss to her forehead, waiting until her breathing became fluid and even. "I hope so," he murmured more to himself than to her. "I certainly hope so."

Eleven

They woke up just in the nick of time the next morning. Nigel counted himself lucky they'd woken up at all, considering how…active they'd been throughout the night.

They'd made love once, twice…he'd lost track at three. And that didn't include the time he'd stirred her from sleep by lapping at her honeyed sweetness and pleasuring her with his mouth. Or the time she'd awakened him by returning the favor.

Which made it a miracle that they were up now, dressed quite fashionably, and on their way to the charity runway show that was scheduled to start in a little under two hours, without looking like the walking dead. He was wearing a simple tan suit, white dress shirt open at the throat in deference to both Miami's weather and its casual, oceanside style of dress. It had taken him all of twenty minutes to shower and get ready.

It had taken Lillian slightly longer, but the added time had been well worth it given the results. Her hair was a mass of pale brown waves, drawn up at the sides and held in place while the rest fell down her back in a loose, sexy ponytail. Her makeup was light and flawless, showing no underlying signs of her lack of rest. And she was wearing a short, brightly flowered sundress that definitely hadn't come from the Ashdown Abbey collection. It was, however, perfect for the Florida sunshine, and she looked good enough to eat.

He rather wished he could skip the fashion show altogether, drag her back to the hotel suite and do just that. It took a number of stern mental lectures and dressings-down to keep from telling their driver to turn around and return them to the Royal Crown.

He was Ashdown Abbey's CEO, after all; he was required to be there. And as upset as his father was already with the company's performance since opening storcs and a manufacturing plant in the United States, he doubted the old man would be happy to hear Nigel had blown off a big event to spend the day setting the sheets afire with his lovely new personal assistant.

But despite all the reasons he knew he couldn't, he still wanted to. Especially when he reached for her hand in the lift on the way down to the car and she let him take it, leaving her fingers in his on the walk through the lobby, then again in the limousine. And when she sat mere inches from him in the back of the car—still a respectable distance, but much closer than she had the previous night.

They arrived at the event location and joined a line of vehicles waiting to discharge their passengers. People were pouring into the giant white tent set up for the runway show. Slowly, the limo moved forward until it was at the head of the line, and the driver came around to open the door and let them out.

Nigel stepped out first, then assisted Lillian, keeping her

close to his side while camera lenses approached and flashes of light went off all around them. Today's show wasn't exactly a red-carpet event, but there were enough big-name designers showing and celebrities in attendance that it brought out a crowd of paparazzi and legitimate media alike.

Nigel smiled, nodded, played the part, all the while guiding Lillian through the throng with nothing more than a hand at her back. He was careful not to touch her anywhere else or give any hint to the public of the true nature of their relationship. Or what could be considered the true nature of their relationship after the way they'd spent last evening, at any rate.

It seemed to take forever to make it through the tent, stopping every few feet to say hello or speak to people he knew, people who wanted to know him, or simply big associates it was best to share pleasantries with. Until finally they reached their reserved seating near the runway.

Before sitting down, Nigel took Lillian's hand and leaned close to whisper in her ear. "I need to go backstage and check on preparations for the show. Would you like to come with me or stay here?"

Her fingers tightened around his and she looked more excited than he would have expected, her eyes lighting with anticipation. "I'll go, if that's all right," she replied.

He led her along the long, long frame of the raised runway, weaving around bystanders and finding the entrance to the rear staging area tucked off to one side. Backstage was a mad mass of wall-to-wall people rushing here and there, yelling, calling out, trying to hear and be heard over the cacophony of noise and other voices.

He had a general idea of where the Ashdown Abbey staff and collection were set up, and headed that way.

When they reached the proper area, models were at different stages of hair and makeup and dressing in the chosen Ashdown Abbey designs that would be walking the runway today.

At the center of it all stood the head designer of the collection, Michael Franklin. Calling out instructions, pointing this way and that, keeping everyone on task. As frantic as it looked, Nigel knew from past runway shows that it was all a sort of controlled chaos. Once everything was ready and the show was underway, Michael and everyone else would sit back and declare that things had gone off with nary a hitch.

When the designer spotted Nigel and Lillian standing at the edge of the activity, he lowered his arms, took a deep breath and bustled over. *Time to put on a confident air for the boss,* Nigel thought with amusement. Though he wasn't the least alarmed by what he was witnessing. In his experience, what was taking place behind the scenes of the runway was perfectly normal, Michael Franklin perfectly capable of choreographing the necessary stages of preparation.

"Mr. Statham," Franklin greeted, shaking Nigel's hand.

Nigel said hello and reintroduced him to Lillian before asking how everything was going.

"Fine, fine," Franklin replied. "We're short one model, though," he added, glancing to see if she might be somewhere in the crush of people surrounding them. "I'm sure she'll be here, but if she doesn't show up soon, we'll be pushing back the prep for the champagne gown. We had special hair and accessories lined up for it, since it's our final design to walk the runway."

Nigel pursed his lips, wondering if he should put voice to the idea flashing through his head. It was brilliant, of course, at least to his mind. But he wasn't so certain Franklin or Lillian would agree.

Mistaking his drawn brows for upset, Franklin rushed to reassure him. "Don't worry, Mr. Statham, everything is under control. We'll get the model here or find another. If I have to, *I'll* squeeze into the dress and walk it out there myself."

"Actually," Nigel said, deciding to take a chance Lillian

wouldn't slap him for his presumptuousness with so many witnesses standing around, "I have a thought about that myself." Turning to Lillian, he took her arm encouragingly. "Why don't you stand in for the missing model?"

Her eyes went wide, her face pale.

"What? No. Don't be ridiculous."

"What's so ridiculous about it?" he argued. "You're beautiful, poised, more than capable. And we both know you look amazing in the gown, since you wore it to the cocktail party just last night. I'd say it's an ideal solution."

Before she had the chance to say anything more, he turned back to Franklin. "Send her to hair and makeup and get her into the dress. Make sure she looks like a million bucks. She'll be the perfect close to our portion of the show."

"Nigel," Lillian said, shaking her head, looking on the verge of panic.

He leaned in, pressing a kiss to her cheek. "You'll be fine," he assured her. "Better than fine, you'll be marvelous."

When she still didn't look convinced, he added, "Please. We need your help."

He heard her sigh, knew she was on the verge of acquiescence and didn't give her a chance to change her mind.

"Go," he commanded, pushing her toward Franklin, pleased when the man wasted no time grabbing her up and bustling her off to get ready.

With a smile on his face and heady anticipation thrumming through his veins, he made his way back out front, taking his seat and awaiting what he suspected would be the best runway show of his life. Career aspects be damned.

Hours later, Lily was still shaking. She'd never been so nervous in her life. Not even on her first day pretending to be a personal assistant for Nigel.

What had he been thinking? She wasn't a model. Far from

it. She was a designer, for heaven's sake. Her place was well on the other side of fashion—behind the scenes, not out in front, walking a runway with hundreds of eyes riveted on her and flashbulbs going off in her face every tenth of a second.

Not that Nigel was aware of any of that. But that still didn't give him the right to dress her up and shove her out there without warning.

She'd survived, of course. She even liked to think she'd done an exceptional job. At least she'd stayed on her feet, hadn't fainted and had made it all the way down the runway and back without falling off into the crowd of onlookers.

But what if someone recognized her? From the audience or later, from all of the pictures and video clips that were sure to be circulating across the globe.

Too many people knew her as Lily Zaccaro. Even with her hair a little darker than her natural shade and heavier makeup than usual for the runway, somebody out there was sure to notice her and wonder what she'd been doing walking the runway for one of her competitors.

With luck, they would call her cell phone to ask what was going on. But much more likely, they would call the apartment and end up talking to either Juliet or Zoe. Her sisters would be clueless, but they'd begin to put two and two together, track her down in Los Angeles and blow her entire ruse as Lillian George.

Nigel would be furious—for good reason. But worse, she would be kicked out of Ashdown Abbey. Before she'd figured out who was stealing her designs.

Dammit. How did she get herself into these predicaments?

Running her fingers through her hair, she shook it out of its overly sprayed upsweep until it resembled at least a modicum of normal, natural, non-runway style. She was out of the champagne-colored gown and back in the sundress she'd been wearing when they first arrived.

The makeup, however, would have to remain until they returned to the hotel suite and she could take some cotton balls and about ten gallons of makeup remover to it. Not that she looked like a clown. It was just that everything—eyeliner, shadow, mascara, blush, lipstick—was thicker and heavier than usual to be seen from a distance and on camera.

She was about to turn away from the oversize mirror and head back out front when a pair of hands spanned her waist and warm lips pressed against the side of her neck. Her gaze flicked to her reflection, and now Nigel's, close behind her.

"You were wonderful," he spoke near her ear, barely above a whisper. "I knew you would be."

Stepping away before someone noticed his familiarity with the person who was supposed to be simply his personal assistant, he added, "That model never did show up, so thank you for saving the show."

"You're welcome," she said with a touch of reluctance. Then she turned to face him, crossing her arms and hitching one hip in annoyance. "You might have *asked* if I wanted to play supermodel before pushing me out onstage against my will. Do you have any idea how petrified I was? You're lucky I didn't throw up on one of the other models or pass out right in the middle of the runway and ruin the whole show."

To her surprise, he chuckled at her aggravation, a wide smile stretching across his handsome features.

"Nonsense. You were exceptional. And I can't imagine anyone else looking as lovely in that gown…not even a professional model paid to look good in designer creations."

As much as she wanted to hold on to her mad, his flattery was working. She was glad she'd been able to help out in such a way when he'd needed her, happy that he was pleased with her performance.

But that didn't change the fact that she was in trouble. Bad enough they'd slept together last night. That she wanted it to—*hoped* it would, even—happen again.

Now she needed to worry about someone recognizing her and figuring out what she was doing playing out a second identity. That *Nigel* might realize what she was up to and hate her forever.

Her heart gave a painful lurch. She might be lying to him. What they had might be casual, temporary and doomed to be short-lived. But the thought of him finding out who she really was, what she'd been doing pretending to be his personal assistant all this time, nearly brought tears to her eyes.

An ill-fated romantic fling she could handle. Seeing a look of betrayal, possibly even disgust, in his eyes after what they'd shared… No, she didn't want her time with him to end like that.

Which meant she needed to be very careful from this point on. She needed to guard herself against any further attachment to this man. Whatever else transpired between them, she couldn't let it affect her emotionally.

Most importantly, though, she needed to get back to the Ashdown Abbey offices in Los Angeles and find out once and for all who stole her designs for the California Collection.

Oblivious to the twisting, hazard-strewn path her thoughts were taking, he ran his hands down her bare arms, threading his fingers with hers. "If you're ready, we can go. We'll have to make pleasantries as we weave our way through the crowd out there, but the car is waiting to take us back to the hotel."

"Don't you need to stick around awhile?" she asked. "Rub elbows and talk up the company to key account holders?"

"Already done," he replied. "I spoke to several buyers just after the show, while you were changing back into street clothes, and anyone else who might be interested in acquiring our designs has my card. They can call me at the office on Monday."

"That was quick," she said. "I would have thought you'd need to spend the rest of the day schmoozing."

He offered her a gentle smile. "Sometimes I do. But for the most part, these types of events drag on for the public's enjoyment. Those of us who are there for business tend to know each other, look for each other and get straight to the point. Besides," he said, leaning in and lowering his voice to a sultry whisper, "I don't want to be stuck out there, making nice with mere strangers, when I could spend the rest of my time in Miami alone with you."

A flush of longing washed over her, making her catch her breath. She licked her lips, waiting until she thought she could speak without sounding like Kermit the Frog.

"So," she said carefully, "we'll be headed back to Los Angeles soon?"

"Tomorrow. But that gives us the rest of the day and this evening to enjoy the sand and sun."

She cocked her head, unable to keep her mouth from quirking up at one side. "The sand and sun, or our suite back at the Royal Crown?"

He returned her grin with a wink and wicked twinkle to his hazel-green eyes. "I'll let that be your choice, of course. Though I know which I'm hoping for."

She shook her head and chuckled, unable to resist his inherent charm. The man was entirely too tempting for his own good. Or hers.

And though it might not have been the wisest decision for her to make, especially given her current situation, she *wanted* to spend the night with him. Another night, just the two of them alone together.

While she realized it would essentially be digging herself even deeper into her deception and making it that much harder to walk away, she wanted as much time alone with him as she could get. Secret minutes, private hours, cherished memories to carry with her the rest of her life.

She might not have a future with Nigel—how could she when she'd been lying to him ever since they met?—but she could have this. The here and now. And if that was all she could lay claim to, then she was going to grab on with both hands and savor it for all it was worth.

"All right," she told him slowly, teasing him a little. "I'll tell you what. You can take me to lunch, and I'll let you know afterward what I want to do next."

He gave her a look, one that said he intended to do everything in his power to convince her to make the right decision. The one that led straight back to their hotel suite and ended with them both sweaty, naked, wrapped together like kudzu vines.

She shivered a little at the slideshow of pictures that ran through her head. Oh, yes, they would get there. But it wouldn't hurt to make him worry a bit about the day's outcome first.

Turning in the opposite direction toward the curtained-off entrance between backstage and the show area, he offered his arm. As she took it and they started walking, he said, "Fair enough. Just remember that I haven't quite gotten my fair share of time in that big bed back at the hotel. It would be a shame to fly home before I've gotten to use it properly."

Lily bit down on the inside of her cheek to keep from laughing aloud. The campaign to spend the rest of their time in Miami safely ensconced in the suite had begun already, it seemed. Although she didn't see why they had to restrict their activities to the bed he was so preoccupied with. After all, there was also the sofa, the desk, the balcony, the shower, the bathroom vanity…

Leaning into him, despite the fact that someone might see

and perceive that there was more going on between them than mere boss-and-secretary professional relations, she said, "I'll keep that in mind."

The sofa, the desk, the bathroom vanity, the shower and the bed. They'd hit every place but the balcony, at least in part, before checking out of the hotel Sunday morning and boarding the jet back to Los Angeles.

Lily knew how dangerous it was to let herself get so carried away with Nigel. Had reprimanded herself several times while locked away with him, doing all the things she told herself she shouldn't. But she just didn't have it in her to stop before she absolutely had to, so she'd decided to adopt a don't-ask-don't-tell attitude. She wouldn't ask herself why she was letting things go on this way when she knew how they were going to end, and she wouldn't tell herself later what a fool she'd been for letting her time at Ashdown Abbey and her feelings for Nigel Statham get out of control.

Which was how she ended up agreeing to have room service deliver lunch after the runway show instead of eating in a lovely, public five-star restaurant so they could spend more time together, alone in the suite. And how she allowed him to sit so close to her on the flight home, interspersing business talk with naughty whispers about his favorite parts of what they'd done together and what he'd very much like to do in the future. Not the far distant future, but soon after they landed.

As hard as she tried to resist, she even let him talk her into going home with him from the airport. It was a terrible idea. One that could only get her deeper into the hole she was digging for herself. The same hole that was quickly filling with quicksand, threatening to pull her under.

But there was something about his fingers trailing along her bare thigh just beneath the hem of her skirt...his warm breath dusting her ear, sending ripples of sensation all the way down to her toes. It stirred up too many memories from their time locked away together in the hotel suite, and made her weak and susceptible and eager to make more.

So she let herself be persuaded. Let him lead her from the jet to his waiting Bentley, let him *not* drop her off at her apartment, but take her home with him instead, her heart in her throat the entire drive.

She'd expected some dazzling but garish mansion in Beverly Hills, complete with swimming pool and a home bowling alley or some such. Instead, he led her past a uniformed doorman into a very nice redbrick apartment building not far from the Ashdown Abbey offices. Definitely a few steps up from the one where she was staying, especially when she discovered—of course—that his was the penthouse apartment.

The view was spectacular, as were the layout and furnishings. Not his own, he'd explained; he'd rented it that way, but they suited him perfectly nonetheless. A lot of chrome and glass and neutral colors, interspersed with splashes of bright color.

He gave her all of ten minutes to process her surroundings while his chauffer brought in their luggage and he poured them each a glass of wine. Then he'd led her to the bedroom, where he'd proceeded to give her the grand tour of his king-size bed, ocean-blue satin sheets and the eggshell paint of the ceiling over her head.

He'd kept her there for hours…not that she'd minded. Then when she began making noises about going home to her own apartment, he'd insisted she stay for dinner. She'd refused, at least until he'd offered to cook. That was something she just *had* to see.

Unfortunately, she'd also had to eat it with a smile on her face, since she hadn't had the heart to tell him his culinary skills needed work.

After that, he'd very deftly seduced her again, keeping her distracted and too exhausted to protest until morning. Of course, in the morning, they'd had to go into the office.

Thankfully, she'd had enough clothes with her from the trip that she hadn't had to wear the same thing two days in a row. And Nigel had been kind enough to drop her off a couple of blocks from the Ashdown Abbey building so it looked as though she'd arrived by herself, then followed behind several minutes later.

From there, they'd proceeded to fool around in his office, exchange heated glances even when they weren't alone, and—to Lily's consternation and self-reproach—practically move in together. It was comfortable and a lot easier a routine to fall into than she would have expected. At the very least, she found herself spending entirely too much time in Nigel's presence and sleeping over at his penthouse.

Time she was spending getting swept up in the fantasy of spending the rest of her life with this man, inching ever closer to the edge of falling for him once and for all. But *not* getting any closer to discovering the thief of her designs. Every minute she was with Nigel was one she didn't use to snoop around or pore through Ashdown Abbey records.

After nearly a week of sneaking around at work, of them acting like boss and secretary with a professional relationship only, then using the evening hours to act like a couple of randy teenagers—or worse, star-crossed lovers in some romantic chick flick—Lily realized she had to get back on track.

She considered herself extremely lucky that nothing had ever seemed to come of her jaunt down the runway in Miami. Apparently, everyone—even the media—had been more focused on the debut designs than who was wearing them. And the big hair and heavy makeup had certainly helped.

Because no one had ever called to ask what she'd been doing there, or pointed at a photograph from the show and commented that one of the Ashdown Abbey models looked an awful lot like that Zaccaro chick from New York.

Thank goodness.

But even if she couldn't bring herself to break things off with Nigel entirely, she did manage to clear her head enough to insist on spending the night at her own apartment for a change. *Without* him joining her there.

Lily hadn't taken her personal cell phone with her to Florida, only the one provided to her by Ashdown Abbey for company business. And she'd been so distracted by her impromptu stay at Nigel's penthouse that she'd forgotten to grab it the single time she'd managed to swing by her own apartment. It was still in the nightstand beside her neatly made, narrow twin bed, exactly where she'd left it.

So when she finally got inside her apartment, alone, and was able to take a breath, clear her head and focus again, she found her voice-mail box full. As soon as she turned the phone on, it started beeping with notification after notification that she had messages waiting.

Suspecting what she would hear and who most of them would be from, she almost didn't want to listen, but knew she had to. Kicking off her heels, she moved around the living room, gathering papers and folders and notebooks even as she dialed in for the messages.

Sure enough, several were from her sister Juliet. *Where are you? Why didn't you say where you were going in your note? Why haven't you called me back? Please call me back. We're worried about you. Where are you?*

Lily's heart hurt more with each message, guilt biting at her as her sister's voice grew more and more frantic.

Then there were the ones from her private investigator, Reid McCormack. He was anything but frantic. In fact, he sounded downright furious, and darned if Lily could figure out why. He worked for her, after all. Shouldn't *she* be the one to get upset at his lack of progress rather than the other way around?

But while his first couple of voice mails were polite enough, simply requesting an update or letting her know he'd found no connection between Ashdown Abbey and the theft of her designs in New York, they quickly deteriorated into demands for her to return his calls and threats to put an end to their association if she didn't soon come clean with her sisters.

She rubbed the spot between her brows, massaging away the beginning of a headache. This was all supposed to be so simple, and now it was so complicated. She was supposed to be the only one involved, at risk, and now things had spread to encompass so many others. People she cared about and wanted to protect.

With a sigh, she glanced at the phone's display and did the math for the difference between West Coast and East Coast time. If she waited just a little longer, she might be able to call the apartment back in New York and leave a message for her sisters when neither of them would be home. That would give her the chance to reassure them—especially Juliet—that she was fine and hoped to be home soon without having to explain where she was or what she was really up to.

Because if Juliet or Zoe answered, there would be no end to the number of questions they would ask. They'd grill her like a toasted-cheese sandwich, and she just *couldn't* tell them the whole truth. Not yet.

Which brought her to the next and most important item on her must-do list. She *had* to figure out how Ashdown Abbey had gotten enough of a peek at her designs to incorporate them into their California Collection.

Tossing all of the paperwork she'd gathered so far from the annals of Ashdown Abbey on the coffee table in front of the sofa, she trailed into the bedroom and changed from the sundress and sandals she'd worn home from Florida to a pair of comfortable cotton pajamas. Then she returned to the front room, started a pot of coffee—which she suspected would be only the first of many—and hunkered down on the floor cross-legged, with her back to the couch.

Given all the snooping she'd already done and information she'd collected, Lily didn't understand why she couldn't figure out who the design thief was. It had to be there, buried, hidden, eluding her. Worse, she felt as though the answer was *right there,* just out of reach. If only she knew exactly where to look…or exactly what she was looking for.

What she needed was a second set of eyes. Her sisters—Juliet, at any rate—would be terrific at poring through the pages and pages of data. But hadn't the entire point been *not* to get her sisters involved?

The detective would be another excellent choice. But Juliet had contacted him right after Lily had, and now he was smack in the middle of a conflict of interest. From his perspective, anyway—not from Lily's, and she hoped not from Juliet's once she found out what was really going on. It did explain Reid McCormack's souring disposition, though.

On the heels of that thought came another wave of guilt. *All right, all right,* she told her nagging conscience. Grabbing her cell phone, she dialed McCormack's office number first. The better to *not* catch him and be able to leave a message he could listen to later…when she wasn't on the other end of the line, a cornered recipient of his wrath.

And thankfully, it was his voice mail rather than his real live voice that answered.

"Mr. McCormack, this is Lily Zaccaro," she said. Quickly, succinctly, knowing she didn't have much time before the system cut her off and wanting to sound very sure of herself, she continued, "I'm sorry I haven't contacted you, but I got your messages and promise I'm nearly done here. I'm not going to give her any details about my whereabouts, but

I will call Juliet and let her know I'm okay. And I'll explain everything as soon as I get back to New York. I'm sorry if this is causing you problems, but please don't say anything to my sisters—not yet. Thank you."

Heart racing, she hung up, hoping she'd said the right things. Hoping she'd bought herself a little more time and extinguished at least a bit of his anger with her.

She thought about calling her sister next, but it was Sunday afternoon, and though the store was open, the three of them usually took that day off. The chances of both Juliet and Zoe being home were too high. She would wait until tomorrow, when the two of them *should* be back at the boutique and unable to answer the apartment phone. Her message would be waiting for them when they got home, though, which should make them feel better about her health and welfare.

That decided, she went back to flipping through papers and her notes, studying each carefully, just as she had several times before. The letters were starting to blur together, the words branding themselves in her brain. And yet she was clearly missing something or the mystery would have been solved by now.

For the next few hours, she kept at it, sipping coffee to stay alert as she organized and reorganized, straightened and restraightened. Sighed and sighed again.

She was going over the specifics of the California Collection—memos, instructions, supply lists and sketches—when something caught her attention. Sitting up straight, she leaned forward even as she brought the printout in her hand closer.

Down in the far left corner, in teeny-tiny print smaller than a footnote, was a number. Or rather, a resource code, with numbers and letters mixed together: CA_COLL-47N6BL924.

It meant absolutely nothing to her, except that it seemed to be an identifier for the California Collection. And like one of those 3-D magic mystery image puzzles, she might never have seen it if exhaustion wasn't making her eyes cross and vision blur.

Grabbing up the next page, she glanced down and found the exact same thing. And on the next. And on the next. And on the next.

Her pulse jumped in anticipation. This could actually be something. Of course, she didn't know exactly what and wasn't even sure how to find out.

But on a hunch, she ran for her laptop, popped the lid and booted up. Thanks to her position as executive secretary/personal assistant to the Man in Charge at Ashdown Abbey, she had all the log-in information to tap into the computer system from home—which she'd done numerous times after hours as part of her amateur investigation.

Once she was in, it took her twenty, maybe twenty-five minutes just to locate anything even remotely related to the code, and another ten or fifteen to track down what the jumble of letters and numbers meant.

It was, she discovered, an identifier for all of the sketches and other information related to the California Collection. And miraculously, it brought her to a compilation of scans of the original sketches for the California Collection.

They were definitely rougher sketches than the ones she'd been studying all this time, done by hand in charcoal and colored pencil and with computerized drawing pads and the like. All grouped together, they were miniscule, but thankfully she was able to enlarge them and even run them across her screen in a slideshow fashion.

A flare of annoyance raised Lily's temperature several degrees. If she'd thought the final results of the collection were similar to her work, the original sketches were practically carbon copies. Someone had initially pitched almost her *exact* creations, and they had somehow—thank heavens for small favors, she now realized—been transformed into garments more suitable to Ashdown Abbey.

Refocusing her attention away from her fit of temper, she began to scan every detail of the designs and right away noticed that each of them was signed with the same set of initials.

IOL.

Lily's brows knit. So often with design teams, no one took or was given full credit for initial ideas. She'd suspected someone of using her designs as suggestions for aspects of the California Collection, but not that a single person had offered up complete, nearly identical sketches for all of the designs, which had then been applied to the overall collection.

Apparently, she'd been going at her little investigation all wrong from the very beginning. The thought made her want to smack her head on the nearest hard surface, even as she admitted a newfound respect for folks like Reid McCormack, who did this sort of thing professionally. Clearly, she was better off locked in her studio with bolts of fabric and thread in every color than out in the world playing amateur sleuth.

Not that she could quit now. She'd come too far and was finally, *finally* on the verge of figuring out this whole ugly mess.

It took a minute or two more of tapping at the keyboard, but she found the entire list of employees connected to the California Collection and started scrolling through. No one, *no one* with the initials IOL that she could see. Dammit.

Teeth grinding in frustration, she drummed her fingers on the coffee table and tried to think of what to do next.

Bingo! Payroll records.

Accessing the human resources files, she found the record of every single employee working at Ashdown Abbey, regardless of his or her position. From Nigel as CEO all the way down to the custodial team that came in nightly to clean the offices, she scrolled through every single name, looking for one to match to those three initials.

A ton of *L* surnames popped up, only a few first names that started with the letter *I*. But she kept going, holding her breath in hopes that the mysterious IOL would pop up and bite her on the nose.

And there it was. Her fingers paused on the touch pad, stopping the document's movement. She blew out a breath even as her stomach plummeted and her heart hammered against her rib cage.

Isabelle Olivia Landry. IOL.

Bella.

Lily leaned back against the edge of the sofa, feeling all the blood drain from her face. Bella? Zoe's friend Bella?

Sure, the thought had crossed her mind—*briefly*—after they'd run into one another, but she'd never truly believed anything like that could be possible.

Could she really have done this? To her friend…her friend's sisters…her friend's company?

Why would she have done such a thing? And how did she manage it?

It made sense, though, didn't it? The longer Lily thought about it, went back in her memory, the more things began to fall into place.

Bella and Zoe were friends. Bella had visited Zoe not all that long ago. She'd stayed at the loft with them, toured the connected studio where they worked from home and the space where they worked in the back of the store, too, she was sure.

She couldn't blame Zoe for showing her friend around, either. Lily and Juliet had both given tours to friends, sharing their work space as well as designs they were currently working on. None of them would ever think a *friend* would steal their ideas and try to pass them off as their own or sell them to another designer.

No, this betrayal lay solely at Bella's feet. But Lily still wanted to know how she'd managed it. And *why.*

Had she memorized so much from just a casual glance, or had she sneaked around behind their backs and literally stolen designs, perhaps traced or copied them to take away with her?

Tears pricked behind Lily's eyes even as her fingers clenched. She was sad and angry at the same time. Relieved to have the mystery solved, but dreading what was to come.

Because she had to confront Bella now, didn't she?

Or maybe she shouldn't. Maybe she should turn over all of this evidence to the police. Or Reid McCormack so he could investigate further and gather even more evidence against Bella.

Gather even more evidence. So that they—she—could prosecute someone who at one time had been a close friend of her sister's. The very thought made her want to throw up.

But it had to be done, didn't it? Even though now that she knew the truth, it felt like rather a hollow victory.

And yet it was the whole reason she'd run away from home in the first place. Left without telling her family where she was going and sent poor Juliet into such turmoil over her whereabouts…flown to Los Angeles and gotten a job with a rival clothing company under an assumed name…let herself get carried away by her feelings for Nigel and fall into an affair with him that was going to end badly…so badly.

If she didn't take action against Bella for stealing her designs, all that would be for naught.

Wouldn't it?

Twelve

There were some things makeup couldn't hide, and the shadows under Lily's eyes were two of them. She couldn't remember ever spending a worse, more sleepless night in her life.

For hours, she'd paced her apartment, chewed at her nails, despaired of what to do. Confront Bella herself? Call Reid McCormack for help? Or go home and tell her sisters everything? Maybe talking it through with her sisters would help her decide what to do, and since Bella was her friend, Zoe really did deserve to have a say in the matter.

But no matter what she did where Bella and Zaccaro Fashions were concerned, she found herself having an even harder time figuring out what to do about Nigel.

Oh, how she was dreading that. So many times during the night, she'd considered flying back to New York without a word to him or anyone else at Ashdown Abbey. And in fact she'd started packing her things, because either way, she knew she would be returning home sooner rather than later.

The thought of seeing Nigel again filled her with equal parts excitement and trepidation. Excitement because every time she saw him brought a thrill of delight and desire. Trepidation because she'd been lying to him all along and might now have to come clean, telling him everything.

He would hate her, of course. Hate her, be furious with her, possibly blow up at her before having her dragged from the building like a common criminal. Which was no less than she deserved, she knew.

Her pulse was frantic, beating louder and louder in her ears the closer she got to her desk and the door of Nigel's office. Before leaving her apartment, she'd called Reid McCormack again, this time glad when his secretary put her through and he picked up in person.

He'd been short with her at first, on the verge of reading her the riot act, she suspected. But she'd quickly redirected his anger by filling him in on what she was really doing in Los Angeles and what she'd discovered. They made an appointment for her to bring everything she'd found to his office the following week, where he could look it over and they would decide what steps to take next.

Then she called her sisters. For a change, she'd actually been hoping one of them would answer, but with the time difference between New York and California, she'd gotten only voice mail both at home and on their cells. Instead of the message she'd planned to leave before figuring out who was behind the design thefts, she'd told them where she was and that she'd be home within the next few days.

She hadn't told them *why* she was in Los Angeles or why she'd taken off the way she had, but assured them she was fine and would fill them in when she got back. In fact, she'd ended her message with *there's a lot we need to talk about.* And, boy, was there ever. She only hoped this entire situation wouldn't end up putting a rift between them.

And then she'd picked up her purse and the letter it had taken her most of the night to compose. The ink of which her sweaty palm was probably smearing into illegibility at that very moment.

Her breathing was coming in shallow bursts, her stomach churning and threatening to revolt with every *boom-kaboom-kaboom* of her aching, pounding heart. But as much as it pained her, as much as she wanted to turn tail and run, this was something she had to do.

Swallowing hard, she laid her purse down on top of her—or rather, the future personal assistant's—desk and turned toward Nigel's office. The letter clutched in her hand was wrinkled almost beyond repair. She'd better do this before it became completely unreadable.

Shaking from head to toe, she reluctantly raised an arm and knocked. Nigel responded immediately, calling in his deep British accent for her to come in. His voice snaked down her spine, warming her and causing a shivery chill all at the same time. Pushing the door open, Lily walked inside, her footsteps as heavy as lead weights.

The minute he spotted her, his face lit up…and Lily's heart sank. He was so handsome. So charming and masculine and self-assured. And lately, he'd begun looking at her like she could come to mean something to him.

He was certainly coming to mean something to her. More than she ever would have thought possible, given the fact that she'd originally come here thinking he might be behind the thefts of her designs.

Now it was breaking her heart to think of leaving him. To have to tell him who she really was and why she'd truly been working for him.

She'd tried to deny it, not even letting the thought fully form itself in her mind, but she'd fallen in love with him. With a man who, in only moments, would come to despise her.

"Lillian," he said, and the sound of her name—even her fake name—on his lips nearly brought tears to her eyes.

Pushing back his chair, he rose to his feet and came around his desk. He reached her in record time, before she could register his movements and attempt to stop him. He gripped her arms, leaning in to kiss her cheek and then her mouth.

Heat suffused her, threatening to fog her brain and drag her far, far away from her determination to come clean and tell Nigel the truth. She couldn't help but kiss him back, but curled her fingers into fists to keep from wrapping them around his shoulders or running them through his hair.

Whether he noticed her reluctance or not, she couldn't tell. He was still smiling when he pulled back, which only made her insides burn hotter with regret.

Nigel reached up to brush a stray curl behind her ear, offering a suggestive, lopsided grin. "Did you come in early for our little game of Naughty Secretary?" he asked. "I can't think of a better way to start the day, and would be happy to sweep away all my work so we can make proper use of the desk."

Her throat grew tight and closed on her next breath. She shook her head and blinked back tears.

At her response, his eyes narrowed, his expression growing serious.

"Lillian," he said again, taking her hand and giving it a reassuring squeeze. "You don't look well. What's wrong?"

Clearing her throat, she tried to find her voice, praying she could say what she needed to say without breaking down completely.

"Can I speak with you?" she began, the words thready and weak.

"Of course."

Still holding her hand, he led her to one of the chairs in front of his desk, guiding her into it before turning the other to face her and taking a seat himself.

"What is it?" he asked, concern clear in the hazel-green depths of his eyes.

Hoping he wouldn't notice that she was shaking, she held the letter out to him.

"This is for you."

While he began to open the envelope and take out the piece of paper folded inside, she rushed ahead, knowing that if she didn't get it all out before he began to react to her letter of resignation, she never would.

"I've been lying to you," she said. "The whole time, I've been here under false pretenses. My real name is Lily Zaccaro, and I'm part-owner of Zaccaro Fashions out in New York. I came to Los Angeles and started working for you because someone stole some of my recent designs and used them to create your California Collection. I probably should have handled things differently. I'm sorry," she hastened to add before pausing only long enough to take a much-needed breath.

"I know you'll hate me for this, and I don't blame you. But I want you to know that I didn't do anything to harm you or Ashdown Abbey. I poked around *only* to find out who might have had access to my personal designs and was also involved in the creation of the California Collection. That's all I did. I didn't come here to spy on your operation or steal company secrets or anything like that, I swear."

Eyes stinging, she blinked back tears. Swallowed past the lump of emotion growing bigger and bigger in the center of her throat.

Where only moments before Nigel's features had been relaxed and soft with pleasure when he met her gaze, they were now stone-cold and harshly drawn with both disappointment and betrayal. He stared at her letter in his hand as though it didn't make sense, and she didn't know if he'd heard a word she'd said...or if he'd heard every one and couldn't bear to look at her because of them.

She sat stock-still, afraid to move, afraid to breathe. Simply waiting and bracing herself for his reaction, however ugly it might be.

And then he raised his head, his eyes locking on hers. What she saw there stabbed her straight through: hurt, confusion, betrayal.

"You're leaving," he said, his tone flat, utterly hollow. "You're not who you proclaimed to be, and now that you've gotten what you came for, you're leaving."

She didn't know which was worse—having to explain her actions or hearing him summarize them so succinctly. Both had her stomach in knots of self-loathing.

All she could do was croak out a remorseful "Yes."

The silence that ensued was almost painful. Like nails scraping down a chalkboard, but with no sound, only the uncomfortable tooth-rattling, grating sensation.

A muscle jumped in his jaw, his mouth a flat slash across the lower half of his face. His gaze drifted away from hers, locking on a point at the far side of the room and refusing to return anywhere near her.

One minute ticked by, and then another, while she searched for something, anything to say. But what more was there? She'd already confessed, told him who she really was and why she'd pretended to be his personal assistant. Whatever else she came up with to fill the heavy weight of dead air would only make matters worse.

So she held her tongue, waiting for the dressing-down she knew was coming and that he had every right to level at her.

Instead, he stood and rounded his desk. Still without looking at her, he took a seat in the wide, comfortable leather chair and placed his hands very calmly on the blotter, palms down.

"You should go," he said finally.

Lily licked her lips, swallowed, wished her heart would slow its erratic pace inside her chest. She opened her mouth to speak, even though she had no idea what to say, but he cut her off.

Gaze drilling into her as he raised his head, his voice trickled through her veins like ice. “You’re leaving. Your letter of resignation has been turned in, and I’ve accepted it. You should go.”

It wasn’t at all how she’d expected things to go. She’d expected angry words and raised voices. Hurt feelings and terrible accusations. This calm, quiet, resigned response was so much worse. Chilling. Heartbreaking. And so very, very final.

With a sharp nod, she gritted her teeth to keep from making a sound. Especially since she could feel a sob rolling up from her diaphragm.

Pushing to her feet, she turned and walked to the door, relieved when she made it the whole way without incident. Reaching out a shaky hand, she gripped the knob and tipped her head just enough to catch a glimpse of him in her periphery.

“I am sorry, Nigel.”

Not waiting for a reply, she slipped out of the room and moved toward the elevators as quickly as possible, hoping she could make it inside before she completely fell apart.

Thirteen

One month later...

Lily stood behind the counter of the Zaccaro Fashions store, staring out at the porcelain-white mannequins wearing her designs; the displays of other items, like Juliet's handbags and Zoe's *daZZle* line of shoes; and the handful of customers milling about. A sting of pain made her drop her thumb from her mouth as she realized—not for the first time—that she'd bitten the nail down to the quick. All of her formerly beautiful nails were like that now—short and mangled thanks to her apparent need to work off stress by destroying any chance at a decent manicure.

Clutching her hands together behind her back in an attempt to stop the troublesome habit, she turned her attention to the front of the store. Maybe she should rearrange the window displays again. She'd redone them twelve times in the past four weeks, when normally they changed them only once a month or so.

Her sisters were beginning to think she'd gone off the deep end. She knew this because Zoe had come right out and said, "Lil, you're going off the deep end," just a few days ago when the smoke alarm in their apartment had started shrieking yet again because she'd put something on the stove, then walked away and forgotten what she was doing.

She wished she could claim it was the spark of creative passion distracting her and making her borderline psychotic. What she wouldn't give to have new design ideas filling her head and the need to get them down on paper or fitted onto a dress form keeping her up at night.

But no. Since returning from Los Angeles, she hadn't sketched anything more than pointless, shapeless doodles that had nothing to do with fashion design, and she hadn't sewn a damn thing. She'd tried, but her heart…her heart just wasn't in it.

She was beginning to think it was because her heart was still in Los Angeles with a certain British CEO who probably wished he'd never met her.

Her chest tightened at the thought of Nigel and the expression on his face just before he'd told her to go. That she wasn't welcome in his office, his company or his life any longer.

Well, he hadn't said the last out loud, but it had been implied. And she'd heard him loud and clear.

She'd hurt one person in all of this mess; she was just grateful she hadn't hurt more. Upon her return to New York, she'd spilled her guts to her sisters. Told them everything, from the moment she'd realized her designs had been copied, to her brilliant plan to find the thief on her own, to her ill-fated affair with Nigel. And as much as she hadn't wanted to, she'd broken the news to Zoe that her friend Bella was behind the thefts.

Just as she'd expected, Zoe had been devastated. And angry. And guilty that she'd been the one to bring Bella into their apartment, their studio, and give her access to their work to begin with.

But Lily and Juliet weren't holding anything against Zoe, in the same way Juliet and Zoe didn't hold it against Lily that she'd kept such a secret and run off to Los Angeles without giving them a clue as to what she was up to. It wasn't as though she'd known what her friend was capable of.

And after a long, exhausting discussion that had lasted well into the night, all three of them—Zoe included—had agreed to turn the evidence and information Lily had dug up over to Reid McCormack to let him do some further investigating. Juliet had even offered to take it to him personally, which surprised Lily, since she'd expected her sister to be angry with the detective for pretending to look for Lily while actually covering for her. That had taken a bit of explaining on Lily's part, too.

Then, if Reid thought they had a strong enough case—and they all knew cases like this, concerning "creative license" or the theft of ideas, were hard to prove—they would proceed as necessary, even if it meant taking legal action against Bella Landry. As upset as she was, it was still something Lily would hate to have to do.

Thank heaven for small favors, she supposed. Her broken heart would eventually mend, and the guilt she felt over betraying and lying to a man she'd come to care for—a lot—would eventually dissipate. She hoped. But she didn't know what she'd do without the love and support and forgiveness of her family. Especially her sisters, who were also her best friends.

"Lily!"

Lily jumped at the sound of her name being called very loudly in her ear. She blinked, turning to find Zoe standing beside her, looking extremely put out.

Brows drawn down in a frown, hands on hips, she shook

her head. "I swear, you're about as useful as a zipper on a pillbox hat these days."

Then she sighed, her tone softening. Tipping her head, she said, "There's someone over there who'd like to speak with you."

Lily followed her sister's line of sight, her heart stuttering to a halt when she saw Nigel standing by the far wall, studying the shelves that displayed some of Zoe's finest—and most expensive—footwear designs. Seeing him again made her breath catch. She forgot to inhale for so long that her chest burned and her head began to spin with little stars blinking in front of her eyes.

"What are you waiting for?" Zoe hissed.

Lily shook her head, swallowing past a throat gone desert dry. She couldn't move. She was locked in place, even as every bone in her body turned to jelly.

With a sound of disgust, Zoe put a hand in the middle of Lily's back and urged her out from behind the counter, then gave her a small shove in the right direction for good measure.

"Go," she told her in a hushed voice. Then, in typical Zoe fashion, she grumbled, "And don't screw it up this time."

Nigel watched Lily walking toward him from the corner of his eye. He wanted to turn to her, cross the rest of the distance between them, grab her up and never let go. Instead, he remained turned slightly away, fighting to school his features, keep his heart from breaking out of his chest.

Blast it all, he'd missed her. As angry as he'd been at her… as hurt by the fact that she'd lied to him, pretended to be someone she wasn't…he'd still missed seeing her, touching her, hearing her laugh, watching her lips curl into a smile. Every day since she'd left, he'd wished she were back…then cursed himself for being such a weak, pathetic fool, so easily swayed by womanly wiles. Again, since he seemed to be falling into many of the same pitfalls with Lily as he had with Caroline.

Yet here he was. He'd flown all the way across the country to see her again. And to get some answers to the questions he'd been too bitter and infuriated to ask before she'd walked out of Ashdown Abbey and returned to her real life in New York.

The question was, could he ask them and wait for her response without reaching for her and saying to hell with anything else?

When she was only a few feet away, he turned to face her fully. The sight of her punched him in the gut. If he'd been breathing to begin with, the air would have puffed from his lungs in a whoosh.

Fisting his hands at his sides, he forced himself not to react. Outwardly. She didn't need to know that inside, a team of wild horses was running rampant through his bloodstream.

She stopped. An arm's length from him, which didn't bolster his resolve in the least.

"Nigel," she said on a shaky breath. Then she licked her lips nervously. "I mean, Mr. Statham."

Her tentativeness had a calming effect, letting him know she was just as unsure of this impromptu meeting as he was.

"Nigel is fine," he told her, resisting the urge to shove his hands into his pockets and rock back on his heels. They were a bit beyond polite social etiquette, after all. "Is there somewhere we can talk? Privately."

Licking her lips again, Lily glanced around. There was a handful of shoppers in the store and a blonde who bore a strong resemblance to Lily—a sister?—behind the counter, staring at them curiously. When she caught Nigel's eye, she glowered at him. Definitely one of the sisters.

After Lily had confessed her true identity, admitting that she'd lied to him, he'd been furious, determined to find a way to punish her for her deception. So of course he'd hired a private investigator to discover as much personal information about her as possible.

She came from money, but had worked to open this store on her own, without a handout from her parents, who could easily afford it.

She had two sisters—one older, one younger—who were partners in the design business. They'd gotten involved after Lily had graduated from design school, but seemed to be no less talented. The oldest sister, Juliet, designed handbags and other accessories, while the youngest sister, Zoe, did shoes. Extremely sexy, fashionable shoes, most with enough heel and sparkle to be noticed from a mile off.

Lily designed all of the clothing for Zaccaro Fashions—and she did it quite well. If he'd known about her talent before all of this, he might even have offered her a design position at Ashdown Abbey. She certainly would have been an asset to the company.

And something else he'd been forced to admit after he and the private investigator had both done a good deal of research: she was right about her designs being copied at Ashdown Abbey. How it had been allowed to happen was still a bit of a mystery, but he'd found enough—a link between one of Ashdown Abbey's employees and Lily's sister Zoe, as well as a distinct similarity between Lily's natural design aesthetic and Ashdown Abbey's recent California Collection—to feel confident it wasn't simply a matter of coincidence.

With a tip of her head, Lily gestured for him to follow her, then led him to the back of the store and through a doorway marked *Personnel Only.*

He was surprised to see that it was part storage space, part workroom. There were sewing machines, cutting tables, dress forms and supplies set up, but no one was using them at the moment.

The door clicked shut behind them, and Nigel turned to face Lily, who was standing with her back to the closed panel, hand clinging to the round brass knob.

Taking a deep breath that raised her chest and drew his attention to her breasts beneath the brightly patterned top he now recognized as one hundred percent her personal creation, she said, "Why are you here, Nigel?"

Right to the point. And regaining a bit of her natural confidence, he noticed. Just one of the things he admired about her, and had from the beginning.

"I thought we should talk," he answered honestly. "You ran off so quickly we didn't have a chance to discuss your true reason for being at Ashdown Abbey."

Lily opened her mouth, clearly eager to set him straight, but he held up a hand, stopping her.

"I know—my fault entirely. I told you to go, and at that point, I was too stunned and angry at your confession to hear the whole story. But I've had some time to think and to calm down, and I have some questions that only you can answer."

She considered that for a second, then offered a small nod. "All right. I really am sorry for what I did, for…lying to you. I'll tell you whatever you want to know."

As simple as that, and suddenly he couldn't think of a bloody thing to say. His mind had been spinning with questions for weeks, his body tense with the need for answers. Now Lily was standing in front of him, ready to bare her soul, and all he really wanted was to close the distance between them, clutch her tight to the wall of his chest, and kiss her until the rest of the world melted away.

Minutes ticked by, the silence almost deafening. Her glossy, periwinkle eyes blinked at him, waiting.

Blowing out a breath, he stiffened his spine, telling himself to man up and do what he'd flown all this way to do.

But again, only a single thought filled his head. Not the

desire to kiss her…that was still there, but taking a close backseat to the one question he most wanted an answer to.

"Our time together," he began, forcing the words past a throat gone tight with emotion. "In Florida, and then after we returned to Los Angeles…did it mean anything to you, or was that, too, part of your strategy?"

Seconds passed while she didn't respond, and his heart pounded so hard he feared she could hear it from halfway across the room.

Finally, her lips parted and air sawed from her lungs on a ragged stutter. Eyes glossy with moisture, her voice cracked as she said, "It meant…everything."

Relief washed over him. Relief and…so much more.

"Oh, Nigel." Lily sighed, dropping all semblance of distance—physical or otherwise—and rushing to him. Her fingers wrapped around his forearms, digging through the material of his suit jacket to the muscle beneath.

"I'm so sorry about everything. I was only trying to find out what happened with my designs. I knew they had been stolen, but I didn't know how or by whom, and I knew I would sound crazy if I started tossing out accusations without proof. I just wanted to poke around a little, see what I could find. I *never* meant to lie to you…not really. And I never, *ever* meant to hurt you, I swear."

She shook her head, glancing away for a moment before looking back, the tears on her lashes spilling over to trail down her cheeks. Nigel felt emotion welling up inside his chest as well, and swallowed to hold it back.

"What happened between us…" she continued. "It was never part of the plan, but I'm not sorry. My feelings for you were completely unexpected, and they made everything so much harder, so much worse. But they were very, very real."

Releasing her hold on his arms, Lily stepped back, not sure if her admission had made things better…or worse.

She felt better now that she'd had the chance to tell Nigel the truth, to tell him how much their time together had meant to her. Not because of her "investigation," not because it absolved her of guilt, but because she'd wanted him to know all along that their relationship hadn't been a casual one. Not to her.

He might not share her feelings. For all she knew, she had been beyond casual to him—disposable, even. But she didn't want him to think, even for a minute, that she'd slept with him as a means to an end. That seduction had been just one more way of using him, lying to him.

At the very least, she'd been able to tell him as much and wouldn't have to live the rest of her life with it hanging over her head. Already, her conscience was lighter for having come clean.

Now only her heart was heavy from having him for such a short time, then losing him to her own stupidity.

Taking a deep breath, she braced herself for whatever his reaction might be. Laughter? An angry scoff? An arrogant quirk of his brow when he realized he'd managed to make another of his personal assistants fall madly in love with him?

Not that she could blame him entirely for the last, if that was the case. She wouldn't be surprised if every person who'd ever worked for him had fallen for him. She'd worked for him only a few short weeks and had fallen head over heels.

The good news, she supposed, was that she had the rest of her life to get over him. It promised to be an agonizing forty or fifty years.

But he didn't laugh or scoff or raise an arrogant brow. He simply held her gaze, something dark and intense flashing behind his hazel eyes.

Resisting the urge to squirm, she linked her hands in front of her and said, "I'm sorry. That was probably more than you wanted to hear. And you have more questions."

Another minute ticked by while he stared down at her, making beads of perspiration break out along her hairline.

Finally, he cleared his throat and gave his head a small shake. "I have to say, I'm disappointed."

Her heart sank. She'd bared her soul, confessed all, come close to throwing herself at him and begging him to love her in return. And he was disappointed.

"Did I mention that you were the best personal assistant I've ever had?" he continued, oblivious to the sobs filling her head as every hope, every dream, every might-have-been died a painful death inside of her.

"And now I find out that you're actually a fairly successful fashion designer in your own right, not a personal assistant at all. You know what this means, don't you?" Without waiting for a reply, he murmured, "I have to start over, interviewing for a new assistant."

He sighed. "I suppose it's for the best. The gossip mill tends to run rampant when executives begin dating their employees. It may not be so bad if we're simply so-called rivals in the world of design."

Lily blinked, feeling as though she'd lost time. He wasn't making sense. Or maybe she'd blacked out for a moment and missed a chunk of the conversation that would help her understand what he was saying.

Hoping she wasn't about to make a giant fool of herself, she mumbled, "You don't have to worry about any of that. I won't tell anyone about our involvement. No one ever needs to know what happened."

A single dark brow quirked upward. "Well, someone is bound to figure it out eventually when they see us together."

Lily tipped her head, frowning in confusion. And her confusion only deepened when he smiled at her. A kind, patient smile she would never expect to see on the face of a man who hated her.

"I had a lot of questions in mind when I walked in here," he told her. "More, probably, than you can imagine. But only one question really matters, and you answered it."

He took a step forward, his hand coming up to stroke her cheek. Her lashes fluttered, pleasure rolling through her at even that brief contact. While he spoke, his thumb continued to brush back and forth along her skin, making her want to weep.

"For the record, it meant something to me, too. Our time together. I've never gotten involved with an employee of the company before. Certainly not one of my assistants. But you…" He shook his head, one corner of his mouth tipping up in a grin and desire flickering in his eyes. "You, I just couldn't seem to resist."

Lily didn't know how she managed to remain upright when her whole body felt like one big pile of sand. Laughter—happy, weightless, delighted laughter—bubbled inside of her, building until it couldn't help but spill out.

Smile widening, Nigel leaned down and kissed her, his lips warm and soft and familiar. For long minutes, she clung to him, unable to believe he was really here, kissing her, telling her these things, making her think maybe, just maybe they had a shot.

All too soon, Nigel lifted his head, breaking the kiss, but not letting her go.

"I think I've fallen quite madly in love with you, Lily Ann Zaccaro. And I'd very much like the chance to start over. No secrets, no lies, no ulterior motives. And no mysterious hidden identities, regardless of how adorable you might look in those sexy-librarian glasses of yours," he added, one corner of his mouth twisting with wry humor. "That is, if you're willing."

"Willing?" she squeaked, barely able to believe *he* was willing to give her a second chance after how she'd deceived him. Or that he was so quick to admit he'd fallen in love with her, when she'd been all but certain feelings like those were hers and hers alone.

If it was true, if he was truly in love with her, she was willing to do just about anything to make things work.

He nodded solemnly. "It won't be easy, considering that we're both tied rather strongly to opposite coasts. But thankfully I have access to a corporate jet and am not above abusing the privilege. I also suspect it will require rather a lot of romantic candlelit dinners. Probably a bevy of bold, romantic gestures on my part. You know—flowers, expensive jewelry, blowing off business commitments to spend amorous weekends in exotic locales. And you'll be expected to *ooh* and *ahh* appropriately at each of them until I've won you over completely. Do you think that's something you can handle?"

Lily laughed. *Giggled* might be a better description. She couldn't seem to help herself. "I'll certainly try," she said, striving to match his falsely sober tone of voice.

"I was also thinking we could work together to get to the bottom of how your designs ended up being used at Ashdown Abbey," he said, brows pulling together in a frown as he grew truly serious for a moment. "I've already suspended Bella Landry's employment at the company, but I can't outright fire her without proof that she stole designs from you and applied them to her efforts for us. Especially since she's denying the accusation. We're looking into it, though. We'll turn over every rock and review every slip of paper in the place until we get to the bottom of it, I assure you."

"Thank you," she murmured, touched by his earnestness on her behalf.

"I'm spearheading the investigation myself, but I could use a bit of help from you, since you're the one most familiar with the designs that were stolen and how they were used in our collection. Fair warning, however—it may require spending a lot of hours alone together, many of them running into the wee hours of the night when we may grow tired and feel the need to lie down for a spell."

At the last, he waggled one dark brow and offered her a lopsided grin.

Once again, a chuckle worked its way up from her belly. She'd never expected him to be able to make her laugh so much, especially when it came to something so serious.

"I'll keep that in mind," she replied, her own lips twitching with amusement.

"I also thought you might consider coming home to England with me."

At that, her eyes widened.

"My father has been complaining for months now that I've gone soft, let your American ways dictate how I run the company. I'd like him to meet you, see just how much I've decided to embrace America—and you."

He offered her a wide and wicked grin. "I actually think he'll be quite taken with you. And after he hears what you did in order to protect your company and designs, I'm pretty sure he'll decide you could be a *good* influence on me."

A beat passed while he let her absorb this latest pronouncement.

"What do you say? Willing to give it a go and see if we're as compatible outside of the office as we were as boss and secretary? And if you survive a visit with my parents, perhaps we can discuss making our relationship a little more… permanent."

Ten minutes ago, she'd thought he hated her. Ten minutes before that, she'd been considering joining a convent and devoting herself to a life of silence and chastity because she'd known she could never be truly happy without him.

Now, she was *too* happy not to agree to almost anything. Even meeting his parents, a prospect that she wasn't ashamed to admit scared her half to death.

"I'd say it sounds like you want to use me for some sort of personal gain," she teased after a moment of collecting her thoughts. "But then, I guess I owe you one on that score."

He tugged her closer, until her breasts pressed flat to his chest and his heat seeped through their clothes straight into her skin. "Very true. But only if you love me as much as I love you."

"Oh, I do love you, Nigel. I really, really do," she admitted, the words filling her with emotion and causing them to catch in her chest. "I still can't believe you're here, telling me you feel the same. So I guess my answer is...*yes.*" Yes to everything, always, as long as it was with him.

He kissed her again, quick and hard, pulling her against him so tightly, she could barely breathe. Not that she needed air when she was with him.

"Brilliant," he said, sounding slightly choked up himself for a moment before clearing his throat. "Although you should know that I'm not at all opposed to you using me again in the future. Preferably when we're alone and naked. Feel free to use me however you like then."

"Really?" Her gaze narrowed, all kinds of delightfully wicked thoughts spilling through her head.

"Well..." she said, dragging the word out, flattening her palm against the hard planes of his pectoral muscles hidden beneath the thousand-dollar-silk-cotton blend of his suit jacket and dress shirt. "I'm pretty sure my apartment is empty. Zoe is working here at the store, and Juliet is off for the day with her fiancé. We would be completely alone. And if you like...naked."

A devilish glint played over his features, sending a shock of eagerness down Lily's spine.

"I hope this means you're offering to use me again. Slowly and for a very long time."

"I think that can be arranged," she told him in a low voice.

Going on tiptoe, she pressed her lips to the corner of his mouth, his jawline, just beneath his ear. "And then you can do the same to me."

Wrapping his arms around her waist like a vise, he lifted her off her feet and started toward the door, kissing her along the way.

"The key to a successful relationship is compromise," he murmured. "And sharing. And mutual sacrifice."

"And being naked together as often as possible."

Teeth flashed wolfishly as he grinned, swooping in for another ravishing kiss.

"That would be my very favorite part."

* * * * *

MILLS & BOON®

The One Summer Collection!

Join these heroines on a relaxing holiday escape, where a summer fling could turn in to so much more!

Order yours at **www.millsandboon.co.uk/onesummer**

0616_MB523_OSA